WATER BABY

edited by John Murray

P A N U R g E
PUBLISHING

Brampton, Cumbria
1995

WATER BABY

first published 1995 by
Panurge Publishing
Crooked Holme Farm Cottage
Brampton, Cumbria CA8 2AT

EDITOR John Murray
ASSISTANT EDITORS   Jessie Anderson
Annie Molloy
PRODUCTION EDITOR Henry Swan
COVER DESIGN Andy Williams
EDITORIAL ASSISTANT Janet Bancroft
Typeset at Union Lane Telecentre, Brampton, Cumbria CA8 1BX
Tel. 016977 - 41014
Printed by Peterson's, 12 Laygate, South Shields, Tyne and Wear NE33 5RP
Tel. 0191-456-3493

ISBN 1 898984 20 4

**All fiction is unsolicited but must be accompanied by
SAE or IRCs or be a disposable photocopy. Work is considered all the year
round, and talented new writers are especially encouraged to submit.**

British Library Cataloguing in Publication Data.
A catalogue record for this book is available from
the British Library.

PANURGE PUBLISHING
Crooked Holme Farm Cottage,
Brampton,
Cumbria CA8 2AT
Tel. 016977-41087

*Panurge Publishing gratefully
acknowledges the assistance of the
PAUL HAMLYN FOUNDATION
1994-1995*

P A N U R g E   Anthology Number 23

ANNE-FRANÇOISE PYSZORA	*Husband And Wife*	5
PETER J. JOHNSTON	*Where The Bunyip Lives*	9
JACK HARTE	*Bike*	16
ELIZABETH HOWKINS	*Any Old Fart In A Storm*	27
ALBERT LEVENTURE	*Researches Between Screens*	31
JONATHAN TREITEL	*Sealed Room*	38
JOEL LANE	*Every Form Of Refuge*	45
TAMAR YELLIN	*The Other Mr. Perella*	57
STEPHEN BLANCHARD	*The Chicken Doctor*	67
CLIVE MURPHY	*To Gilbert And George Or Who Needs Enemies ?*	74
LINDSAY STANIFORTH	*The Stumblingstone*	81
MICHAEL EAUDE	*Long Before Either Of Them Were Ready*	86
KAREN ROSENBERG	*Eulogy By Phone*	93
STEPHEN ORMSBY	*Up To The Eyes*	116
JOHN RIZKALLA	*A Touch Of The Warrior*	124
JACQUELINE DEAKIN	*A Response In Kind*	138
ANTONY JOHN	*untitled*	143
PABLO PALACIO (trans. by Stefan Ball)	*A New Case of 'Mariage En Trois'*	152
JAMES HANNAH	*This Way Up*	157
SIOBHAN O'TIERNEY	*Smiling Through It All*	162
PETER DORWARD	*Drowning In A Light Sea*	171
DEREK GREGORY	*Water Baby*	185
JULIA BROSNAN	*To Sink A Brew*	192
BRIAN HOWELL	*The Imagist*	196
Publishing Against The Grain		
NICHOLAS ROYLE	*State Of Independents*	64
First Person		
MARGARET FORSTER	*Success*	111
Front Line Fiction/Egypt		
LULU NORMAN	*Albert Cossery*	178
Photographs		
PHILIP WOLMUTH		11, 33, 163, 186
Subscriptions, Back Issues, Quizzes		8, 56, 66, 85
Contributors, Letters		4, 26, 63
SPECIAL SUPPLEMENT	**Lancaster Competition**	203 - 240

CONTRIBUTORS

FIRST PUBLISHED STORY

Jacqueline Deakin is a trained solicitor and lives in South London. **Peter Dorward** is a London doctor born 1963. He has worked in Bolivia and Nicaragua. **Michael Eaude** works as a translator in Barcelona. He was born in 1949. **James Hannah** is our youngest ever contributor, only l9! He is a student at the University of Wales. **Anthony John** was born in 1965 and lives in Leeds. **Peter J. Johnston** is a 64 year-old Australian living in Clapham. He has had stories on Canadian radio. **Albert Leventure** is a bibliographer and essayist who lives in Oxford. **Stephen Ormsby** was born in 1961 and lives in Lewes. He is working simultaneously on three novels and pretending to translate Tibullus in the local library. **Anne-Françoise Pyszora** was born in 1963 in Surrey and is now a translator and a film critic in Berlin. **Lindsay Staniforth** lives in Bath and was born in 1951. She has had poems in the *Spectator* and *Literary Review*.

OTHERS

Stefan Ball lives in Oxfordshire and translates French and Spanish. **Stephen Blanchard** is a London postman born 1950. His Chatto novel *Gagarin and I* was much acclaimed last year. **Julia Brosnan** is 34, lives in Manchester and has had fiction in *Writing Women* and *The Big Issue*. She writes articles about nuclear weapons and nuclear families for *The Guardian, Everywoman* etc. **Albert Cossery** is hard to get hold of in English translation but try *Proud Beggars*, Black Sparrow Press(USA) from a good import bookshop. **Margaret Forster** spends half her time in London, half in the Lake District. She is a distinguished novelist, biographer and reviewer. She hates short stories as a fictional form; both as writer and reader. **Derek Gregory** edits *Tees Valley Writer* and had a fine story in Panurge 18. **Jack Harte** is a Dublin writer whose collection *Murphy In The Underworld* (Glendale Press l986) was much acclaimed. *Homage* was published by Dedalus in 1992. **Brian Howell** has had work in *Panurge, Darklands* and elsewhere and has been offered a place on the UEA MA. **Elizabeth Howkins** won a prize in the Stand Competition 1993 and appears in *Move Over, Waxblinder!* She lives in Bryn Mawr, USA. **Joel Lane** has a collection *The Earth Wire*, Egerton Press. He lives in Birmingham and has been in *Panurge, Ambit* and *Darklands*. **Clive Murphy** lives in London and has published three novels as well as numerous recorded histories. His story appears in *Move Over, Waxblinder!* **Lulu Norman** had a Cossery translation in Panurge 17. **Siobhan O'Tierney** lives in Powys and has had stories in the *Irish Press* and *New Irish Writing* and on RTE. She was born in 1960. **Pablo Palacio** was born in 1906 and died in l947. He published two novels and a story collection and has only appeared in English via Stefan Ball's magazine translations. **John Rizkalla** has had stories in *Panurge* and *London Magazine* and a novel out with Bodley Head. **Nicholas Royle** founded the Egerton Press and the Darklands anthologies. He reviews for *Time Out* and *Independent on Sunday* and his novels are out with Penguin. **Karen Rosenberg** is an American living in Vienna. Her stories have been in *Metropolitan* and *Timber Creek Review*. **Jonathan Treitel** is a well known Bloomsbury novelist. **Tamar Yellin** lives in Keighley and has had fiction in *Writing Women, London Magazine* and *Best Short Stories 1994*. **Philip Wolmuth** will be working in Syria and Jordan later this year.

Anne-Françoise Pyszora

Husband And Wife

Gerd and Hannah, born and raised in Berlin, were wedded in a church in the South of France because they wanted their wedding to be unforgettable. It was that, alright. Two days after the ceremony Gerd had a heart attack. At least that's what he thought it was - sharp pain needling around his heart and shortness of breath - but when he went to the hospital and had electrodes stuck to his chest, the graph came out perfectly normal. The French doctor suggested indigestion and it was true that Gerd had indulged daily in *soupe de poissons* and in all kinds of meat with rich sauces and in creamy desserts. But that was the point of France. That and the room they had rented in a villa called La Mirabelle. It was behind the closed aqua shutters that Gerd and Hannah's child was conceived. The dark green palms rustled outside like paper in the wind, the sun struck through a crack in the shutters, a single shaft of white light, lying like a knife blade across the terracotta floor.

The child was born in a Berlin hospital after forty-eight hours labour. Hannah was so exhausted she lost consciousness at the moment of birth, but Gerd was there. It was a wonderful but terrifying experience for him: the purple creature sliding out, blood-stained and floury and ugly as sin. Hannah left a trail of blood when she went to the toilet afterwards and collapsed on the floor in a second faint. The nurses fussed about the blood on the sheets.

Eventually Gerd and Hannah found what they had been looking for - a three roomed flat within commuting distance of Gerd's office. It was January when they moved and the winter was severe. The wind was sending the snow-grit scudding like sand in sweeps across the pavements. The canals were frozen, turning a blind eye to the sky. There was no central heating in the flat, just a coal-burning stove in every room. Gerd had hired four Polish workmen to paint the walls and sand the floors and tile the bathroom. But the workmen had underestimated the time it would take to finish the job, and when Gerd and his family arrived every room was full of rubbish and there was no space for their furniture. They moved the rubbish out into the hallway, clearing one room in which to put their things, and fell into bed at midnight, their throats sore with the dust they'd been breathing all day. The baby woke up five times that night. Hannah got up every time because Gerd had to go to work the following day.

Gerd rode into work on the underground. He disliked the

crowded, closed-in feeling of the steel carriage. He was afraid that the train would get stuck in a tunnel, that the passengers would get panic-stricken. Every morning and evening he felt fear tightening in his chest.

At the office he felt better. He loved to see the work piled on his desk and to hear the patter of his secretary's fingers on the computer keyboard. An American company had expressed an interest in a product from Gerd's department. He began to compose a letter of reply in English. It took him a long time, looking up every word in the *Langenscheidt* dictionary. The phone rang, people came in to talk to him, his secretary brought him a cup of soup and a roll, and he got involved in a discussion about instant soup with her. By the time the letter was ready, it was afternoon.

Hannah had a lot to keep her busy too. She was up at six when the baby woke. She changed his nappy, dressed him warmly in his day clothes and made breakfast. When Gerd had left for work she washed up in a bucket. There was, as yet, no sink or cooker in the flat. Their money had run out after they'd paid the Polish workmen. Hannah cooked over a plug-in electric ring. She went out in the morning to buy organically-grown vegetables from a special shop. She wrapped the baby up, put a hot water bottle beside him in the pushchair, and went out into the freezing glare of the Berlin January day. No new snow had fallen for three days but the pavements were still rutted in ice, the kerbsides were deep in tyre-tracked slush. It was difficult to manoeuvre the pushchair over the lumps and bumps. The baby had a slight cold at the moment, a cough and a temperature of 38°C, but she had to take him out shopping with her. She couldn't leave him in the flat alone. She was in constant attendance to the baby's needs. She could not sleep when she was tired, she could not take a bath when she needed one, she could not eat in peace, or dress, or read or think. The baby's shrieks drove into her brain day and night. Perhaps he was teething, perhaps he had bellyache, perhaps his cold bothered him. When it came down to it, no one really knew why babies cried. They just did. It was their sign of life, their mark on the world, their statement of identity.

When she was angling the pushchair back in through the front door, past the rubbish she and Gerd had piled neatly against the wall, the baby had a coughing fit. Hannah frowned and picked him up. Her heart beat swiftly with anxiety. She held him and he coughed against her shoulder. Then she noticed a piece of paper pinned to her door:

PEOPLE WHO CANT KEEP CLEAN AND TIDY BETTER GO BACK TO WHERE THEY CAME FROM someone had scrawled in large childish handwriting. Hannah took the note down and screwed it up. On second thoughts, she flattened it out to show Gerd.

Gerd was trying to fax his letter through to New York. The number was permanently engaged. He tried to phone the New York office but couldn't get through on the phone either. He replaced the receiver and the phone rang. It was his wife to tell him about the note from the neighbours. She seemed unduly upset. He told her not to worry and that he would be home soon. "We'll drive to the countryside at the weekend," he promised her. His secretary came in to tell him the fax had gone through. He was well-satisfied with his day's work.

On the way home he ran into his ex-girlfriend by chance. That is, he saw her sitting inside a lighted café when he was on his way to the tube station and he went in to talk to her. He ordered a beer and a big plate of fried potatoes and bacon. Gerd had quite forgotton how attractive his ex-girlfriend was and he couldn't help feeling jealous of her new boyfriend. It was a good feeling sitting there in the café talking to her, watching her fingers on the stem of her glass and remembering how intimately he had known those fingers once. They talked for a couple of hours and kissed in parting. Gerd was in such a good mood that he bought a bunch of flowers at the tube station to take home to his wife.

The flat was in darkness when he arrived. He thought Hannah must be putting the baby to bed. He switched on the kitchen light. A half-eaten cheese roll was lying on a crate which served as a table. No sign of supper. Not that he was hungry after the potatoes and bacon. He looked in the bathroom and the other two rooms. The flat was abandoned.

The phone rang. It was his wife. She was at the hospital with the baby. He was running a temperature of 41.3°C and was having difficulty breathing. She had tried to phone Gerd all evening at work because he had taken both sets of car keys with him and there was no money in the house for her to take a taxi. The baby was in serious danger, she said. Gerd promised to get to the hospital immediately. He replaced the receiver and looked out of the window. It was dark outside. At the corner of the street was a bar. An illuminated white and red sign hung above the entrance. He watched a man emerge and walk down the street. He watched a car back into a parking space.

Three people got out, slammed the doors shut and disappeared into the house opposite. He looked up at the sky, clear and black, and he saw the lights of an airplane travel slowly across the gap between the buildings. He did not move.

Subscriptions and Resubscriptions

If you need to resubscribe there will be an appropriate reminder in this issue you have just received. **Please resubscribe as promptly as possible. Subscription revenue is literally our lifeblood.**

Standard Subscription / Resubscription (two issues)
Panurge anthologies come out every April and October promptly. Panurge 24 appears April 96. **All cheques to Panurge, Crooked Holme Farm Cottage, Brampton, Cumbria CA8 2AT UK.**

☐ £12 UK   ☐ IR£15   ☐ £15/$18 Overseas ☐ £20/$25 Air Mail

Peter J. Johnston

Where The Bunyip Lives

He was only an old tramp and he hadn't attracted much attention. Anyone who bothered to think about it at all supposed he camped down by the water tanks beside the railway yard. Most of the vagrants passing through Willandra ended up there. They had water and shelter from a few twisted dust-laden trees and the elevated water tanks. In times of drought, when household supplies ran low, the townsfolk themselves had to cart their drinking water from the railway tanks.

When the loungers on the pub verandah saw the old man coming down the main street towards the pub, they took little more notice of him than they would of a stray dog, or a strange horse. Diversions of any sort were equally welcome in Willandra. He shuffled along with his eyes on the ground, each shoe raising from the powdery earth a miniature dust-storm that whipped off behind him. His dark trousers were white to the knees with dust. Despite the heat, which kept every other living thing off the street, he wore a tattered army greatcoat, fastened with wire. Under a greasy felt hat his face was so bearded and dirty it was impossible to see his features.

When he mounted the three wooden railway sleepers that served the pub for steps and clomped on to the thin boards of the verandah, Skipper, the McEwan's mongrel dog, came out from the shade under the building and followed the stranger along the verandah, sniffing at his trouser legs. As the old man reached the screen door of the bar and swung it open, Skipper commenced an uncertain growl deep down inside. But he was too old, and the day too hot. He let it rest there, reluctantly.

*

Bimbo executed a graceful dive off the edge of the verandah into the dust. Janice McEwan, who believed she was his mother, had placed him on the very edge of a loose board. The old tramp had trodden on the other end of the board and sent Bimbo flying into the air. "You naughty dolly," she scolded. "You can't go swimming today. I won't let you." She spanked the doll's bottom and placed him carefully back on the same board. She hoped the old man would soon come out again.

At the other end of the pub verandah, in the shade of the massive rain water tanks, Sandy Quinlan drained his glass. "Ain't seen 'im around before; 'ave you, Frank?"

Frank finished rolling a smoke. He was a small man, foxy-faced, unshaven and dressed in a particularly dirty railway uniform. Beneath the jacket, from which all but one of the brass buttons were missing, he wore only a grubby singlet, so transparent from oil-stains that the dark hair on his chest showed through. He spoke around his cigarette.

"You'll see 'im come flying back out that door in a minute though, if he's trying to bum a drink off old McEwan." The men grinned.

"Remember a few months back," one said, "when the shearers from Wagga was 'ere? 'E chucked one clean through the winda behind the pub."

"Was shut, too... Wonder Stan never charged 'im for the glass."

"I saw that. The old bugger 'ad settled his bill for the month's bender before Stan threw him out. If I know Stan, 'e'd 'ave added on the cost of the winder in advance."

"*And* a few quid for 'is trouble, as well."

The men laughed, but their humour was mixed with respect and a certain uneasiness.

Stan McEwan wouldn't stand for derelicts hanging around the pub. Willandra had survived without a policeman for the past fifteen years mainly because the McEwans had kept a respectable house. In the hard-drinking outback towns, where fights were a commonplace at any time and almost a ritual at weekends, the pub at Willandra was a notable exception. McEwan ruled the drinkers as if they were inmates of a brutal prison system. At the first sign of trouble, he would heave his huge frame over the bar and lay about him with fists like frozen legs of mutton. He often exceeded the strict demands of peace-keeping and administered beatings that in other communities would have landed him in jail. But the inhabitants of those parts fought their own battles, and lived for the day when McEwan would meet his match.

The laughter died away and no-one spoke. The heat-laden silence returned and pushed everything down flat, subduing all life and movement. Down the street, only little whirlwinds of dust moved, chasing each other briefly until, overcome with the general sluggishness, they rested on the earth. The loafers at the end of the verandah might have been a group of statuary. Only the droning flies moved.

"Will you show me where the Bunyip lives, Frankie?" Janice

Joanna, Southwark 1991

Philip Wolmuth

piped up. She'd grown tired of waiting for the old man. "Skipper knows, but he's too old. Will you take me where he lives, Frankie? Mummy won't; she says there ain't any Bunyips."

Frank smiled awkwardly, showing teeth like a rotting fence. He was an irredeemable bachelor, wedded to beer and hard work, and children embarrassed him, but Janice was too young to notice that he was ugly and not at all clean. She knew he was gentle and she was attracted to him.

"Not now, love. It's too 'ot for Bunyips. They don't like the 'eat. It...er,...it melts 'em."

"Where do they live, then? Paddy Davis says he saw one in his Dad's barn."

"He never saw a real one, I'll bet. They only live where there's trees. Out there by Wilton's Wood now, that's where you'll see 'em".

"Will you take me?"

"Sometime, love. Not tonight. There's a train in. Uncle Frank's got to work."

Sandy Quinlan said, "Uncle Frank's a kinda expert on Bunyips. 'E sees 'em going home every night. Don't ya, Frank?"

"Mostly when 'e wakes up," another man said. The half-dozen drinkers were amused by this, but not Janice. She looked at Frank curiously.

There was a brief babble of raised voices in the bar. Mrs McEwan shouted, "Get out, ya bloody old looney," and as if lashed by the words, the old tramp hastened out, with shoulders hunched into his ridiculous coat as the words fell across his back. The men saw that his lips were moving convulsively. He clumped along the verandah, down the steps, and had turned the corner of the building before the screen door jerked open again and Mrs McEwan sailed out. She was a large woman at any time, but now she appeared huge, swollen up with indignation.

"Bloody old..." Her eyes fell on Janice, who ran delightedly to retrieve Bimbo from the pool of dust. "... so and so," she ended lamely. "I won't have them lunatics here. I never noticed 'till he started talking to hisself. Dirty old wretch, I don't know why they're not all locked up. Give the place a bad name; hanging around here. I'll call Stan if he comes back. He'll settle him!"

The men said nothing. Some of them liked to see Mrs McEwan in action. It was usually colourful but harmless. Stan was a different

12

matter.

Mrs McEwan had to see something react to her tantrum. "Get around the back, Janice... And get cleaned up for dinner," she snapped. "You're covered in dirt."

Janice was. Bimbo had taken yet another header off the verandah and landed in a sea of dust. Janice had dived into rescue him. She looked up at her mother and started to explain: "But Bimbo might've drownded if I..." but one look from Mrs McEwan withered the words on her lips. Now she, too, hunched her little shoulders and, trailing Bimbo by one leg, went around the corner of the pub out of sight, the way the old man had gone.

*

The afternoon train had come and gone, and Frank had locked the station buildings and was going back across the road to the pub when he saw that something was wrong. Mrs McEwan and a group of women were standing on the pub verandah talking in loud voices. On the dusty footpath below them, a huddle of children managed to be arguing among themselves while staring up at the women, like a restive audience waiting for a play to begin. There were no men in sight.

"*You* haven't seen 'er, have you?" Mrs McEwan was the first to see Frank and she detached herself from the group.

Someone shouted, "No. We've looked, we've looked."

"Seen who?" Frank asked, although he knew as soon as he saw Mrs McEwan's angry tear-stained face. "Janice?" he said. "No, not since this morning. She was playing out 'ere." He indicated the spot where the children now stood. They moved away as if it were infected, and stared down at it.

No one, it seemed, had seen Janice since then. While Frank had been attending to the train, coupling and uncoupling wagons in the goods yards, Willandra's dozen or so homes had been alerted. Children had been marshalled and interrogated and out-buildings searched. Stan McEwan had driven over to Goolwindi to fetch the policeman, who never answered his phone on Sundays. The rest of the men were dragging Simpson's dam, a muddy pond half a mile from the town. People had always said that one day a child would end up in there.

A boy was running along the verandah. "'Ere they come, 'ere they come." Two furious streamers of dust announced the return of Stan and the policeman. The two vehicles were moving very fast.

13

Suddenly silenced, the crowd of women and children moved out into the road. They knew something had happened.

"That old tramp's got her." Stan's sweaty red face threw the words to the waiting crowd. "This kid's seen 'em. Tell 'em what you seen, sonny." No-one had noticed the boy. An Aboriginal half-cast of about ten, he sat shrunken and frightened on the edge of the front seat. Yes, he'd seen them, he said, an old man in an army coat and a little girl, hand in hand. They'd gone past the Blacks' camp about dinner time. They were going towards Wilton's Wood.

Frank got in with O'Connor, the policeman, and the two cars started at once. When Frank looked back he could see a group of women assisting Mrs McEwan up the steps. She was in a state of collapse.

"We'll go past Simpson's dam and pick up the other blokes," O'Connor said. "We'll find the kid all right. But God help that old bastard if Stan gets his hands on him."

*

Wilton's property lay about a mile from the town. In one corner, where the land fell away to the creek, was the extensive stand of Athel pine, Wilga and mallee scrub known as Wilton's Wood. Out of a queer mixture of laziness, and respect for this native forest in a virtually treeless countryside, Herb Wilton had never had the heart to commence clearing this quarter of his land. It was a refuge for the few lovers in the area - and they were few, or travelled far - for tramps, and a mecca for small boys from the town. When the sun blazed down and baked the open fields, it could be as cool and dark as a cathedral.

It was already getting dark when the cars of the search party arrived. With a few brief instructions from the policeman, they fanned out singly through the trees. When the others had been gone about five minutes, Stan McEwan returned alone to his car, unlocked the boot, and took out a double-barrelled shotgun. He put two cartridges in the breech and hurried away after the other men.

*

Janice and her companion sat down on the crest of a ridge over-looking the weed-choked swamp which Herb Wilton, having piled some earth in the creek twenty years before, grandly called his Dam. She was eating the last of the old man's biscuits. The two were silhouetted against the bright orange and blood-curdled western sky.

"I'm going back home now," she said. "It's nearly dark and

14

Mummy will be cross."

They had spent the afternoon wandering among the trees and the open spaces carpeted with fragrant pine needles. Janice had never been in these woods before and she was fascinated with the place and with her new friend. He had shown her the tiny mouse-holes in the sand where the sandpipers lived and the little willy-wagtails in their spotless white waistcoats. They had sat motionless and watched baby rabbits gambolling in their playgrounds near the burrows. An opossum had scampered almost to their feet, and stared at them incredulously before washing his face with fussy concentration. Janice had completely forgotten the Bunyip.

"Are you coming?"

"Them Willandra people don't like me. I'm staying here," the old man muttered.

"But where will you sleep?"

He looked about. "I'll sleep with them rabbits," he said.

*

There was a shout and a crashing of feet through the dead branches below the ridge, and Stan McEwan burst through, running up the bank.

"You swine!" he shouted.

The old man leapt to his feet, his face aghast. He was as terrified as a rabbit in a trap. He lurched against Janice, who had also half-risen, and he sent her sprawling. As he made off down the hill, his broken hob-nailed boot came down heavily on her arm. Hurt and frightened, Janice wailed.

Her father skidded to his knees in the dust beside her, "That old man hurt you?" he barked.

Janice nodded and sobbed: "Yes." Stan snatched at his gun and went down the bank, in the wake of the old man.

Ten minutes later, just as O'Connor and Frank, drawn by the girl's hysterical sobs, were starting up the ridge towards her, there came the single blast of a shotgun from the dense scrub around the far end of the swamp. The trees all around burst into a flower of screeching white cockatoos. Their screams drowned out almost at once the sound of a man crying with pain.

Jack Harte

Bike

The women of the house held a meeting. They decided that some things had to go. My wife, her two sisters, and my two cousins decided that the house was becoming cramped. They were right, of course. Add a male partner and an average brood of three children to each of those five females, and you will begin to understand the problem - all crammed into one house. I must clarify that it is a big Georgian house in Leeson Street, three stories over basement, with high ornamented ceilings in every room; yet the concentration of so many people into it gave the effect of a tenement - it is probably the only tenement in modern Dublin!

I don't own the house and I don't know who does. It was, so to speak, dropped in my lap. When I first came to Dublin, to take up a menial clerical position - a position I have occupied to this day - I rented the room on the ground floor inside the front door. The rest of the house was similarly let to students and young professional people, as they were described in the letting advertisements, and the Landlord called every Friday evening between seven and eight o'clock to collect the rent. As I was so conveniently situated inside the front door and always about on a Friday evening, not having been a drinker in those days, a practice grew up whereby other tenants left their rent with me as they exited for their weekend carousals. I became an unofficial rent collector for the Landlord, who neither thanked me nor rewarded me for my services. We never engaged in conversation while he took the money and counted it. I never even knew his name.

Then he stopped coming. One Friday night he failed to arrive, and I never saw him again. The other tenants continued to leave their rent with me, something that worried me enormously, especially when the money began to overflow the drawer in my sideboard. In fear of a robber, I opened a bank account and deposited all the money I had collected, including my own rent. For several years this continued. And, accordingly as tenants left finally, they handed their keys to me. I was prepared to accept responsibility for minding the rent money, but not for re-letting, so eventually I was living alone in an empty Georgian house.

That was when I decided to get married, and took a wife. She moved in with me to my room and enjoyed the thrill of the empty old house for a while. Unfortunately, she soon grew lonely and prevailed upon me to allow her mother and two sisters join us. There were so many empty rooms at the time that I had no logical basis for an objection. So they joined us. In time the mother died and the two sisters got married. Their husbands moved in as well. With three couples breeding, the house began to fill with little ones. Then two of my cousins came to Dublin to work in the Civil Service and I rented a room to them. I was glad of this little private income at the time because I had commenced the practice of drinking. However, when these two got married they persuaded me to give them a second room, and they stopped paying me rent altogether.

With the proliferation of human life in the house, it was not surprising that the women complained of cluttering. The council of war demanded that I consign to the dump all the junk that was lying around. To make it convenient for me, they produced a notice from the Corporation that its disposal teams would be making a special collection of Household Junk on the following Tuesday. This notice came once a year and it had always been used in attempts to pressurise me into getting rid of the many old artefacts that had come into my care along with the house: objects such as broken armchairs, a Victorian hall-stand with shattered mirror glass, and, particularly, the old bicycle that was parked on the landing of the first floor. My reluctance to dispose of these items did not stem from any sentimental streak in my nature nor from any attachment to the antique; it stemmed from my overwhelming sense of responsibility for all that I was holding in trust, and my overwhelming dread that one day the Landlord would return and expect to find the house exactly as he had left it. My anxiety to maintain the role of faithful custodian was even more acute, since I no longer had the accumulation of rent to hand over to the Landlord on his return. Ever since my two cousins had ceased paying me rent, I had been making withdrawals from the bank account to finance my custom of drinking ale in the evenings.

However, on this occasion the women made a more aggressive assault than usual on the old rusty bicycle. They claimed that the children were constantly crashing into it and gashing themselves; they claimed that some day one of the children would die of tetanus or another unspeakable disease, and that it would be my fault because I didn't shift the rusty old bike.

Convinced, partly by their argument and partly by the thought that I might be able to sell the crock for the price of a few pints of ale, I

---

concluded an agreement with the women: I would dispose of the bike, on condition that they did not press me to interfere with any of the other items on their hit-list.

Bald William, the local grocer, obliged me by putting my 'For Sale' notice in his window, and within a few days I had a response, a telephone enquiry, an interested customer. I had to give her precise detail of every part, from the size of the wheels to the shape of the mudguards, and she seemed in no way put off by my frequent mention of rust. When I described the extended height of the handlebars emerging from the long neck in the frame of the bike, she became quite breathless.

"A High Nellie! Is it really a High Nellie?"

I had never heard of such a model, but reassured her that it was, since it seemed to be a good selling point.

She arrived the next morning to inspect the bike. She was pushing a buggy into which was strapped a tawdry but healthy-looking girl-child of one year or thereabouts. Following her was a slim nubile girl of nineteen or twenty. The woman herself was of indiscriminate age, but old enough to be an unlikely mother of the infant. The nubile girl sat on the granite steps pushing the buggy to-and-fro while I fetched the bike for inspection. In the glare of daylight it looked a sorry sight indeed, the prevailing rust having reduced the chrome parts and the once-painted frame to the one dirty brown colour and the same rough texture. I now despaired of striking a bargain, even though I had previously pumped the wheels and ensured that it was functioning in all the expected ways. I decided I would settle for the price of four pints, my usual night's quota, if she would be prepared to take it off my hands.

She went into a rapture when she saw it.

"It is. It is. A genuine High Nellie," she exclaimed. I thought perhaps I might have a week's drinking after all. She examined it, back and front, top and bottom, with as much reverence as if it had been ridden by St. Patrick when he was chasing the snakes, or by Brian Boru when he was routing the Norsemen. She certainly didn't play a cool hand when it came to bargaining.

"I never thought I'd see one again," she said earnestly. "My first bike was a High Nellie. It was my present for my fourteenth birthday. I went everywhere on it. When I came to Dublin I brought it with me. I cycled it for years. Then it was stolen. I could never bring myself to buy another bike."

"Would you like to take it for a spin, and try it out?"

"Could I? I'll just ride around the block. Lisa will keep an eye on Annmarie." She nodded in turn at the nubile girl and the infant.

I carried the bike down the stone steps, handed it to her, and held the gate open to allow her the liberty of the streets.

She mounted the bike as if she had never sat on one before, but when she had gained her legs she pedalled with confidence down the road.

I went back to make small talk with Lisa. She was very pretty with a delicately-cut oval face and tightly-cropped black hair. She was ornamented with a diamante stud in her nose. She was a student of theology, she told me, in from the country. She had been sent by her parents to the home of Phyllis and her husband, in reply to an advertisement in a local paper; the arrangement was that she performed a certain amount of child-minding and domestic duties in return for accommodation and meals. She spoke with a quiet but assured voice. Her choice of theology as a discipline was easily explained. She was not preparing for a church career, nor was she a devotee of any particular religion. She was sent by her family to study at the University, but when her academic qualifications were assessed she was offered a place only on the course for which there were no takers - theology.

Annmarie had begun to whinge a little and Lisa was pushing her gently to-and-fro, humming soothingly to her.

I was very taken with the girl, and enjoyed our little discussion very much, even if I was on edge looking up the street and down the street for Phyllis's return. The small talk was exhausted, and I tried out a few theological topics, the existence of angels and the usefulness of the Mandala for achieving spiritual enlightenment. When the second hour had passed and I had begun to feel out of my depth in our discussion of the phenomenology of the spirit, my patience expired, and I decided to go and look for Phyllis. I told my wife to take Lisa and Annmarie inside and give them some tea and bread. Afraid that they would take flight as soon as my back was turned, I was determined to hold them as hostages until I got my bike back, or the price of it.

I got her address from Lisa and set forth. My first worry was that she had met with an accident, caused perhaps by a mechanical failure of the bicycle, and I wondered what my liability would be in such circumstances. I called at the police station and at the hospital, but there was no report of an accident.

I then called at her own address, surmising that she had been unable to re-trace her steps to my house - an unlikely explanation, as I lived on one of the main thoroughfares of the city.

Her husband answered my knock. He stood squarely in the door, dressed in shirt and trousers, in stockinged feet. His stomach pouted above his taut belt. There was a strong suggestion in his contrary expression that he had been roused from a nap. I explained my predicament. He scratched at his bald head and down the back of his flabby neck as if he were searching for some elusive itch. He didn't appear concerned, just annoyed in an intensely petulant way.

"Damn the woman anyway. She's getting sillier by the day." He spat out the words in no particular direction. He offered no further comment on the situation. I grew uneasy. Anxious to withdraw from this confrontation, I decided to cut my losses.

"I suppose I had better send the child and Lisa back to you."

"Damn the child. If she gave it to you, then you keep it. But send Lisa back to me. I want Lisa back, do you hear?"

I muttered a goodnight and withdrew. This was certainly a dilemma.

Night had fallen by the time I returned home. I found Lisa and Annmarie still sitting in the kitchen waiting for their crux to be resolved. The hostages had become refugees. I explained to Lisa, as diplomatically as I could, that Phyllis had hijacked my bike and had abandoned the two of them; they were not wanted by her husband, either - I simplified this aspect of the crux, as I was certainly not going to surrender Lisa, unless I was ridding myself of the child as well.

I got ready the spare room in the basement, the only unoccupied space in the house, which I kept in reserve for the occasional visits by my relatives from the country. I installed Lisa and the baby. They would be comfortable there, and the women of the house would see to their needs. It would take me some days to decide on a course of action, as I seldom made a good decision in haste.

The following night I consulted a drunken judge who patronised the same pub as I did. He seemed to think that I had entered into a contract, had acquired some assets, and was entitled to liquidate them. When I asked him for some suggestions as to how I might liquidate my assets, he became totally incoherent, lay his head on the counter, and began to snore. I could sell the baby on the black market. There were stories of small fortunes changing hands in such deals. That was a real possibility. I wondered what she would fetch. What then would I do with Lisa? Sell her too? But then white slavery was so much out of fashion in Europe. Unless I did something quickly I would be at a considerable loss, as they both had healthy appetites.

The more I thought about the problem, the more muddled my mind became, the more my sense of grievance against Phyllis gnawed at my spleen. I was riled by the ever-present awareness that she had bested me. I imagined her gloating over her success, laughing in scorn at my gullibility. Her image haunted me night and day, so that I finally recognised I had only one course of action open to me, to track her down and force her to compensate me for the lodgings in addition to paying a substantial price for my bike.

Living in the centre of the city has its advantages. You strike up relationships with all kinds of interesting people, such as winos, newspaper sellers, the skinheads in Stephen's Green. It was to this network of friends that I now had recourse. I had difficulty in formulating a clear picture of Phyllis, but I had no problem describing the bike. And it was the bike that my friends succeeded in identifying. Within hours reports of sightings began to flow back to me. All over the city it was being spotted - fleeting glimpses of it careering down thoroughfares, disappearing around corners, emerging from side-streets, always being pedalled vigorously by a woman, sometimes described as middle-aged, sometimes as young, sometimes simply as a woman.

For two or three days I did nothing but try to correlate the information that was coming back to me through my network. No pattern was emerging, and I could only marvel at her energy and wonder how soon she would collapse.

She didn't collapse, but she certainly started to slow down. Sightings were now beginning to cluster and concentrate in the Temple Bar area, the new Bohemian quarter of the city. The bike was being spotted chained to a lamp-post outside a public house or being walked up the cobbled streets after closing-time. It was time to move in for the kill.

Temple Bar was one area of the city that was unfamiliar to me, and I made my way slowly and cautiously from pub to pub. The patrons were invariably young, and casual-looking, making it all the more difficult for me to be inconspicuous. I dressed like the natives, in blue jeans and plaid shirts, and usually slouched on a high stool by the bar conducting mono-syllabic conversations with the barman.

My guile and perseverance eventually brought success. Lurking in a pub early one evening, I saw her tethering the bike to railings outside. I was petrified. I felt like a hunter across whose path a magnificent deer has strutted so close as to make a mockery of shooting. She came in the open front door, exchanged a greeting with the burly bouncer, who was picking up glasses and re-arranging the chairs where people had just left. She walked past me over to a corner of the lounge; three women welcomed her with animated voices. From the corner of my eye I watched her every move. She sat down with her back towards me and ordered a pint of Guinness when the lounge girl approached. After a few minutes I took my own pint and sauntered over to occupy a vacant seat behind her, between her and the door.

One of the women had just attended a lecture on Existentialist philosophy and she was filtering her newly acquired wisdom through to the others, pausing regularly to imbibe more Guinness.

"You can do whatever you want to do," she declared in a high-pitched voice that trembled from intoxication. "You can be whatever you want to be. It's a simple matter of choice."

"Absolutely true," agreed Phyllis taking a slurp from her pint. "You can do anything you want."

- Not on my bike, you can't, thought I, and not while I'm feeding your child and your child-minder.

After a while her three companions got up to leave. In turn they embraced her.

"Good luck, Phyllis. Have a nice trip."

Where was she going? I was seized by panic. When she sat down again she re-located herself with her back to the wall. She was now sitting alongside me, and couldn't avoid noticing my stare as she watched her companions depart. She glanced at me in half-recognition as if I were some face from her distant past. I sensed that she did not associate me with an event which was not yet a fortnight old. Perhaps my clothes or the changed surroundings had dulled recognition. Or perhaps she had lost all control of her faculties!

I nodded at her and edged closer along the bench seat. She became slightly nervous, but held her ground. Whether it was because of her hair which she now wore loose, or because of her heightened complexion induced by alcohol and all that physical exertion, she certainly appeared much younger than she did on our last encounter.

I passed a compliment on the pub, to which she nodded her agreement. I still could not determine whether she recognised me or not. There was silence once more.

Then she turned squarely and emphatically to me. "Isn't it marvellous what they're doing with the Temple Bar?"

"Yes, marvellous, indeed," I agreed, without the remotest idea as to what marvellous things she was referring.

"It really has such character, and it's so alive now. It's marvellous."

"Yes, marvellous," I agreed again.

"We miss out on so much of life. It's so important to have a place like this at the heart of the city, pulsing with life, full of people, exploding with ideas."

"Yes, yes, absolutely essential."

"Everywhere you turn in the Temple Bar you find people expressing themselves, in music, in art, in writing, or just in the sheer joy of living."

"Are you involved in the arts yourself?"

"No, unfortunately," she laughed, and took a deep swig out of her pint. "I'm involved in the joy of living."

"But you must do something. What about work? Family?"

"I'm finished with all of that," she declared, as if a cloud had appeared on the horizon, but a cloud she was not going to allow overshadow the sunshine in her mind. "I'm off on a long trip. I'm catching the boat tonight. Holyhead. I'm going to cycle from there to the south coast of England, down through the Wye Valley and Somerset, places like that, places I've always wanted to see. And it's so easy on a bike. You just sit up and keep pedalling. From the south coast I'll catch a ferry to France. Then down to Paris! I'll spend some time there, a week, maybe two. Off again down to the Alps, Italy, Florence, Rome. Were you ever in Rome?"

"No," I replied, and in truth had never experienced the slightest desire to go there, always associating the place with pilgrims and the Pope flapping his arms from his top window. However, my reaction to her eulogy was one of vast and intense resentment, so vast and so intense that it took me by surprise. How dare she? The sheer effrontery of it! It wasn't just the bicycle she had stolen from me; it wasn't just her tricking me into assuming her responsibilities; it was the audacity of the woman. She had no right to do these things, no right even to think such thoughts. It was a threat, an insult to me in a way that was too deep to articulate, too deep even to fathom.

"Rome must be marvellous," she rambled on, patently unaware of my dark thoughts, unaware of the seat I had slowly edged out across her direct path to the front door. "All those paintings, and sculptures, and buildings! Isn't it fascinating to think that, once you land on the coast of France, there is a road all the way to Rome. In the days of the Empire they used to say that all roads lead to Rome. Now there is at least one road that leads to Rome, and I intend to cycle every inch of it."

"Will you stop there? Will you come back then?" I asked, wondering at what stage she planned to resume her responsibility for her child.

"Not at all," she was quite peremptory. "From Rome I will go down to Brindisi, and there catch a boat for Greece. I believe the islands are marvellous, especially Crete. And there are very few cars, so it will be ideal for cycling."

"And I suppose from Greece you will go on to Turkey or Egypt."

"I hadn't thought of that. But you're quite right. A person should see Istanbul, and the Pyramids too."

"After that the Himalayas, and India!" She looked at me sharply when she detected the tone of cold mockery in my voice. I launched a direct assault. "What about your daughter? Are you going to put a chair-seat on the back of the High Nellie and bring her with you? Are you going to pay me for my bike before you wear it out on the highways of Europe?"

She continued staring at me as if she were trying to make sense of my outburst. Then she stood up indignantly. I stood up just as indignantly, determined that she should not escape this time. My knee was firmly behind the seat which was blocking her flight-path. As the bike was chained to the railings, she had no hope of shaking me in any event.

"I am going to the toilet," she declared in an aggrieved tone, and plonked her handbag down on the table. I slowly sat down again. She could hardly set out for Rome without her handbag. Nevertheless, I eyed her closely as she made her way to the toilets, and didn't take my eye off the toilet door while she was inside.

Eventually she emerged. She went straight over to the bouncer who was lounging at a table talking to patrons. She tapped him on the shoulder, and I watched him bend his ear to her and then turn to stare at me, while he listened to whatever tale she was telling him. He nodded seriously, his brows tightening around the glare he had directed on me.

Then she swaggered over, followed purposefully by the bouncer. She grabbed her bag from the table without saying a word. Her bearing, her swagger said everything, said that she had won the battles and the war without a single formidable engagement.

As she turned to leave, the bouncer put his hand roughly on my shoulder.

"You stay there," he snarled. "Or, if you insist on leaving, you and I will take a few steps down to the police station. It's a damn shame that a young lady can't enjoy the freedom of this town without being troubled by your likes."

I sat back in a state of dismay. The 'young lady' was quickly outside, unchaining the bike, mounting it, and cycling down the street so fast that her hair was blowing behind her. Somerset, the White Cliffs, Paris, Rome - how dare she? In the following minutes I made several attempts to rise, hoping to head her off at the ferry, but each time I was arrested by a threatening glance from the bouncer. Eventually it was too late She had given me the slip. I lapsed into a night of heavy drinking.

When I finally drank my head clear, I spent several hours contemplating my predicament. My first instinct was to follow her without delay, on the next ferry, through England, through France, Italy, wherever she went, as a weasel follows a hare, never wavering, never losing determination, until I nailed her, devoting the rest of my life, if necessary, to the task of thwarting her.

But, a few pints later, my reasoning had come full circle. I decided to let her go, to let her away with the damned bike, and to forget her. There was no point in letting the injury fester. I would keep Lisa and the child. The house was big enough, the room was free, and my relatives never called anyway. I would give up drinking and take an interest in theology. I could have long discussions with Lisa in the evenings instead of going to the pub; that would save enough money to support her and the child. I might even marry her. Why not? In my house who would notice another wife, another family? If Lisa had any scruples we could both convert to one of those religions that allowed bigamy. Why not? Wasn't it Phyllis who said you could do anything you wanted to do?

LETTERS

Themes

I notice Panurge often has a theme in an issue - any forthcoming themes for a writer to aim at?

Chris Alsop
Chapel-le-Frith

No, the named anthologies are only for shop sales purposes i.e. to get past the booksellers who don't like colourless titles like Panurge 23. *We don't edit by theme, though by a fluke a lot of* Panurge 22 *was about mystery and the occult. Ed.*

Too Quick

Rejection I can take but the sound-barrier breaking speed my subscription cheque appears to have been grabbed and my story read and swiftly rejected has left me breathless. Are all your many submissions responded to with the same remarkable alacrity? Your perfunctory note is evidence of your haste. No spaces between full stops and commas. Small 's' at the beginning of a sentence. No full stop at the end of a sentence. And you yourself are an author and teach Creative Writing!?

Anthony Attard
London N2

Only Mr Attard and Brian Darwent of Panurge 21 *Letters page have ever complained about our quick service. Otherwise we have had hundreds of authors writing in to say thanks for a quick personal response. As for my manky manual typewriting I don't see its correlation with editorial rigour any more than AppleMac'd rejection slips denote a heartfelt approach by a computerised editor. When a*

magazine takes three months to turn down a story it's because it has been sitting there unopened and unread for two months, three weeks, in my view. Mr. Attard even objects to getting his first subscriber copy of the magazine too quickly. If he was trying to edit a magazine on the shoestring budget we do, he would be pleased to send out books by return of post too. Ed.

Censorship

'had it been written by a man I wouldn't have printed it'. Your comments, Letters Page Panurge 22. Care to expand on that remark?

Richard Griffiths
Ware, Herts

Val Warner and Dick McBride have also complained about my 'gender censorship' and I deserve all I get for expressing myself so hastily and badly. What I meant was that I sincerely believe that C. Hauch's very strong and harrowing theme (the poignant struggle between the prudish and sexually active 'halves' of a 19th C female Siamese twin) could only have been adequately written about by a very sensitive and gifted woman writer. Val Warner of South London vehemently believes otherwise and on reflection I think maybe Zola or D.H. Lawrence might have managed it. But most contemporary male writers choosing such a theme would have emphasised the prurient leering aspects I think; a sort of slurping imitation McEwan or M. Amis. However had a gifted male writer sent in something as sensitive and unleering as Christine Hauch then of course I would have printed it. Ed

Elizabeth Howkins

Any Old Fart In A Storm

On the day that Milton was declared brain-dead, seven unattached females of a certain age shot craps for his body outside the I.C.U. Gerda was nervous as she blew on the dice, sending a wad of sugarless gum pirouetting through the morning air, redolent with room-freshener and pee. The faint moustache above her lip quivered in annoyance. She felt that her claim was paramount and viewed her participation in this tasteless, Runyonesque competition with barely harnessed disdain.

She needed a date for her thirtieth high school reunion. The situation was critical. You can't just rent a date like you rent a bike, she thought, unless you want a gigolo with pointed shoes and a waxed moustache. Having been voted the senior most likely to succeed, it was unthinkable for her to attend the gala if she could not even succeed in getting a date.

Hilary, on the other hand, felt that her claim was stronger. After all, hadn't she graciously, if reluctantly, given up a septuagenarian with a steel plate in his head and a quadruple bypass in his chest, handing him over to her friend Louise who was terminally ill with an exotic skin disease that caused her to shed her epidermis bi-monthly in five inch sheets. Louise had made it clear that she felt that her impending death gave her a pressing claim for male companionship. Hilary wasn't sure about the validity of this argument, but she stepped aside gracefully when Louise threatened to blow her head off as she had nothing to lose. Hilary had also felt that her failure to defer to the terminally-ill might be viewed as petty or mean-spirited in some circles and, basically, she was a compulsive pleaser.

Mia also felt that her claim could not be ignored. She wanted Milton so she could have him stuffed and sit him at the dining room table, in full view of her neighbors as they passed by her picture window. By appearing to break bread with her nattily-dressed, if somewhat incommunicative companion, Mia hoped to derive a certain cachet from the fact that she now had a man in her house and was no longer dining alone. It was her hope that the sight of her masculine dinner companion would earn for her that extra measure of respect that might prompt her neighbours, with their frenetic Chihuahuas and Shih Tzus, to pass by her begonias and to cease using her lawn as the communal pissoir and plop place of choice. With a man in the house, she reasoned, one acquired a certain protective accoutrement of mystery and power.

Mia didn't really mind if Milton were a bit stiff and unresponsive as long as he looked reasonably life-like and fashionable from a distance. She did feel that stuffing him properly would be the biggest challenge. But, as she had had a class in taxidermy at School Night, where she successfully stuffed three skunks and an owl, she felt that she could cope nicely. After all, Milton was not that much different from a coyote or a skunk. He was merely somewhat bigger. And she also had a lifetime of stuffing Thanksgiving turkeys behind her.

However, as the crap-shoot progressed, minor sniping became a problem. Gerda began to quarrel with Trixie who only wanted Milton for a one-night stand her - ex-husband's wedding - and felt that, as undecomposed men were in short supply, no one should be afforded the luxury of Milton's companionship for more than an evening or two. In her view, Milton should be passed around like a Mongolian hot-pot and should be the property of all. No one person should be permitted to hog.

Jill was so desperate that she told Mia it was unfair and unreasonable of her to demand a full man when it was so obvious that she could clearly make do with a part. After all, Jill reasoned, Milton would only be seen at the table from the waist up. She considered this to be a flagrant and blatant waste of half a man. However, since the crap-shooting committee was unable to agree on a plan for utilizing the bottom of the body, it was decided that it would be impractical to sever Milton at the waist, and negotiations bogged down temporarily while someone went out for cokes.

Then, someone suggested that Mia was being stubborn and unreasonable as, it was pointed out, she could achieve her goal of heightened self-esteem more efficiently by placing the bottom half of Milton on a ladder in front of the window, thereby accomplishing her desired effect of impressing her neighbors with a masculine presence and, at the same time, freeing the top half of Milton for front-line duty elsewhere.

Trixie then argued that she could utilize the top half by sitting it in the limo and taking it to the wedding, but she would then have to explain why her date could not get out of the car. Thus, the feelings of the group, passionately presented to Gerda by the crap-shooting committee, were delineated and clarified and a conclusion reached: no one woman should be narcissistic enough to demand or expect the unrestricted right to hog a whole man.

But Gerda countered that she held seniority by reason of age and degree of desperation and that she was entitled to a whole man. Her appeal was impassioned, buffered by examples of precedent both literary and legal that no princess in any fairy tale had ever gone to a ball with half a prince and that cutting up corpses was punishable by jail. Why, she demanded passionately, should she accept half a man anyway; after all, when she ordered a turkey, the butcher did not deliver a legless fowl. One expects a Christmas turkey to have all his salient parts and a Cornish hen, to have two legs, so, it is not unreasonable, she argued, to expect a man to have a bottom and a top. Mia, drawing on her twenty years as a member of the bar, was then quick to point out the weaknesses in this analogy.

"Whenever you order a turkey or a chicken," she interjected smugly, "you never get the head."

"Look," said Trixie, "let's work this out. Men aren't exactly a dime a dozen. We can't turn on each other like a pack of starving wolverines. We are ladies, after all. Several of us have doctorates. Maybe Mia could get by with the bottom and I could manage with the top. Maybe, to prove that I am reasonable and willing to compromise, I could even get by with one arm provided it was night time and my escort didn't leave the car. After all, the wedding guests will only be viewing us from one side. I can wrap Milton's arm around my shoulder and, with my body strategically placed, I might even be able to conceal the absence of his head. Can anybody use the other arm?"

"Maybe Mia could get by with just one arm too, by sitting on a couch in front of the picture window, so the neighbors can see an obviously masculine arm strung about her shoulders like a shawl," Gerda said, with a pretense at being helpful.

"You forgot one small problem," Jill said timidly.

"What's that?" Trixie snorted.

"He won't have any head, only an arm, won't it look funny?"

"She won't need a head if she sits to the side of the couch," Trixie countered, never at a loss for ideas. "It will be assumed that his head is behind the wall. We all have to be flexible and bend a little."

"I've had it!" Mia shouted. "Flexibility has its limits. If you take away any more parts, I'll be left with an ear and a nose!"

At this point, Mabel, who had been unable to tag any visible parts, became desperate and offered to take Milton from the knees down. Trixie impulsively offered to settle for a foot. Just as the argument

Elizabeth Howkins

began to heat up, the doors of the I.C.U. opened behind them. Mia grabbed Nurse Mallet by the arm.

"Is it over yet?" she said.

"Oh no, dear, the most extraordinary thing has happened," Nurse Mallet said, waving a paper in front of Mia's face.

"What's that?"

"It's his breakfast order, dear, he filled it all out himself."

She began to read "...blueberry pancakes, no butter, sausage and bacon, two bagels, six eggs, over easy, three bowls of oatmeal..."

"Stop!" Mia screamed. "He's brain-dead. He can't order breakfast!"

"Sorry, dear, the machine malfunctioned. We made a little error. The deal is off. He isn't brain-dead at all. He was only drowsing. We'll be taking him off life support in a few days and he should be out of here in about a week just as good as new. I'm going out for a ciggie."

Nurse Mallet moved off down the hall. Not a word was spoken. Not a glance was exchanged. But somehow, through some finely-tuned extra-sensory camaraderie, they all knew at once exactly what had to be done. Gerda, their acknowledged leader, by reason of seniority of age and abrasiveness of tone, separated herself from the group and passed through the doors of the I.C.U. She presented herself as Milton's sister, come all the way from Pago Pago to buck him up with a chat. She slipped quietly into the cubicle and, in a supreme exercise of situation ethics, she calmly pulled the plug.

"*De minimus non curat lex* - the law does not concern itself with trifles," she muttered as she exited skilfully amid the clanging bells and buzzers, barely brushing the crash-cart with her designer jeans.

Panurge 24 (April 96)

Ron Berry's wonderful story about a Rhondda Valley pit disaster. Lots of excellent fiction from first-time writers.

Albert Leventure

Researches Between Screens

> *Would an event that can be anticipated and*
> *therefore apprehended or comprehended, or*
> *one without an element of absolute*
> *encounter, actually be an event in the full*
> *sense of the word? There are those who lean*
> *toward the assumption that an event worthy*
> *of this name cannot be foretold. We are not*
> *supposed to see it coming. If what comes*
> *and then stands out horizontally on the*
> *horizon can be anticipated then there is no*
> *pure event. No horizon, then, for the event*
> *or encounter, but only verticality and the*
> *unforeseeable. The alterity of the other -*
> *that which does not reduce itself to the*
> *economy of our horizon - always comes to us*
> *from above, indeed, from the above.*
>
> Jacques Derrida

My dead father speaks to me in the present tense of memories that were not to be.

Seated at the kitchen table, he holds between the index finger and thumb of his right hand a photograph. Before him, and arranged in an arc across the formica surface of the table, are more photographs, although to describe these objects in this manner is to confer upon them a dignity, a prestige, which they neither solicit or enjoy. They are, quite simply, 'snapshots', and in lacking artistry, they forfeit artfulness.

These snapshots all depict in an assortment of settings the same two figures, a woman and a child. In one, foregrounded against a screen of trees, the woman, in her late thirties, is seated on the grass in Kensington Gardens. She is wearing a light-coloured two-piece suit; her hair is windswept. Her left arm supports the infant; the hand resting against his right thigh. Both figures are looking into the camera.

Another picture portrays the couple, perhaps a year later. Now the setting is less expansive. The park has been replaced by a modest domestic garden. Lattice fencing and brickwork dominate the rear of the picture. The woman's right hand encircles the child's bottom;

her chest and shoulder act as a buttress for the remainder of the boy's weight. Most of her body is covered by a floral apron. She is laughing. Sunlight has made the child's hair white.

Further snapshots chart the boy's development. No longer in need of the mother's physical support, he stands unassisted and upright outside a tent, its flap open and revealing a groundsheet. He is in the uniform of a cowboy and holds a teddy-bear. In the background, an aviary is visible. Branches from an apple tree in the adjoining garden spill into the one where he is posing.

Several years have now elapsed, and in a garden where a rose bush is in full bloom, the boy struggles to pacify a tabby cat which fills his bare arms. A crude extension to the house, in the form of a wooden outhouse with a corrugated iron roof, appears in the left of the frame.

The garden with the roses, the tent, the profuse lattice work, was located in north-west London. It was there that I was unmanned in a cheerless house by civil affection and the common kiss; where on winter evenings, before a coal fire, a middle-aged woman, sitting at a table, patiently and expertly cut from cheap paper military medals, starfish and flags, which I, sprawled on the floor, pasted into scrapbooks. In these rooms, unnaturally darkened by sickness, infant hands experienced the tender enslavement of sheets, turning the pages of encyclopaedias, their red covers burning bright on the wordstained counterpane.

Neither the picture which my father is holding, or the ones scattered on the table, occupied his attention. What absorbs him resides outside the room. When these visitations first occurred, I thought my father was arranging the snapshots in what he considered to be their chronological sequence, but this was not so, as I was later to realise; their principal function was not to captivate, but to allow deviation to take place.

*

"Would you draw the curtains?"

I did as he requested. The effect of sitting within a hand's reach of a person who had been dead for more than twenty-five years was eerie and quietly spectacular.

"You were very young - five or six. I don't suppose you remember?"

From childhood, continuing through adolescence into early adulthood, the memories I had retained of my father had been

Eva and Jane 1991

Philip Wolmuth

fragmentary, evanescent, and invested with a spurious autonomy; the consequence of my inability to anchor them in any satisfactory matrix of continuity. What remained was the potency of these images to charm and to claim residency within me.

There existed, however, a lack of a particularly singular kind. For no matter how great my concentration, no matter how intense the longing, I always failed to recall his voice. I had no abiding impression of whether it was gentle or harsh, whether afflicted with a speech impediment or bearing an accent, grandly copious or hesitant in expression. In the brief time that he shared with the woman he married, and the child he fathered, it was as if he had been mute, or I, deaf.

I directed my attention to him, and to satisfy his curiosity proceeded to enumerate the incidents that I had carried with me from infancy to the present day. "I remember the smell of burnt wood."

"Burnt wood?"

"Yes. You were removing paint from the toilet door with a blowlamp."

"Oh."

He looked at me quizzically, intently. I resumed the inventory. "I remember you singing sea shanties - at least I think I do. I remember the aviary with all the budgerigars, and you placing your hand in the nesting boxes; and the large tank of tropical fish. I remember playing on a trolley in a warehouse in Shoreditch. I suppose it must have been a day when you took me to work with you. Perhaps it was a Saturday morning? I also remember you sitting at the table in the living-room, a ledger before you; you were adding up columns of figures."

The attempt at reconstruction was obviously as tedious for him to hear as it was for me to reassemble and communicate, for his interest had shifted away from me, and his eyes were following his fingertips as they traced lines across the table. I discontinued the itemising and took a handful of cherries from the colander.

*

"As a young man I had wanted to go to sea. I would look at contemporary prints of those magnificent China clippers, and study all the old shipping routes. Their very names entranced me: the Dutch East Indies, Java, Sumatra, Saskatchewan, Nantucket. How those names resonated when I was a youth. I memorised the names of every piece of rope that formed the rigging. Do you know how many sails a full-rigged ship had?"

I confessed my ignorance.

"Twenty-eight," he enthused.

I listened as he spoke admiringly of the sea-faring abilities of the Phoenicians. Sitting there, dressed in a pair of grey flannel trousers, a sports jacket, and a white shirt unbuttoned at the neck, he conformed in all physical characteristics to the man my untutored eyes had rested upon from the family photograph albums that used to entertain me as a child.

At the age of forty-nine my father had died of a cerebral haemorrhage.

"A stroke, and then he was gone," my mother would, with deceptive casualness, confide to relative, friend and acquaintance alike.

"Fine mariners. Without compasses - they got their bearings from the North Star - they sailed. Wonderful traders: myrrh from Arabia, precious stones from India, gold and ebony from Africa, carpets from Persia, slaves from the Caucasus. Their towns were all ports: Acre, Byblas, Tyre, Sidon. Such colourful names."

The enchantment he received from the construction of his desire passed into something more sombre.

"But then I met your mother. We were both working at the Met. She was operating the spotlights. The Met. It's gone now, but you know that, of course."

I looked up and across to the person whose presence had been absent in the shaping of an individual's growth. Had I disappointed him by my pained civility, by my incapacity to feign surprise that I should be sitting in a room with someone whose funeral had taken place shortly after I had started primary school? Father and son? Yes, but each less than a stranger to the other, without affinity and quite ignorant of the path to the other's heart. I thought of my mother, and how familiarity, the closeness of physical proximity, had prevented intimacy from occurring; and how this familiarity first gave host to impoliteness and, eventually, to detachment.

*

I recalled how, after the first visitation I received from my father, I had instinctively dusted the surface of the table at which he had been sitting, and sprayed the room with air-freshener; then, gently closing the door behind me, walked along the hall to my bedroom, being particularly careful not to disturb my mother as I passed her room, concerned that her discomfort would prevent her from finding the fullness of rest; that she would be compelled to leave her bed and, unknowingly, embark on an unforgettable journey; one that would begin with her opening the kitchen door onto an impossible scene.

*

Except for the packing cases containing her clothes, and the tufts of cat fur that have become attached to the floorboards, my mother's bedroom is bare. Yet death was abundant in this room, as it was elsewhere in the house; its remains were everywhere to be seen.

Because death belongs to the living, insofar as it remains *our* speculation, and it is our speculation that offers the proposition that death is that which does *without something*, I would tell myself that now my mother lives within me, I have become her place of rest, and while I believed such a conviction leaned towards the truth, it was never a cushion against the comprehensive hurt I experienced in the weeks following her death. That which is unavoidable does not necessarily preclude surprise. Perhaps this is another way of saying that knowledge does not prepare us for its consequences, that there is lack in knowledge itself.

Did she, I allowed myself to wonder, because of the severity of her isolation, retrace her steps to a time near the beginning, when eventfulness was found in the unhurried exchange of glances, in the comforting pressure of another's hand upon her own; a time when the body was not set on its irrevocable movement towards the finality of repose, before the turn towards death was completed? Did she remember the period of courtship with fondness, the temporary uncertainties and the promises that were given and withheld in the giving of the promise? Perhaps she relinquished her hold on the past's tender associations to concentrate her meagre energy on the days remaining open to her?

It seemed to me that every move my mother made entailed a loss, as she travelled from the London boroughs of Bayswater to Paddington to Kilburn, from home owner to tenant in a rented property, from financial independence to impecuniosity, from pregnancy to childbirth, from spinster to wife, and from wife to widow, to a body that no longer bore the weight of its existence.

*

There were masks on the walls in the room with the white piano. One, she told me, was a self-portrait, painted at the age of seventeen. Sexually indeterminate, it possessed affinities with a death mask. It

36

was here, in these rooms, in this place that I had come to as if led by a trail of breadcrumbs, that I reconstituted the fragments which formed the final, dismal days of my stay in a house where my father, dead for a quarter of a century, returned to share with his son a dream he had both nursed and buried, and the woman, his wife, my mother, whom he never encountered on his return, and was therefore spared re-experiencing the violence of separation which is constitutive of encounter.

In an upstairs room we listened to the workman's shovel striking gravel; from the window we watched paving stones being lifted and rolled to rest against the base of a tree. I was to learn from her that the first teaching the other gives me is the fact of her teaching. Although I could not have access to the knowledge she held at a distance from herself, even though the incomparable guidance I was to receive could not even be said to be useful, it was from her that I was taught about the gift and the gift in giving. That if it is humanly possible for us to give, then we are obliged to give more than the hand can hold, and not because of the weight of number. If we are capable of giving at all, we give from a necessary blindness, for we know not what we give and we are at a loss to know where what we give falls.

*

And now the truth - that crack in the eggshell - is between us, an unnegotiable distance has occurred. What is left is what remains, rememorations and reliquaries, the ruins of my own making: the tobogganing on Primrose Hill, the amusement arcade on Brighton pier, the Irish coffees at a restaurant in Victoria, her playing a Bach prelude, the two ferry tickets to Brownsea Island, inserted between the Egyptian banknotes and her design card, in the brown leather wallet that once belonged to my father, and the wedding rings abandoned by hands.

I have felt the anguish of anticipation on every occasion when I have entertained the thought of meeting her again. A chance meeting would seem as improbable as one that had been meticulously arranged. What if we met again and I saw nothing of myself in her? This would not signify that my vision had become impaired, but to see her again in this way would be to experience a form of second sight. It would, I have come to believe, indicate that I was approaching recovery, a recovery that would prove to be incapacitating.

Jonathan Treitel

Sealed Room

I met my wife during the War of Attrition. I married her after the Yom Kippur War. Ruth was born during the Invasion of Lebanon; Boaz in the second year of the Intifada. My marriage goes on. If our country were another country, the markers on the course of time would be trivial, pleasant happenings. We would say that such-and-such an event took place while Maccabi Tel Aviv was European basketball champion, or when Israel at last won the Eurovision Song Contest, or in the month I painted the kitchen blue...

I first committed adultery with you in a comparatively peaceful epoch, when our troops had withdrawn from Lebanon, almost; and the territories were as calm as they were ever going to be. I was doing my reserve duty. I was wearing uniform stamped in five places: PROPERTY OF THE ISRAEL DEFENCE FORCES - so you can be sure I was not to blame. My body was camouflaged so as to pass for desert. The soles of my boots were deeply grooved to grip the ground. My bootlaces were threaded through the eyes and wound seven times round the top and knotted at the back as per instructions so they shouldn't snag on anything and come undone. This is what the army does: it tries to remove individuality - so of course everybody fights back with small acts of defiance. The youngsters on call-up go about badly shaven, or don't tuck their shirt in, or affect a gold amulet dangling in their chest hair. Actually many of them, between childhood and adulthood, are happy to float in the womb of the IDF - but it is conventional to pretend to dislike it. Department stores and stationery shops, the length of the land, sell greeting cards with comical illustrations to be given to the teenagers beginning their service - a sketch of a raw recruit being bawled at by a sergeant-major, say; ten thousand soldiers will receive the identical card, each with an individualised message scrawled in the middle. When they leave, they will be sent a card with a picture of a bird fluttering from its nest, a rocket taking off ... At my age then, I was already too old to be sent reassuring cards, and my individuality was both firmer and more difficult to assert. I was assigned to a desk in the quartermaster's office at a base halfway between Dimona and nowhere, with my Uzi to the right of me and a Japanese calculator on my left; my round reading glasses were always sliding down the bridge of my nose; a fine white sand was always flurring around my ankles; there were always more accounts to be checked.

And then, one hot afternoon, ... I remember I was auditing an invoice for a bulk order of canned beans; another one for anti-aircraft ammunition; cheese; grenades; bread; barbed wire... I was thinking about the waste of it, the endless consumption: iron rusts, missiles are launched and burn up during training sessions; lunch metabolizes into shit and water and carbon dioxide... When you came in.

You also were on reserve duty. (Which was strange, because you could have claimed exemption on account of your children.) You had been doing one of those jobs women are allotted in the IDF, involving shouting at men for hours on end. (We need to bring our mothers along, even when we fight.) Your throat was sore. I offered you a soothing pastille. You sucked it. And I too, although my throat was perfect, dropped a pastille on my tongue. I remember we talked about our children.

We talked about our children in the hut in the desert where the fan whirred endlessly and rocked on its base to blow at me then you; me and you; me, you... and white-hot light was seeping in through every crack. We talked many times, as often as we could be alone together. We decided we would not break up our marriages, for the children's sake. We would be lovers, of course, because nothing could stop that; yet the old marriages would last a little longer. But when the children would be mature enough (a certain number of years in the future then; we had chosen a date) at last we would live together, and everything would come right.

The first time we met, you spoke in a scratchy croak because you had to; and I replied in the same voice. Our whispers were scented with camphor and eucalyptus. On later occasions also, we conversed in gasps.

And then it came to pass - not exactly on purpose - that my Boaz was born. The date of our would-be happy ending was pushed farther off into the future, into one of those scarcely imaginable years in which the science fiction novels I read in my own childhood were set - when everybody would wear identical aluminium clothing, inhabit space stations, and fear only Martians.

*

Let's talk about our children. This morning I was bathing Boaz, my three year-old. I washed him; I soaped him; I helped him push his yellow plastic Tyrannosaurus Rex beneath the surface, and laughed with him when it came bobbing up. I waved the big soft towel before him like the future, and wrapped him all around in it. I dried him. He

39

was so beautiful I wanted to cry.

I took him back to his room. His room is furnished with soft, harmless things: a cuddly bear, a bean bag, a poster of Bugs Bunny ... When you have a toddler you suddenly realize the world is crammed with dangers. Even your own home is a hissing nest of death traps: you must ward off each one. The toilet bowl is to be covered lest the child slip in and drown. The electricity outlets have to be plugged so he won't poke things in. A steel bar had been screwed across the sole window in his room, small and high up though it is. I sat him on his bed. I told him a story about a foolish brave boy who exchanged a cow for a bag of beans; I made him smile. I climbed on his bright green chair and gripped the steel bar with my left hand as I crisscrossed tape over the window so that, if the worst came to the worst, the pane, hopefully, would not fall in.

He burbled something to me. I tried to explain what I was up to; but I'm poor at justifying my actions, as you well know. He was puzzled. He questioned me. He stammered, 'Missile.' I remembered how proud I used to be when one of my children had learnt a new word.

*

And two hours later I was driving into Jerusalem, to meet you.

*

Every house, every apartment, every school, every office, every hospital, every factory, now has a sealed room. Plastic tape covers the cracks and crevices. Frowning instructors on the television have shown us how to convert a normal room into a special one; a free leaflet in Hebrew, Arabic, and Russian contains several helpful diagrams. One calls it 'sealed' but of course it is not - not perfectly, that is; a little something might always drift in. In my home we had decided to make Boaz's room the sealed one - because it's high up, and has the littlest window, and so as not to frighten him too much. When the warning comes on the radio and the siren goes off, I and my wife and my Ruth who is a big girl now have to squeeze into his childsize room, and attach his mask first and then the others (the instructions are to put his on last - but no parent would ever do that), and sit on his bed or the beanbag, or the floor, or remain standing, waiting, conversing until the conversation dies away, listening to the radio for further news, staring at his grotesque, chewed, beloved brontosaur, glyptodon, mastodon, pterosaur ...

*

It was dusk. I was speeding down King George Street, and then turning sharply right and right again into Jaffa Road. I was on my way to the heart of the city, to the rendezvous. A mass by Palestrina was playing on the car stereo (I had chosen something as unconnected with the present as I could); a choir of boy sopranos was singing a phrase in Latin I couldn't make out. Every time the voices rose to a quavering peak I imagined it was the siren blasting its terrible warning. There had already been several missile attacks - nobody killed, few injuries - in Tel Aviv, Haifa ... not here, not here...

The Old City. It loomed above the dim roads astir with a little traffic. It looked like a port seen from the sea, or the hulk of a big ship. Let the city be one of the grand transatlantic liners of yesteryear. (Strange how Jerusalem should evoke maritime images, despite and perhaps because of the scarcity of water here. The righteous king Hezekiah dug a well deep within the city to resist siege. The well still exists, though each year the water table sinks.) I thought of those bittersweet shipboard romances you read about in novels and watch on film: he and she suppose they are in love, but when the time comes to step on dry land again - with umbrellas furled under arms, wearing going-away suits - they see each other as strangers and know they must part ... Yet we did not part.

Suppose the siren really should shriek. I mentally ran through the procedure. One is supposed to turn off the engine and the heater, so nothing will attract a heat-seeking homing mechanism; and put on one's mask. The effort is to make one's vehicle, one's surroundings, oneself, exactly like everywhere and everything and everybody in the land: then there is no special reason why fate should pick on one ... on me ... on you ... Now is the wrong era for love. Fear makes us want to shed our egoism, our (the word should exist in a lover's lexicon) tuism; to switch off our heart so no love-seeking homing mechanism will find us out and destroy us.

*

I phoned you this afternoon, after bathing Boaz. He was tucked in his bed. I'd told him a story about a boy who climbed a beanstalk; I'd begun the tale of the three bad wolves but no sooner had the first beast begun to huff and puff than my son fell asleep with his mouth open. Meanwhile my wife had been in my study, in search of a safety pin, rummaging through my bits-and-pieces drawer. I mumbled to you urgently. We had to meet. We had to meet soon and there, now and here. My wife had discovered something. I wasn't sure exactly

41

what. Perhaps fate advances like a supersonic missile - you hear the engine-whine only after the explosion.

*

I was on my way toward 'our place'. Nowhere else came to mind. It was where we had always rendezvoused in the early months of our covert adultery, before we had become efficient and hired a room of our own. This location was simultaneously on the roofs and the ground of the Old City ... The paradox dissolves: adjacent districts are built on different levels; the Jewish quarter rears up over the souls of the Christian ghetto. It had been a canny place to meet, because on the one hand few people we knew had any likelihood of passing that way, and on the other hand there were many adequate reasons why we both might have been walking through separately, en route from one part of the city to another, and have met by sheerest chance. There are many exits and entrances to our place. In the old days, before the Intifada, you or I used often to step through Jaffa Gate, past the Armenian tourist shops where they vend jocular tee-shirts, antique oil lamps, olive wood crucifixes and menorahs, then twist left and right up steep alleys, over a glorious rug, worn steps, sometimes a stretch of sand where the paving had been taken up to lay pipes for water or cables for electricity ... and climb a fire escape to the place. But this route had become risky, what with the demonstrations and the strikes and the hatred and the tear gas ... Or (and this had become the standard way in) we could reach it via the reconstructed Jewish quarter, striding beneath the pale cool arches of First-Fruit Street. Let me fix my mind on our place, as it was back then. Prickly pear cactus grew wild against one corner of the roof/ground, bearing a watery untouchable fruit that was too much trouble for anybody to bother picking. A yeshiva was established at one end: we could often hear the students praying, or studying in a chant composed of variations on a theme of interrogative sounds. Dress shops and a costume jewellery shop were below: we glimpsed through skylights the tops of shoppers' heads passing under our feet. Also down there: Muhammed's Video Parlor; triumphant beeps signaled the destruction of a flying saucer. Usually a couple of soldiers were posted somewhere in the vicinity; they smoked and chatted, ignoring us; each time it was a different pair.

This place, as I have said, was where we met, kissed, and moved on together to some hotel for a few hours. We tried so many hotels. The Christian one where they disapproved of us. The Armenian one where (worse!) they clapped and offered arak. We liked the one where nobody appeared to care; we entered by way of a cafe where old men in kefiyahs sat playing backgammon and sucking hookahs. We also stayed at the tourist hotels; sometimes we'd speak English at the reception desk and pretend to be Americans. Oh, you'd even dress the part, in shorts and amazing sunglasses; you'd pretend to crave Budweiser and enquire about the results of baseball games; you described everything as 'quaint' and 'cute'. When I'd finally lead you into the bedroom, you'd burst into belly-laughter, helpless with it. I'd have to undress you, my darling American tourist ... Of course our act fooled nobody ever.

*

A solo alto sings ... And the siren whined.

My instinct was to press the accelerator, to speed away from the danger zone, to escape. With conscious effort I braked; the car drew up at the curb. I put on my mask. I waited. How intolerable just to hang about: I drove off slowly, contrary to instructions.

And, cautiously looking around, I saw that all the other drivers were doing likewise - stop; mask; move - the same sequence of thoughts had passed through all our minds.

The music rose to a climax: the massed choirs sang some refrain I couldn't catch. And the siren projected its aria. And all this was background music to the old city heaving anchor and setting out to sea ... I wondered what music was being heard in other cars - heavy metal; Yemenite folksong; Beethoven's Fifth - stirring or calming, or affecting in some unimaginable way other people's minds, lending an emotional coloring to what is beyond emotion. I switched off the stereo. On the radio a nervy voice was telling us to be calm.

No pedestrians were out. I peered into the other cars. Masked figures turned to gaze at me; they could be freaks, houyhnhnms, or the inhabitants of the Jerusalem a million years in the future when homo sapiens will have evolved into an ideal race, lacking fear and love. Slowly a Subaru coasted by containing four Hassidim identifiable only from their frockcoats; their beards were concealed within their masks. A creature on a Vespa was weaving through the traffic: its torso wore a Mickey Mouse tee-shirt. I thought of certain old illuminated manuscripts of the Haggadah; because of the prohibition against depicting humans ('Thou shall not make to thyself any graven image ...') all the figures - Moses and Pharaoh, slaves and overseers - were depicted with beaked, bestial heads.

43

I parked, I walked alone to Jaffa Gate, in through the dark silent ways. I remembered my phone call to you a few hours earlier: I had blurted something and you had murmured something. It was dangerous to fix this meeting here and now - but everywhere is always dangerous - and anyway what choice do we have?

*

I wait for you in our place. The yeshiva is silent; no electronic racket from the video game parlor below. No soldiers are on guard duty here. The spiny fruits of the cactus gleam in the corner - ah, it's just a trick of light: the plant was weeded out long ago. Part of a moon, and stars.

I wait. I imagine you coming for me. You will be masked as for a masked ball. I think of Longhi's superb oils: Venetians in black costumes are on their way to a palazzo where they will undertake fantastic sensual affairs with anonymous strangers whose faces they will never see and whose identity will always remain secret. The temporary partners will descend into separate gondolas and never knowingly meet each other again.

*

Suppose a missile filled with deadly gas were to descend nearby, killing the two of us. What delicious irony ... Then I think of my Ruth and my Boaz.

*

A dog howls. It is kenneled on top of a shack on top of a roof; nowhere else to keep it, I suppose. But the dog doesn't know - it thinks it is protecting the whole black night set with stars.

*

You will come. A trim figure in jeans and sweatshirt and mask. I will hug you. And then a thought will cross my mind: am I sure this is really you? It could be another woman, here for a different assignation. Maybe a crazy American tourist. Or an Arab - who knows? - a spy radioing secret messages to Iraq. Or perhaps even, were I to tug off your monstrous mask, underneath it I would discover the head of a monster indeed.

*

You have not come yet.

*

We should be inside a sealed room - and this is the only sealed room we have: this space between the city and the sky.

Joel Lane

Every Form Of Refuge

Rumour is another world. Like tabloids or soap operas. People at work were talking about Matt's affair with Kathleen before it had even started. And once it was over, the same people claimed they'd always known that nothing was going on. How could two such different people get involved? But I could see what had made them try. Each was looking for a sort of missing element: a way to change.

Matt had joined the company a year before, fresh out of college. He was a quiet bloke, read the *Telegraph* and usually wore a suit. Whenever I looked at him, I thought of Billy Joel's line about some people seeing through the eyes of the old before they ever got a look at the young. He had a signed photo of Margaret Thatcher at home. I'm not kidding. But he hated Yuppies and the cold opportunism they represented; somehow, he thought the true face of Conservatism was different from that. I thought he was a fucking idiot, politically speaking. But a decent type, all the same. Kathleen was a newcomer to the company, up from London after four years in advertising. She was three days older than Matt, but looked much younger because she was skinny and pale. She always wore bright, multi-coloured clothes, and had a crystal laugh that threw fragments of light around the office. She was vivacious and funny, and slightly wild. But very insecure. They both were.

We worked in the publishing offices of a mail-order catalogue firm. They'd found us a new building in the jewellery quarter. New to us, I mean. It looked like a condemned cinema, with fake-marble columns on a white panelled façade. The interior had been rather hastily redecorated when we took the lease. Once we'd settled in, problems literally came out of the woodwork. We were getting used to finding our desks littered with what looked like coffee granules. So far, poison and mousetraps had achieved nothing. We were working to fortnightly deadlines, with printers who were both incompetent and mendacious. It was no wonder, in these conditions, that office gossip became somehow detached from reality. Or that some of us, particularly Matt and Kathleen, developed a kind of strange humour. *How many printers does it take to change a lightbulb? Two: one to take out the dead bulb and put in a live one, then another to come back at the last minute, take out the live bulb and put the dead one back.* Stress humour, I suppose you could call it.

Matt and Kathleen often went for a drink at the end of the working day. They lived on opposite sides of the city, so it was easier to do that than go home and meet up later. Sometimes I joined them, though I rarely went the distance as far as alcohol was concerned. They both drank as though they were empty vessels needing to be filled. After three or four pints, I normally pleaded fatigue or urgent hibernating and left them to it. Wherever we went, Matt would always use the jukebox to set the evening's mood. His favourite band were the Eagles - 'Desperado' and 'Take It To The Limit' in particular; songs of romantic longing and lonely survival. I prefered 'Lyin Eyes', with its deeply ironic sympathy for the betrayer. Some of the current bands had a similar haunted vibe: REM, Pearl Jam, Soul Asylum. One evening, the three of us were listening to 'Runaway Train' and I saw Matt and Kathleen blink away tears at exactly the same moment. That was one of the few times that I believed they might make a go of it: the fact that they didn't seem like a couple might not stop them belonging together.

That spring, the climate seemed to be going through an identity crisis. One day would be warm and bright, the next filled with rain, the next bitterly cold. In the mornings, sunlight coming through the windows created a deceptive warmth. When you left the office, the wind hit you like guilt. The mice increased their activity; and after a week when half the employees were off with mysterious skin rashes or stomach disorders, the management announced we'd be moving out in the summer. Matt and I shared an office on the first floor. Kathleen dropped in on every available pretext. She was fighting a continual battle of nerves with her supervisor, an older woman who had made the department her personal empire. Middle management seems to be full of people like that. Matt was trying to change his image: he started wearing black jeans and tight pullovers. He was learning to play the clarinet, a subtle instrument I'd always found disturbingly like the human voice.

Kathleen was always chatty in the office, but went quiet on leaving. Then later she'd brighten up again, as if she'd remembered how to smile. I thought it was strange that she managed to promote our catalogues with so much energy, when she had such a strong dislike of capitalism. "You have to make a living," she said with a characteristic shrug. "I've always fitted in where I didn't belong." Sometimes she talked about her life in London: how she knew various 'alternative' rock musicians and was friends with the head of a famous indie label. I saw no reason to doubt this. Londoners always seemed to be meeting famous people. Somehow, I felt it was better not to ask why she'd moved away. Whenever we talked about music, or films, or books, I was struck by how similar her taste was to mine. Though she was much closer to Matt, their lack of common interests seemed to create a tension between them. There were other problems too.

I remember one evening when I came back from the bar, clutching three pints of Bass, to find Kathleen crying into Matt's pullover. As I reached the table, she looked up. The tears made her eyes seem huge, like empty sockets. "It's all right," she said. "Don't worry... It happened a long time ago. Can't be changed." Matt embraced her gently. I walked over to the jukebox and selected half a dozen tracks, taking my time over it, flicking through the track listings in search of some half-remembered piece of music I couldn't identify. It was around then that they started going out together for real.

And a week later that they split up for the first time. Matt came into work looking like he hadn't slept: pale, unshaven, his clothes rumpled. We were very busy that day, so his relative silence didn't stand out; but there was something in his voice, a kind of bitten edge, that made it seem unwise to speak to him. Or even to ask what was wrong. Kathleen came in only twice, to ask for copies of the pages we were setting. Matt didn't look at her. He left early. The next day was much the same, though Matt attacked his work with a little more confidence. Just after he went home, the phone on his desk rang. It was Kathleen; I told her she'd missed him. "Damn," she said. "What time are you going?" Five-thirty, I told her. "I'll speak to you then."

We walked into town, and had a drink in one of those sad little pubs off New Street Station that nobody goes to. Kathleen said she'd backed off from Matt, and he hadn't taken it very well. "Now he won't even speak to me. But... I just can't handle going out with someone at the moment. It's not him. Or it's not his fault. He's like a child sometimes. Or I am, I don't know. It was OK when it was just casual. I'm not afraid of sex. Just of responsibility." There was a lot more like this: join-the-dots explanation, both revealing and vague. She told me her ex-boyfriend had followed her from London; he'd borrowed things from her and sold them to buy drugs. "When I found he'd stolen some of my jewellery, I went mad. Gave him a box of razor blades and said, if you want to kill yourself do it cheaply. He cut his wrists. The scars look like bracelets. His flatmate found him, just in time. Now he uses that to hold onto me. He says *I'll die without your help*. Guilt, freedom. Freedom, guilt. Matt thinks he can protect me from these things. But he can't, and sometimes it's more like..."

"Like he thinks you can protect him?" She nodded sadly. "Perhaps you're seeing too many parallels between the past and the present?" That was something I knew a lot about, having been unable to trust anyone since my boyfriend ditched me two years before. He'd worked with me, so I knew about the problems of going out with a colleague - or rather, of working with a lover. Sometimes it's better for life to be compartmented. Kathleen and I talked a while longer, going through the options - everything from quitting the company to going steady with Matt. She decided to take the middle course: meet him for lunch and try to be friends. I wished her luck. "Everyone's capable of madness," I said. "Doesn't mean everyone's mad. It just depends on what happens to them." She smiled, and I could see layers of experience shifting in her face. We walked out to our respective bus-stops, waving goodbye across a crowded street. These days, 'rush hour' seems rather a sad understatement.

I was off work the next two days, a 'holiday' that was secretly a bit of freelance moonlighting. Then came the weekend. So it wasn't until Monday that I found out Kathleen and Matt were back together. Even then, it wasn't obvious: glances, a shared laugh, the occasional touch. Their faces had brightened somehow. That evening in the pub, Matt told me they'd spent the weekend together. When I say 'pub', we were actually in the bar at the back of the Midland Hotel. At six o'clock, it was rapidly filling up with the kind of shabby-suited respectable drunks who work in the city centre and never go home before chucking-out time. The three of us drank several pints of industrial-strength real ale, watching Pearl Jam and Nirvana on the video jukebox which nobody but us was putting money into. When Matt was at the bar, Kathleen said to me: "I can't take my past out on him."

Later but still before nine, Kathleen made a phone call from the metal-screened payphone in the hallway. Matt said he knew she'd talked to me the week before. "Did she tell you about Sarah?". I shook my head. "That was one of the things on her mind. An old friend of hers who kept borrowing money to buy heroin. She tried to drown herself when Kathleen refused to go on helping her. Now she's disappeared somewhere in London, and Kathleen thinks she might be dead." I shut my eyes, trying to hide my confusion. Fortunately, alcohol is a good screen. When you and the person you're talking to are both drunk, it's like double glazing. I wondered what to say when Kathleen came back.

But she didn't sit down again. "I've got to go," she said. "Sorry, Matt. I'll call you first thing in the morning. That's quite a good thing to call you, actually." Matt laughed without much conviction. She leaned over the table and kissed him, then smiled at me. "See you, Tim." Then she was gone, dodging through the crowd of piss-artists like a sparrow dressed as a peacock. A few seconds later, Matt jumped up. "Back in a minute." I saw him walk across the room to the telephone. Because this was a hotel, the bar had a proper BT phone rather than one of those shit portable ones, the kind that gives you no change back and cuts you off just before your money runs out.

A couple of minutes later, he was back. A deep frown joined his eyebrows together. "Tim, this is really odd. I suppose it's my own fault for being a paranoid fuck. But... there was something a bit funny about that phone call. I just went and pressed the last number redial button. Stupid thing to do, really. And a voice said 'Blind Moon'. Must be a bar or something. A male voice. I said I was trying to trace a missing person, Jane Starling. He said 'She doesn't work here.' I said thanks and hung up. Have you ever heard of a place called Blind Moon?"

I shook my head. "Who's Jane Starling?"

"Just a name I made up. That's all. God, I hate feeling suspicious. Not knowing what to believe." For a moment, the drunken stubbornness in his eyes gave way to a real unease. But another pint lightened his mood. He was in love, after all. When I got home that night, I looked up Blind Moon in the phone book. There was no such place, at least not locally. Maybe it was unlisted; but who ever heard of an unlisted bar? Then again, I suppose you wouldn't.

A few days later, the three of us went to a Chinese restaurant in Moseley. We were joined by Lee, a friend of Kathleen's. Another Londoner in exile. I wondered if she was trying to pair him off with me; but we didn't really get on. He was a fast-talking, hyperactive

Cockney with bleached hair, who worked in a music studio and had an ego roughly the size of Canary Wharf. As well as the palest blue eyes I'd ever seen. The meal was like a complex game in which various dishes were passed around the table, sampled and remixed. The conversation was simpler: it consisted of Lee talking and the rest of us making the odd comment. He was full of anecdotes about the London club scene and the various well-known people who frequented it - their music tastes, sexual preferences, drug habits and HIV status. At the time, it seemed unlikely that so many singers and actors had entrusted their secrets to Lee. Unlikely for several reasons. Afterwards, I realised it was all rumour dressed up as personal experience. Just outside the window, I could see the restaurant sign revolving in the wind: the words TAKE AWAY and LOTUS HOUSE alternating at a speed that made me feel sick.

Afterwards, we went back into town and visited a series of pubs. They became more crowded and more blurred as the evening wore on. At some point, Lee asked me what the Birmingham gay scene was like. He'd only been here since January, he explained, and usually went back to London at weekends. "Maybe we could meet up some time next week, and you can show me round all the local places?" I assented, though I didn't feel wildly enthusiastic about the prospect. On the off-chance, and following the warped logic of alcohol, I asked him if he'd heard of a place called Blind Moon. Kathleen and Matt were off somewhere else at this point. He looked at me in a way that was both cautious and surprised, as if I'd revealed something about myself. In a different, slower voice, he said: "It's in Digbeth. Near the coach station. But you'll only find it if you're lost." He looked away. Over the white noise of the pub crowd and the sub-Spector histrionics of a Meatloaf ballad, I could hear Kathleen's distinctive laugh: a mixture of high and low registers, like a mother and a child sharing the same joke.

Things got stranger when we ended up in the Midland Hotel bar, in time for last orders. Kathleen spent a while talking to the young barman, out in the hallway. Then she came back, giggling and clutching a scrap of paper. "He wants me to give his number to one of you two," she said, looking from me to Lee and back again. "I don't know which one." Lee glanced at the barman, said "Well, I'm up for it," and went over to speak to him. A minute later, he reappeared. "You dozy woman," he said to Kathleen. "It's *you* he's after."

50

Kathleen laughed. "Never. No way." But I noticed she'd kept the scrap of paper. Matt, who didn't seem very wide awake, wandered off for a game of pinball. I should have gone with him and asked if he was all right. But I felt too drunk to move. Lee was saying something about "you and Gary, last night". In one of those moments that's like crossing a border, I turned to look at him. He was talking to Kathleen. "Stuff being sold in that pub even I'd never seen. Cheaper than London, I'll give you that. How some of those kids made it home I'll never know." He turned to me and shrugged. "I was out with Kathleen and her boyfriend last night. This really wild place in Erdington. Bit scary in a way. She tell you about it?"

I shook my head. She'd told Matt that she'd had to stay in and work on some accounts for the publicity department. It was all to do with preparing spreadsheets on the computer. For a moment, I had to put my hands over my face. When I looked up, there were rainbows in the corners of my eyes. Kathleen was resting her chin on her hands and smiling at me. As I watched, the smile spread over her face like a thin film, from the forehead to the neck. It caught the light, so that the whole of her face shone. Then it broke, leaving a kind of raw blankness. A complete lack of identity. I got up and staggered away, pushing through the crowd to the toilet. The rusty mirror put bloodstains onto my reflection. I kept my hands under the dryer until they stopped shaking.

That weekend, the need for a drink never left me. I'd fallen into alcohol dependency two years earlier, and it had taken me months to break free. Now that pair were dragging me back through the neck of the bottle. It would have to stop. I tried not to think about Matt and Kathleen, and ended up thinking about my parents instead: their terrible marriage and confused, piecemeal divorce. Sometimes childhood is like toxic waste. It's not buried deep enough to be safe, but you can't risk digging it up again. You never get a second chance.

I don't know what I was expecting when I went into work on Monday. But Matt was fine. In the course of the day, as Kathleen consistently failed to drop in or even phone him, he became a little anxious. We'd both seen her in the building. She'd passed me on the stairs, smiling and saying "Hi!" without pausing to talk. A sort of pointillist friendship. I wondered if she mistrusted me because of what I'd learned about her on Friday. If so, it was nothing compared to how much I mistrusted her. I didn't know what to say to Matt, and somehow convinced myself that it was better to say nothing. At lunchtime, I wandered around the jewellery quarter, looking at the old façades of renovated or derelict buildings. A shop was being gradually demolished: only the frontage remained between the road and a heap of scattered rubble, half-dressed in tarpaulins.

On my way through town the next morning, I ran into Lee. "Hi Tim, how you doing?" he said. "I was going to call you today. We'll have to go for a drink next week - I'm going to London tomorrow. But I'm meeting Kathleen for lunch today. Why don't you join us?" I said I'd speak to Kathleen about it. "See you then." The early morning sunlight glittered in his hair. I saw Kathleen by the photocopier in mid-morning. The first thing she said to me was: "Lee said to give you a message. He had to go back to London last night, but he'll call you next Monday."

I said I'd seen him that morning. "In fact, he said he was meeting you for lunch today." Kathleen nodded without surprise. "Yes, that's right," she said, and went back to her photocopying. I thought of the boys in camouflage jackets you saw walking through the shopping precinct. How something meant for disguise actually made them stand out.

At the end of the afternoon, Matt phoned Kathleen's extension; but she'd already gone. "It doesn't look good," he said. I had to agree that it didn't. But the following day, she didn't come in at all. Matt considered phoning her at home, but it didn't seem likely to help. After all, her flatmate Sally would contact us if anything was seriously wrong. The next morning, Kathleen's supervisor told him she'd spoken to the flatmate. Apparently Kathleen had disappeared. She'd taken her clothes and basic possessions, left a share of the month's rent and gone. There were still things of hers all over the flat - TV, books, records, posters. Sally had no idea who to pass them on to. Matt spent the day in a state of shock, mechanically doing trivial paperwork and checking through computer files as if in search of some hidden information. Halfway through the afternoon, he disappeared for more than an hour. Then he came back with a thick sheaf of computer printouts. "What do you make of these?" he asked, passing them to me.

The immediate answer was, not much. The first lengthy printout was a series of letters and numbers arranged in groups, such as MN GMNI 15.2 and SN VNS 23.1. The letters MRS suggested a woman's name; but then who was MRCRY? The numbers, I realised, were dates in the recent past or near future. Then I saw the word ORION and realised this was some kind of astrological chart. Alongside the details of planets and constellations, a few everyday words were printed: LONDON, WEST B., LEEDS. Then I flipped over a page and saw the words BLIND MOON, next to yesterday's date. I looked up; Matt was watching me intently. "I printed these off her computer," he said. I wondered what she'd called the files, but didn't ask.

The other printouts were all biographical information. Each one started with a woman's name and date of birth, then a series of facts about her life. It was like a CV, except for a few bizarre personal details: *First sexual experience; Recurring dream; Things she can't remember; Worst and most secret fear.* There were six of these profiles. All the women had the same date of birth, nearly 23 years ago. The fifth was called Kathleen Marr. The sixth was called Jane Starling. I looked back up at Matt. "I swear I made the name up," he said. He'd gone very pale, and clearly hadn't been sleeping well. One thought was lodged at the back of my mind and wouldn't go away. It made no sense for Kathleen to store anything vital on her computer. These were old machines: they had no security, and were liable to crash at any time. So she'd installed these files with the intention of wiping them. But had she done that so she could refer to them every day while pretending to work? Or had she typed them out in order to test her memory?

Matt called in sick the next day. I suspected he'd been up all night, probably with a bottle of Jack Daniels. I'd have to call him at the weekend, check he was okay. But first, I wasn't going to let her vanish if there was any way of finding her. It was Friday; there was no entry for today on her astrological chart to provide a clue. Even then, I knew it wasn't really her I wanted to find. There was no way of recalling her to things she didn't belong to.

By ten o'clock, I'd visited every pub or bar that I'd been to with Matt and Kathleen. There were quite a few. I was drinking in order to blend in, and my sense of purpose was getting blurred. There was nobody I recognised as having known Kathleen. Even the barman who'd fancied his chances with her at the Midland Hotel was off tonight. Every now and then, I asked someone if they knew a place called Blind Moon. All I got was blank looks. Eventually, I walked down the steps at the end of New Street and past the empty stalls of the open market, frames of scaffolding and canvas like boats in a harbour. It was a cloudy night; only a few stars were visible. Beyond the market, the road led sharply downhill towards Digbeth Coach Station.

As I walked, I thought about compulsive liars. I'd met quite a few, and they didn't usually disturb me. There was one man who'd spent an evening telling me about his fabulously successful acting career; we'd gone to a pub that had signed photographs of famous actors all over its walls, and he'd complained that they'd taken his down. I later discovered he was a spot-welder. Then there was a very depressive boy who told me he'd been systematically abused as a child. It was only when his stories began to involve Satanic rituals and serial killers that I began to have doubts. The things people made up seemed to be either triumphs or traumas. But I was beginning to wonder if something else might lie behind it all. There was so much about life that didn't add up or make sense. Maybe we needed someone to take the blame for that. Someone to be the liar, so what we said could be the truth. But what would the world have to be like, for everything a compulsive liar said to be true? Like I said, by this time I was pretty drunk.

It wasn't until I reached the coach station that I realised how unhelpful 'near' was. In the waiting hall, a few drunks and vagrants were passing the time. An old woman was holding a bottle wrapped in a shawl, like a baby. An acne-scarred boy was trying either to score or to sell himself, I wasn't sure which. Possibly both. I didn't think these people would be able to help me. Just up the road, there used to be a fairly rough pub called the Barrel Organ, where I'd gone to see local bands play bad rock and have plastic glasses thrown at them. Now it was an upmarket Irish tavern, repainted in green. Everything around here changed hands before long: shops, pubs, offices, warehouses. According to rumour, the National Front met here in an unmarked building. These tall brick façades, blackened by heavy traffic, looked capable of concealing more or less anything. What could I do? I retreated into the Irish pub for a quick half, then wandered down a side-street, found another pub and repeated the process.

It was darker here; the buildings were older, and a series of low bridges (presumably for local goods trains, and presumably now defunct) made the streets look like the view through a bad pair of binoculars. Through the windows of derelict houses, I could see piles of rusty scaffolding. I walked at random until I found another pub. It was almost empty; the barman was putting chairs on the tables, but he let me have a pint of Bass. There was an outside toilet behind the pub: a tiled wall with a trench set in concrete, no running water.

After that, for a while I didn't know where I was. As my head slowly cleared, I realised there was nothing about Kathleen that couldn't be explained as mental disturbance. So well hidden that it drew other people in. The thought was quite a relief. No doubt she'd had a bad childhood. That seemed obvious. I didn't want to think about my own. Not now. It was time to head back towards New Street, assuming that I still had enough money for a taxi. What road was this?

At the corner, an old-fashioned nameplate was fixed to the wall. But it had been sprayed black. I could just see the letters stand out from the plate, but there wasn't enough light to read them. Then I realised it wasn't a street nameplate at all, but a blank circle with words embossed on it. A fire escape led up to an unmarked door; above it, there were two lit windows. I reached up to trace the letters on the sign.

When I knocked at the door, it opened. The interior was a café with black leather seats and gentle lighting. Photographs with mirrored surfaces were scattered over the walls. There were several tables, each with a group of people engaged in quiet conversation. What I had at first taken for music was, in fact, the sound of their voices echoing and overlapping like waves on a rocky shore. I bought a cup of coffee and sipped it. My head felt strangely clear. A man at the nearest table caught my eye and pointed to an empty seat. I sat down gratefully, though something about the light made these people look wrong. They had the fixed stares and jerky movements of people suffering from a chronic lack of sleep.

Their conversation drifted around me, words rising into focus and falling again. I kept my eyes on my coffee; its surface was cloudy with steam. "Kathleen is changing trains," a woman said. "There's no choice. The timetable is set." There was a mutter of agreement. Someone else added: "She always travels light. With a background like hers, who can blame her? She never had a childhood. That's why she couldn't keep the baby." The discussion continued. I looked around the table. Even close up, these people seemed unreal. Their faces were half in shadow; I could see pale skin stretched over frames of bone. They all wore the same clothes, made from

55

something like felt; it rustled as their hands moved. They were still talking about Kathleen. Were they rehearsing her script or putting her case? The café was like a film set. But it was also like a courtroom.

By the time I'd finished my coffee, the narrative had changed. They were talking about Jane and her life in Newcastle. "Her boyfriend beats her up when he's drunk. There are stitches in the left side of her forehead, like silver in a broken rock. She tells people she was mugged." *Come on,* I thought. *You can do better than that.* As if I'd spoken out loud, they all turned to face me. I saw edges of bone glinting through dry flesh. The man sitting next to me put his hand on my arm. "Do you want to be someone else?"

"No," I said. But they could tell I was lying.

BACK ISSUES AT ROCK BOTTOM PRICES

Some of the Best New Fiction of the Last Eleven Years.

Tamar Yellin

The Other Mr. Perella

He first called up my mother in the spring of 1972, and a completely unexpected 'phone call it was. She would not know him, he said, and he hoped she would not think him rude, but he had discovered our name while leafing through the local telephone book. He was investigating his family background, and wondered if there was any possibility of our being related.

We are rather proud of our name, which, while not unheard of in this country, is unusual enough to confer a little spurious mystique. In fact, his name was not identical to ours. It was spelt with only a single l, while ours had two ; the pronunciation, however, was the same. Nevertheless, the lack of the second l seemed to militate against there being any close connection.

My mother put on her best voice : Mr. Perela had a deeply refined accent, and she was a snob. On the same grounds she was reluctant to reveal very much. Our own genealogy was hardly in Debrett, and she was not going to ask him if he was Jewish.

But that much was obvious. He plainly did not expect it. And when, from her series of hints, he inferred our origin, his reaction was an explosive and delighted : "Oh! But that is wonderful. Simply wonderful!" And he insisted that we come to visit when we were next his way.

"You see," he confided, in the course of their tumultuous conversation (we were soon to learn that waves of emotion crashed perpetually through the soul of the other Mr. Perella) "I know nothing about my own history, absolutely nothing."

When my mother put the 'phone down she was slightly breathless. My father, ever calm and analytical, commented : "He sounds a little mad."

"Yes," she agreed, her eyes moist as though she really had just received a communication from a long-lost relative, from beyond the grave. "A little eccentric. A little desperate. But," she added, and this for her was the clincher, "he's a gentleman." It was largely at her insistence that we passed his way rather sooner than we might otherwise have done.

He lived in a large house near the sea, set back amongst tangled gardens on an isolated road. As we drove down the long rough driveway we exclaimed frequently, overwhelmed by the evidence of so much wealth.

So much former wealth, I should have said, for both house and grounds showed signs of having known better days. The windows were rotting in their frames, the garden a glorious wilderness ; long strands of ivy ran across the gravel and embraced the sundial near where we stopped. And the owner himself, who half ran towards us as the car drew up, was worn out like his property : bald and bespectacled, decent in a frayed waistcoat and faded corduroys, but curiously old-fashioned and neglected, like a man left behind by time.

He greeted us with the enthusiasm of a lost relation, pumped my father's hand, kissed my mother's, and professed himself charmed by the presence of three such beautiful children. I had never heard anyone speak in quite that way before. His Englishness was so exquisitely concentrated as to seem foreign.

The house smelt of mice and mould, and the narrow hall contained so many indeterminate objects we were obliged to squeeze our way through ; in fact the entire place was crammed with junk and clutter like a vast attic. Our host flung back the door on room after room. We glimpsed tapestries, uniforms, weapons, a stuffed moose head, a hurdy-gurdy. Finally we reached a wide sunny living room with French windows and enormous pictures ; there, on a broken-down Chesterfield strewn with Indian shawls, were two children, older than us : a boy and a girl, as untidy as everything else. The girl wore a buff-coloured smock and purple stockings, and had long unruly hair ; the boy lounged against the back of the sofa with his hands thrust into his trouser pockets, gazing at us through a donkey-fringe. Mr. Perela introduced them as Miles and Flavia, his children ; and while Miles tossed back his hair and flung out a hand to be shaken, Flavia bounced out of the room to fetch tea.

An unaccountable silence followed. Mr. Perela gazed uneasily at his son. Then he said, without preamble : "For God's sake, Miles, sit up straight. Don't they teach you any deportment at that bloody school of yours?" The words were spoken in a bantering, half-humorous way, but none of us were deceived. Miles looked sulky and shifted an inch in his place ; my mother began very quickly to make small-talk.

Flavia had baked a ginger cake in honour of our coming. As she set out the tea things and handed round plates, I admired her completely adult poise. She must have been about fourteen, but she had the gestures of a woman, spoke like a hostess, and had not the least hint of diffidence in her manner. Even her untidy red hair seemed deliberate, fashionable.

After tea we left the adults to themselves and explored the house. Miles disappeared off almost straight away. "He and father hate each other," Flavia said. "It's a bore." We played the hurdy-gurdy ; it produced a blurred, chaotic sound, at once comical and sinister. She began tossing things out of an old ship's chest : a wig, a doll with a soft body and china face, a pasha's switch made from a horse's tail. Everything here was touched by ghosts and belonged to the past. Flavia herself was ghostlike, other-worldly.

I picked up the switch. "Are all these things yours?"

"They're father's. He collects them. He goes to auction sales and buys mountains of other people's junk." She made a mock yawn. "He's such a bore about it!"

She took us up to her bedroom. It was cold, and to my notions, miserably bare. Flavia bounced onto the bed, and, to our well-concealed astonishment, pulled a squashed packet of cigarettes from under the pillow. "Do you smoke?" She shrugged her shoulders as she lit up. "At my school literally everyone smokes. You can't really avoid it." While I examined the items on her dressing-table - lipstick, powder, earrings, a string of hippy beads - she talked to my sisters who made a pretence of being more worldly-wise than they were : how her parents were divorced, how she attended boarding school, how she spent the Easter holidays with her father and Christmas with her mother. As she leaned back against the wall I noticed the gleam of a gold cross against her throat.

We ran outside into the garden.

The idea was to find Miles and torment him, but there was no sign of him in the broken greenhouse, on the wrecked tennis court or in the woods. The floor of the woods was scattered with narcissi and nascent bluebells ; they sloped a little in the direction of the cliff, and looking back at the house it too seemed to lean forward slightly, as though the whole property were sagging gently towards the sea.

I lost the others and found Flavia on the cliff. "Look," she said, pointing. "You can see the moon." Its pale three-quarters hung against the clear blue sky. "Do you think the moon is a man or a woman?" she asked.

"A man," I answered decidedly.

"Oh, no, she's a woman!" She frowned. "Sometimes I talk to the moon. Sometimes I talk to her all night. I pretend she's my mother." She turned to me with an appraising look. "Do you think we're related?" I shook my head. "No, I don't think so either."

When we returned to the house the grown-ups were already on the whisky and sherry. My father, who never drank, looked awkward cradling a cut-glass tumbler in his hands. The other Mr. Perella was leaning over my mother, who turned the rough-edged pages of an enormous book.

He looked up and his eyes crinkled behind his round glasses. "I see Flavia has been performing the role of hostess," he said ; adding severely : "Splendid, splendid."

All the way back to the city we discussed the idiosyncrasies of the other Mr. Perella. He was both quintessentially English and essentially foreign. He had attended minor public school ; fought in Burma ; endured a disastrous marriage. For years he had tried to trace his family without success. Now he was, as he put it, 'alone.' His children did not seem to figure in this isolation. Pouring out his heart to my mother, whom he found immediately sympathetic, he confessed that his life was ending as it had begun : in exile.

"As Jewish people, I am sure you understand," he had concluded. And then he added : "But you have so much history. I envy you your history."

This flattered her. She had already constructed many romantic notions around the English aesthete, the well-educated exile with the impeccable accent and the blank past, the lonely house on the cliff top crammed with mementoes of other people's lives. In the lights of the passing traffic my mother's face glowed and darkened with the mystery of it all.

*

Some time later the other Mr. Perella came to visit us. He came alone. My mother dressed up the spare bedroom to receive him.

I believe there was some disagreement between my parents over the wisdom of taking this course. My father was not enthusiastic. He had few romantic illusions, and feared our guest might outstay his welcome.

The other Mr. Perella looked taller and more fragile out of the context of his house, and more than ever like a visitant from another time. He gave off a peculiar odour too, not a human smell at all, but one of damp wood and dust : the smell of a genuine relic. Meeting me again, he graciously kissed my hand. I giggled ; he did not smile. Rather he looked disgusted.

He stayed for a week. To a child - perhaps also to a host - this seemed an inordinate length of time, long enough to feel as if I should always come home from school to find him reading, his finger pressed to his brow, under the standard lamp in the corner of the lounge. I got used to his smell and his green waistcoat and the fragments of black hair - nose-clippings - which he left in the bathroom. He listened to me play the piano with a concentration I had never felt from my teacher, and made me recite, under the standard lamp, the things I had learned in school.

"So you want to be a writer," he reflected, passing his fingertip over the bridge of his nose. He never looked at me directly, giving off an air of diffidence, even fear, which I was too young to interpret. "In that case there is a book you must read. It is the greatest novel ever written, and no-one can be a good writer unless they have read it. I will lend you my copy, but only on the understanding that it is a loan and not a gift. It was given to me by a very dear friend who is dead, so you must absolutely promise to return it." He brought out the book, which was not so much thick as heavy with the weight of hundreds of tissue-thin pages, and had a green cover embossed with gold. He showed me the dedication, written in already faded ink : From Charles Douglas to Anthony Perela, June 1944. I accepted it with the understandable reluctance of a child accepting a book which they must both read and return. It was *The Charterhouse of Parma.*

What was his history, what was his secret? Perhaps he had none, and the days my mother spent chasing embassies and writing letters and investigating records, unknown to me, were wasted on a man who had no secret and no history, a man from nowhere. A man whose very identity was his need to belong.

*

He did not visit our house again. Sometimes he telephoned. "Oh," my mother would say, her hand covering the mouthpiece, "it's the other Mr. Perella!" Over the years we saw him occasionally, always, it seemed, on impulse or by accident, so that I never happened to have *The Charterhouse of Parma* with me and was unable to return it ; but more than this, I was unable to do so because I had not read it yet. At every encounter I sat rigid under expectation of being asked about the book.

My mother grew older, was widowed ; he grew older, grew ill ; they shared not only a common affection but a common understanding of the cruelties of time. His children were adults now : Miles had gone off to India with a backpack and Flavia was something Bohemian in London. He continued to seek out putative relatives in Paris, Rome, Amsterdam ; he created a network, a directory of Perellas, even discovered a branch of our own family we did not realize we possessed, but he never found any who would own him as kin. The last time we saw him was at the Royal Hotel in Scarborough, in their elegant dining room. It was the perfect setting ; he and my mother talked until the remnants of the buffet were cleared away and the waiter swept the floor with an old-fashioned roller. He looked ill, obviously and slowly dying. Towards the end of their conversation he put his fist gently to his chest - he wore the same green waistcoat, I noticed - and said, in his husky, learned tones : "I suppose what I find so hard to accept is that I am really going to die without ever knowing who I was. I mean, I should be old enough to accept that by now." And after a moment he repeated, with lowered eyes, "One should really be old enough to accept these things."

My mother must have grown to love him, this relative who was not related, this lost Perella. She placed her hand over his. It was one of the few occasions on which he permitted himself to be touched. "What nonsense, you know exactly who you are," she said, smiling. "Stop looking for evidence that you're someone else."

He gave her a sharp look, and after a moment he removed his hand.

There was a finality in that last goodbye. My mother was weeping a little. They knew they would not see each other again.

Dimly I sensed it too. "I never gave him that book back," I said as we emerged from the gilded splendour of the foyer into the chilly afternoon.

"I wouldn't worry about that," my mother replied.

And indeed I still have it, on permanent loan. It seems to me, on the rare occasions when I pick it off the shelf, that the burden of guilt makes it peculiarly heavy. Perhaps this was one of the few things he possessed which were actually his own ; and he gave it over into the irresponsible hands of a child. There is no comfort in pretending that he would have wanted me to keep it, since he stated categorically that he did not. Nor can I help wondering about the consequences, for my writing skills, of the fact that it is still unread. But in this respect, perhaps, it only represents the withheld revelations of all the other unread books.

At least, whenever I look at it, I remember him.

LETTERS

Gender Bias

Nearly twice as many male writers as women writers in Panurge 22. If this continues, here's one subscriber you have lost

Daphne Maughfling
Sevenhampton, Glos

I wish the balance was better myself though as fiction editor Lorna Tracy finds with Stand, we get a lot more submissions from men than women, even though we do regular promotions with Writing Women and QWF to try and rectify matters. However to assert a few publishing realities: i) We recently printed a first book of 14 stories, a thing that few other publishers are doing these days, in the form of Julia Darling's Bloodlines. We offered it at concessionary direct mail rate to Panurge readers via Panurge 22. The response was not brilliant (more men than women bought it)and I feel that plenty of women readers of Panurge think less about gender solidarity than Daphne Maughfling might suppose. ii)In Panurges 20 and 21, in 1994, we printed 14 stories by women of which no less than 10 exceeded 5,000 words long. There is definitely no other British magazine doing that kind of job for women writers; not even Writing Women and QWF, as they simply don't have the space for long substantial stories. Ed.

Non-fiction

It's your magazine and you can print what you like but I buy the magazine for the fiction only. Is Margaret Forster's piece going to be fiction?

Bernard O'Brien
Yelverton, Norwich

No, sorry it's not. Since the reintroduction of regular publishing and first person articles in Panurge 19, we have had two letters of complaint and about fifty praising the various non-fiction pieces. Ivy Bannister of Co. Dublin would actually like more articles but I think the 10% is about right. If it's any consolation to you, it's proving absolute murder trying to get small publishers to talk about themselves. Polygon, Fourth Estate and Al Saqi have all been approached and have all failed to respond to the invitation. They aren't even interested in free advertising which is baffling, is it not? Ed.

63

Nicholas Royle

State of Independents

Dick McBride's collection of reminiscences and advice on writing and small-scale publishing/distribution ('Whizzkiddery', *Panurge* 22) was both interesting and infuriating. It raised a number of points to which I, as a writer and publisher/distributor, felt I had to respond, both on behalf on individuals such as myself and any aspiring writers and or publisher/distributors who might have read the piece and taken its advice to heart.

First my credentials, such as they are: I've been writing for 12 years and have sold around 80 short stories. My first novel, *Counterparts*, was published in a limited edition by Preston-based writer/publisher Chris Kenworthy's Barrington Books in 1993. It is a mark of Barrington Books' professionalism and achievement that the novel was widely reviewed and subsequently picked up by Penguin - their edition appeared in March 1995 and will be followed by my second novel, *Saxophone Dreams*, in March 1996. I also found time to edit two short story anthologies, *Darklands* and *Darklands 2*. And I stress 'found time to', because, like the majority of writers in this country, I write in the morning, in the evening and at weekends. For eight hours or so in the middle of the day I go out to work and earn a living. I don't resent that; it's just the way it is.

'If you are a writer,' McBride remarks, 'time shouldn't concern you; you can always make time. As a matter of fact, time is expendable.'

Absolute nonsense, clearly.

For all of us time is precious. We spend it because we have to - that is the nature of time. But that does not make it expendable. Especially for a group of people who are always striving to fit more hours into the day. It's a lucky writer who earns enough from his/her writing not to have to go out to work as well. For those of us who squeeze in a couple of sentences before breakfast and try to average a paragraph or even a page when we get home in the evening, time is a valuable commodity.

And one factor which helps us make the most of it is computer technology, which McBride treats with withering scorn. Not only does my Apple Macintosh LC save me time when I'm writing (in the ease and speed of rewriting, the printing of manuscripts and archiving material), it also enables me to run a very small but quietly successful independent press with high production standards. I started Egerton Press in 1991 in order to publish *Darklands*.

'Don't try to compete with the big boys; don't try to make your book look like theirs,' writes McBride.

Darklands competed with the big boys and won the British Fantasy Award for Best Anthology. *Darklands 2*, also published by Egerton Press, repeated the success of the first volume and then Hodder & Stoughton bought the series. With those first two books I was outputting hard copy to send to the printer. By 1994, when I published award-winning poet and *Panurge* contributor Joel Lane's first collection of short fiction, *The Earth Wire and Other Stories,* I was simply sending the printer a disk. When the job was done and the printer told me the pages had been badly trimmed so that the text was a centimetre higher on the page than it was supposed to be, I accepted his offer to reprint the entire run. He knew that there was no reason why the standards set by a small independent publisher should be any lower than those of a conglomerate.

McBride's nostalgia for mimeographed pages and stapling guns is just that: in 1995 we can produce beautiful books that are a credit to their authors. Joel Lane contacted me when I sent him his first copies of *The Earth Wire* and said he didn't think he would ever be the author of a more beautifully produced book. It was kind of him, but I'm glad to say I think he's wrong. Many publishers - Penguin, Viking, Cape, Picador, Flamingo and especially Vintage - are producing extremely attractive books these days and there's no reason at all why a small publisher cannot match them in terms of quality, production and design. Goldmark Books of Uppingham publish one book every five years or so but the standards are as high as you'll find anywhere in British publishing. Goldmark's first edition of Iain Sinclair's *White Chappell, Scarlet Tracings* is one of the most treasured books in my collection.

McBride advises underprinting rather than overprinting - 'one way of saving trees,' he says. 'If you think a book might sell 500 hundred copies, print 400 not 600.' Follow his advice on this one and you've had it. Always print 100 more than you think you can sell, because that's how many you'll need for the press, other media and complimentary copies. You'd be surprised how soon this lot adds up. With a good cover design and authoritative high production standards you can ensure people will at least pick the book up in bookshops. If you've sent out a few dozen review copies to the right people, you've also a chance that those potential customers don't just put the book right back down again. Think about it: with thousands of books published every year, the average punter is more likely to buy your book if he/she can recall its being favourably reviewed. And, assuming you've published a limited first edition, your author's not going to find it easy to sell the mass-market paperback rights unless Vintage, say, can stick a few good reviews on the back of their own edition. As my former agent told me on numerous occasions, *Counterparts* might well not have sold on to Penguin were it not for the good reviews that greeted the Barrington edition. Chris Kenworthy made sure anyone who might possibly be interested in reviewing the book was sent a copy. I follow the same line with Egerton Press, often sending copies to specific reviewers as well as literary editors, even if that means sending three copies of the same book to the same paper.

As a publisher/distributor your responsibility to your author only starts with your acceptance of his/her manuscript. If you can't deliver the goods after that, they're better off without you. There's no advantage in producing the 'cheapest edition possible of the book you want to bring out' - it does no one any favours. Go to town on the book. Do a number on it. Your author will always be grateful. I know I am.

'Counterparts' by Nicholas Royle is published by Penguin (£5.99). 'The Earth Wire and Other Stories' by Joel Lane is published by Egerton Press (£8 incl p&p from 5 Windsor Court, Avenue Road, London N15 5JQ).

Not A Pushover Quiz

Answer to Panurge 22 Quiz. It was **Francis Ponge**, dubbed by Sartre the 'poet of existentialism', who wrote a novel all about soap. **Michael Eaude** of Barcelona got there first, followed by Dai Vaughan and Maggie Mountford.

Panurge 23 Quiz. Pretty easy this if you are a keen cook. Which Nobel literature winner wrote a very good oriental cookery book? Answer to Not a Pushover Quiz, Panurge, Crooked Holme Farm Cottage, Brampton, Cumbria CA8 2AT. Deadline 5.11.95. First correct answer gets a £20 Book Token.

Stephen Blanchard

The Chicken Doctor

We had chickens before we had the dog and the dog is dead. We kept them in the back garden in a coop with a chicken-wire run. The passing of the chickens made the dog possible but eventually the dog died and the garden is gone now as well as the house. The chickens are gone, the house is gone, the dog is dead.

It was a long garden and a fair-sized house. Though I never went inside, the coop would have been high enough for me to stand upright. After that I grew quickly and by the time I was twelve I was almost as tall as my father who was anyway unusually short.

"He'll outgrow his strength," my mother predicted. "Already he has a cough."

My aunt said, "It's his nature to be tall, Eileen. Just thank God he'll take after our side of the family."

My mother was tall but had married short. She had a part-time job in the bakery, five mornings a week. Aunt Irene was unwed and fond of the chickens. She fed them and cleaned out the coop and run. She dug their droppings into the flower beds. On fine days when she was not overlooked she sang in a low light voice -

> *We have some chickens in our backyard*
> *We feed 'em on Indian corn*
> *And one's a bugger for giving the other*
> *A piggy-back over the wall.*
>
> *

Everyone kept chickens and then they didn't. One year it went out of fashion and you can walk through the town now and not see a single hen.

While the birds were still there I had a cough which kept me from school. Maybe I'd outgrown my strength. I'd put my hand against the lamp and see the shadows of my bones, the webs between my fingers filled with yellow light.

*

"The birds have stopped laying!" Aunt Irene said. She stared about the kitchen as if she was short of breath.

My mother was soaking the dried peas. "They can't have! Sometimes they hide them."

"You can't tell me that! I've looked in all their places."

My mother puzzled over it, though she had no love for the chickens. "Then a cat will have frightened them. Or a fox. They'll start again when they're settled."

Aunt Irene soaped her hands under the tap. I noticed a curl of white feather at the back of her hair. She cupped cold water to rinse her face and then stood back from the sink, gasping.

"Those hens are getting old," my mother said. "We've kept them for too long. And what's the use in keeping chickens when eggs are cheap?"

"Why there's nothing like your own eggs!" my aunt protested. "And what if there's another war?"

*

A week went by and the birds still wouldn't lay. On the Friday afternoon my aunt put on her hat and kid gloves. She wore the dark suit she kept for visits with a rabbit's-foot brooch in the lapel.

"You'll make yourself foolish, Irene," my mother warned.

Aunt Irene smoothed the wrinkles from her gloves. "There's nothing foolish in seeking advice."

She left the house, locking the front door behind her and dropping the key back through the letter-box on its twine. My mother frowned at the rattle it made. "Irene's gone to see a *man*," she told me.

"What man?" We were passing the time playing dominoes on a corner of the living-room table.

She made a hissing sound. "Some fellah about those hens of hers!"

I picked up my pieces. We were playing nines and I found them difficult to handle. Despite my height I had my father's small hands.

"Irene wants to live in the past, she wants to turn back the clock," my mother went on. "The truth is she's never forgiven me."

I did not ask what for. I had an instinct when to stay silent. With angry sweeps of her arms my mother shuffled the counters left on the table, making them slide and clatter.

"So then who is this man?" I asked when she'd finished.

Her eyes still had a glare to them. "Oh, someone she's been told about. Someone good with birds... Now who has the double-six?"

"Not me," I said.

She put down the six-and-five. I followed with the five-two. She hesitated, her tongue in her cheek, and then laid the six-and-one. "You see the world is on my shoulders, Leonard! I'm that tired after

68

that job and all they think about is getting more work from you. Your dad makes his contributions but it doesn't go far. While Irene messes with those chickens. They are what's called a mania with her."

*

Aunt Irene came back in the evening and tugged off her kid-gloves. It had been raining. Her rabbit's foot shone with drops of water.

"His name is Kruger," she told us.

My mother was making batter in the kitchen. She walked through wiping her fingers on a cloth. "This chicken-doctor?"

"Yes, that's who I meant."

"Is he Polish?" my mother asked.

"Not necessarily."

"You would think so with a name like that!"

Aunt Irene lifted one shoulder. "Polish or not he's coming to-morrow."

*

My father was short but had dark close-wove hair and strong curving teeth. His face was pale and well-shaped. On fine Saturdays we'd walk through the town looking in shop-windows and then go on to the flower-gardens or the pier.

"If he asks any questions," my mother said, "just say you don't know."

"What sort of questions?"

"Any questions! It doesn't matter what sort!"

It was early March but sunny. Dad and I sat on the pier. The warmed woodwork had a tarry smell. On the weekends you could hire deck-chairs.

"The hens have stopped laying," I told him.

He laughed at this. "Keeping chickens is old-fashioned, Leonard. You see eggs were scarce during the war but there's no need for it now. I could go into a shop this afternoon and buy a hundred eggs!"

The way he said it sounded brutal. I wasn't comfortable in the chair. I leaned forward and then back. The frame squeaked as it adjusted. "They're getting a chicken-doctor," I said.

He shook his head and took his newspaper from his pocket. "I suppose that was Irene's idea! I'll just have five-minutes nap now, Leonard. Here's sixpence for the telescope."

I took it from his hand. "Thanks," I said.

"Thanks what?"

69

"Thanks dad."

He stared at me cleverly against the light. "Look, here's a trick I learnt in the army."

I'd seen it before and it wasn't really a trick. All he did was separate the front page from the paper, put it over his face and fall asleep. After a while I left him in his chair. I thought I'd save the money he'd given me and so instead of looking through the telescope I walked up and down the pier watching the shine of the brown water between the gaps in its boards.

*

The chicken-doctor was an old-looking man with a thin neck and long-lobed ears. He sat at a corner of the kitchen table eating a sandwich my aunt had cut into four small sections. He wore a collarless shirt and a dark jacket with stained lapels and looked about the room as he chewed, at the shelves of pots and pans, the sink, the glowing element of the paraffin-fire. He was bald except for tufts behind his ears and his forehead was divided by a deep upright line so that even when eating he seemed ferocious and frowning. A leather bag with a zip-fastener stood close to his feet. The zip was part open and I saw the silvery top of a thermos flask and some contraption of striped canvas and wire struts.

"Leonard," my aunt said. "This is Mr Kruger."

"Youngster," Mr. Kruger said, his mouth half-full.

His look made me feel awkward. "Where's mam?" I asked.

"Your mother's movements are a mystery," Aunt Irene said. "A conundrum within an enigma."

Mr. Kruger drank tea and read his paper. When my mother came home she beckoned Aunt Irene into the living-room and half-closed the door.

"You didn't have to give him the ham, did you? Luncheon-meat would have done just as well."

Aunt Irene looked distressed. "You are always begrudging, Eileen! I didn't want to seem paltry. With him being a foreigner."

"You were denying it before! He can't be a foreigner one day and then not!"

"I was denying nothing, Eileen. Only did you see that mark in his forehead? Well that was a wound. They stitched it up but he says there was a hole you could dip three fingers in."

My mother sucked in her breath. "What have I to do with people's wounds! Has he seen the hens yet?"

Aunt Irene lowered her voice. "He said he didn't need to. He says he'll watch over them tonight."

"How do you mean, watch them?"

"I mean he'll be staying in the coop."

My mother stared towards the gap of the door. She might have seen Kruger's foot seeking the warmth of the paraffin fire.

"He's brought a flask," Aunt Irene went on. "And even a kind of stool."

"But what will he do in there?"

My aunt clasped her hands, working her elbows so that the palms rubbed one against the other. "I think that's his business, not ours."

*

Mr. Kruger sat in the kitchen until it was almost dark, reading with his legs stretched out. We watched the TV. In the quiet parts I heard the slip of his paper. Then he cleared his throat and stood up. There was a soft chime of metal as he picked up his leather bag.

He came to the door, filling the opening with his dark bagging suit, his war-wounded face. *"Mrs,"* he said.

My mother was Mrs. but he meant my aunt. She turned down the volume of the set. "Is there anything you'll need Mr. Kruger?"

My mother kept her eyes on the silenced screen. She made a noise by sucking her cheek.

"No Mrs, there's nothing," Mr. Kruger said.

"Then Leonard will take you outside."

My mother made the same noise again but did not speak. I took Mr. Kruger through the backway. There was enough light left to see by and a half-moon above the line of broken glass on top of the back wall. The hens made their soft noises. Mr. Kruger took the canvas contraption from his bag and fashioned it quickly into a small stool with a canvas seat.

"How many birds?" he asked.

When it came to it I wasn't sure. "About a dozen," I said.

He nodded and sniffed the air through his narrow nostrils. The coop smelt of shit and damp ashes. I lifted the latch and let him into the run.

"Thank you boy."

He had to crouch, carrying his bag and his canvas stool in the same long hand. His dark shoulder made a tight silvery sound against the wire. The hens began to stir straightaway and when he opened the narrow door of the coop they started one of their panics, shrieking and striking the walls with their wings, sending up a spray of grit and white curled feathers. The chicken-doctor paused for a second, his hand on the frame. Then he nodded to me and stepped through into hysterical darkness.

*

At this time I was growing so quickly that my father seemed to be shrinking. "You'll soon top me at this rate," he said.

"My mother says I'll outgrow my strength."

He winked at me. "She's fond of her pronouncements."

We sat side by side on the striped deckchairs. The sun was out again but the air was cooler than the time before.

"Your mother and I," he said, "have been talking lately."

I felt the chicken-flesh rising on my wrists.

My father sat forward in his chair. "How would you like it if we got back together again?"

"I don't know," I said.

He frowned towards the other side of the estuary. Spokes of light were moving over the water and you could see trees and the roofs of houses. "Why you must know! You must have your views on it one way or another!"

I wouldn't look at him. I spied down through the slats at the swilling brown water. The iron piles of the pier made a faint tinkling sound as if particles of rust were flying like gnats about their hollow insides. Eventually he held out his hand, turned it so that I could see the sixpence among the creases of the palm.

*

The hens started laying in the middle of the next week. The eggs were fewer than before and their shells were thinner. Sometimes they'd break at a touch.

"And they don't taste the same," my mother complained.

Aunt Irene looked surprised. "Why, what do you mean?"

"Only that boil, fry or poach them they have a funny taste."

My father took a job in Middlesborough he'd seen advertised. It was an engineering job where his height was not a disadvantage. He sent money through the post for a while but then stopped.

"It's not worth chasing these things up," my mother decided. "Who needs bloody men when we can manage as we are."

"Two fellahs are coming for the chickens," Aunt Irene said. "They said they'll be here at half-past two."

"So," my mother said. She pursed her lips and glanced at the

72

clock. "Then shall we go out now or wait in?"

Aunt Irene lowered her eyes. Since the trouble with the birds she had turned gentler and more private. "I'll deal with it, Eileen. The lad could do with some fresh air. And it won't take them long to wring their necks."

*

I helped to pull down the coop. We rolled the wire for the scrapman and made a bonfire of the woodwork. There was a smell of burnt feathers and the smoke lifted dark and oily. The day after my mother bought the dog, a parti-coloured cross-bred bitch. I took it for long walks, my cough disappeared. In the autumn I started a new school and wore a tie and a black blazer.

"He'll be a fine fellah," my mother said. "If he keeps his shoulders back."

I didn't see the chicken-doctor again, only his funeral. Aunt Irene pointed out a black car splashed with mud on its underside.

"That's Mr. Kruger," she said.

My mother pretended not to remember the name. "Mr. who?"

"The chicken-doctor, as I'm sure you recall."

We watched the car as it turned right into the main road. The dog sniffed towards it, pulling on the lead. There were no flowers on its roof and nothing was following behind.

"Only it was years ago," my mother said.

"They say he died of a stroke. He's being buried on the rates. No family here you see."

"No flowers," my mother said. "Only the chickens will be sorry."

My aunt looked at her sideways. "These strokes are terrible things!"

"I'm not saying they aren't, Irene. But I still think those eggs tasted funny."

The hearse had disappeared now and cars and buses were passing the top of the street. My aunt put a hand to the side of her face as if the flesh was tender. "Yes," she said. *"Bitter*-tasting."

Clive Murphy

To Gilbert And George Or Who Needs Enemies?

1. *From an actress*

3 August

Tits, dogshit and more dogshit. There's Nice for you in a nutshell, darlings. Oh, and <u>winos</u> - lots and lots of them, pissed as farts, reading Simenon under the lauriers-roses (pink elephants?). Are you still on the wagon?

A bientôt,
Lallah

2. *From a failed writer, HIV positive, brave*

Thursday, August 5th

Dear G & G,
    Writing this on, well not actually <u>on</u>, the Port Jetty. Gay Switchboard said I could come here and come here I have - three times in the last two hours. Who says Englishmen can't have multiple orgasms?
    Sea defences - huge slabs of rock, cement etc. - have been chucked here higgledy-piggledy as if by Messrs Cyclopes on an off day. First you think you're alone. Then you become aware of nuderies and ruderies in every nook and cranny. A camp trio is cavorting under my very <u>nose</u>. One arrived all piratical with, believe me, a parrot on her shoulder. Another sported ribboned culottes and clutched a chihuahua. The third, in a sailor suit and a cloud of scent, was dragged into sight by two huskies - I'm sure she got the idea from Vogue.
    My feet are <u>killing</u> me. Penetrated by the spines of sea urchins when I crawled down to bathe. *"Il faut plonger!"* screamed the trio, waving well manicured hands like windscreen-wipers. *"Vâches!"* I screamed back. "I <u>can't</u> dive! Why didn't you tell me sooner, you two-faced mother-fucking daughters of Gomorrah?" Much pouting of lips and heaving of shoulders. The parrot

74

squawked and I distinctly saw the chihuahua wince.

That pink and white striped blazer I bought at Austin Reed's summer sale was a *succès fou* last night at Le Rusca where Jacques, the oh so dishy proprietor, dimmed up (is that the opposite of dimmed?) the lights to admire me. He's put N.Y. posters, mostly men in undies, on the walls and, in one corner, the statue of an uncircumcised peasant boy playing a flute.

Tonight it's wank-wank-suck-suck over the car park in the Boulevard Saint Jaurès. Tomorrow the Cap de Nice by day and, by night, Le Blue Boy Disco. Isn't Gay Switchboard just a <u>mine</u> of information?

Forgive all this silliness. Be thankful you have one another and aren't Jewish.

                    Love
                    Ben

P.S. According to my phrase book, *'Je suis ici pour les affaires'* means 'I am here on business'.

PP.S. Has my absence from London left a gaping hole?

3. *From a social worker*

                                        Nice
                              12 August 1993

Dear Gilbert and George,

I am writing to you in layperson's terms about a matter which concerns me as a professional carer and as a human being. The letter is unofficial i.e. off the record.

Hilary Johnson has brought it to my notice that you employed her as a model during July. To be photographed so often and to be paid, however little, for her pains, has boosted her morale no end. In fact, she has begun to think of herself as quite a star. I shall not inform her Social Security Office of this transaction or they might query her allowance.

You do realise, don't you, that Hilary is not a boy? I only mention it because my No. 1 has advised me that your work so far has never depicted the female sex. I am pleased if you have consciously decided to break new ground. Women get a raw enough deal as it is without famous artists such as yourselves deciding to ignore them. Only the self-confidence the likes of you can instil in this future citizen will bring her round to a less rebellious attitude.

Needless to say, there is still much room for improvement. Strangers who don't realise, as we do, what a sweet girl she really is can react against her without mercy. Do you know Nice well? I imagine you do, given your work is represented here in a major museum. The other night I took her for a *boisson* to Le Pub Opéra at the corner of the rue St. François-de-Paule and the rue de la Terrasse and, whether because of her tattoos or her nodding to a rhythm on her Walkman, we were refused service. I doubt if that would happen in England. Still, it may have taught her a useful lesson. In her present emotional state, though, it may equally have reinforced her bitterness because she has now started crunching her Coca Cola cans before she's even drained them of their contents. This is a sign I recognise of old and all I can do is spoil her a little, indulge her physical appetites e.g. her fondness for Chicken McNuggets and Chicken Cheeseburgers at McDonald's, for parachute lifts, water-skiing and wind-surfing in the bay. The parachute lifts are a real favourite. Imagine a motorboat dashing here and there dragging our Hilary aloft across the blue! At 200 francs a turn, three to four times a day, I'm glad it's not me that's paying. But I do think that the Social Services in offering these holidays to deprived youngsters are on the right track. Till we came to Nice I'd no idea Hilary was such a tomboy.

Please don't give up on this girl in the coming months. I mean, should you decide not yet to find a place for her in your pictures, might she help you to prepare and assemble your materials in the studio? Apart from your reputed generosity to AIDS victims, I know so little about you. Hilary is hale and hearty and in her adolescent prime. She trusts you and I'm sure you won't let her down. I have asked her to spend some of her pocket money on sending you a card.

> Yours respectfully,
> Pattie Purefoy
> Welfare Officer

4. *From a juvenile delinquent*

miss the Boys in pRick lane spose patties OK in small dosus wish tho shed foRget heR sopeBox she pReechus even when shes plasteRd

76

she nids a paRm tRee up heR Fanny
see yeR
Hil XOXO

5. *From a fellow artist*

Hôtel Massenet,
Nice
18th August

Chers máitres,
I note that your photo-piece 'Flower Worship' at the Musée d'Art Moderne is dated 1982. *Plus ça change.* What are your future plans? No more postcard collages, I hope. I always find them too close to my own territory for comfort. For my next 'Beachcomber' exhibition I've chosen the twelve or so *plages publiques* below the Promenade des Anglais. This evening the Plage du Centenaire yielded a baby's bottle, a doll's arm, a piece of elastoplast, a plastic cup, a French letter (unused, *arome vanille*), a Galeries Lafayette carrier-bag, a shoe, a pair of briefs and a copy of Nice-Matin whose front page advertises an appearance of Charles Aznavour (thought he was dead) in Golfe-Juan. Stick them on a beach mat, and Bob's your uncle: more 'conventional detritus transformed into ironic cultural statement' and another twelve thousand quid in the kitty. Not quite so pricey as your good selves, but then I don't work such long hours, do I? And I don't employ models or studio and secretarial assistants.
Does it ever occur to you that we're overpaid? Not a stone's throw from where I'm dining - the Mississippi - sorry, does the name distract you? - there are portrait artists, African drummers, fire-eaters, puppeteers and clowns working the shit out of themselves for a handful of francs. In the Marché aux Fleurs I've observed a first rate water-colourist who's lucky if he gets four hundred francs for a little masterpiece ... Have I made my point? I shall shortly be driving to Cannes to pit some of my ill-gotten gains against the croupiers of Jimmy Z's. Have I doubly made my point?
Given your own all too sound financial position, I cannot understand why you refused to join me here if only for a couple of days. Don't you ever give your earning power a rest? Do you dress in those prissy, buttoned-up suits because you're inwardly busy playing bank tellers counting your estimated and actual earnings?

Frankly, I'm finding our friendship rather one-sided. You won't gamble. You won't read or go to exhibitions* for fear of being influenced. Perhaps you won't even take a short holiday with me away from that gloomy, shuttered house of yours because you are afraid that, if you stopped to think, you might die of shame. Or are you afraid that the purity of the Riviera light might expose you for what you are, careerists seeking maximum publicity, male M/ madonnas in sheep's clothing? I can't, for much longer, endure your joylessness, your lack of warmth. I wonder if your wide-eyed good manners are no more than the snobby detachment of two insufferable prigs pretending to be naive when they're merely naff.

Yours, you'll decide, in envy and self-loathing,
Rupert

*You attend your own, of course. You'll be dropping by at Peking or Shanghai when your 'work' goes on show there next month, won't you? Why, by the way, should I have to learn about all this from my dealer? Why are you so fucking cautious with me? Very Chinese of you. I've no doubt whatever that in China you'll go down a bomb - personally at least.

6. *From a lounge lizard*

Hôtel de la Gloire,
Place Masséna,
06000 - Nice
Saturday

How wise of you to remain aestivating in Spitalfields. Awoke, Morning One, to find myself twice bitten - great purple blotches on neck and shoulder. *"Les méduses!"* cried the femme de chambre. "Since when have jellyfish been a hazard of your hotel?" I protested. Whereupon she became coquettish, then jokey: "Lovebites? ... Vampires?"

Be good,
Fergus

Tell Clyde and Phyllis that *filet de St. Pierre rôti et sa fondue de tomates au basilic* are as nothing compared with their Market Caff's good old r.b. and Yorkshire pud.

I'm in the devil of a fix as usual. Please, please, please send me the sterling equivalent of FF.8,000 as soon as ever poss. I'll try to repay you mid-September. Take this as an IOU.

7. From an educator

Nice
27.8.93

Hi Gilbert! Hi George!

Gwen joins me in thanking you for allowing us to share your superb collection of ornaments and 'icons' and for wining and dining us so royally afterwards at your local Music Hall. How fortunate you are to have this wonderful reminder of pre-war England in a predominantly Moslem district. What do your Bengali neighbors make of 'Down at the Old Bull and Bush' and 'Knock 'em in the Old Kent Road'? And why don't we see more Bengalis in your work? Forgive the latter question. Perhaps they've refused you or else you've a *coup de peinture* in store for us. Not that 'peinture' is quite the right word, is it? You don't paint in any accepted sense, just as it's no secret that you can't draw.

You mentioned that several of your acquaintances would be in Nice at the same time as ourselves. We have not, to our knowledge, met any of them. What a pity you didn't provide us with letters of introduction. You also mentioned that your 'Flower Worship' is on display at the Gallery of Modern and Contemporary Art. My wife enjoyed it more than I. I do not respond to your choice of color. As a matter of fact I'd have expected, rather, to find an example of your *oeuvre* at the Naive Art Gallery. I consider your outlook and execution essentially simplistic.

You told us how your relations with the established church have been tarnished by the opinions of a former rector of your parish who thinks of you both, despite or because of your Christian references, as pornographers and blasphemers. I reject this crude assessment. I regard you as deeply religious. Indeed I feel it my duty, in view of your great wealth, to point out that, here in Nice on the hill of

Cimiez, a Biblical Message Center has been built to house the seventeen Chagall paintings inspired by the books of Genesis and Exodus and by the Song of Songs, which the artist and his wife donated to the French Nation in 1966. I can vouch that it is a place of tranquility and that its atmosphere engenders peace and spiritual calm in the hearts of visitors with many of whom Gwen and I communed. Surely it is not beyond the bounds of practicality that you persuade some future rector to let you do the same for Christ Church, Spitalfields? This might help to mitigate the effects of the predicted race wars in the area and to lay the evil shade of Jack the Ripper. You must also design some stained-glass windows. I know that Hawksmoor 'were he living at this hour' would not disapprove. Chagall expressly designed stained-glass windows for the concert hall of his Center, and I gather Christ Church is already used for Musical Festivals as well as for Evangelical Christian Worship. I should mention that the Center is at present holding an exhibition of 12th to 19th Century Byzantine and Post-Byzantine Icons. Given you are iconologists, whether as investors or lovers of a genre or both, I suggest you read *L'Icône* by Michel Quenot. It is not unusual, I hear, for exhibitions with a religious theme to run in tandem with the permanent Chagall collection. I can see no reason why your own lovely home in Fournier Street might not become a public shrine in tandem with your church.

But I speak of years and years ahead. In terms of your true potential you are still crawling in the nursery: before handing in your dinner pail you must develop and mature.

Meanwhile, Gwen and I bless your endeavors, present and future. This letter is our last while vacationing in Europe. Tomorrow we fly back to Wichita where my students await me. Please remember these 'two old fogeys' in your prayers as we shall remember you. Always follow the paths of goodness rather than self-righteousness. Always use your talent to assuage the suffering of humanity at large.
                    Yours in Christian love,
                    Arthur and Gwen

You have our home address. Don't wait till Christmas to reply. Write to us in detail in the fall.

Lindsay Staniforth

The Stumblingstone

"Mother wants to see you in Longsuffering."

Such a summons was not common, but always dreaded. No-one came out of Longsuffering the same. Although on occasions the news was good - a scholarship, a translation to prefecthood - mostly behind those doors a blow fell. Sophie was tenderly led there to learn that her father had died suddenly; Anna was escorted from it in silence to pack her case and leave, instantly expelled for a sin nobody knew. Girls who were bullies came out cowed into clumsy kindness; slatterns emerged into campaigns of smartness; idlers were somehow goaded into effort. There were usually all the signs that tears had been shed. But the process was never discussed, in spite of the furious curiosity of the excluded.

The sisters had the practice of naming rooms after the fruits of the Spirit or the Virtues. When my asthma was bad one term I had to sleep in Mercy, along the sisters' landing. I'd rather have been with my friends in St.Cecilia's, up near the Seven Showers bathroom.

There were rumours about the nuns having baths - that they had to be covered with a sheet, and that there were no mirrors (that one was probably true) - and that all underwear had to be held in common and was distributed at hazard. And bad jokes - "Well it said St. Michael on his underpants", or "Where's the soap?", "Yes, doesn't it?" - that had to be thought about, though one laughed anyway, in case incomprehension brought mockery.

We had a horrified fascination and sometimes respect for the signs of the mortification of the flesh the nuns exhibited. It strikes me now that Mother's whiskers, which we shuddered at when we had to kiss her on the cheek on Founder's Day, must have been an agonizing and deliberate denial of vanity. And they said that when the porridge was burnt and we wouldn't eat it (shades of Lowood!) the sisters ate it, for days, till it was finished, that it might not be wasted. We were awed by this ability to deny the flesh, but ferociously resentful when they tried to inculcate the same virtues in us. The worst thing of all was the rule that allowed us to send only one pair of knicker linings to the laundry each week. If for some reason the laundry refused to deal with them, the offenders were called out of a meal and had to queue up to be interviewed one by one by the hated Miss Haywood, who would return the offensive garment to its owner unwashed. The shame of being called out to this queue was the purest of torments.

81

Thirty years later the hairs on the back of my neck prickle as I remember the humiliation of a careless bloodstain.

The rumour was that Miss Haywood had applied to be a nun but had been turned down because of her vicious streak. Time has not mellowed my view of her; she should have worked in a concentration camp. She had a pinched loathing of the young and fresh, a total cynicism, and a venomous tongue. Once in the Library she found a bookmark, a tracing of a Perseus, that I had admired and left in the book: someone had been drawing cruel caricatures and leaving them around for the victims to find, and this 'evidence' condemned me in her eyes. She spat accusations at me until my sight blurred. I remember reeling from the room in sick shock. I had not been allowed a single word in my own defence. There was a solidarity amongst us which was unusual in our detestation of her: once, after she had told us a thousand times to be more quiet in meals, we simply kept total silence. The girls on her table had to be the bravest. After a few moments, and asking a question or two which elicited no reply, she stood up, taking her plate with its bread and marmalade, and walked out. As she left the refectory, conversation sprang up. I wonder now how she must have felt as she retreated. We were made to apologise, of course, but she moderated her demands for quiet after that.

They put me up a year one summer term, me and two others. My best friend, Jennie, wasn't moved. The new form sent us to Coventry completely. It was the most lonely term of my life.

All of the new form were dancing in a pageant up at the Abbey. They had rehearsed for this for months in the Lent term, and had Anglo-Saxon costumes of surpassing ugliness. For three weeks they were out every night until half-past ten, and came back chilled and whispering excitedly about the boys they had been smiled at by. Most of them were in love with Caedmon, who was about nineteen, and a real actor.

Night after night I lay in the little dormitory, in the middle bed of the row of three, alone. In theory this should have been no problem: the most serious rule of all at the school was the dormitory rule. From the bottom step of the staircase, upwards and always, there was silence. There was no occasion when it was permissible to talk, no excuse one could offer for being caught communicating in words. We became adept at signs, expressive faces and gestures. Anyone caught talking was in trouble, and had let down her form and dormitory shamefully.

Nevertheless, I crept out of bed and tiptoed slipperless to the last dorm of the Northern Saints' wing. The cool summer evening greyed the long corridors, but the sisters were all at the pageant or in Compline, and the cheerful sound of television came from Matron's flat.

With my old form there was the welcome and the warmth I had been looking for. We huddled around, whispering and suppressing giggles until it ached, briefly liberated from the pious oppression of the school, and with the moment heightened by adrenaline, the knowledge of our own naughtiness. Was it a 'midnight' feast, sharing birthday tuck? Was there a school scandal I have now forgotten? All is blocked out now, except the moment of pure terror as we heard the heels of Miss Haywood clacking down the corridor, the cul-de-sac, the only escape route.

"Dive!" (We knew all the warning words without sibilants.)

There were eleven beds in the dorm, but we were twelve, and I the last-comer, the outcast. The heels approached with agonising slowness. No cupboards, no useful curtains, and under the beds trunks blocking all hopes of a hiding place.

Toni Rees had a quilt over her sheets and blankets. She was frozen in feigned sleep. I pushed, pleaded - "Move over!" - and was in, my weight tightening the blankets over her, and froze myself, holding my breath to hear the heels stop and a terrifying silence begin.

She stood, silhouetted in the archway, assessing the atmosphere of the silent dorm, searching in the shadows for evidence. Then the lights clicked on, and after another minute the voice cracked like a shot -

"Out of bed, everyone."

Myopic, and dazzled with the sudden light, I could not see the expression on her face, the fact that she did not see me slip from beneath the quilt while Toni had to wriggle free of her blankets. But I could feel the intensity of her stare as we stood, side by side and petrified, on the wooden floor.

"Antonia and Katherine. *In the same bed.*"

Memory blanks out the next bit. My next frame is the two of us standing on the sisters' landing, waiting in silence for the headmistress to return with the dancers. Bare feet numb on the brown lino, shivering and dizzy with cold and terror.

When the sisters returned, in silence after Compline, they had clearly been apprised of our crime. They stared at us coldly and didn't even make the tut-tutting noise that was the only sound they allowed themselves after nine. Banished, trembling, to our cold beds, the night was sleepless with dread.

Then began a time that was arid with fear. Everyone was forbidden to speak to us. I was accustomed to this, but Toni found it hard, and was angry with me anyway. Once, I tried to apologise, cornering Sister Christian and stammering repentance, but she shook her veiled and wimpled head and said it had gone beyond a sorry. Neither of us knew why we were outcasts: the dormitory rule was often broken, and although the miscreants were punished, the process was immediate and recognisable - their school badges were taken away, or they were made to waitress on the juniors' tables. But we were waiting, it seemed, because Mother was away.

At last the summons came. In prep, heads bowed obediently over Geography, we were called out by Sister Christian and led like lambs to Longsuffering. At the threshold she tapped and waited, then at an inaudible summons held the door wide and made us go through, closing it with a threateningly quiet click behind us.

Mother sat at a table with two train tickets in front of her.

"Sit down." We sat.

"Do you know why you are here?"

Which of us answered? I don't remember, but we said, "Yes, Mother, we broke the dormitory rule."

"Tell me what happened."

That had to be my turn. I tried to explain clearly how I had been lonely, had gone to talk to the friends I had been torn from, had dived into the nearest bed when we had heard the footsteps coming. I faltered to a stop.

There was a long silence. I could not look at Mother.

"Is this true?" She was not only asking Toni for corroboration, she was asking me too, to perjure and damn myself, or to examine my conscience and declare that I had spoken the whole truth.

"Yes, Mother," and then we had to look into her great searching eyes.

A long pause. She picked up a piece of paper and placed it thoughtfully on top of the train tickets.

"You can go. But you will never talk in the dormitories again."

*

We left, dizzy with relief that the axe had somehow not fallen. Baffled and bruised, we were gradually readmitted into the life of the school. I don't believe Toni and I ever spoke to each other again. My end-of-term report mentioned nothing that had to be explained to my parents.

And it must have been about four years later, when as a senior of sixteen I heard the gossip about the last games mistress and the Upper Sixth, that it broke over me in a flood of understanding and shame and fury, what we had been silently accused of, and how the wisdom of Mother had eventually seen that it was ignorance, not guilt, which had made us incapable of defending ourselves.

Pushover Quiz

Answers to Panurge 22 Quiz. The four Georges were George Orwell, George Moore, George Gissing and George Meredith. Lots of people got it but first there was **Gary Couzens** of Aldershot who got a £20 Book Token.

Panurge 23 Quiz. A major 20th C English novelist sometimes named his characters after organic chemicals. e.g. Joe Aldehyde and Mr Mercaptan. He also wrote a book about improving your eyesight without using glasses. He also suffered a major house-fire. Who was he?

First correct answer gets a £20 Book Token. Deadline 5.11.95. Answer to Pushover Quiz, Panurge, Crooked Holme Farm Cottage, Brampton, Cumbria CA8 2AT. UK.

Michael Eaude

Long Before Either Of Them Were Ready

1963.

Once before Jim had been summoned to the Head Man's study. For a ticking-off, along with a whole group of boys called out in Assembly for throwing snowballs too near the windows. They knew it was only for the Head Man to let off steam. But Jim had never forgotten the feeling of dread in the corridor while they waited. Tall corridor five times his height, walls of stone with small high windows, designed to be austere and dark. The duty senior paced like a parading horse, to keep them in line and silent. He turned and snorted at the faintest shuffle or whisper. Fear. The feeling of fear that is physical. Jim Johns, young boy, wanted to shit. He wished he'd gone before, but he hadn't wanted to. Clench teeth and buttocks. Hang on. Suffering is a training...

Slowly boys went in, and came out smiling and jaunty. One cracked his knuckles in scorn. Like a chicken-leg snapping. The duty senior muttered and frowned. And then stiller silence over the shortening queue, as they heard through the door distant cracks, like a nail being thoughtfully, rhythmically driven. A well-known hard boy emerged. Holding his arse with both hands, biting his lip, he ran past.

Later Jim put himself near the hard boy, who was telling his friends it was nothing. But Jim remembered a glimpse of a weal like a fierce red crayon mark when the boy pulled down the back of his trousers to show.

*

1948.

Major Johns felt the weight of what had to be done. It was so tiresome. The day was humid so that just sitting immobile in his office under the fan, his groin's hairs dampened with sweat.

When Jango nodded through the door, the Major waved an arm at him, as if to say: "Send them home. I can't be bothered." Jango disappeared. The Major continued to sit for several minutes, until he adjudged everyone had been kept waiting long enough to notice. He rose slowly and strolled across the dirt yard to the court-room.

Below the verandah, the brown river rolled over the smoothed giant boulders. The jungle stretched insolently into the haze. The Major hitched up his shorts, inserted his stick under his left upper

86

arm and stepped into the room. "Stand," screamed Jango. The Major winced: 'damned excitable bastard,' he thought. His face of course remained stiff. Everyone stood. The Major took his seat at the raised table under the furled flag and picture of the King. "Proceed," he thundered with the authority of his office.

*

1963.

"Dub us a flame, Horsman," Jim said. They lit their cigarettes at the door of the classroom on the top floor of the empty new wing. They watched the boys tramping back from the sports fields. Dark starting under the trees. The two sucked madly at the fags, shielding the glow behind their hands. They felt the illegitimate excitement. They too should be down below, muddy, wet, tired and healthy.

Steps in the corridor. Heard a moment too late. "Scarper," hissed Horsman. Panic. They threw down the butts, rushed out. Jim turned back to scrub them out with his shoe. Horsman was away down the far stairs.

"Boy! Here you, boy!" The step hurried. "At once. Stop! Do you hear?" Jim heard, but he was away. In the half-light, he thought he hadn't been recognised. Down the corkscrew stairs, then out into the yard, suddenly casual, hands in pockets, mingling, but staying close to the wall. As he left the yard to final safety, he was thrilled to hear distant shouting.

*

1948.

"Oh darling, I'm so glad you've got back early."

"Managed to keep everything running to time. How's my little poppet?"

The Major sat and tickled her chin while she knelt before him on the floor. They had been married six months. She had returned with him after his last leave. Now he couldn't imagine staying a week in this godforsaken corner of the Empire without her.

"I'm perfectly fine now my walrus is here." She stroked his moustache. "But my darling looks so tired."

"It's damned hot."

"Always hot."

"Unpleasant business. Punishment stakes. Chap keeled over. Jango had to throw a bucket of water over him."

87

She put her hand to her mouth. "How perfectly ghastly for you! I know you hate these beastly floggings so much."

"We have to set a standard. Without discipline..."

"Don't talk of it, darling," she shuddered.

The young woman, whose skin and bone he thought of as silk and china, scratched his rough neck and whispered:

"Walrus wouldn't ever discipline me, would he?"

"Of course not," he smiled.

"Not even when I'm a naughty little girl," she whined.

"I like you when you're naughty. Come here," he said and kissed her, on the lips and then all over her unbelievably soft skin.

The Major noticed a bead of sweat trickle down her forehead into her closed eyes at the moment of his ejaculation. And just when he wanted to be aware of nothing but these moments and sensation of her so wonderfully close... Escape, escape! To now, to now ...then he thought of the sweat on the flogged man's face, his tight-closed eyes, the marks that scarred his smooth skin as he lay in the dust. He cried out.

"There, there," she patted him. "My dearest darling." A mosquito on the ceiling stared down into her expressionless wide blue eyes and had to fly away.

*

1963.

The Head Man was a thin ascetic man with straggly grey wire for hair. He spoke in a stumbling fashion.

"I'm afraid this is a case of doing, er, what I say, not what I do." He grimaced. He was known as Drag, when he was not the Head Man, for his habit of always dragging, cheeks dipped, on a fag.

"As I say, I don't take the view that cigarettes are..." he coughed "...evil. But school rules are school rules, you know. And I take a dim view of a boy who can't face the music if he's caught doing wrong. Running away. Not what we expect. Fathers don't pay good money for boys to run away."

The boy, head down, hands clasped on his abdomen. "Yes sir."

The Head Man walked about. "Our purpose...training... expense...parents...country...principle...leaders, I mean, morally speaking."

"Yes sir."

The pattern of the carpet on the floor, expensive, inexplicable in

88

pattern and addictive to the eye, was for the boy to be the pattern of these words.

Turning away to the sliding door of a homely jumbly cupboard, like the corner of a garden shed or cricket pavilion. Heaped in the corner, thick canes, thin canes, old split canes, new shiny canes, some straight sticks, some with curved handles.

Jim thought of his father. Summer afternoon, deck-chair, puffing a pipe, red-haired hand clasping in peace a thin china cup. He was ashamed his father would be disturbed by knowing he was here.

"I can tell you," said the Head Man as he selected a stick, "this will hurt you a lot more than it will me." The Head Man coughed at the little joke and looked slyly at the boy, who nodded but could not bring himself to laugh or look away from the thick polished stick, hard and glistening like a snake.

The boy bent over the musty armchair, as he was told, resting weight on the forearms. He thought and felt nothing. Only the physical sensations of now. A faint breeze on his bare thighs. He waited. Slowly his buttocks relaxed. It would be alright. He wasn't going to shit himself. The worst had already happened, the anticipation, that now was nearly over. He was to be beaten by the Head Man. So. It had happened to others. He heard the whistle of the cane in the air. He felt his pants tighten over his arse. His penis began to fill with blood.

*

1948.

If only time could have stopped now, pure moment out of time, cool late evening with a long gin in the hand and his beloved asleep in the room behind the verandah, in trust. But the place intruded. Loiterers chattered beyond the garden wall. Mosquitoes. Pictures he could not forget of the man flogged that morning.

Sure that she slept, the Major slipped out of the garden gate, down the track into the town. By the court-house a group of young men lounged about. Gentle hissing voices and laughter. He passed by on the other side, apart, glad there was no street lighting. He thought of the unseen group of men as the men he had seen by day in the fields, in hat and loincloth only, oil shining on their shoulders and backs.

At the bridge he stopped and listened to the river and was calmed by its equality.

"You want," stated a voice. He went with the boy to a hut.

"No," said the Major when the boy struck a match to light a candle.

The Major lit a cigarette and saw the boy's face before he blew out the match.

"You want."

The Major took off his belt, lowered his shorts and commanded the boy to thrash his buttocks. The pain made him feel alive.

People still talking after the crack of the leather. No real quiet, no peace. Another match. His own hairy red hand passing bank-notes. And out in the night again. He felt tired.

For several days the Major simulated a mild fever and slept apart from his wife, though he yearned to be with her. Each day he examined in the mirror his secret, to check if he could again lie naked with his beloved.

"When you feel better, darling walrus, will you make me a baby?"

*

1963.

He stood up slowly, as if he feared he'd strained his back, and unleashed a searing pain across his bum. He bit his lip and unwanted tears dribbled down his face.

"Look up, boy," said the Head Man. "No hard feelings." Jim shook the hand that was proffered him. "I trust I won't see you here again for anything like this."

"Thankyou sir," he mumbled. He ran past the queue of boys who stared at him. Later he showed the six neat red stripes to friends.

"Does it hurt?"

He shrugged. "Not too bad." He felt strong.

Horsman had some cold cream in a round blue tin. Under the stage there were old mattresses from a forgotten play. Out of bounds; safe enough at certain times. By the second day his arse was throbbing all over and starting to turn purple. Then Horsman rubbed on the cold cream gently and thoroughly. Jim pushed up his bum in satisfaction. It seemed worth the beating to feel such sensation.

Horsman went on rubbing, across, up, round and round, pushing and massaging. Suddenly, without thinking, Jim came.

"Oh thanks, Horsman, that feels so much better."

"Least I could do, old man, seeing as you got nabbed not me."

"If I get whacked again, I'll feel better, knowing you'll soothe it for me. You will, won't you?"

"Of course, and you can do it for me."

*

1978.

They made love. Unbidden, unwanted, unavoidable, flashing pictures of distant sex clicked through his mind as he caressed this woman he felt so much for. He breathed in deeply her skin, her smell, her presence. But he saw a nameless woman bending over, her knickers pinching her buttocks: she winked naughtily. A man he thought he knew looked back over his shoulder at him with a watery eye. A porcelain-doll face of a woman he wanted to smash in bits. A tear ran down her face. The swish of a cane. Jim came, in a rush, long before either of them were ready.

He lay with her before the light of a gas fire on a winter's night. They didn't touch. They lay without speech on the bed. The woman rolled toward him and rubbed his chest. He turned away with a twitch.

"No, it's no good."

"Have it your own way," she snapped and jumped off the bed. "My God, what's the matter with you?"

"I'm sorry."

"It's no good being bloody sorry; you're, you're always one step away, it's as if you live behind a brick wall."

"It's not that bad," he muttered.

"It fucking is! You don't have to suffer it. You want to get in touch with your feelings."

"I'll be off then."

"That's typical."

"What?"

"Get a problem, get a crisis, and you're off."

"I thought that's what you wanted."

"I want to sort it out. Don't you?"

"Well, yes, but we can't get any further tonight."

"Oh piss off then."

*

At home he banged his fist against the wall. When he climbed into bed, he lay on his back staring at the ceiling and imagined himself being open and honest. He imagined himself telling his lover about

91

the sexual images that forced themselves involuntarily onto him, his history. He came for the second time that night, imagining the wonderful intimacy and excitement as he explained, even embellished, what he knew of himself.

Karen Rosenberg

Eulogy By Phone

"Please get it," said my mother and shocked me, because I hadn't noticed any sound at all in the apartment. I guess my grandfather's death had driven me to thoughts louder and more urgent than a bell. "I have to start folding up his clothes for charity, I simply cannot comfort Uncle Izzie or Mo right now." But it was yet another miniature anarchist - my grandfather's movement produced a lot of short old men.

"I heard," he said, not adding what and from whom, "and I want you to know that we have called an extraordinary meeting in his honor for next Saturday, I hope that you can come into town. It will be a small memorial to everything that Solly Pakentrager stood for - we think it would be most appropriate to review your grandfather's philosophy since his biography is known to all of us, so to go over the assorted names and dates would be superfluous and, frankly, boring. Instead, we've arranged a medley, so to speak, of his favorite themes, the ones he sang out with an admirable bass. He never intervened just to remind us of his presence - he always stepped forth clothed in a quotation, to display another's wisdom. (He had a showy modesty about him, your grandfather.) It was impossible to overlook his curiosity which opened the most far-fetched sources. I met Laotse courtesy of your grandfather, one night over herring, since it was cheap in Poland. China appeared unexpectedly in Yiddish - having passed through German first, I think, but by now I have forgotten the route.

"My presentation (and I want your advance approval - I value your opinion, Judy) will concern freedom in the family. I'm sure that you're acquainted with that topic, he couldn't have omitted it in his sunset talks with you. Of course I've heard all about the dent that you both wore in that greenish - or is it greyish? - settee next to the homemade whatever-you-call-it, that gigantic glass box that blocks the window, you know the one I mean, his agricultural experiment."

"The terrarium," I offered.

"Ah yes, I thought it was Latin or maybe Greek, he liked that kind of learned expression, your grandfather. At any rate, Judy, you remember how he'd recite Multatuli's sixth parable on authority in his most Biblical tone of voice? Now I've prepared a little English translation that I'd like to try out on you if you have a minute. I'm afraid it won't be up to the level of your grandfather, who chose the

93

holy Shelley as his stylistic model - my language is much more proletarian, I mean pedestrian. Clarity is all I'm after: now just interrupt me please if there's something that does not make sense." And he orated and intoned:

'It was the parents' first child! The mother was carried away with joy, and the father too eyed it with heartfelt love.

"But tell me, will it always remain so small?" the mother asked a genius. "Then again, you know what?" she went on, "I really don't know if that's what I want after all. I'd love to see it as a grown-up person, but on the other hand it would be a pity if it became completely different, so that I couldn't carry it any more or feed it from my breast."

"Your child will become a complete human being," replied the genius. "It won't be fed from from your breast for very long. There will come a time when it won't be carried in your arms any more either."

"But Mr. Genius," the mother cried out in fright, "will my child up and leave me? When it's able to walk on its own, will it go off? What must I do so my child doesn't go away when it's able to?"

"Love your child," said the genius, "and it will not move away from you."

And so it came to pass. And that state of affairs lasted for a little while. But then a whole lot of children were born. And a lot of parents found it very difficult to love all of those kids.

Then a commandment was thought up which was supposed   to take the place of love - as is the case with a lot of other commandments. That's cause it is easier to issue a command than to give love.

Honor thy father and thy mother.

But the children abandoned their parents as fast as they could. So a promise was tacked on to the order:

Then you'll have long life!

Some children remained with their parents! But they didn't stick around in the same way the first mother had in mind when she asked the genius, "What must I do so my child doesn't go away from me just as soon as it is able to walk?"

And that's the way it has stayed until today.'

"Are you still there, Judy? You must have a cold - you're sniffling an awful lot."

"I'm OK," I answered, silent on my tears.

"That's good, you should dress warmly, there's some flu going around - they're blaming it on Asia this time. Isn't it a bit too miraculous that no serious illness originates on our great continent? But don't worry, I never believe half of the libel in the newspapers. Listen, it isn't necessary to comment on my translation immediately, I know it's hard to take it all in on the phone. I tell you what: I'll send it to you so you can look it over, and don't be shy about your criticism. 'A good writer deserves a careful editor' was a line your grandfather drilled into me. Now you've inherited that task along with his library. He trained me to take suggestions with grace - or to feign equanimity, if I couldn't do any better. I don't say I live up to his expectations, but I always try."

"Jesus," I responded, and not to his request. Some news had been obscured by his antique and awkward phrases: a catastrophe was coming to my one-room apartment, my possessions would soon be outnumbered. I hadn't seen a will, where did he get such private information? "Are you absolutely sure about those books?"

He was consoling but insistent.

"Don't ask me where your grandfather's instructions are written, it's hardly my business. But when your mother threatened to throw out (God forbid) all the mildewed paper - and I admit it smells a little sour - due to her allergies, your grandfather (of blessed memory) told Dr. Weinberg, or maybe it was another comrade-in-ideals, that you were the only extant relation he could trust. I know that it's a heavy responsibility, so don't worry yourself even a little: we will help you transport the boxes up to wherever it is you live, just get some from a liquor store, they won't cost you a cent, shopowners are always happy to get rid of cardboard before it has to be it broken down, bound up and carted away - I know, my brother-in-law ran a fruit and vegetable stand for years right in your neighborhood, in fact, where the Mi-T-Fine grocery is located now. My son has a pick-up truck and two hefty boys whom you might like to meet anyway, they're both around your age and (if I may say so) exceptionally physically attractive.

"But anyway, Judy, for this tribute to your grandfather that I've been telling you about: would you please pull out the selected works of Multatuli in German, the translation by Wilhelm Spohr? I think you'll find it on the bookcase by the writing desk under Douwes

Dekker. Don't worry about the author's many names. You'll recognize what I am looking for by Fidus' illustration on the flyleaf: just keep your eye out for a manly lion who looks dissatisfied, though God knows why, when he's cuddling a shapely nude (who could miss a picture like that?) and bring that volume to the ceremony on Saturday. But be careful with it please now, the leather binding is disintegrating and tends to leave red stains which won't amuse your mother, I am sure, if they appear on her beloved furniture. I suggest putting it in plastic, but watch out: not a sticky bag."

How did he know that my mother's collection was turning back into petroleum? Perhaps my grandfather had told that Dr. Weinberg or another close comrade. I could see it was going to be a part-time job dealing with this unwanted legacy. I was already lending out rare holdings - pretty soon I would have to keep a written record (a log? a file box, maybe) of who had what: name, address and even next of kin, so I could beg the relatives to send me back a book after its aged reader had croaked.

"Don't you have a copy of Multatuli's works yourself, if you made that nice translation?" I asked in my sweetest tones, hoping to avoid a tedious task.

"Not of the German," he answered abruptly, hitting a shrill note. "I used the French by Alexander Cohen, the Flemish anarchist who joined the monarchists eventually, so now I have to check his every sentence carefully." And then he softened a little, maybe because I was bereaved, adding politely, "But I expect you've heard his story."

I was forced to admit I hadn't and he paused, I guess for reflection.

"Ah yes of course," he soothed me, "I understand: your grandfather probably preferred to shield you from that history. It does get a little nasty at points."

I asked him what he meant and he returned to his higher pitch, the tone of disapproval.

"Emile Henri... Vaillant...Ravachol - doesn't that series say anything to you? The trial of the thirty - no? Not even Johan Most?"

Again I was obliged to confess my ignorance.

"My God, he really left you completely in the dark, didn't he? I must admit I am a little surprised at him. Ask your mother," he advised, as if I were a child who hadn't yet been told where babies come from. "She is sure to know the book by Rocker. Ask your mother, Judy, it's better that she tell you everything. Tell her I referred you to her." And he got off the phone.

Oh great, I thought. My grandfather is newly dead. My mother has shut herself inside a closet. My profession has just changed to head librarian. And now I have discovered a large and mysterious omission from my upbringing. I went to the kitchen to eat my way out of this dilemma. But after looking at the store-bought solutions there, I decided to make myself some bread instead. Pounding flour, water and milk together to form a tough, resisting whole appealed to me.

"Do you keep yeast in the house?" I knocked on my grandfather's former door.

My mother opened just wide enough to expose her hair, dishevelled from bending. "Why should I?" she answered. "I haven't baked for decades." And then she paused, as if remembering. "That's it, not volcanoes - I don't want to talk about his visions of violent revolt, I'll leave that to his fanatical old friends. But yeast - you'd think it had been created expressly for his pleasure, put on this earth for him. 'Yeast means change is wild, waiting in the air and soil, caught in trees and eaten by insects, unseen and almost everywhere,' he repeated till it became a kind of incantation."

Then she reviewed her eccentric education by my grandfather, a method different from the one he practised on me.

"He would wander over to the encyclopedia and read me how Pasteur convinced the world that fermentation was brought about organically by life, not by mere mechanical combining. Sugar becomes alcohol and carbon dioxide, one substance is transmuted into others, he would report with satisfaction, as if that proved him right in all of his ideals. You want to know how I made sense of his infatuation with leaven? I think the raising of dough, the bubbling of beer was due not just to gas, as far as he was concerned: it signalled an intellectual activity. Nature was a mind for him, producing new ideas in a kind of chemical activity. After all, his thinking worked by chain reaction - it proceeded in regular, indeed predictable, stages. Maybe he abstracted from his own experience and imagined the world as Solly Pakentrager's head, greatly expanded.

"You can imagine how it went: after reading the encyclopedia entry on yeast, he'd slide right into Yeats, following the alphabet, and tell me of that Irishman's friendship with William Morris, the author of some kitschy verses set to music, listen to the chorus.

97

Hark the rolling of the thunder,
Lo the sun and lo thereunder
Riseth wrath, and hope, and wonder,
and the host comes marching on."

This she sang, framed by the low doorway, unabashed, as if death
had levelled her decorum.

"The toiling masses will storm the citadels of power, Morris
predicted - I'm telling you in case you didn't get the meaning. Not
that I question your intelligence, Judy. It's just that all the Biblical
language isn't easy to decipher (you can see that for yourself) and it
was particularly impossible for a child. But I wasn't left to scratch my
head over anything - your grandfather had his interpretation all
worked out for me: no leaders appear, and no politicians either, in
this poem because the slaves of labor don't need them to rebel.
Morris, he insisted, was an anarchist in all but name.

"'The workers' point of observation stands above the parapets of
party,' your grandfather would then declare, translating of a line from
Freiligrath's 'From Spain.' Next, he'd laugh at Herwegh's weak
protest that 'the gods themselves came down from Mt. Olympus to
fight upon the parapets of Party.' For starters, he informed me that
there aren't any gods in Greece, the firmament, or anywhere else.
And, secondly, the German Social Democrats only talked big:
'Kautsky, Bebel, Liebknecht (the elder) - not a Jupiter among them!'
he would thump. The trouble with your grandfather's intelligence is
that it jumped like a hopscotch player from box to box. This game
went on for hours, until I learned to walk right out of the room,
sometimes while he was still reciting.

"But inadvertently I still picked up a lot - too much. My head is
packed with poems, maybe now that he's dead I will be able to
discard them once and for all. I tried my damnedest when he was still
alive, God knows - I wanted to move out of the nineteenth century,
but he kept reminding me of lesser works of justly obscure authors. I
tell you, I must know more third-rate left-wing verses than anyone
my age who isn't a world-famous scholar.

"My problem has always been the same, starting with my
childhood," said my mother, now resting wearily on the threshold.
"People think I'm capable of writing the book they can't. I won't go
into all the many examples in my life to date, let's just take your

grandfather for now. He had very specific requirements of me: the arguments I should put forth were entirely clear to him, all that remained for me to do was simply to copy them down. That's the secret of Mozart's method, he told me - the scribbling of his symphonies went so very fast because he had already composed them in his head from beginning to end. Between your grandfather and me, we would amount to Mozart, I guess, but I was allotted the much less exciting part of genius.

"What had unjustly been omitted from history, what I was charged with restoring, was the importance of theatricality. 'Listen,' said your grandfather as he fed me milk and cookies after I'd come home from school, 'I will give you an idea, and you can use it free of charge. Why did we fight for May 1st as a workers' celebration? Not just to have a comfy day-off strolling with the wife and kids, greeting the neighbors with a nod - that can be accomplished on any Sunday, there would be nothing special about the holiday if that were its essential goal. No, we wanted a rehearsal for seizing the streets; a march was necessary to give the proletariat (an old-fashioned word, but I stick to it deliberately) a foretaste of the time when they would determine whether the traffic could proceed or not. Put this on paper when you get older, Sally: people need practice in rebellion, they have to start with as little as one day a year, and gradually build up their stamina.'

"'In the beginning was the deed!' His exclamation point was a forefinger poking my shoulder. 'Only a fool or a communist could think that it is possible to overthrow the government after hearing a few speeches, no matter how talented the orator. Watching marathons is, likewise, lousy preparation for running a race. We believed in training the muscles, getting the body accustomed to revolution.'

"'Give us credit - this was modern theatre!' Poke. 'We wanted to obliterate the distinction between actors and audience, now isn't that quite avant-garde? Our idea was to hold open meetings where questions rose up from the floor. Rely on representatives and of course you'll not develop the public's capacity for eloquence in language and power in movement - we spurned all parliaments because the pulling of a lever in a ballot booth requires almost no energy. Ask too little from the citizen, and that's exactly what you'll get! Courage must be built up slowly, from baby sacrifices to heroic deeds. The Young Ones said: Seize May Day from the work week, let that be your first act in reclaiming the time that you have sold too cheaply considering it is the only life you own! But don't quote me on that,' he added, 'I've never read their little ten-penny brochures, you will have to check the German for their precise expressions.' So guess which language I had to learn in school."

But I won't reconstruct the entire conversation between my mother and me since we talked indirectly, almost in abbreviations. Though raised separately, we knew the same utopia of Young Ones in Friedrichshagen. To present it in full would strain my memory, as if I had to take a quiz without the opportunity to cram, and I'm not sure it was ever laid out logically for me anyhow. All I can do now for you is to reveal how it formed itself in my imagination, and that will have to suffice.

*

In the 1890s, Friedrichshagen was a little town, accessible by railroad from Berlin, but much too inconvenient to be expensive. Some streets were still unpaved, some cottages still thatched - "the country," said the urban writers who moved there. Yet every night a dark orange glow insisted that a proletariat existed. A pine moor lay nearby (but please don't ask how those two words combine, I haven't even seen a picture) and there was a lake where discarded snake skins and water fowl could be inspected among the reeds. A philosophical stroll was sometimes followed by a snack and beer at a little restaurant with a veranda, but mostly newcomers held a kind of open house, dropping in on each other almost daily to drink some wine and chat. When I asked my grandfather how they got much done, he admitted they repeated themselves in print and the only first-class mind among them, a playwright by the name of Gerhard Haupman, lived in far greater seclusion further down the line.

Yet if they sometimes got tired of each other's jokes, my grandfather did not confess that to me. They needed each other desperately, he said: in Berlin, at society parties, they would stand out as unbecomingly odd because they had refused on principle to encase themselves in paramilitary suits. Only among themselves were their soft, wide felt hats and silk scarves, tied in a loose bow, acceptable. Such was the costume that even Kafka wore in Prague - he, too was one of us; you might well be surprised to discover how many people of that era I'm related to. Martin Buber, Knut Hamsun, August Strindberg - they may not be famous any more, but they were to my grandfather.

Their dress expressed rejection of rigidity - no stiff bowlers, starched collars, tightly-buttoned gloves - but otherwise I can't say exactly what they meant by freedom and, at that point, maybe they did not know either. The Young Ones is what these anarchists were called within the Social Democratic Party, as if age was enough of a distinguishing mark. And, in fact, they played the kids, with tricks and tantrums; experts at staging scenes, they knew exactly how to get the daddies mad.

They would climb on chairs at the Social Democrats' party conventions - to which they had not been invited - and interrupt the speakers in loud voices to charge them with betraying the working class by settling for small reforms, like petty-bourgeois shopkeepers. When the chairman had them forcibly evicted and threatened to summon the police, he played the part The Young Ones had just assigned to him: the stuffy advocate of law and order, the enemy of open debate and change. Their improvisational skills evoked by grandfather's admiration - he could tell a good show just from the reviews. "We make up in theatre what we lack in numbers," he declared frequently. "When the police attempted to trap us (which happened a lot, of course, since that was their occupation) we were likely as not to plan a dramatic counter-scheme. But you know the tale of the three Young Ones."

And this was my David versus Goliath which I begged for when I couldn't fall asleep.

Once the Berlin police tried to establish an anarchist magazine devoted to dynamite in order to discover who was attracted to such means. Names and addresses were what they were after, and subscription lists provided a convenient way of gathering data both exact and up-to-date. It may sound clever, but in fact it was a very unoriginal idea, my grandfather noted with contempt: a Parisian journal called 'The Social Revolution' had been started earlier with the money of some English lady who turned out to be a front for the French police. And we (in Germany) were well aware of that recent history, even though it took place in another language: internationalism is our credo, you know.

Anyhow, the plot was foiled when the anarchist who was recruited by the Berlin police to serve as editor/informer - one Thomas Mackner - told his colleagues among The Young Ones about the sordid scheme. Together, the men decided to take revenge in a harmless but pointed fashion.

One day Mackner invited the head of the Berlin police department to a rendez-vous. The setting was a fairground of some sort - if I recall correctly, an industrial exposition of the electric wonders of progress in the century. And who should show up at the appointed hour but some anarchistic Friedrichshageners - Landauer, Spohr, and Widner. None of the plainclothes cops in the area had noticed their presence, because the three had made themselves unrecognizably older with false beards and wigs. Mackner politely introduced his comrades to the embarrassed police commissioner, who took to his heels post-haste and ran away - he was not supposed to be consorting with the enemy, especially in very public places, I was told. The sight of his behind in motion gave the three men joy.

And you'd think that they had won first prize for costuming at some kids' Halloween party, they got so much satisfaction out of their outlandish dress-up: a photograph of the pranksters in their homemade disguises was published in 'The Socialist,' a weekly that they edited, along with a report of how they managed to make great fools of the Berlin police.

At that my grandfather generally said good-night, but one loquacious evening he added an epilogue: soon afterwards that issue of 'The Socialist' was confiscated, the three Young Ones got their houses searched, the newspaper's files were seized, and a trial was set in motion. Evidently, the police commissioner lacked a youthful sense of humor. But my grandfather still considered this a tale fit for a child, because angry, vengeful Prussian justice presented absolutely no threat at all to Friedrichshageners. After refusing to pay their taxes, they were apt to invite the tax collector in for champagne, according to Spohr. And my grandfather had still more proof of their magical untouchability.

There was once a Young One named Bruno Wille who believed that God was nothing more than the feeling of oneness with all things and beings which wafts over you sometimes, especially in love. An atheist, some called him, but Wille denied it - why should God just be the usual old man with a long white beard? he asked. Although he was forbidden by the school authorities to teach the children of the Free Religious Congregation, he persisted, knowing that would mean a fine or jail.

According to my grandfather, Wille was gregarious and this protected him from many an adversity. Before a court official could impound his property, a writer friend in Friedrichshagen demanded it in payment for a still-outstanding debt. And then kindly lent it back to Wille indefinitely. ("Get the trick?" my grandfather quizzed me, grinning triumphantly at the Young One's cleverness.) A judicial representative who was well disposed to Wille begged him merely to promise that he'd pay the fine sometime in the future - that way his arrest could be avoided. But Wille stood on principle. Jail held no fear for him, in fact he "felt something of the curiosity of a child who sits in a theatre looking at the curtain and imagining what strange pictures and faces will appear." In my grandfather's hands were Wille's memoirs in old German script; I suppose I own it now.

Where this German resister ended up was in the basement of a building behind a pub. That neighborhood jail might have been no worse than an old-age home or the army, as Wille had anticipated, but to me it seemed considerably more comfortable. His wife was allowed to equip the place with carpets, curtains, and the major arts, represented by a zither, a well-stocked bookshelf, and a drawing by Fidus; I think she also brought a hot lunch daily though I may be making that up. But I do remember that the door to his cell wasn't always locked: on Wille's birthday, famous Friedrichshagen friends and a few Berliners entered with gifts - flowers, Burgundy, cigars, some book by Kant and a china cat (my grandfather translated every word for me when I looked even mildly fascinated).

And not only could people come right in, Wille was also known to go out. When the favorite doctor of the writers' colony insisted that the prisoner needed outdoor exercise, Wille got permission to gather mushrooms which his wife would cook for him. Wille slowly picking at the roots of trees while minded by his jailor, Mr. Bolle, must have been a most uncommon picture - the owner of the nearby forest found it so amusing that he didn't even mind that they both were trespassing on his land.

You'd think from Wille's telling that prison was a series of fun and games. There was the time that Bolle and his family kindly took Wille and his wife for cake and coffee in an outdoor restaurant. The exuberant prisoner could not resist playing hide-and-seek on the way back, until his wife insisted that he drop the childishness. (She played the heavy in this book, and later they got divorced.)

Another example: Wille was also able to go home for a weekly bath which his jailor waited through with remarkable patience. One day, however, when Wille was still under water, Bolle was summoned to round up a gang of poachers. Trustingly, he left the keys to the prison with Wille, who used the opportunity to spend an afternoon with the playwright August Strindberg, then visiting in Friedrichshagen. Towards evening, they all wandered over to a nearby bar where Strindberg made up verses while somebody played the piano. ("Spontaneity!" my grandfather would shout.) It was Wille's conscientious wife who insisted he return to jail, and they went home together to get the key. Wille stood outside to catch it as she threw it from a window, but it apparently got caught on an intervening tree and couldn't be found till morning. "What if some poachers had been arrested and I'd had to lock them up?" asked Bolle in the memoirs. But no one was caught because a shot that went off during the search had forewarned the gang. My grandfather liked jokes at the expense of police.

Instead, it was the assistant warden, the man who ran the pub which contained the backyard jail, whom Wille got into trouble. Insisting that he had shoulder cramps, the prisoner managed to receive permission to go rowing on a nearby lake for exercise. The assistant warden lost his policeman's cap - it fell into the water - and so had to walk bareheaded with his charge back to the jail. This infringement of the regulations for uniforms was reported to a higher-up and elicited a reprimand, while Wille got away unscathed. As usual.

But his worst sin was similar to the heinous crime of Landauer, Spohr and Widner. It also involved photography: a carefully composed shot of Wille and his wife behind the barred windows of the local jail, but visited by many well-known Friedrichshagen literati who stood out in the courtyard, was sold in Berlin with the caption 'Freedom of conscience in Prussia.' It became so popular that the bureaucrat in charge of religious affairs got wind of it and Wille's jailers stood in danger of being fired. If there's one thing that got government officials mad, it was being laughed at - perhaps it was to end their own embarrassment that they finally granted Wille an indefinite leave from prison.

"Show a sense of humor," he once told his jailer. The Friedrichshagen I was offered was a town where laughter was required. The more pompous and rigid the officials, the more happy-go-lucky The Young Ones had to act. It was as if any sense of pain had been banned from crossing into the suburb and all complaining was taboo. Maybe they were posing because their homes were practically public: aficionadoes of the arts and anarchists from all over were almost always sleeping over and mooching meals; city workers were invited en masse for the picnics of the Free People's Theatre; Fidus, who lived nearby and liked to play the piano, came for musical soirées; some guy whose name I have forgotten was treated to an eight-day birthday party; and the police paid for reports about who said what to whom.

And it was just as strictly and repressively jovial at the offices of 'The Socialist' in Berlin. When Spohr and Widner tried to get Landauer's goat by calling him a "damn Jew" and a "crafty rabbi," he always responded with loud pleasure. At least that's what Spohr wrote in 1951, now I can lend you his reminiscences in German if you don't believe me. I know it's improbable that - after everything that's known, shorthand, as Auschwitz - Spohr could tell this anecdote without a word of apology. But I assure you he was proud of the good-humored, undogmatic repartee of his circle.

I distinctly remember wiggling as my grandfather set this ideal before me. For years I felt inferior to their cheerful acceptance of martyrdom - I probably still do. Although I tell myself that Wille never broke his irony because he might scream with fierce frustration, although I bet each Young One was terrified of being called a sissy, although I'm pretty sure that all their drinking was due to more than joviality, I suspect nonetheless there's something weak in me because I cannot imitate the jaunty Friedrichshageners.

"Maybe the memoirs were one long invention and Wille only wished he had toyed with his jailers," I protested once, when I was old enough to consider this possibility.

It got me out of nothing. "Then imitate the fiction," responded my grandfather, smiling at his cleverness or mine, I could not tell which. Given his ability to think up arguments like that, it's no wonder that my mother learned to walk into another room. My mistake was sitting on the sofa till I dented it. I had to practice my childish arithmetic on questions by my grandfather: if 'The Socialist' had thirty-one editors in five and a half years (because the courts held them responsible for the contents of their newspaper), what was the average length of time each spent at his post before he had to face trial?

$$12 \times 5 = 60 + 6 = 66 \div 31 = 2.129 \text{ months}$$

He would trot me out at meetings of his comrades to perform, as if I were a violin prodigy precociously acquainted with the sonata, and they would applaud.

"Now don't scare the child, Solly," I remember hearing from Uncle Mo, who had a disease of age my grandfather called 'classless thinking.'

"It's better she should know the penalties early," he replied. "Spare her any illusions. Then let her decide."

But if those were his principles, why did he paint prison as the ideal university - a place of philosophical quiet where one could finally complete a dreamed-of project, free from the daily distractions of a fashionable world? Why did he declare in no uncertain tone, "It was in his jail terms that Gustav Landauer studied Shelley who freed him from the pseudo-scientific system of Marx with its predictable historical progression"?

There was no point waiting with passive impatience to be released, thought Landauer inside his cell (according to my grandfather) when at least the small beginnings of freedom are forever available, even under obvious oppression. What the medieval monk had found within thick monastery walls, the modern individual could seek inside his skull - there is always some less-troubled spot one can withdraw to. (This he wrote the lover of Richard Dehmel, a woman named Hedwig Lachmann - you can find the letter in Martin Buber's collection.) Even Wilhelm Spohr, no Landauer, made prison profitable! For a single speech at a May Day rally, which Spohr claimed was much less angry than most of his listeners, that Young One served a year. ("A one-to-one correspondence," joked my grandfather, pulling out pencil and paper to teach me that mathematical sign.) Aside from bedbugs, which Spohr burned out with a petroleum fire, his major problem was leisure even longer than the novels of Dickens and Scott. So he decided to teach himself Dutch.

For Multatuli's sake, of course. Discussions in my family seemed to rotate around this ancient star, as if he were a distant sun. The dilettantism of our living room was only apparent - his gravity held the very disparate interests of my grandfather from flying apart. Before being sent to prison, Spohr had produced a German version of Multatuli's ten parables on authority for 'The Socialist', but - not knowing the language of the Netherlands - he'd used a French translation as his source.

It was from a Parisian magazine where anarchists shared pages with poets, playwrights, and painters. Everybody who wanted to feel avant-garde read it, or browsed through it at least. That's why I am indirectly related to Mallarmé, Camille Pissaro, and even a premier of France, once a reviewer of literature, named Léon Blum. They may not be famous to you, but they were to my grandfather.

For my thirteenth birthday, my grandfather gave me one thick, white sheet of paper on which he'd written out a stanza of Richard Dehmel's 'Song to my Son' followed by 'To My Children' by Multatuli, as if the author was one and the same. It read:

> 'My son, one day
> when your aged father talks to you
> of filial duty,
> don't obey him! Don't obey.

You're still small and right now you wouldn't get what I'm about to say, but one day you'll read my words, so here goes: if I ever appeal to my paternal authority in my dealings with you, jeer at me!

If I ever try to force you into a subordinate position...make fun of me!

If I ever demand love from you...because... because...(how can I express this?). Love...because of something that took place when I wasn't thinking about you in the slightest. Love...because I did this thing before you came to be. Love...because...

Fill in the blanks, kids, you'll be able to when you're mature enough to read these words by your father - fill in what I'm leaving out!

So if I ever demand love from you, using *that* as my reason...sling mud at me!

Just laugh at me, make fun of me, sling mud at me, if I should ever demand subordination or love...for *that* reason!

Better to believe that one part of the ten commandments was mistranslated. Really and truly - I'm not kidding! Take my word for it, it goes, *"Hate your father, then you'll have a long life!"* Just check it out!

I'd like to see the Lord and Master who could prevent you from loving your mother by promising you ten full lifetimes in ten countries at the same time. With or without the Biblical text, for or against the Biblical text, with or without a commandment, she and I will still manage to win your love by giving love. Anyone who can't do that has no claim on love!

Your 'subordinate position' will continue only while my intellectual powers are greater than yours, because I came here a few decades earlier than you. You'll soon make up for lost time, and I'm afraid that's largely because I've often stopped on my way!

Kids, you'll have nothing to thank me for - nothing but what I did for you *after* you were born, and not that either. Love is its own reward.

You know, it would be great if you were far enough along to read my *Ideas* and everything I'm saving up for you and only you. Gee, I can imagine it now:

"We love you, Dad, but we would have loved you even if you hadn't been our father!"'

I assume my grandfather spoke through Multatuli because he couldn't find better words. There was humor in this Dutchman's sententiousness which made it bearable, his sentimental message contrasted with an understated tone. The man on the phone was wrong: my grandfather was conversational in writing and left the big words for speeches, don't ask me why. Perhaps he wasn't sure if his English could compete with Shelley's and didn't want to see it saved on paper in the same home library, close enough for detailed, precise comparison.

"By the way, I was wondering," I tried to sound casual while not looking at my mother. "Just who was this Alexander Cohen - I mean, I know that he was Multatuli's translator into French, you don't have to tell me that. But there was some trial of thirty people he might have been one of. And, you know, I was never told about Vaillant, Henry, Ravachol -"

"Why not throw in Johan Most too, while you're at it?" she glared at me. "Now this! That's all I need right now, to give my daughter a crash course in The History of Terrorism, Part One: Nineteenth-Century Assassinations. I should sit down with you in the kitchen - no, better, on that disgusting, ragged sofa by the bookcase (he wouldn't let me reupholster it, although I begged him time and time again to let me have it measured for a cover, at least - he called it "comfy," can you believe it?) and translate Rocker's paeans to the heroes. No sir, you won't get me to make more propaganda for their deeds - I want them out of my house once and for all. Didn't I have enough terrorism in the family when your grandfather was still alive? And don't object: you haven't known him as long as I, he had calmed down considerably by the time that you arrived on the scene.

"Tomorrow I'm discarding every last brochure, all those chipping leaflets that he hoarded so tenderly. Out goes Kopelov's *Once Upon on a Time in America* with its sweet reminiscences in Yiddish of how he met his wife. Just listen to this, Judy, listen hard, before you start your charmingly naive investigation.

"It was an interminable, stuffy summer in New York City - it must have been in 1887, because Kopelov was fuming that some anarchists out in Chicago were about to hang for a bombing they hadn't committed. But you've probably heard of the Haymarket martyrs, as your grandfather always honored them - he enjoyed stories where his people could play the role of innocent victims; what he forgot to mention were their calls for blood, or (sometimes) even their bloody deeds.

"Anyway, Kopelov was feeling guilty - get this - because he just couldn't find the courage to avenge the court's injustice by engaging in some act of violence of his own. First of all, he didn't have the money to buy the necessary equipment - I hate to think what that might be. And then, poor guy, he didn't feel confident that he could plan and execute a crime all on his own. A friend (I seem to have forgotten his name, but it doesn't matter - another anarchist) who had a family declined to help, even after listening to inspiring examples of the burdens born by wives and children of revolutionaries. So Kopelov was left to reproach himself about his lack of will-power and faith, since he wouldn't act alone.

"Lack of faith - can you believe it? If there's one thing he could boast of, that was it. 'If you want pleasure, don't look to fancy clothes which will soon wear away or pass out of fashion,' Kopelov's father told him, 'try self-sacrifice: the more a good deed costs you the better - your efforts will live on in your memory and give you joy.' The sons - and that includes your grandfather, my girl - might have thrown out God, but that is all they managed to abandon.

"I will give Kopelov credit for just this much: he figured out he never escaped the magic family circle. Listening to Johan Most attack the sins of kings, he noticed the pose of a Biblical prophet, and when he saw the radicals with boards for louder clapping, he recalled Purim celebrators greeting the evil name of Haman with the racket of rattles. After learning that one of his anarchist friends (his name also escapes me, but it isn't important) was once a Hasid, he figured out that the two groups held a lot in common: not just all that sentimental fanaticism, not simply relaxed and yet intense community, but that peculiar joyful openness so disconcerting in adults. I tell you,

Judy, if these revolutionaries had not seemed so damned happy, they would not have won all that attention, which was entirely out of proportion to their meager numbers. It was the ecstasy that was so very seductive - who doesn't long for its oblivion?

"So anyway, when a third friend of Kopelov (I can actually remember his name, but why trouble you with it?) came to visit that oppressive summer and saw sleepless self-doubt, he said, 'I want you to meet two sisters.' And sure enough, one soon became Kopelov's wife, in a ceremony without a rabbi, of course. Now please don't tell me that you need to hear much more about such people - this touching romantic story of blood on the marriage sheets instead of blood on the streets should be enough.

"I advise you not to ask more questions or you'll find out a lot you'd rather not know. I say that for your own good, Judy - you have more important tasks than to exhume this unproductive past. Tell people that you want to learn about the anarchists and they'll wonder if you're one of them - or worse, they will assume it without asking. Then suddenly you are associated with death by the dagger and dynamite - you who've never even heard of Vaillant, Henry, Ravachol. Stay out of it, I tell you, better to fritter away your time on home movies or unprofitable literary journals. All that may be foolish but at least it won't destroy your reputation for sanity. But anarchism..."

Her honor could not bear the weight of more detail. She turned her back. I heard the clang of hangers in my grandfather's closet as she prepared to discard.

Success

Margaret Forster

It must be my upbringing. All true Cumbrians view the very word 'success' cynically, with deep suspicion. Using it about anyone can be both a sneer and a challenge - 'success' is always something that has to be proved and even then will be quite often laughed at. Such a healthy climate to grow up in - I love being a Cumbrian: impossible to flatter; well aware that what the rest of the world calls 'success' is really just a farce.

But quite a seductive farce when first it began to play for me, against all the odds. I can't say I always wanted to be a writer. I didn't know they existed, they were all dead, surely. There weren't any in Carlisle, anyway. When a teacher at Ashley St. Infants flourished my little compositions, and said she was sure I was going to be a writer, I was embarrassed - for her. A doctor, a teacher, that would have made sense, but what was this thing called a writer, eh? It did occasionally strike me that somebody must have written all these books I devoured, but I never thought of them - the writers - as earning a living, as serious people.

I didn't try to write until 1960, after Oxford. My hero was Balzac and what I wrote was a long saga set in France entitled *Green Dust For Dreams*. Oh dear me ... I couldn't type (still can't) but I felt I couldn't submit my MS in handwriting , even if it was the pride of Carlisle High School, so I typed out 400 pages with one finger, single spacing. What a sight. Then I sent it to a literary agent I'd read about, a young man called Michael Sissons, just starting off. He wrote me what I realised many years later was a perfectly nice, even encouraging, letter saying he thought my writing showed promise, though he didn't think this particular novel would find a publisher. Why didn't I come see him? But I am a Cumbrian, I saw straight away he was only being kind, and I couldn't bear it, so I tore the thing up. End of attempt to be a novelist.

Only it didn't work, sulking like that. The old excitement kept returning, the old conviction that I could do this too, that I wanted to do it, and do it well. I was working now, as a teacher, but at the weekends I started another novel, deliberately different from the Balzacean effort I'd attempted. This was more *Catcher in the Rye* (it was 1962), a frivolous, slim story called *Dame's Delight*, about me at Oxford. I despised it even as I wrote it but it was so beguilingly easy to write, just a game. I tried another agent this time, too ashamed to bother Michael Sissons again. Graham Watson, at Curtis Brown, said at once he'd have no problem selling it.

He was right. Tom Maschler, at Jonathan Cape, snapped it up - success! Oh heavens yes, definitely, but I kept very, very quiet about it, knowing the Cumbrian rules: no boasting, no fancying myself. I got an advance of £250 which made the success - sssh! - real. Then I went to meet Tom in his office in Bedford Square. He wanted some bits taken out of the novel. I had a scene where the heroine goes to a gynaecologist, graphically described, and he thought it 'too strong'. A few years later and it wouldn't have been strong enough, but in 1962 it wasn't decent to use words like vagina. I took out everything he suggested - since I didn't care at all about what I'd written, since it was all just meant to be funny, there was no principle involved. Unfortunately, I didn't take out the right bits. Tom gave the novel to Norman Bognor, a young American, to edit, and Norman didn't spot the libel possibilities. At proof stage, someone else in the firm did. Tom called me in and yelled at me. Hadn't I realised that since I was just down from Somerville, and this novel was first person, then the Principal of my college and my tutor and certain others could be identified?

No, I hadn't. They were caricatures, the people in my novel, they bore no relation to real people. Tom marched me to see the lawyer Michael Rubenstein who laughed and said he thought the novel very funny, I was not to worry, a letter to Dame Janet Vaughan and to Barbara Harvey (my tutor) and to whoever was the mother of the character Amanda, in the novel, would sort the whole thing out. Hardly able to speak for suppressed tears - I was damned if I was going to cry in front of Tom Maschler - I asked what kind of letters? Oh, simple ones, just in effect saying 'this is not you, but if it were thought to be you please say you wouldn't sue'. Dear God ...

Dame Janet and Miss Harvey replied coldly and bitingly. They were disappointed in me but they would not deign to sue. But the mother of Amanda, a character based very loosely on my best friend at Oxford, rang her lawyer at once, and said she'd sue unless a certain incident was removed forthwith. The 'incident' was crucial to the little plotting there was. It involved the seduction of a fourteen year-old by her headmaster and was the funniest part of the novel. I had to take it out and then cobble together what was left as quickly as possible. Success? I'd never felt so miserable, such a failure. The £250 advance promptly went on legal fees with the threat of a bigger bill to come.

Dame's Delight, published finally at the beginning of 1964, got quite a bit of attention and some good reviews as well as some bad ones. I did lots of interviews - radio and television as well as newspapers and yattered on about what a con Oxford was, which was good copy. In publishing terms, the novel was a success alright, but it did me terrible damage. It set me off on a path I didn't want to follow, but still tripped down, because I'd started out on it, and hadn't the courage to turn back and take another. For almost a decade I continued to write flippant novels that were counted *successes* but not to me. One of them was *Georgy Girl*. which was made into a film. A film? Oh my - how could anyone deny that this was SUCCESS indeed?

It certainly felt like it at the time - I couldn't believe my luck. It wasn't the money (£2,500 in 1965, a veritable fortune) nor the hobnobbing with the stars (though a photograph of me with James Mason completely overwhelmed my parents and fairly shouted SUCCESS for their lass) but the thrill of knowing that what I'd written had sparked off so many other people's ideas. It was a good film. When my name went up on the screen I was glad it was dark, so that no one could see my blush of pleasure and pride. I hadn't written the whole script myself - it was a shared credit, Peter Nicholls was brought in to get it right, which I'd failed to do. I definitely hadn't been a success as a screenwriter, a useful discovery to have made so early in my career.

So there I was, aged 28, generally reckoned a success in my chosen field. For the next decade I went on writing novels, all supposedly successful, in that they were published and reviewed and sold well enough. I was making my living as a writer but I wasn't the writer I wanted to be. It was my own fault. Then, in 1978, I wrote a different kind of novel, *Mother Can You Hear Me?* The flippant tone had gone, the neat plotting. It was a dark novel, full of a good deal of anguish, quite a dreary read. It was full of pain, my own pain, and I felt brave revealing it. It attracted some very interesting, violently hostile reviews from men, and some very sympathetic ones from women. Commercially, it was my first failure, remaindered very quickly. But I was pleased, since this was the sort of stuff I wanted to write, and at last I'd done it. No more rubbish, I promised myself, no more jolly little entertainments, and I think - I hope - I've kept that promise.

I suppose I've missed out a crucial bit, the effect of turning to biography in 1973. I'd reached the stage of having children at school all day and suddenly had all this lovely time - 9 a.m. to 3.30 - after shoving the writing into corners for so long. But I couldn't write novels all the time - one a year was enough, the ideas anyway didn't come faster than that - so I turned to biography as an alternative, a sort of second string, and one that would be radically different, combining as it does research and studying with the writing. My first effort, *The Rash Adventure,* about Bonnie Prince Charlie, wasn't very good - I'd such a lot to learn - but I loved the doing of it and it was an immediate success in a way no novel had been.

Now this is interesting, the difference in a novel being a success and a biography being one. Biography, I discovered, commands more attention and respect all round. It took me twelve novels to get solus reviews - and not always solus, my novels were (and are) still quite often done in a batch, with three others - but with my first biography *all* the reviews were solus and long. Literary editors love giving space to biography, reviewers love reviewing it, and so the evidence of a certain sort of success is always greater. Not only did it improve my writing, knuckling down to the intense discipline of biography, but it seemed to put me into a different category. The ghost of the awful *Dame's Delight* was finally laid, and I'd redeemed myself. I was seen to be serious after all. And when in 1979 I did a cod 'biography' of Thackeray my stock soared immeasurably.

This last decade, I've settled down. Middle age is brilliant - *all that time!* Three children grown up and gone off, and without my family to put first at all times, there are no obstacles to writing as much as I want, for as long as I want. It is now that I feel, at last, successful, to have pulled it off, to have the way of life, a writing life, that I want. This successful feeling has nothing whatsoever to do with winning prizes or being a bestseller, or having any kind of name, if only in the tiny literary world - it's to do with that disappearance of frustration which I felt so strongly for so long. No one can be successful if they are not comfortable with what they are turning out - God knows how J. Archer & Co. survive (but then they aren't

Cumbrians and may be deluded) - and it has taken me a long time and many failures to reach that position.

I haven't, of course, yet written a wholly successful book. The nearest I've got with a novel is *Have The Men Had Enough?* I thought I'd done it with that one - been entirely successful in what I'd wanted to write - and it was agony realising when I read it in proof that no, I'd just missed it, I hadn't quite got there. The nearest with a biography was Daphne du Maurier, the book I've been the most passionately involved with ever - oh, I adored writing that one, it was heaven (or Daphne) sent. But a couple of damning reviews among all the glowing ones echoed my own secret judgement - a good bit of work but not the success it could have been, because somehow I didn't quite capture the essence of Daphne du Maurier. It's painful to admit this measure of failure but it is true.

So the striving goes on, the desire to write a book of which I can be proud, a book that doesn't leave me with that sickening feeling of an aim not quite achieved. Back in Carlisle, growing up in the 1940s and 50s, I don't think I ever thought of success as anything more than an escape to another kind of life, and that always seemed to depend on money - money to have a house, money to travel, money to be independent. The money came, or enough of it to give me all those things. I've never despised it, never said money is not an important part of success. But I didn't need to make money to show myself it isn't the most important part. I always knew money, prizes, plaudits were the *fun* part. They make a writer happy, they are comforting, encouraging. But there is no success like one's own conviction that something good has been written.

I'm waiting for it, quite contentedly.

Stephen Ormsby

Up To The Eyes

My father didn't love my mother, but he could look at her for hours. If, that is, he happened to be at home: more often than not he was away. He worked at the Foreign Office where, as an observer, he was likely to disappear at any time, usually at that moment of calm which precedes an international crisis.

He never saw a crisis *en famille* until my mother died and, as far as I remember, there was never an angry shot fired in our house. The war-instinct was firmly suppressed. That was the trouble, I think. Too much peace. Nothing was ever said to provoke, the adults never fought, and any cross-talk from my sister or myself at the dinner table was instantly quelled by my mother's pacific gaze. No one had a temper. My mother was a Scot, but not at all fiery. She was, in her own words, a 'daughter of the Lowlands', gentle and non-combative. My father's glacial attentions never appeared to unsettle her. She was used to being looked at. As a young woman she was relentlessly photographed, and I still have a scrapbook of these magazine portraits - first Ascot, Royal Caledonian Ball - each with its heaven-directed glance, the carved eternality of Georgie Burne-Jones, remote and beautiful. That's what she was in life: a study, a representation. I only wish I had tried, as I'm sure my father did not, to talk to something other than her image.

But it wasn't only my mother who turned to clay under my father's watching eye; we, the children, were subject to that professional scrutiny. To be fair it often had a smile in it, a sort of contained benevolence, and for this reason perhaps neither my sister nor my mother found it as loveless and disinterested as I did. Certainly my father admired - he admired everything, or looked at everything in the same practised and uncritical way. Perhaps it was a natural consequence of his training. I never knew. None of us did, because my father's work was, of course, secret. But, like any small boy, I wanted to know a few of father's secrets.

As a rather big boy (just turned fifty, in fact) I have begun to look into them again. I've had to. For the past few months I've been in the grip of an emotional crisis of the kind that compels one to look into these things. It started in a recognisable way - little tics and compulsions - then I began to spiral down into an infernal twilight in which I was barely able to see my way minute by minute. I developed a fear of being seen. I would wake, and still do, with a feeling of deathful dread, inertia, pain, at the thought, unconscious or otherwise, of exposure. The dawn, rather than bringing relief from the terrors of the night, delivered me into a day during which I believed I was certain to be discovered: it was a time of cold surveillance, stark appraisal. Until now I had worn a mask and been recognised in it, year after year. Now, as it surely had to, the mask had slipped. The terrible secrets of the son were at last coming to light, there for all to see.

So I am looking for my father, not in order to blame him for my present condition (he's no longer here to be blamed), but simply to understand. I'm being helped with this process by a nice lady I go to see in Huntingdon; my 'counsellor'. I couldn't do the work alone. I've been too much alone.

*

What, then, do I know of my father? In strictly biographical terms he was always 'up to the eyes' (my mother's words) in matters of state. For most of his adult life he was attached to the F.O., always in some junior capacity. His schooldays were seemingly as uneventful as my own. I imagine him as a listening, watchful boy at the shoulder of the history master, or the captain of the first eleven, in the background, taking it all in. Photographs of him at this age tell me little. We never talked much, and the one story he told of his early life was a dull one. A week or so before he sat for his scholarship he became ill, some sort of nervous trouble, he said. In the sanatorium there were books by Ruskin and Dante Gabriel Rossetti, and these he duly absorbed. He had a photographic memory and when he came to sit the paper it was on *The Crown of Wild Olive* and *The Blessed Damozel*. (I can remember him smiling as though there were some great moral in this.) After university he met my mother, in London, and somehow, perhaps with a meaningful glance, proposed to her. That was in 1938. My sister was born in 1940, I was born in '42. I know my father spent the latter part of the war at the Vatican trying to determine Papal attitudes to an Allied occupation of Rome, but when the war ended it seemed that Bevin had no use for my father and his kind, so he spent much of that period, my early life, abroad pursuing 'business interests'. I have never discovered precisely what these were. The most important thing to me at the time was school. I used to receive faceless letters from him, hoping I was doing well. He never visited. Yet I always had the feeling that he was still watching me, somehow, from afar.

117

*

I'm back there now, at the same school, teaching music. I came here about five years ago after a succession of jobs. I've always taught. I won't say it's a natural thing with me, nothing is, but it's what I've done. I've felt at home in schools, among teachers - until now. In an objective sense I know I'm teaching still. This is what others see. What they don't see is how terrible, how impossibly difficult the work has become. The words I use sound wrong, every gesture has become strange, hollow, magnified into absurdity. The music, even the most familiar piece, has an implicit and horrifying message. The pupils watch me. Each day requires greater and greater courage. I've never been so afraid, so sick-afraid, since I was a boy. Then, as now, I didn't know why. Surely if one was afraid one must be afraid of some*thing* or some*one*? I could only think of my father who, as so often, wasn't even there.

The terror, it would appear, is of the unseen; of myself.

During the holidays it's worse. I spend, or rather waste, my time wandering listlessly round old record shops, antique fairs and the like, trying to discover, to make contact with what I was before the change, before I began to feel like this. All the things I cared for have been screened off, silenced. How did I manage before, what *was* all that? The lady in Huntingdon has been an enormous help. I saw her card pinned to the noticeboard at school. It was she who introduced me to psychodrama.

A friend of hers operates these theatricals in a secluded wisteria-clad old priory in Suffolk and I was assured that, in these productions, I would be caused to remember that human puzzle, my father, and that this could only do good. I had my doubts. Actually, I was terrified. Of course, I felt that I was to be exposed, once and for all; that seemed to be the purpose of these curious events. Psychodrama. The word alone made me tremble, reach for a glass. But it was, the lady assured me, a rewarding experience if only I was prepared to fully enter into it. And so I came to spend all my weekends in old farmhouses or priories, performing scenes from my familial 'tragedy' with complete strangers who seemed to become lovers at the end of each act. It was, alas, an illusion - the closeness, that is. Despite the postcards and letters I could never bring myself to see these people again.

There was one, disastrous exception.

At a special week-long performance I met a young woman, Rosie, a beautiful waif, entirely alone in the world (or so I dreamed). She was about twenty-two. It was a puzzle to me that someone so young should be there. Her dark history had emerged during one of the sessions and the guilty party, her stepfather, was ritually dismembered and buried at the crossroads in a sort of corporate hierurgical mime. (I learned later that the man had done the work himself, in prison, with paraquat.) Rosie screamed in triumph. It was operatic; it was *The Antigone*. We were all, particularly the men, very taken with her. I was in an enchantment. When the week was over I decided I must see her again. I had her address - everyone had everyone's address - and, almost delirious with hope, I jumped into my car and raced over to the West Country.

She lived, it transpired, in a hippy settlement near Taunton with (needless to say) her mad boyfriend, a sort of shaman cum warlock-in-residence to the local community. He answered the door, and when I asked for Rosie, he stared. Nothing was said. He simply stared. I ran to the car and, a mile or so later, got into a spin at seventy.

This is the pattern, then, of my life; being drawn to people, then having to *with*draw, often at speed, when I discover things are not as I have imagined them. It's rather as if I'm looking for a particular face in a given crowd, or hoping to see in the one I eventually choose all the things the others lack, my own included.

But I never find my face.

What am I looking for? I wish these feelings had an object, I wish there was one woman I burned to possess, even once, long ago. The truth is I've loved none of my faces. After school, when I found I wasn't homosexual, I very nearly got married. Actually I was in my final year at Oxford when I met Marion. She came up and spoke to me after a concert I had organised. Then I saw her all the time. It began to seem like fate. We embarked on our own Classic Tour, got drunk and, in a mood to laugh at ourselves, began to talk about marriage. Or she did. I even took her home to meet my father and he seemed to warm to her, in his way. Not *warm*, exactly, but he did a lot of gazing, like a sort of elderly Eros with sight restored. But he had only recently lost my mother. Marion was a Scot, a Catholic, with dark red hair. We looked at the family photographs. I hadn't noticed the resemblance until then. A week or so later I fled to a music college in Paris, and since that time, with the exception of Rosie, there have been no more faces to speak of.

119

*

Strangely it was my father who arranged for me to have music lessons - piano, then cello - to celebrate the fall of Attlee's government. He didn't care for music (perhaps for the reason that he couldn't see it), but he seemed happy for me to learn. Sometimes he would watch me practise, admiring the cello, the sweep of the bow. I think this troubled me much more than any public performance, and during my last bout of psychodrama I relived an episode that everyone considered to be deeply significant, so much so that my entire life would appear to have been determined by it.

It happened during a school holiday. I think my father had been home for a while. It was just after Suez, and he was being 'rested'. I remember I had gone to bed, or, rather, I was sat on the bed, fingering the neck of the cello he had bought for me. There was a knock on my bedroom door. My father called my name, and I felt suddenly afraid, icily afraid, and guilty, sitting there in my pyjamas. Then he did something he never did, he actually came into the room and stood looking at me, fondly, or at least with kindly consideration. Then he did a stranger thing. He came over, walking stiffly as he did, and stood near me, straightening my jacket collar and patting my head. Everything seemed slow, and I listened to the breaths coming thickly above. He had been drinking. When I looked up there was a brightness in his eyes. I glanced away, disturbed somehow. "Clean hands?" he said. "Yes, sir." "Good man." Then: "Don't be too long into bed."

Don't be too long into bed. The words chilled me, and the smell about him, on him, seemed to get stronger every moment; that was what made me shrink away, want to hide behind the neck of the cello. I felt sick and faint. "Beautiful finish," he said. I knew it was the smell of a woman who was not my mother; a languid, musky, dangerous smell, a smell of heat and life. I remember it now, how it made me afraid. He had been with other women, and though I didn't know what that meant, I knew enough to trust my own sense of disturbance. I glanced up again, then at his hands. I don't know why: to be certain, to feel finally afraid. But I could sense it in him, not the last gleam of desire, or the memory of pleasure - something worse; as if he carried in him a vision of lust, nothing of himself at all. He had taken no part. He had merely been a watcher at some dark festivity.

I enacted paroxysms of frightened rage, tortured grief, howling for my betrayed mother. Not at the time, of course. No, last month, somewhere in Essex I think it was. The group was very much interested. It was the best I had done for them.

I knew, have known, I think, for a long time, where he went that night, but didn't confess my father's secret to my fellow actors. There was, I remember, even talk at school at the time about a certain address in Camberwell. It became a 'private' joke. One boy, a Cabinet Minister's son, had seen a letter. Children find out about these things; perhaps they have to, it's their fate. But it was long after that when I read my father's private papers that I discovered for certain where he had been. I think now that my father was sent there, once again, to observe, to be refreshed, perhaps, for future service to the nation. But my father having *fun*... The mind trips, blanks at it. My father at an officially sanctioned Bacchic orgy (for I'm sure that's what it was), a sort of priest or bawd, overseeing, recording...

His account of the visits to that house are meagre; bare details about the building, a Georgian terrace not far from the Green, and a remark or two about the Dulwich Art Gallery, which he would visit before going to the Kentish Drovers for a glass of vermouth. But for the mention of colleagues (by initial) and what he calls 'the hetairai', there is no description of what went on in that place. Perhaps he was being discreet. I think it's more likely that it meant little or nothing to him. Yet he felt bound to set down something of the experience. Habit, perhaps. Someone, after all, will always feel bound to make a record, mark a reflection.

My father, then, was a voyeur in the purest sense of that word, and his voyeurism was high-minded, dispassionate, dutiful. He was quite genuinely a *seer*, one who saw, and that was the beginning, the end of his pleasure.

All well and good, until another nasty thought occurs: that he watched in a like manner at my own conception.

*

And is this enough, I wonder? Is it possible that my father's watching and setting down is the root cause of my malady? The Huntingdon lady thinks so, though she's reluctant to concede that I am ill. We scrupulously avoid using words like breakdown, monomania or depression. Instead, I elaborate the many variants of my fear; that I am going to be exposed, suddenly, to a general, hostile, condemnatory gaze, as a pervert, a misfit, an impostor, one incapable of feeling. Is there a more vulnerable creature than the single middle-aged man? A boy put a note into my bag only recently - just some scribble, a childish *cri-de-coeur* - but I broke into a sweat, terrified that another member of staff would see it. I burnt it at once in the chemistry lab. But any of the boys might simply make up a story, and it would be over: my life discovered, entered into; newspapers, the cold eyes of the lens. And, should I escape that fate, there will always be someone to see...

What, exactly? I don't know. But if I am alone I must watch over myself. This is worse, this is to understand the real nature of loneliness; not the kind that drives you to turn on the television, have a drink, talk to a neighbour, but the deeper sort, almost pathological, where one is forced to watch, in complete isolation, over the wastes of oneself; when dreary scenes from the past appear in grey and sudden flashback, when a terror comes of the very space in which you watch and have being, like a darkness, an anti-light, which passes through the familiar, everything known, illuminating those fastnesses of dark, the empty places into which the phantasms must soon enter; they will come; you sit and wait...

The Huntingdon lady nods and smiles, and, yes, I seem to feel better afterwards for having spoken of these things, for having struggled to arrange these strange realities into patterns that might be discussed. It's rather like composing; first comes the dream, then the need to express it by means of a notation quite alien to its scattered form. That's why I love music; it combines all the ways of telling without words. Music meant nothing to my father and, though he appeared to be dreaming often, he was really unable to dream. He was too busy, always too 'deeply involved' with affairs of state.

But I cannot accept my father's deep involvement in anything. When I think of him I think of shallowness; shallowness of feeling, shallowness of effect. His mind was a film waiting behind the shutter, and I am one of the images, incorrectly processed. He died only last year after a short illness. Perhaps the suddenness of it affected me more than I ever imagined it would. I don't know what he saw at the end. He became detached from this world (if he could ever be said to have been a part of it). His eyes were open, but he had stopped seeing. We didn't talk, really. He spoke of my mother once or twice, as if they had some vague arrangement to meet. Apart from my sister and myself there were no other visitors. No one remembered him. All his fellows were either dead or had forgotten their one-time colleague.

Now, as with my mother, only photographs remain. But it is in these pictures that I seem to find his true self, particularly in the eyes, the look of them. There he is, frame after frame, very nearly looking the part of the black-hatted statesman. At a glance it might be Eden, or any of his Cabinet. In one set he appears sober and uncomfortable in the Hong Kong Club of 1946; in another, all smiles at the Raffles Hotel in Singapore. Then here he is at a cricket match in Calcutta, looking entirely at his ease, or as much as he ever did. There is an attractive woman at his side, speaking to him. He is not looking at her, nor at the play.

Where is he looking? Could it be that he has at last sighted the land of his unknown desires? Is his ear ravished by the sound of the flute and the lyre, as it was at that house in Camberwell? If only he had left a reliable account of his feelings I might know, but there was nothing, nothing of real interest in the pages he left, not a line to enable me to uncover that secret of his. The more I think of him, of his life, the more I'm forced to conclude that his visual sense made no passage to the dark continent of his emotions. My father faced dangers, he saw men killed; but in times of peace he became hidden, to himself, because he was afraid to look inward, to that place where we can't hide, where there is no abroad, and no imperative to share what we have seen. To himself he was blind; and, like me, always out of sight of love.

John Rizkalla

A Touch Of The Warrior

The day he had limped out of prison his Angolan guards had taunted him, vowed that he would never again be able to enjoy a night's uninterrupted sleep alone. They were right: he did miss the coughing, spitting, farting, the grunting of unshared pleasure. But tonight back home in Maman's house it was his sister Hélène who kept him awake, criss-crossing the room, dragging his foot. She and Ruth.

Had he the right? The courage? Even enough stamina left? God, how his age had come to scare him!

"Why did you come to Versailles, Thomas?"

"I grew up here. I'm over forty. I need a home, a family..."

"Fat lot you cared about either for the past twenty years!"

Was it really as long as that?

"Did you miss me?" he smirked.

"I thought you had another six years to your sentence."

"The Angolans decided on a sudden amnesty. They're making friendly noises to the west."

"Nobody here cares about the likes of you. You got paid."

"I spent it all; that and the years." He pretended to smile.

She relented a little:

"I tried to get you out. But nobody would touch the case."

"At least I survived. One of the others died in prison."

"Well, my life has changed too. I've done with nursing. I've had to retire. But I don't live alone. I have a companion. Ruth. She's over thirty." Hélène watched him warily. "We worked together in the same hospital. She's an American from Philadelphia and thank God she enjoys living in France."

"I'll try to do the same. Now, shall I kiss you nicely?"

But Hélène whose arms were full with a terrier she had also acquired in the meantime, pulled away. The animal had bared its teeth, indicating that neither was to be touched.

*

In the first days after Hélène had allowed him back into the house he had drifted from one shuttered room to another. Despite the summer heat they all smelt musty, with not an armchair between them in which he could settle for very long. Too many memories surfaced; splintered, belligerent and vindictive. Maman, Father - too much the Englishman to be ever at ease in France - Hélène, were still fighting to seek an elusive dominance over their youngest. The piano-roll of their strident, off-key voices pursued him, drove him back into the dark hallway. They dared him to do again what he'd done once before years ago, wrench open the door and leave. But one leg couldn't run any more.

"Maman should have fitted glass in the door." His voice had lost none of its boom. "Let some bloody light into the house."

Maman, now happily reborn in Hélène, came from a good tight-fisted Normandy family and would not countenance it. The best Versailles houses would have preferred a drawbridge for entrance.

"Well, Ruth likes it that way," Hélène said slyly.

Ruth was an agreeable surprise: slim, tall, captivating in a quiet way. No make-up, and straight hair, cut too short. Why did she spoil her looks? He'd heard her before he saw her, playing the piano in the salon. It still needed tuning, as it had throughout his childhood, as if to get back at him for his enforced practising. Now he didn't let on he could play, knowing he never would again. He resisted the sob of Chopinesque sentiment, concentrated on watching Ruth. He hadn't been so close to a woman in years. God, she was wasted in this atrophied town!

"Ruth would like it. She works for you."

"On what I've saved! I don't know how I'd keep the house running if Ruth didn't do some nursing. If she ever left..." A stick of an arm tried to reach him. "Has she said anything? You must tell me. You must stop her. Do you hear?"

"Hardly a gentleman's role..."

He slumped in the armchair facing the bed where Hélène took her afternoon rest alongside Whisky, her pet terrier.

"You snake!" she hissed and the dog snarled on cue. "You should be out finding a job."

"What for? To look after you?"

"Ruth will find you one. She knows everyone in Versailles."

"If you give me my share of the house..." he mused aloud.

"You mean sell it? Never! You'll have to see me dead first."

"If that's the best you can offer..." He rose to his feet in disgust. The terrier reared up, jaws open.

"Thomas, I want to die. I'm just a burden to Ruth. I can read it in her eyes. I never dreamt that two such close friends who worked in a war together could reach a point where they wished they had never met. It's horrible!"

There was no denying that. Hélène's disintegration upset him. It was premature, repulsive. Worse it was threatening to deviate him from the purpose of his homecoming.

"We'll talk about it later."

"I won't change my mind. I'll fight you in the courts."

"I suppose that's one way to kill yourself."

"You're no good. You never have been," she yelled.

He limped off, expecting her to unleash the dog on him. But she didn't. Perhaps she guessed he'd have willingly killed it.

*

Hélène didn't eat at night and when Ruth came back from working in the clinic she had to cook for herself, and now Thomas. It was always something quick and easy: omelettes, grilled chops.

"How did you two come to be such good friends?"

"We are, aren't we?" It was as if the fact had just struck Ruth. "The war in Vietnam, I suppose. We worked in the same hospital. Not a military one. Hélène had been in Indochina some years before I arrived. She was invaluable, knowing French and enough Vietnamese to help our medical team. She was very brave."

"I bet. She enjoys parading. Especially down the wards."

"Do you suppose that's how she developed heart trouble?" Ruth chastised him with a smile. But he went on defiantly:

"So that's it. You're nursing her."

"If I am she hasn't mentioned it."

Ruth cultivated a mocking tone. She was self-possessed, subtler than Hélène. Above all she was younger than Thomas.

He relented and apologized: "You think I'm unfeeling, that I don't care."

"You will care now. You've come back, haven't you? The weary warrior is returned."

"It's nothing like that."

"Hélène tells me you were a mercenary. Not even a freedom fighter. Where was it now? Rhodesia, Mozambique, Uganda, Angola. You seem to have been liberating all Africa."

"I think some would say it was the other way. I was never sure." He affected to joke. "Anyway I wasn't that good, was I?"

"Caught, put on trial and jailed. Bam!" She knew it all.

"They could have shot me. But I'd already got my leg shot up. Otherwise that lot would never have managed to capture me."

"You mean your friends deserted you"

It was her pretending to be shocked at the possibility that made him lurch over to the bed and thrust his hand under the mattress. Very well he would shock her. And he did.

"The only friend I know about is this..."

"A gun!"

"A revolver. A 9mm Browning Automatic, to be precise!"

"I hate it. I'm sorry but Hélène and I have every damn right to hate guns. I agree with her. You should never have come home."

She marched out of the room. The impudence! The arrogance! He was quite convinced she would never come back. But in fact things worked out differently.

*

To his embarrassment Ruth did find him work with M. Perron, an ex-patient and secretary to an Old Boys' Association in the nearby Jesuit school. Thomas was aghast at the trivial job.

"Filing cards!"

"He thinks you were in the British army. He lost a son at Bir el Hakim, and that's why he'll take you. No questions asked."

"The only one who'll be pleased is Hélène," he said sourly.

"Yes. That's what I wanted." Ruth was suddenly harsh.

"And did you want to retire to Versailles in this house? You could have opted for a more exciting life," he said brutally.

"I've had my share of excitement. Besides Hélène needed me."

"Needed or needs?"

"Needs then." Ruth paused, eyes hesitant: "The fact is I've booked myself a passage next month on a liner to the States."

"You mean you're leaving Hélène? For good?" He was shocked.

"It had to happen one day."

The idea struck him suddenly. It made him laugh.

"It's not because I've come back, is it? You think I'll look after her. I tell you she only puts up with me because you do."

"You've got to learn to know each other. You never have. I really believe you'll get on the way you ought to." She was embarrassed. "Look, the boat's a whole month off. I could change my mind. I haven't told her yet. So please don't say anything."

His promise, however breezy, breached her reticence.

"Hélène can't face loneliness, or inactivity now. It used to be I who needed all the support." But it was on Hélène that she elaborated. "She wasn't like this in Vietnam. She slept on the

127

roadside, in the rain, ate with her fingers or not at all. She was tireless and so in control. God, she was someone."

Ruth's admiration piqued him.

"So now she's the god who failed."

"You wouldn't know. You've never loved a god," Ruth said.

*

The church clock struck three. Thomas stopped before the window, staring at the massive early Baroque church squatting on an island in the roadway. Each morning Maman had attended Mass there and now, Christ knew when the habit had started! Hélène. In just over three hours she'd be on the street: bowed, slow, old before her time, tapping a stick along the pavement. He was conscious of watching a dying woman. To his shame the prospect filled him with relief.

He switched on the bed-table lamp, the only luxury Hélène had conceded to furnish the room with. Otherwise the iron bed, wardrobe, desk, creamy ceramic jug in enamel bowl (and underneath behind a hanging cloth, the slops pail) had preserved intact all the chill of childhood.

Thomas decided he would have to make his move now or never. What would he say though to Ruth? Would he even need to speak? She would surely know why he had come. In a fever of doubt he slunk along the landing to her room, once Hélène's. Now Hélène occupied the one, further down the corridor, where Maman had eked out her widowhood. Thomas pushed the handle, opened the door. But the bed was empty. He hobbled back to his room, pursued by guilt.

*

Thomas stripped, slumped on his bed. He had to face the truth: Ruth had left her room to be with Hélène. How he yearned for a tent, the open sky, a clean life. How he hated walls; and people were walls. Come dawn he would wrench the front door open.

Then from far away, a long, piteous cry reached him. It filled the house, an orphan cry pleading at every door for entry and finding none. Christ, it was Hélène! Cries, sobs, shouting, the dog yelping! Ruth's younger voice though was more vibrant, cruelly dominant. Then silence. Thomas quivered with fear. He might have been a child again, hearing his parents tear at each other the way he cupped his hands to his ears.

He was trembling, sweating, as nervous as an animal caught in the open, scenting death on the wind. He clamped his arms down on the

128

mattress, secured it to himself. Perhaps, just perhaps, Hélène had died from the struggle, destroyed Ruth. For a moment he saw them both removed, the challenge withdrawn, himself free!

"Thomas!" The whisper crossed the room.

Ruth slipped under the sheets, more naked than he.

*

It was only a week ago that he suspected Ruth was a virgin, and learnt that Hélène had once been in love. That day she had offered him her old Citroen to drive, insisted he and Ruth would enjoy a picnic in the Bois de Boulogne. When after disposing of the bought quiche, the salamis and camembert, shirt undone, he tried to seize Ruth playfully, she jerked away with such violence she upset the bottle of Bordeaux. In something like shock they both watched the wine waste into the ground. She half-whispered:

"I'm sorry. I never could... Not in public, not like this."

She wouldn't look at him. She had shrunk into herself.

"There's no one around. And anyway in France..."

"Oh for God's sake!, why must I be like everybody else?"

She turned away. But still he asked:

"Is there... was there someone else?"

Ruth went searching the ground for blades of grass to pluck.

"Did Hélène never mention Joel?" Her voice faltered and at once Thomas had identified his wall. "He'd been in Indochina with her, long before I arrived. He was our French team doctor. One day we drove out to a hamlet in the hills. The Viet-Cong ambushed our jeep. Hélène and I, even the Vietnamese nurses, would be set free, but not Joel. We argued for hours. Hélène offered to stay with them and nurse their wounded. Suddenly the idea of losing Hélène frightened me so much I said I'd stay too. But it was Joel they needed. So they just took him. We never saw him again."

Thomas brooded. Why had he always considered Hélène lacking in imagination? Now he was discovering her at the heart of a passion that mocked at his own scabrous wanderings.

"Hélène collapsed and I was the only one who could nurse her. It went on for months." Ruth scattered the blades of grass she had gathered and faced him. "She was my child. I grew up. I owe her life, feeling, joy, love..."

"Is that why you're sailing home?" He gripped her wrist.

Ruth wrenched herself free, looked at him pityingly. But, he might have guessed it!, she answered a quite different question.

129

"I shall still love her."

"But will she love you?" he asked in a brutal voice. Then shook his head sourly. He hadn't been thinking at all of Hélène.

*

"You failed to come in to work yesterday." M. Perron frowned through his opaque glasses.

"My sister wanted me to go into Paris," Thomas happily told his half-lie. "I couldn't refuse her. She's an invalid."

"I was on my own..." blinked M. Perron as though this had never happened to him before. Without a transition he added: "So far I have not asked you to write letters for me, although your French is admirable."

M. Perron's voice was thick with catarrh. The suffocating cubicle in which they were standing, even to the stacks of ledgers climbing on each side, seemed to have been absorbing his catarrh for years. Thomas couldn't bear to look at his boss. Instead he pretended to examine the filing cards he should have cleared and alongside which a whole new pile had now appeared.

"The tiniest mistake, monsieur, an apostrophe, an acute for a grave accent in a person's name or address could cost the Association hundreds, thousands of francs. Some of our pupils are now in charge of the electronics business, the petro-chemical industry. One is a cabinet minister..."

The tentacles of the school's influence in socialist France appeared to be directed from M. Perron's dusty cubicle.

"Today attack the yellow filing cards and bring them up to date. Some of those boys have probably died or changed address. Start with the year 1927..."

Thomas might have been one of those same thirteen year-olds.

*

Her white flesh lay interlaced with his own sun-beaten one. Drops of tears still clung to the tips of her eyelashes. But they were not of his making. How easy, simple it had been in the end.

"I told Hélène I was leaving." He shunted the notion rapidly to the back of his mind. "She hit me. Scratched me. Look." He saw, he touched, worshipped a long-neglected nakedness.

"Help me, Thomas. I'll have to leave now. She'll destroy me. And then it'll be your turn. Don't laugh."

But he couldn't help it at first. Only later when light fanned across the ceiling did he realize that in their love-making his own hunger had matched her anger. He bent and kissed where he had hurt her most, and wakened her.

"Why have you made it all so much more difficult for me to leave now?" She pulled him down to her, nibbled at his ear.

"Come back tonight. It'll be even better..." he promised.

She did not return, not that night, the next, nor the one after and thus for a whole exasperating week. Nor did they ever seem to be alone in the same room. Hélène, desperate to appease Ruth, was made to hover about like a guardian angel. Thomas found no way into the tight wall of fussy concern for each other which the two women, in a pretence of reconciliation, had erected.

At work Thomas discovered the cigarette smoke kept his boss away. The man was too timid to protest. Soon Thomas felt only contempt for this insignificant being who had the power to employ or fire who he wanted and decide how much or little to pay them.

One morning before breakfast Thomas was in the kitchen cleaning his revolver. He had just inserted two bullets into the cartridge magazine when Hélène returned from Mass.

"Put it away! I've spent my life repairing the damage that disgusting thing has done to people."

Of course he ignored her. He found it just as disgusting to see her squat down to croon to the dog and fondle it and said so.

"Who else have I got left?"

She poured herself a cup from the pot he'd made. She sat sipping the tea and buttering her biscottes. Now it was the cosiness that revolted him, and he said brutally:

"Ruth and I are lovers."

Hélène gasped, cringed before him. Her eyes filmed with tears. She lifted the dog to her lap, turned its head sideways so sharply it let out a warning yelp. He went on:

"She came to me the night she told you she was leaving."

Hélène nodded. He began to wonder if she did understand.

"Yes. She needs someone strong. I was strong once. But no more. Together, two of you, you'd be strong. Marry her!"

He listened aghast.

"I haven't been honest with you. There's a little money, some shares. You can have it all. That's my wedding present. Marry Ruth and keep her here with us, to live in this house." She grasped his wrist. "All I ask in return is that you leave me my room, so that I can die in it. Afterwards do what you like."

She struggled to her feet, stumbled. His hand shot out to steady her. She was so frail it could have picked up, or just as impulsively put a halt, to that scratching life.

"My lawyer, Maitre Emile, will draw up a settlement. I swear I'll never claim Ruth back."

This she believed rather more than Thomas did.

*

A letter from Maitre Emile confirmed Hélène's new will. There was something too in the mail for Ruth. It was her day off and she was toiling at the sink, her turn to make breakfast.

"There's a letter for you," Hélène said.

Ruth tore open the envelope and let out a cry of delight.

"It's my ticket. I'm sailing in five days. Look, read it."

The other two let the letter flutter to the table.

"You're not serious." Thomas stood up, heard himself exclaim in a hysterical voice, "Christ, I thought we had something..."

"We?" Ruth accused. "You and I? Hélène too? Goddam you both." She snatched up the letter, pushed her way between them.

Seconds later she had slammed the front door.

"Go after her," Hélène urged. "Go now! Catch her."

"What with?" Thomas limped into the hall in disgust.

*

The school building hummed with the petulance of end of year exams. M. Perron was absent but he'd left a note for Thomas.

"Please do not repeat the mistakes you made yesterday."

Thomas crumpled the note. A vision of plenty, Hélène's plenty, suddenly obscured the cubicle. Thomas stared at the pile of green cards that had now replaced the yellow ones, waiting for the red, the blue and mauve years to follow, and lit a cigarette.

"There is no place for the weak in this world." Had he not pursued the principle passionately throughout his life? "There is no place in this world for the Perrons with their cubicle souls."

With a dedication that on any earlier occasion would certainly have gratified M. Perron, Thomas threw the cards pell-mell in a bin, and waited till he had burnt the lot.

*

"I've made onion soup. Your favourite," Hélène greeted him from the kitchen.

He didn't need to ask where Ruth was. The house felt empty. he sat down facing Hélène, tasted the soup. It was excellent. He asked for more. She sat, arms folded, her repentance, like the meal, lovingly prepared.

"I wanted to please you both. But now I know I can't. I can only hope. I've been selfish, possessive."

"Tell it to Ruth, if she ever returns." He banged the table.

Hélène bowed her head. Sniffing, as humble and dutiful as a Vietnamese bride, she withdrew without protest to her room.

Thomas waited for Ruth, slumped in an armchair he had dragged into the hallway. In fact she woke him up.

"Where did you go? Hélène has been worrying herself sick."

"Then she must be feeling better. Her light's out."

She sauntered into the salon.

"I resigned from the clinic then went to a movie in Paris. There was a man sitting next to me who kept trying to put his hand up my skirt... But he was so nervous..." She laughed.

It was a long while since he had seen her so confident, and it scared him. He blurted:

"You will stay, won't you? Please. I want you."

A lone car zoomed past, sucking in the silence.

"I'm tired of helping others. And that's all you really want, Thomas, like Hélène, a prop."

"I've lost my job. I burnt all M. Perron's filing cards."

At last he'd pricked her concern. She turned round angrily.

"Have you gone mad? Do you realize that filing system was his life's work? How could you do such a terrible thing?"

"To retain some dignity." Reckless perhaps, but the gesture rang with the panache of youth. "I was a nothing there. A zero."

"And now you've destroyed him, you're something more?"

"You only want to hurt me because you came to my bed."

"God, is that what you understood?" Ruth pushed past him. "I wasn't coming for you. I was leaving *her*."

*

M. Perron had taken to his bed in a state of double shock. He'd submitted his resignation, confessed to the Rector:

"I've lost the school its whole History."

The Jesuit noted the crisis carefully on his note-pad. He could think of no one to replace M. Perron. It was his turn to confess: "We do have a copy of all your files..."

"And poor M. Perron who had thought his files irreplaceable, now finds he's never been anything more than a back-up system!"

Ruth was sharing lunch with Hélène and Thomas. Her eyes dared them to find the truth as funny as she was pretending.

"So maybe what you did was meritorious," she forgave Thomas. With two days to Ruth's departure no one in the house wanted to upset the other. Hélène leant forward to remind her friend:

"Thomas and I must call on Maitre Emile. He's got the papers ready for signing. I'd like you to act as a witness. Please?"

Ruth blurted out as though Thomas was not there:

"Is that wise, Hélène?"

"Who else is left to me to trust now?"

Their eyes met, would not disengage. Thomas had never felt so excluded. Then Ruth jumped up, clapping her hands:

"Only if afterwards we drive through the Vallée de la Chevreuse and have a meal. I so want to remember its beauty."

So they set off the next day and arrived at Maitre Emile's office just off the Cathedral, too early. The Angelus bells were pealing. It added a festive touch to the coloured market stalls spilling on to the square.

"Drop me first then park the car," Hélène instructed Thomas.

She sat at the back on her own holding Whisky down on her lap. The dog hated car trips as much as it hated anyone coming near Hélène. The moment the back door opened it jumped free.

"Ruth! Ruth! Get him back to me! Ruth!" Hélène was frantic.

Ruth sat rigid and seemed not to hear.

"Judas!" Hélène struggled to get out but couldn't. In her frustration she accused: "Thomas, are you siding with her too?"

He saw Whisky across the square. The scrawny voice behind him was punctuated by Hélène's fist beating his shoulder. He got clear and like a clown dragged his leg in pursuit of the hated animal. It had stopped, turned to bark a warning as he approached then a yard off darted into the front wheels of an oncoming car.

Whisky lay gasping in the gutter, pawing the air. Blood was seeping through the soiled fur. Thomas squatted to pick it up. But in a last act of hatred the head jerked up and bit his arm.

"Christ!" It was pure instinct that made Thomas use the side of his hand, aim a single blow at the dog's neck and snap it.

"You've killed him!" Hélène was screaming down on his head. She snatched up the limp bundle, hugged it. "You've done it to everything I ever loved, or loved me. Out of spite, jealousy."

She seemed to have contracted all of Whisky's loathing.

"You stole Ruth, my love, the last love of my life..."

Thomas raised his hand as if to strike just as ruthlessly. But Hélène dropped the bundle from her arms. Her mouth gaped, her eyes fluttered. Strangulated words, syllables escaped and ended in spittle. Slowly she leant forward to come and rest on Thomas.

*

From the landing he tried to spy out Hélène's half-lit room. He could discern the bed, the short legs, the shape of a doll. Was Ruth going to watch over her all night? He could hear the whispering, the wheedling. He tiptoed inside, halted at the sight of Ruth in nurse's uniform, bending to tuck in the sheet then slowly, intensely kiss Hélène's lips, as one lover to another.

"She's not dead yet," his pain protested.

Ruth looked up, her face flushed. She turned the bed-table lamp to one side so that Hélène seemed to sink into the gloom.

"Dr. Pascal says she could recover some movement of limb, even speech. You can never tell. We'll have to wait and hope."

"That could mean weeks, months." The prospect appalled him.

"Years. We'd better get used to it."

"She'd be better off dead."

"Tell her that!" Ruth said and walked out on him.

Thomas was tempted to turn the light back on to Hélène. Ruth had not wanted him to see. What? He strained to catch a glimpse and became aware of the skeletal face, the lower jaw fallen from the skull, the bared lips on toothless gums, the closed eyelids, the heavy breathing. He turned away, mortified.

He caught sight of a wig left on the dressing table. Hélène was bald! And he'd never once suspected. In fact he'd never cared to think about Hélène, neither the years she'd wasted in this town waiting to bury Maman, nor why she had journeyed out to a distant and bloody conflict that had nothing to do with her? The fact that she would die a stranger to him left him bitter.

"I came back too late. I didn't matter any more to you," he accused out loud. "I was just a means to keep Ruth here."

Yet all the time he spoke he felt this ache, this craving deep inside him to be forgiven - and knew he couldn't be now.

He fled in horror at himself, dragging his useless leg to his own room. It was the end of foreign sunsets, hills to assault, deserts to trek, the taste and comradeship of death. No one would ever hire him again.

If only he hadn't seen Ruth kiss Hélène with such feeling! The only truth was the automatic waiting on the desk. He picked it up, looked into the barrel, pulled the trigger. It clicked.

"I removed these days ago." Ruth's voice ruptured the silence. In her outstretched palm were the missing bullets. "Was there anything in life you ever loved more than killing?"

"I loved you!" He snatched the bullets, flung them out of the open window. "If you'd given me the chance. The two of you." He didn't know how to stop himself breaking down. "I know I can never have you. That ghost in there claimed you years ago."

He covered his face, the sight if not the sound of tears.

"You fool." She parted his hands.

"The way you kissed her..."

"Such an inadequate way to say thank you after fifteen years of being together, don't you think? Thomas! Thomas! How little you understand. And now you're jealous of what she's become?"

"Will you leave?" He was kissing the back, the inside of her hands. "Don't leave me alone with her. Stay till..."

Ruth clasped his head to her stomach. She whispered:

"Last night, or was it the night before?, I dreamt of a warrior who snatched me as his prize and plunder, then in his haste to get away safely, lost me." Her grip tightened, her voice filled with anguish. "Thomas, how will I find my way home?"

"Let me find you. Let me keep you."

It was the turn of his arms to enfold, to imprison her. She had a spasm of revolt. But he strengthened his hold, carried her to his bed, laid her alongside him. He soothed, warmed her in words and touch till she cried out for him to meet her on a new and dangerous shore.

The crash in Maman's room, like the wrath of an ancient god, echoed through the house and summoned them both back to their duty. Ruth, desperately trying to dress her nakedness, was first in Hélène's room. She found her patient dangling over the bed, fingers brushing the floor.

"My God, she must have regained consciousness for a moment and tried to get out." She grappled to raise the inert figure.

Thomas watched in his bare feet, shivering in the doorway.

"Do you think she's had another stroke?"

Hélène still lived, still breathed. Her eyes were open, quizzical, her mouth loose, dribbling uncontrollably. He gazed in fascinated disgust at the fingers clutching, unable to get a grip on death. The irony was that though scarcely aware of it, Hélène had never been stronger.

Minutes later the china figure was propped up, wiped clean, wigged, packed rigid inside the sheets. Then with neither a word nor glance to each other, warily the two finished dressing in Hélène's room. All night, past dawn, they kept vigil waiting and not daring to hope.

Jacqueline Deakin

A Response In Kind

Wilbur Boyle, arbiter of style, poison pen-portraits and practical jokes, stood in Boots wondering whether to buy strip wax or depilatory cream. The glossy curls on his chest were springing up with unwarranted vigour past his mid-day stubble to meet the spiky tufts bristling out of each nostril. His head, in contrast, was stark, his hair-line retreating. At twenty-four, this was sad. It meant that he spent long hours devising ways to prevent an Elizabethan ruff. He had even considered a daily hand-stand in the hope that the stuff would by-pass his neck and come out where it was supposed to - on his crown. He sighed. Wax hurt and cream was messy. It would have to be the scissors and razor again.

As he came out of Boots he noticed Prudence, the accountant with sensible calves, turn down an alley. He was just about to call out when Travers slipped past after her. Travers was the ultimate push-bike courier. Fit, tanned, dark, he swung in and out of the traffic with derisory ease, coasting along in the lust of passing strangers. He monitored his prowess in a myriad wing-mirrors, his reflections his accolade.

Wilbur's antennae, extra-sensory, rather than follicular, quivered. Was this a potential number for 'The Voyeur', his in-house rag-mag? Lust in the lunch hour? As a marketing executive, he was conceptual. All were impressed with his diligence on the screen until it emerged that the little blocks of text he moved from column to column were damning send-ups of the staff's out of hours passions and peccadilloes, and not the company brochure at all. Then everyone had a good laugh until it was their turn to be featured. Then the laugh became more of a death rattle.

Oh this was wonderful! No-one liked a good story better than Wilbur. Travers was straddling Prudence against the wall, pinioning back her arms. Their heads slowly synchronised. Wilbur stared, riveted. Then someone walked into him and left a very decisive mark on his right shoe. Annoyed, he bent down and meticulously rubbed it off. He was 'marketing' after all. He didn't want to look like he had just come out of an alley. Prudence and Travers! What a scoop! Inspired, he actually increased his pace back to his office.

Half an hour later Prudence walked past his room - he always kept his door open.

"Alright?" he called out, cheerily.

138

Prudence turned round and beamed. She wasn't prone to smiling spontaneously. It was quite something. She didn't linger but continued up the corridor, her stalwart calves whisk, whisk, whisking with formidable coquettishness.

A little later Karen, the Personnel Manager, dropped by, wanting him to draw up an advert for a new sales rep. He was pleased to see her. He got on very well with Karen. As he was acutely aware, all good personnel managers know far more than necessary about their employees. What did she know about Prudence and Travers?

The corner of her mouth dipped uncontrollably and she quickly looked down so that her long dark hair swung over her face. Wilbur registered the movement but failed to interpret it.

"You're not still having a fling with Travers, are you?" he asked, stretching curiosity to concern with negligible success.

"No." The reply was muffled.

"To think you thought that nobody knew about you and Travers until that meeting when I passed you a copy of 'The Voyeur'! Do you remember? The meeting went on forever and you couldn't say a word about it until it was over - three hours later. Your face was a picture. It was so funny. I thought you'd burst."

Karen parted her hair and stared at Wilbur appraisingly.

"So did I, darling. So did I." His grin could have been infectious if she hadn't been the cause of it. The Managing Director had found it all very amusing as well, but amusing an MD is no guarantee of a recommendation for promotion no matter how many times he has dined out at your expense.

"Prudence and Travers - unbelievable!"

"Very." Karen allowed herself a tight triumphant smile and turned to go. As she made her way out she added, "Oh, by the way, there's a message on the noticeboard for you."

"Oh good. Thanks."

It could be about any one of a number of fixtures he was organising - go-kart racing, ten-pin bowling, comedy club. As at university, Wilbur arranged work around his social life. He promptly abandoned his survey analysis and made his way down to the Smoking Room. Paula and Colin were in there, examining a document together with scant regard for the boundaries of personal space. But it was the piece of A4 paper on the noticeboard that seized his attention. It wasn't a message. It was an enlarged copy of a photograph of the back of his head. The monochrome reproduction was a particularly effective genre to emphasise his baldness. Like an octopus, the circular naked patch of his crown extended down in long white tentacles of scalp.

The world reeled. No! When had it got so bad? The back of his head was as familiar as a watch-face to everyone else except him. Wilbur felt he had been walking round in a hospital gown for the last few weeks.

There was a snort behind him and as he looked round, Colin whipped his hand away from Paula.

"I was just, um, I was just checking Paula's proof-reading," Colin explained, unnecessarily.

"You haven't got..." Wilbur began.

Paula dropped the papers she was holding and she and Colin both scrabbled to pick them up. Papers reassembled, they faced Wilbur in united pink expectancy.

"A mirror?"

"Not me mate. You want Travers."

"I've got a make-up mirror. Will that do?" Paula fumbled in her hand-bag. "What do you want it for?"

"Oh - my lenses are playing up."

"I didn't know you wore lenses. Are they new? What have you got? Hard or soft?"

"Hard." He grabbed the mirror she was holding out to him and dived out of the room. As the door banged behind him, a great shout of laughter followed him out.

The only mirrors in the Gents toilets were the ones above the hand-basins. He stood, with his back to the wall, angling the hand mirror to catch his reflection in the wall mirror. Then he crouched. Then he stretched. It was impossible. His bum kept colliding with the basins. In the end, cross-eyed, crick-necked and defeated, he went back to his office.

There on the seat he found an anonymous submission for 'The Voyeur'. It was an advert for new members of staff to join the social club, which was puzzling because the company didn't have a social club. There were only thirty or so employees, everyone knew everyone else and he organised anything that was worth going to. The phone went and he put it on one side.

As it was Friday he finished work early but he only stayed for a quick drink with one or two of the lads from 'dispatch'. They had too much hair. He found the length and luxuriance of their pony-tails unsettling.

On Saturday he bought another hat. He was rather proud of his collection but as he tried on a brown and cream art-piece, an urban tribute to Andean trekking expeditions, the thought did occur that his obsession may have contributed to his premature alopecia. He had read somewhere that sunlight promoted hair growth. Perhaps he needed to go someplace hot to kick-start the follicles. After all, he couldn't recall ever seeing a bald West Indian.

On Monday Wilbur resumed his regular routine. He arrived at work at 9.45, sat down with a cappuccino and a warm croissant with jam, and worked his way through *The Guardian*. He always felt 'Creative and Media' on Mondays.

"Wilbur! Where were you Saturday night? I didn't see you at the party," Prudence assailed him gaily.

Party? Prudence? He gawped at her incisive slabs of dentine, beyond her moustache and up to her round dancing eyes.

"Yo! Karen! Wild outfit you were wearing Saturday."

Colin followed Karen and Prudence into his office and suddenly everybody was in there talking about this brilliant party. They had all met up at The Three Bells first. Travers had got done for speeding before he had even arrived and Adam had accidentally deposited his last lump of hash into a charity collection box along with three 10ps and a guilder. Stacey and Kevin were now an item, Mark and Patsy had split, and Mark had brought along the new bar-maid from New Zealand. Then, just as suddenly, they had all gone and he still didn't know whose party it was and why he hadn't been invited.

Gloomily he made his way down to the Smoking Room for a quick cigarette before getting stuck into some work. He followed Travers, taut in black lycra cycling shorts, down the corridor. Paula was standing by the lift door. She smiled at Travers, the doors parted and Travers abruptly changed direction and got in with her. His arm closed around her as the doors shut. In the Smoking Room Colin was examining another document, or maybe it was the same one, in lip-kissing proximity with Prudence. They both looked up with the same silly smile.

Irritated, he lit up and stupidly went over to check the noticeboard. The photocopies, unlike his scalp, had sprouted. His hand rose, of its own volition, to massage the back of his head. Behind him Colin started to hack. Prudence patted his back and tittered. Grimly, Wilbur made his way out. Prudence, frolicsome, was too much. It was all, in fact, too much.

For the rest of the day Wilbur locked himself away and finished a report based on the survey he had been analysing in desultory dribs and drabs for the past fortnight. He was rather pleased how nice it felt to have finished something.

His redemption came at the photocopier. There was a small pile of paper on top of it which turned out to be originals abandoned under the lid. It was no surprise to find the ubiquitous copy of the back of his head. What was illuminating though was that this copy had Tippex on it in the shape of an octopus with long white tentacles. Wilbur felt whoozy with relief. Now he wouldn't have to sit back to front in a passport photograph booth. He screwed the photocopy up and threw it in the bin. In future he would save them the bother.

That evening he went to the barbers and had all his hair shaved off and the next day he went to work wearing a woolly hat, like a tea-cosy on a speckled egg.

Panurge 24

D.J.Taylor on Success. Fine stories from Sally St.Clair, Sarah Spiller, Neil Grimmett and many more.

Antony John

untitled

Elouise watched as he dragged the mattress towards her. Bazza stared from under his eyebrows as he hauled. The mattress was a dead weight against the carpet. He sweated. He wore a shirt, the tails slapping against his naked legs. He gripped the floor through white socks.

He deposited the mattress at her feet. "There!" he said, close to her face. "Mountain to Mohammed. Satisfied? Now get on the bed and get your kit off. I'm in the mood for love."

Elouise turned back to the window. "It's raining," she said.

Bazza peered out. "Where?"

"Raining in my heart," she replied. "Bazza - I feel like we're losing each other." She ran a fingernail down a badly mended crack in the window. "That's us," she said. "Two pieces of broken glass, sellotaped together. See how it's coming apart?"

Bazza sniffed at her. "Have you been with someone else?"

"I've just come out of the bath."

Bazza crossed the small room to a cracked sink in the corner. "I ought to give you a good fisting," he muttered. "Knock you some sense." He began to sort through a line of plastic bottles. Panic crossed his face. "Where's my *Feel Fresh?*" he demanded. "I want my *Feel Fresh!*" Bottles of shampoo and conditioner tumbled to the floor as he searched through them. His face twisted with indignation. "You've used up my *Feel Fresh!*" he hissed. "I'm sweaty. How can I deodorise myself with no deodorant? How can I smell like fresh summer meadows without my *Feel Fresh?*"

Bazza ran at Elouise and grabbed the back of her long hair. "Are you laughing at me?" he asked, pulling tight. "Are you laughing at me behind your hands?" He pushed her face into his armpit. "Sniff that!"

Elouise tripped and fell backwards onto the mattress. Her dressing gown fell open as she hit the bed. Her breasts stared up eyelessly at Bazza and he met their gaze. He lowered his fist.

"Do you like that?" said Elouise with a slight smile. "Do you like looking?"

Bazza nodded.

"Kneel down," she instructed.

Bazza knelt.

"You're a dirty little tyke, aren't you?" Elouise said. "What are

143

you?"

"I'm a dirty tyke." Bazza bowed his head. "I just get confused and then I'm gripped with violence."

"Who's your queen?"

"You're my queen."

"And who's my Lancelot?"

"That's me," said Bazza. "I'm your Lancelot."

Elouise knelt up on the bed, her dressing gown open, and took hold of the shoulders of Bazza's shirt. She pulled the shirt halfway down, exposing Bazza's chest and pinning his arms to his sides. She stared into his eyes and plunged her hand down his Y-fronts. "Well, Lancelot," she said. "You feel that? That's mine that is!"

There was a noise in the kitchen below and Bazza's ears pricked up. "I didn't realise *he* was in!" With his arms still restrained, he bounded over the bed, panting like a dog. "The Babbling Man! The Confused Man!" He tripped and fell, his head thumping heavily against the floor. He pressed his ear against the carpet, his rear end high in the air. "Shhh! Listen!"

Bazza felt Elouise's lips soft against his other ear. "He's our landlord, Bazza," she whispered. "He's coming to get you. We've been here three weeks and we haven't paid him a penny of rent."

"But we've spent all our money on mind-expanding drugs for the weekend," Bazza replied. "Listen - he's coming upstairs!"

Elouise and Bazza froze in silence. Her red hair fell across his face and his taut back. Her hand rested on his shoulder. In the gathering dusk outside the window, a seagull called out as it rose in a spiral above the house. The streetlights lit. The house stood alone, in yellow light. Below a concrete and iron promenade, the sea shifted and dragged.

Footsteps mounted the stairs leading to Bazza and Elouise's room. Elouise followed them with her ears as they approached. Each stair creaked with its own voice. The footsteps halted outside the door. Then they continued up another staircase.

"He's going to the attic!" Bazza whispered.

"That's his dead mother's room," Elouise replied. "She was bedridden and crippled with pain. He was distraught. Death was a real release. He got the house out of it."

Bazza eyed her suspiciously. "You know a lot about it."

"I was in the bathroom when he took me into his confidence," Elouise replied. "Listen - the footsteps have stopped!"

Bazza looked at the ceiling. Silence. *"He's* listening to *us* now. Gives me the creeps."

Elouise had spread herself on the bed. "Make love to me, Bazza," she said. "Make love to me while he's listening."

*

A few days later, Elouise was sitting in the downstairs kitchen at a heavy oak table. She had cleared herself a space amongst the newspapers and books and rotting dinner plates. Behind her, the sink was piled with washing-up. Pot plants, parched dry, hung down from the windowsill. The room plunged into darkness then filled with light as clouds passed across the sun.

"Do you know anything about infection, Mr Featherstone?" Elouise called. She addressed herself to a walk-in pantry. A kettle began to shriek from the stove. "I've heard infection never goes away once it gets a hold. Once it's in there. It just rides through our veins causing untold mischief."

The piercing cry from the kettle became unbearable. A man in his late sixties, with a plume of white hair and gaunt, concentrated features, leapt out from behind the pantry door and seized the handle. His fingers sizzling, he dashed to the table.

"It's just I've got a scratch, you see," Elouise continued, pulling open her shirt a little. "Here, on my left boobie."

Mr Featherstone craned his neck to look and spilt scalding water down his trouser leg. "Ooyah! That's hot!" He dropped the kettle with a crash on the table.

He nursed his burnt fingers, then tipped the contents of the kettle into a large teapot. The water hissed and gurgled. "The tea ceremony," he explained. "So very English. I'll grill some muffins presently." He paused. "I do hope we'll all get along."

"Bazza's upstairs," Elouise replied.

Mr Featherstone's face twitched a little and he pulled at his cardigan. "I do hope you explained to your young man ... the other day ... when I walked in on you ..."

"When I was in the bath?" Elouise asked. "Naked?"

Mr Featherstone flushed. "You should lock the door, you know," he said, avoiding her gaze. "You could cause all sorts of misunderstandings leaving it ajar like that." He poured a cup of tea.

Elouise leaned back on her chair. "You said you had something to show me."

Mr Featherstone's face lit up. "My autobiography, yes! I'm glad

145

you're interested. Most people couldn't give a fig." From a drawer he produced a red folder. "This is my life!" He passed it to Elouise who flicked through with a smile.

"To put it bluntly, I've had a hell of a life," Mr Featherstone told her. "I was a tie salesman to the stars of stage and screen, as well as to your ordinary bloke. Some of the necks I've seen, you wouldn't believe. Sometimes I fancy I'm a suitcase of bright ties myself, ready to throw myself open and bring colour to this drab, cruel world of ours."

"Mind you," he continued, "the world is very different now to when I started out. Then everything was simple. Churchill and Stalin and Roosevelt had just drawn up all the maps. Now everything's breaking up, confused, higgledy-piggledy. People shooting each other for the wrong reasons. Throats slit and children incinerated in Balkan basements. Fascism's all the rage again. Starving faces looming up from the TV. Curtains going up, walls coming down - it's like a house on a sudden precipice. And gun law on the streets of Manchester, it's all getting a bit much."

Mr Featherstone's eyes refocussed on Elouise. "I hope I'm not leaving you behind with all this political talk, love." He took a gulp of tea. "Things are so much more confusing since Reginald Bosanquet left our screens. He was a great communicator. I took a professional interest in him, having once sold him a cravat."

Elouise opened the red folder and flicked the pages close to his face. "Look," she said. "The pages are blank blank blank. They're numbered but there's nothing written."

Mr Featherstone passed a frustrated hand over his white hair. "Of course the pages are blank, I haven't worked it all out yet. It's so complicated. How can I write down what I don't understand?" He took the folder from her. "How can you condense into a few words a man's whole life, and set it against the complexities of post-war European history?" A white page caught his eye. He smiled. "Page 365 - one of my favourites." He removed the page from the folder. "I fall in love on page 365. Myrtle. She had blue eyes and a fragility that tore your heart to shreds. Or was that Hilda?" Mr Featherstone sniffed. "Look at me, I'm beefing. Look - I'm crying." Elouise passed him a teatowel to wipe his eyes. "Mother never liked her because she smoked in the public street and supported women's suffrage. She married a Yank in the end and was blown up by the Nazis."

There was a clatter of boots down the stairs. Bazza pushed his way through the kitchen door. Elouise put a comforting hand on Mr Featherstone's cheek. "I'm sorry," Mr Featherstone was saying. "I'm babbling on. Sometimes my emotions run away with me, like a dish with a spoon."

Bazza circled the table, staring at the back of Mr Featherstone's head. "This is all very cosy," he said. He was wearing a tee shirt and a pair of Army slacks. Mr Featherstone collected up the pages of his autobiography. Elouise watched as he put the folder away. Bazza sat down, his chair screeching along the lino.

"I was just telling the young lady about my life and times as a tie salesman," Mr Featherstone said. "What would you do, son, if you had the chance of a job?"

"I'd be an investigative journalist," Bazza replied. "Or a juror in a case of murder."

Bazza reached across and placed his finger on Elouise's forehead. He traced it down her nose, then along her mouth until her lips were wet with saliva.

"You're the future, you kids," Mr Featherstone was saying. "Sometimes the politicians forget that."

Bazza and Elouise's eyes were locked together. Bazza's finger had entered her mouth and she gripped it with her teeth. She pressed harder as she smiled, and harder still. Flecks of blood appeared on her tongue tip. Bazza smiled too.

Elouise let go his finger. "We know who we are," she said. "We're indestructible. Like Superman."

Mr Featherstone sighed. "Mother always used to say that love was a many-splendoured thing."

Bazza turned on him. "Your mother," he said, "she copped it, didn't she? Suffocation wasn't it?"

Mr Featherstone paled. "Mother did pass away recently, yes," he answered. "Natural causes was the coroner's verdict." He lowered his gaze. "She was a fine woman. Built like a horse. Dominant and brutal in her way, malicious and snide, but still she had about her a woman's vulnerability. You would have liked her. We came here because of her disease. It ate her away. Corroded her bones." He looked up. "We used to lay awake, side by side in the attic room bed, and listen to the sea and the gulls. I'd stroke her hair and tell her she'd be all right. She'd clench her jaw against the pain and occasionally go into convulsions."

"You talk about her as if she were your wife," said Elouise.
Mr Featherstone was silent.

"In agony when she popped off then?" Bazza inquired.

"You understand we're only inquisitive because we want to help," Elouise explained. "Often it can be beneficial to talk things through with friends. It can help sort out emotions and strong feelings."

Mr Featherstone met her eyes. "You're right," he said. "I shouldn't keep it bottled up." He tugged at his lower lip. "I remember her last day. She asked for fried egg for breakfast. I fed them to her from a plate. Her toothless mouth reached out for the fork. She was eating, and she rolled her eyes round to see me, then rolled them back in sheer pleasure as she chewed. I was shivering, the fork rattling on the plate. She motioned to me to have some. I was trembling, but she rolled her eyes in delight when she saw me eat. My throat was constricted with fear. She was ecstatic, grinning, her half-blind eyes staring round the room. I was gagging. The yolk was dribbling down her chin. Inside, her mouth was sticky with the filth of death, tar black, her gums biting down on half-chewed egg. I ran out of the house, her moans calling me back. The sound of the plate crashing to the floor was the last thing I heard. I walked by the sea in the rain. When I got back, she was dead."

Mr Featherstone stood with a stumbling dignity. His face was contorted with sorrow. Outside, the sea thumped against the concrete defences like a head against a wall. He took a gulp of tea.

"That's quite a tale," said Elouise carefully. "Evidently your mother was in a lot of pain and close to death. It's technically illegal, but no one would blame you if you'd ... so to speak ... nudged her on her way."

Mr Featherstone wiped his mouth on his sleeve. He moved, unsteady, out of the kitchen. Elouise listened to the sound of vomiting from the bathroom.

Bazza was very excited. He took Elouise's two hands in his. "We've got him! We've got him!" he said, his eyes wide. "We must break into that attic room. There'll be the evidence in there to wrap up this case!"

The next days passed almost in silence. Elouise and Bazza slept separately, she in bed, he curled in the corner of their room. They ate little. When they met Featherstone on the stairs, they avoided his eyes. He had acquired a haunted, shrunken look.

Only once did Bazza speak to Elouise, instructing her: "Now it's time to shave our heads." She rested her head against his naked chest. She listened to the snip of the dressmaking scissors and her hair falling to the floor. She was empty of emotion. She was content.

Bazza shaved his own head over the sink, badly, blaspheming under his breath when he cut himself. When he'd finished, Elouise ran her palm over his scalp. "It's all tufty!" she laughed to herself.

It was on the fifth day after the kitchen encounter that Bazza and Elouise broke into the room of the dead Mrs Featherstone. The door gave way with a crack. They stood at the threshold.

Before they crossed, Elouise pulled Bazza towards her. "You're a real live wire," she said. "Let's plug you in." She reached up and kissed him deeply. He choked a little and felt her pass a small capsule from her mouth to his. "Don't worry," she said as she broke away. "Just something to sharpen you up." She took his hand and they stepped into the room.

The attic room was empty but for a large brass bed and a wardrobe in the corner. Bazza sank to his knees. "The room's stripped bare!" he wailed. "We're foiled! The scene of the crime has been tampered with. The course of Justice is perverted!"

Faced with the empty room, Elouise too was at a loss. Then a slow smile crossed her face. "Look under there, Bazza."

Bazza crossed the room on all fours and reached under the bed. "The murder weapon!" he cried. He pulled out a slightly grubby pillow. He lay down on his stomach and peered at the carpet as if looking through a magnifying glass. "And fingernails! Broken in the struggle!" Abruptly, he shook his head to clear it. "I'm going to have to calm down. I'm off it." He buried his face in the carpet.

Behind them, the door creaked open on its broken hinges. Mr Featherstone, his eyes heavy with sleep, stood in the doorway. "What's the meaning of all this disturbance at this hour?" He saw the door. "Look at this wilful damage" I ought to give you a good hiding!"

Elouise was leaning over Bazza, whispering at his ear. "Can you hear me?" she said. "I have something to tell you."

"Let the witness take the stand!" Bazza called out.

Elouise held herself steady as she bent over him. "It was a few days ago. I was in the bath, with my knees against the sides. I was washing myself. The door opened and in walks our good landlord,

149

Mr Featherstone." Elouise paused. "Are you getting this, Bazza? I asked what he wanted and he said he'd come to use the toilet. He already had his trousers down. The next thing I knew he was in the bath too."

Bazza let out a low animal moan that startled even Elouise.

She took a deep breath and smiled at Mr Featherstone. "He was on top of me, Bazza. He was moving, and the bathwater started slooshing up and down around us. Slooshing up and down. He fumbled about, but he knew where everything went. I just let him get on with it. He looked so earnest, I didn't want to put him off his stroke. When he'd finished, he sat on the toilet and boasted how he'd bumped off his mother. Then he left."

Bazza was silent. Elouise stood and moved slowly away.

Mr Featherstone had stepped into the room. He walked over to Bazza, spreadeagled on the floor. "This carpet's not for laying all over!" He took hold of an arm and hauled Bazza to his feet.

Bazza stood, his head angled forward, staring at Featherstone. "Where's my *Feel Fresh*?" Bazza asked him. "What have you done with my *Feel Fresh*?"

Mr Featherstone looked puzzled. "Have you been drinking?" He began to tremble.

"Get on the bed," Bazza instructed. "I'll show you not to mess with my woman."

Mr Featherstone backed away. The bed creaked as he climbed onto it and lay back awkwardly. "Do you have a knife?" he asked.

Bazza tapped his crotch. "This is the only knife I need." He leaned forward and pinned Mr Featherstone's shoulders to the bed with his hands. "Get your tits out," he said coldly. "Get your tits out. Get your tits out for the lads."

Mr Featherstone stared in disbelief. "I'm an old man!" He looked imploringly at Elouise, who was sitting on top of the wardrobe to get the best view.

"Get your tits out," she echoed. "For the lads."

Bazza pushed Mr Featherstone further into the bed and stood up. "That's where she lay!" he snarled. "That's where she lay when you done your business." He waved the pillow in Featherstone's face. "We've got evidence! You done in your own mother! She who raised you, she who opened up her loins and bore you into the world. All because the lady was a dribbling diseased wreck!"

"It's true!" cried Mr Featherstone. "I killed her. When she

needed me most, I ran away. That moment of disloyalty was more lethal to her than any number of pillows on her face." Tears fell from his eyes. He wiped his nose on his sleeve. "I never knew my dad. She was my everything. The way we touched, it was more than just mother and son. Punish me! Do your worst! I've been in a Burmese gaol, I know what to expect."

"Knack him, Bazza!" Elouise shouted from the wardrobe.

"You're not even worth punching a hole into," said Bazza in disgust at Featherstone. "I wouldn't mucky up my knuckles doing it." He turned to Elouise. "Come on, doll, we're out of here before I puke my guts."

Elouise jumped down. She kissed Bazza's shaven neck. "Time for bed," she cooed, slipping her hand into his. "Oh - wait!" she cried. "We've forgotten about his autobiography!" She rushed downstairs to the kitchen and returned with the red folder. Bazza threw it to the floor and stamped on it until the white pages were covered with bootprints. Hand in hand, Bazza and Elouise descended the stairs to their room.

"Don't go!" Mr Featherstone called after them. "We've hardly started!" he cried. "Punish me!"

151

Pablo Palacio

A New Case of 'Mariage En Trois'
(translated by Stefan Ball)

They lay with their mouths almost touching, caressing each other. Suddenly Elvira leapt to her feet, wrinkling up her nose and spitting.
"Oh! Oh! Jesus!"
Antonio, unconcerned, knowing that women are prone to make a fuss about nothing, wrapped himself up in the sheets and said between his teeth:
"OK, let's hear it, what happened?"
She grew more and more horrified, emphasised her startled grimace.
"The fly, for God's sake, the fly! It got between our lips."
The Maestro shivered slightly: he had felt a soft tickle move across his lips; then it jumped to his forehead and slid down the profile of his nose; and at last something bulky, that fluttered furiously, invaded without mercy one of his nostrils and, buzzing, banged its body against the sides of all his hidden cavities.
Recoledo sat up on the bed with a jerk and sneezed violently. How awful! Between his sweaty arms there lay a warm pillow and next to him there was nobody.
When he remembered the ardent parts of his dream, he was ashamed of himself. If at that moment he had seen Elvira, he would certainly have asked her forgiveness on his knees. It was an insult to profane her like that, in dreams, when he hadn't even dared to confess his love for her when he was with her. But in the end he was a weak man: what could he do?
With his little finger he began to pick at his nostrils, thoughtfully, and with the index finger of the other hand he rubbed his eyes. Never let anyone know that a man as serious as he would do such stupid things in the dark in this way.
Antonio Recoledo was a rather short individual, stocky and a bit short-sighted. When he went out in the street he always wore a little bowler hat, glasses and everyday black clothing. Aged about forty, he was already famous.
And Antonio was intelligent, always intelligent. His contemporaries said so. He founded two periodicals: *The Beacon* and *The Truth*, in which he campaigned valiantly and justly. He gained his Bachelor's degree and studied as far as the third year of Law, from when his sociological interests dated. His was a talent truly encyclopaedic,

because in those days they really did study. If only we could get back to those days! With the same ease he could talk of Natural Law, Economics and Chemistry, and even of Literature. Of course, sometimes he didn't say the same things as the books, but already Antonio had confided in private to his nephew Juan that the books made mistakes too, and often. Juan called him quietly 'Maestro', and well he deserved it.

Following his leanings towards sociology, a study which has caused a great leap forward in contemporary science, the young deserter from the University shut himself away in a private cubbyhole. At the cost of half his life, half his hair and half his sight, he made himself wise. A laudable sacrifice on behalf of human progress.

The centre of his researches was Woman. He knew the subject off pat. Some were of the opinion that he was more adept than Balzac and more accurate than Stendhal. But the thing that most appealed to them was his healthy optimism. One should be optimistic, of course. Nothing is lost by it, and one gives heart to decent folk.

'Woman, that angel of light,' Recoledo had written, 'made up entirely of feeling and love, sensitive and fragile as she is, is meant for great things. Tolerant and intelligent, to a degree nearly equivalent to that of we men, she will provide, without the slightest doubt, the most solid base of life in the future. At least, philosophers and publicists agree on this point.' Who can deny it? They were beautiful phrases, Antonio's.

With such favourable opinions of the fair sex, he composed his monumental work *In Defence of the More Interesting Half of the Human Species*, which gained him so much fame.

It was full of considered and lapidary phrases, 'disconcerting because of their incisive laconicism, which probe deep into the truth like a scalpel in the flesh of a corpse.' This is what a commentator wrote to him and, as the Maestro had underlined the phrase I think that it was to his liking.

And it was natural that after the publication of his book he should dream of marvels for at least three nights: a man who writes a book is no common thing. He thought of meticulous biographies, of his photograph on the covers of foreign periodicals, and of numerous congratulations from feminist committees - although, to his credit, he was never one to seek out honours. On the contrary, Antonio took every chance he could to throw this phrase into the face of his

153

adversaries, as if it were a punch: 'No superior man... sets out... on the hunt... for vanities!' When he pronounced this favourite dictum, he stretched his meagre body up as far as it would go and shook his index finger vigorously, in a significant way.

Now, with his eyes still swollen from so much sleep, he meditated, full of contrition, on the barbarities in his dream. The committee and the periodicals, that was one thing. But to have included Elvira, such a good girl... Nevertheless, instead of forgetting his dreams, he kept reviewing them, and in his heart he would really have wanted it all.

At that moment, on the point of getting up, he heard a noise. It was the cook who was calling him with her eye to the keyhole and her voice all liquid.

"Sir... Sir..."

The Maestro, putting his hairy legs back under the covers, told her to enter.

Petrona came in with a daily paper in her hand. Her eyes were shining with happiness. With her plump index finger she pointed to the paper and affirmed that what was written there was sublime, that was what Mrs Gertrudis, who read the papers every day, had said to her at the market, and she had bought a copy so that he could see it...

He grabbed hold of the paper, rubbing his eyes again, put on his glasses and ran his eyes along the black lines. Yes, there it was in the books section. After a cough and a spit, he read aloud.

'Antonio Recoledo and his book *In Defence of the More Interesting Half of the Human Species.* We have received the excellent work whose title heads this article, two volumes, published in a limited edition, which we have just had the pleasure of reading. Antonio Recoledo, the author, a young man of special talent, has dedicated all his powers for many years to the study of Woman...'

"Bring my breakfast at once."

Petrona left the room reluctantly.

... 'one of those studies which we feel such a lack of in these days when the young waste their energies uselessly in uninspired literary dabbling, which add every day to the dishonour of our beloved country.' Recoledo smiled with satisfaction; it was so. There was nothing like the newspapers for telling the truth. 'It's high time that the young woke up and followed the valuable path of science, along which travels, in the vanguard, our wise Recoledo, who, despising at all costs personal advantages and vain satisfactions, consumes his best years in the silence of his study, with Benedictine patience. As we are short of space, we will limit ourselves to a simple announcement of the appearance of the work, reserving for another occasion a detailed critique. We predict many triumphs for our philosopher and friend.'

The cook had tiptoed back with the breakfast. Antonio, as if bowled over, was slowly scratching his legs, his eyes wide open. It really was a case of having glory within reach. Why should his dreams remain fantasies? He saw once more Elvira next to him, flattering, smiling, offering him her sweet mouth and intoxicating him with the aggressive splendour of her black eyes. He raised his trembling hands, squeezed two curved hips, two hard thighs, and mad with desire laid Elvira down and kissed her.

Petrona gave a sigh of contentment. Hearing it, the Maestro realised his mistake and drew apart, very grave. This was no longer suitable for a man in his position. But the cook had grown bold, and knitting her arms around his neck and going as red as beetroot, whispered in his ear.

There was a tragic silence. The writer threw himself out of bed at once and stood and stared at her in an atrocious rage, as if he wanted to tear her to pieces.

It has to be admitted that the poor thing had a funny expression, but he was very upset. All he did was glare at her stomach and think of the irremediable death of his one illusion. He would never reach up as far as Elvira. In the end he exclaimed, furious:

"Lies! It isn't mine. You're not going to pull the wool over my eyes, you bitch. Get out at once. You're a bunch of animals, all of you."

Petrona was dumb with terror, not knowing what was happening to her. After an instant she slowly left the room and went to the kitchen, which had a small smoked-glass window overlooking the street.

What was she going to do? She was no novice in matters of this sort, for this was the second time it had happened, and now this child wouldn't have a father either. In truth she wasn't sure who was responsible, but it had to be one of the two. She had told the other one, Emilio, that it was his, and they had agreed that she would lie to her boss. But she had already prepared herself for the idea that Emilio would laugh in her face and head for the hills when he heard the answer Recoledo had given her this morning.

She put her head out the window and leant on the filthy ledge. By chance, Emilio was going by on his way to work. When he saw her sad face and the negative signals she was making with her head, he knew at once what was up. He stopped for a moment, thoughtful; then, coming to a decision, he shrugged his shoulders and went on his way, not saying a word. Only to himself did he sum up the situation:

"Well, the poor thing! As for me, I don't believe her either."

Then, seeing him walk away, Petrona straightened up, very pale, with her hands laced over her rounded stomach. And with all the anger of her impotence, furrowing her brow and grinding her teeth, she spat on the less interesting half of the species: "Oh, you swine!"

James Hannah

This Way Up

→ In order to continually recognize a point on a sphere, one must naturally give it a name, for example, A. In order to locate the point, one must impose upon the sphere a top and a bottom, and a left and a right. Problems then encountered involve ensuring that left remains left and right remains right, whether or not the sphere is perceived the 'correct' way up. The top can be named T, the bottom B, the left L, and the right R. Burdened with these names, the sphere is thus captured. Plotting a line where the top half meets the bottom half and vice versa (call it H, for example), and another where the left half meets the right half and vice versa (call it V, for example), one can locate position A as being a certain distance above or below H and a certain distance to the left or the right of V.

Help or hindrance can be drawn from the exactness of the sphere, and the patterning or other conditions thereon. Some names might come naturally - especially, I might suggest, if the designated point or location is large. A whole central area might be named Centre, or might be prefixed with Central- or Mid-. Smaller areas could conceivably be more difficult to label, but - if the sphere is imperfect- might be aided by local features.

→ Aberystwyth is constantly under siege. On stormy nights, the loudest noise to be heard is not that of the waves collapsing on to the beach, but that of the raking of pebbles as once more the water recedes. On stormy nights, grit from the beach is relentlessly swept by the raging waters on to the seafront promenade. Hywel, a man designated to sweep the grit back on to the beach, does so to the best of his abilities, but only during the summer months when the seaside town is to look its best, to gain as much revenue as possible. Out at sea there is virtually no sound, save the occasional catastrophe of a passing vessel, or the call of floating gulls.

When it lands, a seagull will pick up on its feet a few grains from the ground, and transfer them perhaps to a roof, perhaps to the top of a lamp post. When it returns to its hotel room, a human may knock a few grains from the ground into the carpet. Such involuntary actions as these Hywel is powerless to remedy.

On Aberystwyth seafront, the rigours of the wind from Ireland ensure that many of the buildings are crumbling. One or two are condemned (by official human standards) but make their money while they can by housing students. Keeping up with repairs to these buildings proves too much: one negligible problem will not be fixed with any great urgency, but neglected problems mount up soon enough, and only with the most strenuous effort is the decision made to carry out any repairs. Structural developments in the town take place further back, further east, as they have progressively been since the first buildings were built. All of the seafront buildings are gaily painted.

In the summer months when Hywel - replete with lengthening beard - has picked up his industrial brush once more, he sweeps to the sound of Aberystwyth's detachable ornaments being reattached by other designated persons. Delicately crafted decorative wrought-iron lamps are erected, hanging baskets are potted and watered, coloured lightbulbs are strung from pillar to post. From the pavement, the grit is swept back on to the beach for the rage to flatten, in preparation for the tourists. The flat tops of the permanent street lights keep their grit, but they are tall - maybe three times taller than the average street light - and the grit goes unseen by designated persons and undesignated persons alike. Indeed, only the gulls and insects have the agility to notice.

→ In the average area of forest, the trees will be brought through their particular phases. They will germinate, grow, age, die, rot, fall, and melt away. Thus the ground is unfertilized and fertilized. Depending on atmospheric conditions, this growth may be affected by parasites, causing the trees to die more quickly than they might unhindered. This kind of event is not usual, but is possible. One might call it *unusual*. Some have called it *abnormal*, but the situation can nevertheless be caused by numerous phenomena, and will continue until the balance of, say, parasites to wood, has levelled out, as it must eventually do. Trees felled prematurely (before death) continue to grow.

→ From a handrail on the ship, a limb was beginning to form. Beneath, the water was pushed into a concave, spreading along the hull to the sides and back. It washed up in eddies behind the stern, and once more became calm; as calm as ever it was. Behind the boat and all around, the water cast itself in all directions with all serenity, calmed by the water all around in all directions.

Drops leaked into the cracks of the wood, which were plentiful, and stayed there or were washed out. Those which stayed were soaked into the wood, safe from washing, but were (soon enough) evaporated and returned to the sea once more. As it was dragged through the ocean, the wood rotted.

Beneath the hull fish swam; on the deck people toiled; on the mast gulls perched; behind the stern land cast itself in all directions. Great mountains bubbled upwards and plunged into deep valleys. A farewell to A—. When the land became distant the gull set to the air and returned to its grit.

When the wind died down the progress of the boat slowed, and the deck people began to worry a new worry. A slowed boat meant a less reachable goal, which was sad. When the tempest resumed, they were content to let the worry drop. Pipes were lit and the smoke was diffused in all directions by the milling air. Sea sickness struck some and vomit was spewed over the side into the water. The spew was diffused in all directions by the milling sea. It took a longer time, but soon enough.

Ahead of the bow, land cast itself in all directions. Vast plains stretched out and formed great chasms. A welcome to A—. This was the new location for a new beginning that the deck people sought. A goal reached.

→ Since it had been built, the house had been occupied by the same people. Recipe cards in the kitchen, tools in the garage. *Duck á l'orange et un scie circulaire*. Cutting wood was a pastime. The dust settled everywhere always, so moving it was an idea abandoned. Picture framing was a hobby. Cooking happened regularly, wettening the walls, but the recipe cards were never removed from the cupboard, unless the dust was to be taken out. The table supported an ash tray and a pipe. Ash was burned in the pipe and tapped on to the tray. The tray was periodically emptied, swilled, replaced. The ash was *trashed* and sat amongst the *cola* and *gum* and *candy* and *pretzels*. The *trash* was *canned* in the *trash can* and collected by the *trash man* who was a man who collected the *trash* or *garbage*. The ironing board, when swung down from its niche in the wall, supported the clothes and an iron. Clothes ironed included *sweaters* and *pants*, and when ironed, clothes were stored in the *closet* with the shoes and *sneakers* and *nike air* which cost *eighty bucks*. The rooms inside the house were gaily coloured. They were subtly gaily coloured. *Peach* and *light blue* and *mint*. The paints were in the garage. The *pants* were in the *closet*.

Periodically, a swarm of silver-fish migrated from one side of the house to the other. This was a risky venture indeed, as spiders were plentiful and *pest control* were just a *call* away. But the damp was good for silver-fish, and the books. Bowls of cereal collected them and they drowned in the milk. One of the occupants of the house was not trusted, so his cereal and milk were poured for him the previous night. He would not get more than his share. In the night, silver-fish flicked over the cereal and were drowned. In the morning they were digested.

Then the closet was changed. The shirts and *pants* were gone and the shoes and boots were taken away. There were only blouses and skirts and *jogging pants* and *slacks*. From the shelves, books about golf and football were gone, and there were only church books. The garage was emptied of tools and wood, and the wood shavings and dust were swept into the wind to gather elsewhere. The wind in these parts was gentler. A little gentler. The garage was empty except for spiders and grubs. The garage was not empty. The ash tray and pipe were gone.

These objects - these possessions - gathered elsewhere.

After that there were more flowers and ornaments. More miscellany. The cooking continued and on the walls were church verses where there had been *art*. Things were replaced and were peacher than light blue.

Soon again, these were gone. Soon enough the house was empty and bare. Soon again, soon enough, it was full again with tools and recipe - this time - books. Still the silver-fish migrated, until at least they were dead awhile. And again again.

↓

Awake.

Oh, those were the days. We have such stories to tell!

Do you recall? In the early days you had me hovering over the waves. Oh, I remember those days...those nights.

Does it seem like you have slept? Perhaps because I woke you. It is late.

You had me stuck there, waiting there. You had me waiting for that momentous abnormality, the first boat. But there was nothing I didn't expect. It was nothing I hadn't in mind, that first ship. Sure enough, soon enough, it appeared over the horizon, ambling its way towards; under; away from. And then it was gone. Or, at least, that was all you would have me witness. You were *on your way*, you said. It's easy for you to be embarrassed by what you said in the old days. Oh those nights... But you, you were *on your way*.

So I present you with →.

Or rather, so I present you, and then you present →.

→The air, in those early days - it's easy to be embarrassed by one's early creations - the air was too thin. That ground, what contrast! Miles too hard! (Thank you for the *miles*). Imagine it - being hurled through the air; the freedom of movement was abominable. And the ground - being hurled through the air and being hurled to the ground - the lack of movement was a disgrace. I would be quite abashed.

The water - ah now, there was a positive godsend. Granted, it hung a little too close, it slapped rather of primitivism, but the movement was a joy. In all directions it lapped, every which way.

But let me take you back a short while. For the air flowed all over, it buffeted around, every which way. And the ground, the rock, in just as admirable a fashion it thrust itself every way at once.

→ Put beneath, above, around an arrow, its movements would be the same. Not, then, such an embarrassment.

So now I have made you conscious once more. There is no land, no air, no water. There is no need to name these things. There is never a little bit, for a little is everything. One cannot get close, for one cannot help but view the whole thing at once and in the slightest detail. There's your answer for you. Plunge yourself into rhetoric: there is now only the *Deep*, all around. Deep, no. Neither shallow. But I know you understand, for you invented the word.

→ The *Deep*, it *flows* in every *direction*. The rhetoric, you see, becomes more complex. Back to simplicity.

In the *Deep* you are perfectly comfortable, in all directions.

Except for your imperfection
↓

Siobhan O'Tierney

Smiling Through It All

Every now and again somebody somewhere discovers that the statue of Our Lady in their bedroom or hall or kitchen is shedding tears. The way this country is, it doesn't surprise me. Any day now the stones will cry. When I was young statues never cried, instead we learned about the children of Fatima and Saint Patrick. One story from my reader book, Day by Day, affected me deeply. (I reckon the big traumas in life don't cut so deeply as the minute, almost undetectable ones). Saint Patrick was preaching by a lake one day and hundreds of men, women and children came to hear him. Some of them wanted to be baptised so he stuck his crozier into the ground to free his hands for pouring water over their heads. Unbeknownst to him, the crozier didn't pierce the ground at all but went straight through the foot of a young boy standing next to him. This is the amazing bit, the bit that haunted me for years - what did the boy do? Did he cry out in pain? Did he wince or whimper? Did he swear at Saint Patrick to take his stupid fucken crozier out of his foot? No. The boy did nothing at all, not a murmur passed his lips. When Saint Patrick finished and returned for the crozier he was horrified to see blood streaming from the boy's foot.

"Why didn't you tell me!?" he cried.

"I thought it was part of the baptism," the boy answered, then fainted. Saint Patrick was hugely impressed by his simple faith and courage and told the crowds that this boy's place in Heaven was surely guaranteed. I couldn't get over that, imagine being *guaranteed* a place in Heaven, you could live as badly as you liked and not have to worry about it! I desperately wanted such security though for the life of me I can't remember now what sins I wanted to commit that I was so keen to have my place up above assured first. Of course this story is ludicrous but when I was eight it thrilled me. I wanted to be tested like that boy - I wanted to know how *I'd* cope. At night I'd fall asleep trying to think up ways of accidentally stabbing myself. There was a pitchfork in the tool-shed; I tried to picture it in my foot but just looking at it terrified me, the prongs were so long, dirty and thick. Surely Saint Patrick's crozier would have been much smoother and narrower and cleaner. Surely nobody could remain silent if something like that was slammed into their foot. No, I couldn't bear it. I decided on a little test first. I sat for hours in my bedroom staring at the door and its frame. I opened and shut it repeatedly; it wouldn't

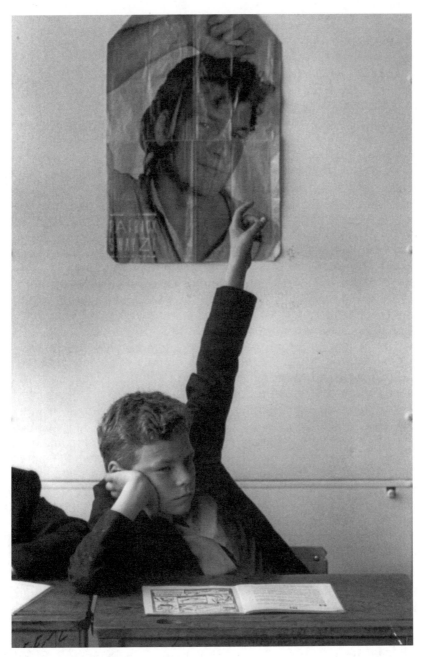

Pennywell School, Sunderland   *Philip Wolmuth*

shut tight, but tight enough. Finally, one day I stood before it and braced myself. Closing my eyes tightly I placed my left hand against the frame, then slammed the door. Aaaggghhh!!! I screamed and screamed. My hand felt smashed to smithereens, the pain didn't stay in my fingers as I hoped it would but went shooting up and down my body, through my arms, legs, shoulders, head, *everywhere.* Nobody ever in the whole wide world had pain worse than this. Mamu came tearing up the stairs panic-stricken.

"What's wrong! What's wrong!" She held my hand over the sink under a full flow of icy cold water and I cried inconsolably. My fingers were swollen and bruised purple, black and blue for weeks after. But worse, what couldn't be seen, was the terrible disappointment at my own cowardice.

It's amazing what you can get your body used to.

Dr Faltry keeps on at me, trying to find the source of my 'addiction' because this story isn't enough. He won't be happy until he hears that my step-fathers assaulted me or the gardener or the milkman or *someone.* He believes he can cure me, I'm on his 3A programme. I have to keep writing in this little book, to see if I can uncover some forgotten episode from my childhood. He doesn't want to read anything I write though, he has promised never to do that. Instead I had to promise to *tell* him ('that's all you have to do, just tell me') any unearthed memories. Three steps to help me become a fully-balanced human being. ????? Whatever he means by that! All I have to do is firstly, *'acknowledge'* myself, only then can I learn to *'accept'* myself and after that it's just a hop, skip and a jump before I'll *'appreciate'* myself. According to Dr Faltry self-appreciation is the only true path to inner harmony, which to me sounds like a newly-repaired church organ. What he doesn't know yet is that long before he'll get anywhere near harmonising me, I'll have him completely screwed up. It's not that I want to but I won't be able to stop myself, no more than I can stop the self mutilation. Mamu was an incurable seductress and that's the only trait I've inherited from her.

12 March

My mother. This is a pain now, every time I try to write about myself, I *always* go back to my mother, that really bugs me. My mother adopted four daughters. Shayoto, my oldest sister is half-Japanese, half-white, and very beautiful. Next is Chemboko, half-Kenyan, tall and willowy, as elegant as a length of chocolate coloured silk ribbon. Next came me, Huapu, I'm half-Nepalese, short and dumpy, but I'm told my eyes are irresistibly alluring, my lips divinely tempting, and my smile is God's finest creation (all direct quotes, honestly). Toquaio is the youngest, she's half-American Indian and possibly the most beautiful of us all. Mamu had to go to Britain to adopt us all. She spent six years there before returning, alone, with her little family of beauties to Kilmaddo, a little seaside town on the south west coast. Mamu (she made us call her that, I don't know why) was the only child of extremely wealthy parents. They were Lapsed Catholics before the word was invented, Mamu told us, and we should all strive to be the same, Lapsed Catholics were more Christian than Roman Catholics. When I told this to my teacher he looked so mad I thought he'd hit me. Soon after her parents died Mamu moved to Britain so we never met them. Mamu was bizarre. We lived in her parents' huge house with enormous gardens. There was a gardener; Paddy, the cook; Mrs O'Dea, and housekeeper called Josephine. They all used to make a great fuss of us. Mamu didn't like any kind of work, she preferred to read, she was always reading. But she did tell us lots of wonderful stories. Ha!

Some locals were bemused and tolerant of our set-up and they treated me and my sisters as a great novelty, they were always welcome at our home. Especially children; our house used to be full of local children playing with my sisters. Others were indignant but we didn't care, Mamu would imitate their voices perfectly and poke fun at them, she could be hilarious sometimes. Mostly it was only men who visited Mamu, but that was fine, they always bought sweets for us. Some stayed overnight or married Mamu, always going to London for the occasion. Once the priest came to have a word with my mother. When I opened the hall door for him he marched in self-righteously, obviously on the war-path. Mamu sent me down to the kitchen to tell Mrs O'Dea to bring up some tea and porter cake, and quietly led him into our sunny front room, where she directed him to sit in the softest armchair. In the company of men Mamu's voice automatically dropped to almost a whisper (I do the same but am working against it). She only liked to sit on the sofa, so big it always made her look even smaller. When he left an hour later all the pompousness was gone from him and he kept smiling at Mamu as if she was his favourite flower-arranger.

13 March

Shayoto and Chemboko were both very fast runners so they always made friends easily, everyone wanted to be on their team. Toquaio is so beautiful that even children were drawn to looking at her; at school girls queued up to be her best friend. I was different, I never get close to people (I find it easier to have sex with men than a chat) but I don't mind all that much. Maybe it was my independence and reticence that made Mamu choose me to unburden her secret to, a couple of days before she died of breast cancer.

I was two when we moved to Kilmaddo (Shayoto five; Chemboko three and a half; Toquaio eleven months) so I have no memory of our life in London. But Mamu often told us about our Papa, her first and most dearly beloved husband, with whom she had adopted us all. He was a celebrated concert pianist and one night she saw him play at a concert in the Albert Hall in London. Mamu fell in love with Papa during the second half of the performance (throughout the first half she thought him far too cocky). Immediately after the concert she told her escort that she had a terrible headache and wanted to take a taxi straight home, alone. No sooner had they turned two corners than she told the driver to stop; from there she ran back to the concert hall and sneaked up to Papa's dressing room. My sisters and I loved this story. Time and again we begged Mamu to tell us what he first said, how he first looked at her and how he spirited her back to his hotel inside an old cello case.

We didn't fret about being adopted, Mamu was great for telling us how much she loved us, how desperately she wanted us, how much Papa adored us. She often said the most wonderful gift in the world was a baby as beautiful as one of us.

I could easily accept Mamu wasn't my real mother and love her all the more. She made us feel privileged to have been plucked from what was otherwise, no doubt, a bleak, impoverished shadow of a life. Paddy and Josephine frequently told us the same, how lucky we were to have Mamu. But, completely illogically, I was convinced that Papa was my own father. Maybe because he was dead and unlikely to appear and shatter my idea of him. He was mine, mine alone to imagine and create as I wanted, with Mamu's stories for inspiration. I loved him more than anybody in this world.

Papa found all our names for us. Shayoto means the dawn of an especially long-awaited day in Japanese. Chemboko means a gift from the Gods in Swahili. My name, Huapu, is Nepalese for a funny little thing and Toquaio is Sioux for most beloved. Mamu would tell us how long she and Papa spent reading through books of names from all over the world to find just the right ones for us. Oh, we were all so special, so chosen, so blessed. Dr Faltry gets bored listening to me recreating my childhood, he can't believe it was all so idyllic. It doesn't fit.

14 March

When I look at Dr Faltry, I look into his eyes and I smile slowly. People smile much too quickly, their smiles come and go all the time, like switches, on and off, worthless from over-use. They don't know how to tease a smile out and hold it. Mamu's was slowest in the world, many long seconds could pass before that thin little solemn face fully relaxed into her wide, joyous, sparkling smile. It would start at her pointy chin, softening it, rounding it out, then her dimples appeared, her cheeks would fill out, and at last her eyes would light up brilliantly. Paddy once described Mamu's smile as a pint of Guinness allowed enough time to be poured properly, slowly filling up the glass right to the top and then the cream settling. When her smile was complete, your heart would soar with relief and pleasure so much you could feel your blood quickening. All the time you couldn't take your eyes off her, in case she didn't quite make it, in case she stopped half way, with only half a smile, leaving you lurched in uncertainty. Mamu rarely smiled at women or children, apart from us. From an early age I knew the power of her smile, I saw that when Mamu smiled at men there was nothing she couldn't ask of them. For years I practised it in a mirror under my bed by torchlight - it's natural to me now. However, I always thought Mamu could choose which men to smile at but now I think she couldn't. It was beyond her not to smile tantalisingly at every man she spoke to for more than a few moments. That's how it is with me, even men I'm not remotely interested in, I find myself smiling at them, so so slowly. When I smile at Dr Faltry his Adam's apple goes all jumpy, and he has to undo his top button and tie, he shakes his head as if to push off some buzzing insect, and he runs the palms of his hands down the sides of his trousers. "Well. Huapu," he gulps. After a few minutes I smile again and that sends him into a fit of coughing, after which he'll lift up my arms to examine the scars.

Mamu had another story but we rarely asked for it; 'the accident';

Papa was looking inside a grand piano when the lid fell down and broke his neck.

'The accident' happened when Toquaio was six months old. Mamu tried to live on in London but couldn't bear it and moved us all back to Kilmaddo. She couldn't even bear to bring any reminders of the happiness she'd lost, and so left everything behind. Mamu did not bring one single photo of Papa. But she told us he was tall and slender, with thick brown curly unkempt hair that she loved to stroke. His eyes were narrow and dark but full of fire. All visible evidence was to the contrary but I believed myself to be the spitting image of Papa, the man who I knew was *really* my father even though Mamu told us he wasn't.

Sharp stainless steel forks are good for parallel lines and if you get the angle right the blood flows out in four beautiful rows. Six inch nails are good too but if you want to cut really deep a Stanley knife is best. Swiss Army knives are easiest to carry around, I never feel comfortable without one in my pocket.

15 March

Mamu's secret. I am not telling this to Dr Faltry. It's none of his business. It's nobody's business. I will not tell him or anyone. Ever! Ever! Ever! She should never have told me. *Why* did she do it! I didn't need to know, I never asked. I won't tell Shayoto, Chimboko or Toquaio, *I'll* never be so weak, not even at death's door.

Today he almost got angry, Huapu, this is no use, we're getting nowhere, you must try harder. I smiled at him and he leaned across the desk to pick up my hands, he held them tightly. Held them too long, lifting them nearer and nearer to his mouth. My hands are alright, I never stab them, only my arms, shoulders, stomach and thighs. It feels like the whole world is squeezing, pressing, pushing me - everything weighing in on me, as if I'm about to be crushed or explode or something, so I cut through my skin and when the blood spills out I feel fine.

Nearer and nearer to his mouth he pulled my hands but suddenly, my fingers only inches from his skinny cracked lips, I resisted. Dr Faltry dropped my hands and looked at me, his eyes wide with alarm. Oh God, he whispered.

16 March

Surprise, surprise, Dr Faltry feels that to continue seeing me is unwise, he thinks the 3A programme might not work for me after all.

That this Holistic Growth Centre might not be the best place. At last, after five days in the loony bin, I can go home! Toquaio will collect me this afternoon. I don't know why I let her talk me into coming here. Why does everyone think my remedy is a problem - it's not as though I hurt anyone else. So what if I'm a patchwork of scars. It's my own body to do what I like with it. I *do not* need help! There is nothing wrong with me. What about athletes, dancers, musicians, anyone who tests their own limits - why doesn't Faltry chase them for his 3A programme? Alright, I am doing it more than ever since Mamu died but it was nothing to do with her. Not really. Anyway, I'd been doing it for years before then with none of them knowing. Bad luck Toquaio found me out. I'm finished with this little book. This little failure of a book which Dr Faltry told me to keep anyway in case I'd like to continue writing in it. Actually I am quite fond of the cover with its lock and key but I won't write anymore.

20 September

I can't believe I wrote all this. What a pretentious opening! Huapu, you little gobshite. Acknowledge myself! Ha! Is it six months already? Little book, I almost threw you out just now. Poor old Faltry still rings me up. Just because I let him take me out to dinner and screw me a few times - he wants to leave his wife and marry me. No way mate. He says he can't concentrate on his work anymore, without me. Heal thyself, Faltry, you big eejit. Mamu couldn't live with men but she kept marrying them anyhow as if every few years she forgot. I don't forget. Mamu was a liar. I am not. I just like carving my body. That's all. I hold down a job, I pay my rent, I do at least half of all the house work and cooking in this flat I share with Chemboko. Yet my sisters think *I* need help.

There's one more thing I'll tell you, little book. My sisters *really* drive me mad sometimes! They way they keep on about Mamu and Papa is enough to drive me to drink. Then I'm going to burn you.

There never was a Papa, never a long, slender fiery-eyed celebrated concert pianist, never a two-street taxi ride, never a cello-case. Never a neck broken under a grand piano lid.

Mamu invented everything.

There are no such names as Shayoto in Japanese, Chemboko in Swahili, Huapu in Nepalese or Toquaio in Sioux, Mamu made them all up. We were her *own* children, *she was our own mother*. She made everything up! Mamu lived six wild years abroad, sleeping with all and sundry. She had no idea who our fathers were, let alone their nationalities. But Mamu mustn't have been as indifferent to public opinion as she always let on to us. And herself. Or else why didn't she return to Ireland with the truth about her dolly mixture of little bastards? Why the elaborate fabrications? Poor Papa, I loved him so much! Much harder than trying to realise he never was my father is trying to realise he never was.

Peter Dorward

Drowning In A Light Sea

On the morning of his death, Alasdair woke from sleep haunted by bad dreams. He lay awake with his eyes half closed, bathing in a March sunrise which shone directly through his open bedroom window. It was cold: his bed faced east, and he always slept with the window open, under a suffocating pile of old blankets, sniffing as he slept at the damp air coming in from the sea. He slept on four pillows, one for each decade that he had lived alone in the house, and thus half-sitting he would fall asleep and waken to the same constantly changing view, through a half-open window with a shattered top left pane, which made the sea and sky appear to him in fragments.

He enjoyed these waking moments, when his mind played games with itself. He thought every morning the same thoughts, thoughts which danced through his memory like brightly coloured insects, fluttering through the decades: his father dropping a coconut after a fair, and its shell shattering like bone, and the sweet milk which bled onto the pavement; or his wife's voice, indistinct now as her face; his brother and their games; Kate, his brother's wife; old thoughts.

He coughed, swallowed a mouthful of spit, and drank the cold air, chasing away the last scents of his half-forgotten sorrow. That's it. That was it. He stretched, enjoying the cracking of his thin bones, and stood naked in front of his mirror on the Turkish carpet which lay beside his bed. Look at the blue eyes: powder blue now, with a film of cataract in the left; grey spines, not hair; the skin which fell from his face; breasts like an old woman's where he'd once been proud of his tennis player's chest; blue veins on his legs; cock like an old horse's; flat belly. He smiled at the old man in the mirror, and the old man smiled back, liking it.

It was the morning following his seventy-fourth birthday. He had sat up until late the previous evening, drinking and eating with his brother and his brother's wife. They had played cards and argued as they always did. They gave him presents and together prepared the meal, talking all the time, following conversations which were as familiar to them as the music of their voices, or the aching of their joints. They had left, said the special goodbyes of the old who had loved one another for many years, and he had gone to bed, unhappy.

He could still taste the wine at the back of his throat, and the tarry thickness of the cigars which every year his brother made him smoke.

171

He blew on the mirror, 'Haagh', and smelt wine and a stale cigar. With his fore-finger he wrote "A" on the film his breath had left, and watched it as it disappeared.

Two of the three people left in the world for whom he still cared.

He shambled over to the window. Its pane was cracked as the leg of a spider. Every morning he told himself that he would replace it, and by the end of every evening he had forgotten. He leaned out, and the cold made him shiver. A bank of grey cloud on the horizon was being chased out to sea, and the sun had already risen above it. A yard or so from the old man's head a herring gull was standing, huge and alien on the gable end, looking out to sea. Alasdair sang some loud and disconnected notes to the wind, and the gull looked at him, unfrightened. It made a fishy diamond with its open beak, and sang its own song; answered him in its own harsh language.

*

Alasdair turned his back on the sunrise. For a moment he felt choked. The combination of oil, grass and wind, the scent of the wild honeysuckle which defied the salt in the air and tapped on his bedroom window, they clawed in his throat, made it tight. He coughed again, and spat the rich phlegm into a glass beside his bed. His was a battle against suffocation. As a child he had played under the blankets in bed, feeling the air grow thick and stupefying around him, and that creeping suffocation was only a game. Now a sudden blast of cold air made him wheeze, and when he tapped the ribs which vaulted the barrel of his chest, it felt hollow under his finger-tip, as if he were only a finger tip away from suffocation. It was a thought which he drove from him - that if he wished he could no longer throw off the blankets which were suffocating him.

He hummed to himself: some sad, flat tune without words which came to him from long ago. He pulled on a crumpled linen shirt and a pair of dusty blue shorts which he always wore when the weather was warm, and went downstairs. Last night's glasses still stood where he had left them, and a colony of ants formed a waving line of bread-crumbs down the leg of the dining-room table. At the place where Alasdair had sat, between a plate of coloured cheeses and an empty bottle of champagne, was a sherry glass half full of water with a pair of freesias in it, one yellow, the other blue.

*

They had arrived late as they always did, burst thunderously into his solitude, pleased to see him.

"Alasdair!"

"Ewan!"

"Alasdair!"

"Kate!"

An old man's ready tears pricked him. Kate was the frailest of the three of them. Earlier that year she had been taken to hospital with her chest, out of their hands and care, and Alasdair and Ewan had sat in their separate houses waiting miserably for her to come home, with nothing that they could say or do but grieve.

"I brought you these." She handed him the freesias, stems wrapped in tin-foil, and a little card.

"You cut them in my garden!"

"Give me a drink, or I'll die before the flowers do. Of course I cut them in your garden. Ewan and I aren't so rich that we can waste money on your birthday flowers!"

Alasdair gently unwrapped the foil from the thin stems, and put the flowers in the only sherry glass he owned. He half-filled it with water from the kitchen downstairs. On the way back up he read the card:

"To Alasdair. May it not be the last."

She had always been the bravest of them, saying things which should never be said.

"Happy birthday Alasdair," said Ewan, handing him a bottle-shaped present, and a box of the cigars which they always smoked on birthdays until they felt sick.

"Thank-you."

"The party!" said Kate.

That was how it had always been, every year for forty years since his wife had disappeared: he alone, birthdays and Christmases, with the only other people for whom he cared. Kate and he went down to the kitchen, and together they chopped vegetables, drank wine and boiled pans of water, while Ewan sat upstairs on his own, reading the money pages in the paper. When they had finished talking and cooking, Kate would produce three fluted glasses which she never forgot to bring, and they would go back upstairs again. Ewan would say 'at last!' put down his paper, and unwrap the bottle. It was always good, expensive champagne. He would ease the cork from the bottle, never wasting a drop of the spit, and fill the three glasses. It was a very formal moment. Together they would raise their glasses, say something funny and dangerous proposed by Kate, and

173

something more formal proposed by Ewan. Together they lifted their glasses and made wild promises to an uncertain future.

*

Kate gave him freesias every year. She cut them from where they now grew: just behind the rusting green gate to Alasdair's back garden where his wife, Alice, had first planted them. She would wrap them in the foil which she had brought and present them to him, always with the same words and same misty thoughts which freesias woke in them. He always left them overnight, inelegant on their long stems, leaning over a half-filled sherry glass, so that their peppery scent would fill the room and greet him in the morning, reminding him.

And then, his house rich with the scent of freesias and stale tobacco, he would seek to preserve them. He had a heavy old book of music which had belonged to his mother, which he would take from the sideboard which contained all of his secrets: things which Alice had given him mainly - a diary, a hat-pin, the unopened letters which carried her handwriting; and open it at a new page. The first one hundred and sixteen leaves of the book had generations of freesias crushed between them, their yellow and blue ink now an antique stain, all their colour gone.

He didn't know why he had done it, every year, for so many years, pressing so many freesias. He had never told Kate about it. And although he knew that it would please her, he knew that he never would.

*

It was almost seven by the time he left the house, turning down the cliff path that started almost by his front door, and going down to the beach. The tide was out and the air smelt of the sea. He always came this way in the morning, to fill his lungs with salt air before breakfast. In winter he would walk the length of the beach, almost three miles, fighting the gusting wind, gazing at the grey water, listening to the strange thoughts which came to him from the other side of the horizon. In summer he would go the other way, down to the old swimming pool, whose stones were being slowly eaten by the tides, where he would sit in the sun with his feet in the water, and sometimes swim.

The sun was up, but the wind made the air feel cooler than it really was, puckering his skin. Rain from the previous evening had made the path slippery, and Alasdair walked slowly, barely keeping his footing on the thin layer of mud. He picked his way down and over the rocks which stood above the strip of beach. He felt the rock cold through the soles of his worn shoes. He jumped the eight feet down to the sand, hesitating for a moment in deference to the age of his bones before doing so. He lay on his back and watched the changing sky, running sand through his fingers, pleased to be loyal to the child who had made that jump, which then seemed so much higher, so many years before.

Something which they had said had disturbed him. He had gone to bed unhappy, and the feeling had still been there in the morning: something more than his child's melancholy on the day following his birthday; or the loneliness which followed him like a shadow, which he had borne for so long that he had come to love it as part of himself. Something frightened him. Something had been said, and his brain, worn like an old gear-box, refused to remember for him. He stood up, brushed down his old shirt and shorts with his hands, and spat on the sand.

*

He and Kate had cooked a fish casserole, full of garlic, bayleaf and tender feelings, and revelled in each other's praise after they had finished. They had sat drinking wine and brandy, and smoking Ewan's loathsome cigars as tradition demanded. They played a game of three handed poker, and Kate lost the family home to her husband, which they settled with an I.O.U. They argued about whether a four of a kind beat a full house, and were unable to continue because no-one really knew the answer. Then they talked about family.

"He's such a materialistic shit," said Kate, referring to their son Berty, who was a psychiatrist. "All he cares for is money and his car. I can't bear even to see him now."

"He's done well. He's solid. You should be grateful. I don't know why you keep running him down."

"And you always defend him!" That was true. He defended their prosperous son against his disappointed mother, and it goaded her.

"He's happy, they're well off, he's a good father..."

"He's a shitty father! He wants to make Kim just like him, all straight lines and dependable attitudes, just like his filing cabinet! No wonder the poor girl ran away!"

"She didn't run away!" said Ewan, beginning to raise his voice.

"Then where is she?" Kate was shouting. Familiar arguments. Ewan had learnt when to be silent.

175

"That girl had too many good influences. A doctor daddy, and a rich grand-pa. She was kept from her wicked old grand-mother!" Kate loved to see herself as wicked.

"What's the law about corrupting grand-daughters, Alasdair?"

"It depends on what you do with them. In your case I should imagine death, or life imprisonment."

"Hardly seems worth sentencing me then, does it?"

"Or they may just take pity on you, and send you to a good home with plastic chairs and carpets which smell of piss and disinfectant, and you can spend your autumn years singing I'm H-A-P-P-Y with a care assistant."

"It does sound heaven. When can I start?"

"Tonight?"

"Seriously," said Ewan, breaking the game which Alasdair had begun, "you should let go. Berty knows what he wants for her. I don't think our advice helps much."

But Kate wasn't listening. She was talking to Alasdair.

"I gave Kim these ear-rings you know. Do you remember the ones which Alice gave me, the glass ones you used to think were diamonds? We're going to get her ears pierced; we're going to go out to feed the ducks or something - whatever you're meant to do with grannies, and she's going to come home with ear-lobes like Liberace's smile. Technically I think it will be an assault. Berty'll have me put away."

She paused, looking at her finger nails, squinting at them through long-sighted eyes. There was no sound, apart from the wind squalling around the gables and the ticking of her watch.

They had decided that they would tell him that night, that they wouldn't leave it, and without meaning to she had said the name "Alice", which was never said, and she had found a way. But with the moment there at her feet, she hesitated to dive in. It struck her, painfully, that it had been years since any of them had said anything important at all. Without any of them realising that it was happening, their own lives had come to consist of memories.

"I wanted her to look nice for Alice. She's never met her Auntie Alice before. She's coming back to see us. She wrote. It arrived yesterday. She told me that she kept writing to you, but that you never replied. She wanted you to know that she was coming."

Ewan looked at his feet, saying nothing.

"You've no idea how much I've missed her."

"Thank you for telling me," said Alasdair.

*

The words and their tune came together. His memories, like the sea-breeze, cutting scales in the water. He stood on the crumbling stone wall at the end of the pool, holding on to a rusting postern which had once controlled the sluice. Opposite he could see the path which he had just come down, cutting across the cliff face where the gulls nested. To the left the gable of his house, and beneath it the sandstone cliffs where he had played as a child with his brother. He had left his canvas shoes on the beach, and walked bare-foot over writhing sea-weed, his feet numb with cold, to where he now stood. He peeled off his crumpled linen shirt and hung it on the postern where it fluttered like a white flag. He stepped out of his shorts and stood naked on the wall. The sun chafed his shoulder blades, the breeze tickled the short, grey hairs of his legs. It was March, and still cold: he had never been swimming by March before.

A gust of wind knocked him slightly off his balance, and for a moment he found himself on tip-toes, on the point of falling forward into the water. He could have broken the smoothness of his purpose. He could have grabbed at the rusty postern for support, stood up again, put back on his shirt and shorts, ashamed of his nakedness, and hoped that no-one had seen the pitiable thing: a naked old man contemplating the water and retreating. He crouched instead, leant forward and dived.

He heard the screeching, gloating gulls. He saw a shoal of fish shimmer across the clear water, and wondered at his huge whiteness crashing through their tiny worlds. From the moment that he hit the water, from the moment that he felt its frozen teeth close on his chest, he knew that he would die there.

And for a moment he resented the passing of his life: that he wouldn't say goodbye to Ewan and Kate and ask their forgiveness for the many things which he regretted; he resented being old and so foolish to throw himself into a frozen sea in March. And then there was Alice, who had abandoned him and was now coming back. He would never see her, never find out why.

The gulls called to him from their nests. His white shirt fluttered from the postern, still warm with his body heat. The tiny fish glided around his body, thinking with the smallness of their thoughts that he might be food.

177

Albert Cossery

Lulu Norman

In the best tradition of French novelists, from Balzac to Proust, Albert Cossery does not sleep at night. I had had strict instructions not to phone before midday, but knew better in any case than to risk disturbing Cossery at sleep. At night, he reads or watches TV, usually with the sound turned down. Recently he was watching a chat show on which the great French actor (and his friend) Richard Bohringer had been invited to appear. Asked what he read, Bohringer pronounced 'I read Albert Cossery'. Albert's phone did not stop ringing for days, much to his disgust, and the newspapers are now fawning over him, as if he's just been discovered - all because an actor goes on a chat show, he complains, 'but of course these people never create, they always follow'. However he tells me with a hint of pride that his new editor has even got him going round bookshops to do signing sessions these days. I can't help laughing: the idea of Albert doing book signings is like Proust going on a sponsored run.

But Cossery is not French, though *Jeune Afrique* has made the point that he is either the most Egyptian of French writers or the most French of all Egyptian writers. Born in Cairo of Egyptian parents in 1913, he was sent to a French school from the age of five and began to write stories soon after, encouraged by his elder brother who had books. In 1930 he went to Paris to finish his studies, before returning to settle there permanently.

He has lived in the same hotel in St Germain des Près since 1945, the hotel where all the notorious young artists of the day shacked up, and in the same room until recently, when the owner abruptly said he had to repaint and then secretly moved him to a smaller one while he was away. Cossery is used to this kind of deception for gain; he knows the owner would throw him out but for Albert's former friendship with his father.

He has never become emotionally naturalised; he may have lived in Paris for forty years but in his work has never left Egypt. He is never tempted to write about the French, cannot be doing with what he sees as the bourgeois character of most French novels; and makes a clear distinction between a writer and a novelist, saying he is a writer and a writer only writes when he has something to say; he has

Albert Cossery   *Gilles Plazy*

no need to write every day. Cossery's work can be seen as the black comedy of man's vanity and greed, played out to hilarious effect at every level of society; it is a little as if Balzac had made an extended sojourn in Egypt and fallen under the spell of its slow rhythms, turning his penetrating eye on the poor and dispossessed of the Cairo slums and those who won't let them be. Albert used to return to Cairo twice a year but since our last meeting his brother, the only surviving member of his family, has died.

His old flames, aware of his sleeping habits, always ring late at night from America to talk over old times and complain of their rich husbands. He was himself married once, to an actress, but it all went downhill once they moved in together. Needing his solitude, he couldn't stand it. 'But people can't bear to be alone; they need to be in packs.' Cossery reserves his greatest scorn for this human herd instinct; when he goes to the Luxembourg gardens he spends the first ten minutes painstakingly removing all the seats from around his preferred spot, to stop people sitting close simply for fear of being alone, of standing out or being in any sense apart.

Cossery has exploited this rich seam from Pascal, that all man's trouble comes from his inability to sit quietly in his room, throughout his work, so that when he states, with a typical Louis XIV flourish, that 'mes personnages, c'est moi,' he is preaching exactly what he practises.

We tend to admire those who can't stay in their rooms, who are restless and ambitious to achieve worldly success and acquire material possessions. Cossery's heroes do not wish to get anywhere in life, their wildest ambition is simply to be left in peace, to have time to think and give full rein to their sensuality; they bestir themselves to action only when this peace looks as if it may be threatened. Like most writers, Cossery claims he always writes the same book; it usually begins with the reluctant hero pulling himself from his torpor, if only to ensure he never has to again.

The hotel is a short walk from the Café Flore. He always arranges to meet at the Flore, where tourists still flock as pilgrims to a shrine, because 'they have to be nice to me here; I'm the only one left.' He sits as inane remarks float past his ear ('This is where Sartre wrote *La Peste* - maybe at this very table!') watching the world go by. He likes to sit outside unless the weather's bad, but the trouble is that when the weather's good, there are far too many people. And what people! He comments that he's run out of adjectives for how disgusting humanity is. From his corner of Paris, the americanization of Europe seems complete; he complains that all the young women don't just talk and behave like Americans nowadays, they look like them too. Democracy, of course, is a joke; he claims Berlusconi and Clinton, its supposed champions, as recent examples, were elected through manipulation, deception and outright theft. Crooks one and all; he is almost as scathing about politicians as he is about publishers.

I remembered our first meeting, when the head waiter had scanned me with a critical eye and sternly demanded if I had an appointment before escorting me grandly towards Monsieur. As we weaved round the tables, my apprehension reached its peak: I had heard that Cossery was proud and bitter, had become arrogant since receiving the Grand Prix de la Francophonie from the Académie Française for his oeuvre in 1990, that he sat here all day long and was only ever heard to utter one word - merde - carefully placed at the end of other people's sentences. I had, however, found him charming if caustic, taking great pleasure in his rude humour, though we had had difficulty talking partly due to my shyness and partly to a throat operation which made his voice more than usually low and rasping - occasioned by smoking too many Gitanes, he said, eyeing my pack (so he'd switched to Stuyvesant.)

Ionesco, that other great master of the absurd, had died in Paris the previous day at the age of eighty-one, which made me unreasonably anxious for Albert; he is also eighty-one, and energetic though very thin and somehow delicate. The incisive lines of his face have softened into curves and the pale spring light made his thin skin translucent; yet he is still very handsome, with a definite twinkle in his eye. He looks both shabby and smart, wearing an old tweed coat and yellow tie, with a frilly thin yellow handkerchief blossoming from his top pocket.

I tell him of my accident, since we last met, when I broke my spine and leg jumping from a wall. He inquires with a note of incredulity: 'Were you escaping from prison?' and it immediately seems the only logical explanation, if only accidents had need of them. I am straight into the Cosserian universe: just then the woman at the next table taps him on the shoulder and complains that the ash from his cigarette is flying into her face. There is a pause. 'Perhaps you have not noticed, Madame,' he answers, 'but there is a gale blowing.' 'Still,' she insists, 'you could tap it downwards.'

181

There is in his speech a regular refrain of remarks like 'il faut rigoler,' 'mais c'est une blague.' This is, in fact, the premise for his novels, in which the line of least resistance happily becomes the most effective method of resisting. His 1964 novel *Violence and Derision* argues the futility in locking horns with your oppressor: when all around is misery and corruption, he suggests, there is no point in violent confrontation, because this takes authority seriously, exactly what it needs in order to survive. Far more effective to undermine by ridicule, and far more natural, since our first reaction to most of our representatives of power is one of laughing disbelief.

He suggests we go to the Brasserie Lipp for supper - all the way over the road - because they'll always give him a table there. He assures me he sometimes goes further afield to eat, but only when friends pick him up in their cars - it takes so long to find a cab (this on the Boulevard St Germain) that it's really not worth the bother. In the restaurant he is anxious I enjoy the food; like a coward I ask for the *plat du jour* simply in order not to have to tangle with another uncomprehending Frenchman over how to accommodate vegetarianism - while Albert tackles the waiter on the grounds that the leaves of his green salad aren't quite young enough.

It was Henry Miller who launched his work in America during the war and later wrote 'I never see anything anywhere like it. All of Cossery's books have a rare, exotic, haunting, unique flavour. (Whatever has become of him I wonder?) He makes one laugh and cry at the same time. I only pray that in republishing this you will make him better known. We don't have this much-needed kind of story-telling in North America...' The writer and critic D J Taylor has remarked that the difference between Cossery and Miller is that Cossery doesn't have a return ticket in his back pocket; hearing this Albert grins broadly. When asked which writers he admires, he only admits to reading Dostoevsky. His work has often been compared to Beckett's but he says 'I could never stand him.'

'J'aime les gens qui vivent leur vie, qui savent vivre.' Like Camus, his great friend. The two would carouse all night, and on their way to bed at dawn have coffee and croissant in cafes where men were having their morning rouge before starting work. They had similar backgrounds and shared the same ideas: 'on rigolait ensemble.' He asks me about London, saying he had a marvellous time there during the war, but did not see anything, due to drinking his way through the afternoons with Cyril Connolly and being led (blind but willing) from place to place by women whose men were at war; but he remembers his first night because there was an air raid. People were banging at his door, shouting at him to get down into the shelter but ('puisque je suis paresseux') he just pulled the covers over his head and stayed put.

He had had a job once, I knew, as chief steward in the Egyptian Merchant Marine on a liner from Port Said to New York during the war. I wondered how this could possibly have come about, and whether it wasn't a hard life. But of course the son of the vessel's owner was his great friend so the work was somewhat cushy. 'Oh I just signed, signed everything, whatever it was, I didn't even look.' Since everything on board ship is done by chits, all orders or questions were easily dispatched in this manner, his indolence undisturbed.

The central idea of *The Idle Brothers of the Fertile Valley* is that doing nothing is a rare privilege and idleness a precious state, or as one character puts it 'you might as well know, when a man starts talking to you about progress, he wants to make you his slave.' The peace of a family who have renounced work and the outside world, and devoted themselves to sleep and laziness, is threatened by the father's sudden decision to marry and the son's endlessly thwarted attempts to find work.

I mentioned my difficulties translating the title, having had to add the noun 'brothers' to the adjective 'idle' where the French has simply the marvellous 'fainéant.' Albert was annoyed and could not accept there being no equivalent; what do you say when you call someone lazy? I went through the list: idler, layabout, good for nothing, sluggard, lazybones, indolent, ne'er do well - all of them too pejorative to work or too abstract to stand alone, coming before 'the fertile valley' which we both wanted to retain. (The Irish, however, have the word fenian, which comes from the same root.) 'Well,' he said, 'that just proves that the English don't understand the concept. They're nothing but workers - look at their empire, going all the way to India to work, to make other people work. My books translate much better into Spanish and Greek because they have the same spirit.'

The writer John Murray (who published Cossery in *Panurge* in 1985 -'they even printed my picture!') has pinpointed the likely reason that Cossery has been neglected in the West: 'His use of irony is one of the most powerful and pity-inducing to be found in any literature East or West, old or new. It is an irony so fierce, an anger so sharply muted by inversion of sarcasm and disgust that it makes the reader's hair stand on end with guilty compassion' - as if we in the West could not take it, preferring our Third World weeping and wailing and down on the ground. It is in our interest: we want them to want what we've got, or at least what we want, or we might have to question our own values. With publishers panting for the next model's life story that will reinforce our slavish adherence to consumer values, this is the last thing they want to know about (let alone publish.)

Cossery himself takes on this theme in his latest novel *Ambition in the Desert*. Its young hero is forced to turn sleuth, in order to preserve the beauty and peaceful way of life in the wretchedly poor Gulf state where he lives, which has escaped the attention of multinational corporations and political adventurers, only on account of there being no oil in its subsoil. He must discover the perpetrators of the inept terrorist attacks taking place in the city, before sympathies or alarm are stirred elsewhere, prompting international attention that can only be damaging. Perversely, it transpires, the terrorism has been promulgated by the prime minister himself, desperate to play a part on the international scene, his vanity thwarted after being eclipsed in Western eyes by his oil-producing neighbours.

Cossery prides himself on his small but dedicated readership and told me there was one thing that had really pleased him : he received a letter not long ago from a man who had read his work during a long illness, and claimed it had cured him, had made him strong again. There is indeed great strength in Cossery's rampant anti-orthodoxy and refusal to compromise; he shows how difference can be the source of strength rather than discomfort. As we walked back to the hotel in the dark, he asked if I had liked the graphic novel of *Proud Beggars* he had given me the last time, which he worked on with the artist and illustrator Golo and was utterly gleeful about. I confessed to having spilt coffee over it, at which he gave a wry laugh, saying they'll pay more for that one day. Golo was so entranced with the story he gave form to, that he went to live in Egypt for good, unable to stop drawing it...'I hear he's very happy there.'

Derek Gregory

Water Baby

I'm sure Stephen didn't really mean to drown Freda and me. We have been, I hope, passable parents. Though we hadn't given him all he wanted, notably siblings, he was, barring a certain aloofness, a much-loved boy of eight.

I first noticed the symptoms in the Fifties. I don't think Freda was sufficiently into child psychology, although she was a social worker. Her courses and conferences hadn't prepared her for this sort of thing.

As often happens these things come out in unfamiliar situations. It was a family holiday. We had been chivvied onto the beach by the landlady as soon as the breakfast cruet had been snatched away. A desparate scenario. Seagulls chewing sodden crisps. Ice-cream all down my trouser leg. It was raining like hell and all the bus shelters were full. But where could you go on a day like this except back home? After a bit it eased up. Stephen played in the sand. He didn't mind the cold. He dug happily while I read the newspaper and Freda knitted in her solitary way.

We kept glancing up to a rotten damp hole in the sky where the sun should have been. It was only a couple of hours later that I noticed what Stephen had done. I could hardly believe it.

At first I thought it was a series of sandcastles made by other people which, by a trick of the eye, seemed to link up right and left of our suntrap. They stretched away in terraces back to where a stream issued from the bottom of the seawall. It looked as if the beach had erupted in a leprous rash of over-filled sand cups.

I put down the paper and straightened up slowly to disperse the stiffness in my knees. Stephen's tiny castles were filled to the ramparts with water. They seemed to pivot in a triangle with their apex at our suntrap. I rose to my full height and looked back to where the stream began. As I swivelled I caught sight of Stephen in the rear. There was a hell-bent look stamped on his little face. I was about to wave to him when he suddenly leaned forward and churned with his spade, thrusting at a particular ring of sand. The seconds seemed to slow and the air bristled as if the metallic clouds were giving up static. Then it dawned on me. Stephen had released the first small torrent of water from a kind of header dam.

What he had been doing over the last two hours I saw only too well. First one castle crumbled. Then, by a domino effect, another.

Dominican Republic 1991   *Philip Wolmuth*

186

The cascade fed a third, and so on. Each castle was artfully placed so the rush of water boosted the next. I just had time to drag Freda from the suntrap before a sizeable flood hit us.

All the time I kept an eye on Stephen expecting a child's laughter at this discomfiture of parental authority. His face held nothing but a dull stare. For some reason this lack of expected response infuriated me and I chased him all over the beach whilst Freda wrung out her Fair Isle jumper. She wasn't very impressed. And my angina hunted about fearfully in my chest.

We didn't chastise Stephen physically. Freda and I had agreed things like that before we started family planning. After all, Stephen was still a child. And it *was* supposed to be a holiday. Also I felt a queer tingle of pride in what he had done. He was a late developer as far as speech was concerned, a bit of a loner. He never confided in either of us, about bullying at school, or the puzzling concepts of the adult world.

"It's his way of revealing his intellect and his preferred instincts," I suggested.

"I expect he's trying to win our approval," grumbled Freda. I sensed that she had 'given him up' long ago, sometime during Stephen's babyhood, her period of 'enforced house arrest' as she called it. She wanted something average and normal. Like a Fair Isle jumper.

I surveyed the punctured, cratered sandscape. I couldn't help admiring his artistry. What might it not hint at for the future? The whole concept was so far removed from a child's teeming and pouring. His mind, I realised, was dominated by the concept of water. From then on I continued to observe Stephen. I noted his lack of eye contact with people, but also the torch-like intensity of his obsession with water. He would play long and quietly in the bath, not because it delayed bedtime, but for the pure joy of shuddering with ecstasy when water slid through his fingers. He was simply entranced by the shimmering jelly of its twitching surface. He ignored toys other than water-related ones. He would drag a stool and stand on it over the sink, running the tap and staring manically at its thin silver rope caught in a sunshaft. Sometimes I crept up and gently held his slim trunk in my palms. It was vibrating uncontrollably. Once he turned round to see if I shared his joy. I tried to appear unconcerned. Now I wonder if I failed him.

When he grew into his matchstick teens I expected he would take naturally to swimming and aqua sports. Not a bit. He was not interested in teams or competition. He was simply fascinated by water, the plasticity of its forms, its noise and weight, the awful power of its moving mass. His only youthful hobby was fishing. He would stand like a lord on the river bank drawing its secrets to his net. He fished where the water moved fastest, rapids for trout, weirs for barbel. Once I accompanied him on a muggy June day. The air lay like a heavy poultice above our heads before the high summer pomps exploded upstream in a tremendous downpour. Water poured down our valley and the river burst its banks even before darts of rain thrashed its surface.

Stephen stopped fishing to watch. Each stalk of grass was festered blackly with insects escaping the rising flood. In the purple light roach skittered, maddened by the harvest of earthworms coiling from the drowned vegetation. Soon the swollen waters stretched tightly over the valley. Finally I had to drag him away as he protested in a heathen outcry.

Whenever I broached the subject of water his face lapsed into a sideways reverie as if I had tripped a primal memory scar. Some years later we took a Scottish holiday. Our moorland walks bored him until we came upon the blue-black burns and tarns. There he swiftly fashioned locks and dams from tumbled stones whilst we ate our sandwiches, watching his progress with shaking heads and oblique matching smiles. If there was a water sprite or dryad about, it seemed to be working its impish way with him as heather and needledross hurried to fill the gaps in his strategically placed rocks, before he finally slipped the key rock which loosened the torrent.

Freda explained to me that water entranced all children. No wonder, she added prosaically, when they had so recently spent nine months in the amniotic fluid.

At school physics was his main subject. He tried for marine biology but found himself, after the summer scramble, on an Honours course in civil engineering. In his final dissertation he won the Schrödinger Prize for his work on computer applications of the catenary principle in suspension bridges. No employment problems. He went abroad after that, head-hunted by a famous firm of international engineers. He never came back to England.

He kept in touch with us via a stream of world souvenirs, batik work from the East Indies, brassware from India, miniature assegais from Africa. We would meet him again, I felt sure, when I took early retirement and we thought about world travel.

Freda was enthusiastic and our first step came by way of Stephen's invitation. His firm had contracted for a hydro scheme on the Watusi River. The official opening of the dam was a year away, in March. Stephen's area of work had been to create the finished blueprints for the coffer dam, a vital, though subsidiary part of the whole operation. Could we make it? he asked.

We flew out a few days before the opening. The smells, the tastes, the sounds of Africa! We picked up a light plane from Lilongwe and skimmed low over the red, shrivelled landscape with the occasional paint-green chip nestling in the giant thighs of its hills. Stephen, our son, would bring fresh green life to the whole of this burnt land.

He seemed older. Freda fussed about inspecting his kit like a sergeant-major. In his photos he had been laughing, arms linked with the construction gang, tanned flesh to the waistband of his shorts, standing in a crowd of camera-shy natives. Not now. When he saw us his eyes reached back into their sockets. The searching dust of Africa had settled into wrinkles and the loose skin on his neck a lizard might have discarded. He still flinched at intimacy. He was now a grown man and I felt a desperation that he would never confide in us during our lifetimes.

"Nothing's the matter," he said without much conviction.

"This country's getting to you," I said. I wiped the red sore band on my forehead. "Low altitudes are no use to a European in this country."

He looked away with his curious apartness. He became animated only when he pulled out the thin drawer of blueprints and explained the enormous pressure of billions of gallons of river water. My mind flew back to the beach and the Scottish highlands.

The day before the opening we all went in the safari truck up to the hills with askaris standing guard on the running boards. Stephen explained the catchment area and pointed out the parts which would be flooded and the irrigation network. His voice was high and his speech trembled. As we drove along my eyes were more on him than on the dried snakeskins of the river beds we passed. Tribespeople along the road were covered with our red dust as we sped along. They carried sugar cane, firewood, and huge precious cans of water. Stephen ignored them, commenting only on the technical miracle beginning tomorrow, which might put an end to this primitive existence.

That night I stared at the coin of the moon through my mosquito net. The mozzies buzzed on the other side anxious for their blood meal. I was just dropping off when I heard footsteps outside. They hit the concrete path in a way that bare feet don't sound like. Something made me get up quickly.

Outside the bungalow, I saw the figure some yards in front going down the path, skirting the native portakabins and making for the transport compound. As we went through, the ghostly shapes of great claws of earth-moving equipment towered on each side ,paralysed without their human operators. By the time we were on the approach road to the dam I was gasping like the old man I was, but Stephen kept his pace striding forward as if on a mission. I had a job to keep him in sight as he doubled through the complex. My fears shaped up as he marched rapidly to the control pavilion. I fought the hot lump in my chest. I was almost running now and my flapping bedroom slippers must have been quite audible to him. He never once looked back.

When he reached the gantry I was only a few yards behind. A night-shift worker, moon-white overalls springing from under his black face, touched his forehead in recognition and stepped aside to let us pass. Stephen took the catwalk two steps at a time and leaped smartly on to the console platform. I had that third stage crushing sensation in my chest which definitely signals an attack - but I heaved myself forward in a last effort as Stephen smacked down several electrical switches in rotation. And when his hand finally hovered over the flume button I was able to clamp his wrist in my hand. My scream racketed through the girder braces like an eldritch shriek.

His face turned towards me pale with sleep, but his eyes were pin-bright and sharp-coned with hatred. I screwed his hand back from the button.

"No-oo!!!" I screamed with all my force into his face.

He was shuddering like a man in a fever. I now held his hand as I had once held his tiny shivering body. Then, for some strange reason, not born of my mind alone, I cried: "Stephen - we love you! We *love* - !" His hands dropped to his side. He was cold to my touch and greasy with sleep and sweat. I don't think in his conscious mind he heard me. In a way I was glad. It wouldn't be a source of embarrassment to us both when he woke.

When we got back to his hut I quickly sprayed his room with a knock-down canister and tucked him into the truckle bed. I bore down on his shaking shoulders but when I put the mozzi net over him it was like drawing a veil over the smudged relaxed features of a baby.

Next morning, after the furnace of an African dawn, but before the sky had assumed its white-hot grin, the wife of the Head of Overseas Operations lifted her lacy gloved finger as we gathered round. In a tentative feminine gesture she touched the red flume button on the panel. A second later there was a roar and a great white cockatoo of foam sprang from the smooth wall of the dam. Freda clapped vigorously with both hands upraised. She looked suddenly proud to have mothered her son. As I gripped his arm tightly Stephen turned his head and looked at me, for once, directly into my eyes. I grinned at him wildly. Admiration for his achievements with water must have shone out of my face. He smiled back as if his body had come to the end of a journey and shed a great weight. Then his gaze went back to the thundering furry spout, and he cheered his applause like a child, as heartily as anyone in that sea of sparkling cries.

Julia Brosnan

To Sink A Brew

Pia finds deep erotic stimulation in right wing ideology. The thrill of preposterous ideas ignites a fire at the back of her head; the anticipation of dark realities effects an axial shift in her groin. It is no surprise to Pia that Fascists wear high leather boots. The links between sex, total control and unbridled power are branded into each of her body cells. She dreams of humping a large Nazi.

Funny then, that she chooses me for a friend. Breezy, cheery, with the belly of a girl fond of biscuits. What's more, I've always voted Labour. Pia says I've only voted Labour once, but being 20, I've only ever *voted* once. Apart from total body mass, age is the only thing I have over her. Two years older and I milk it dry. I have recently been making clumsy and transparently false references to the deep and other knowledge bestowed on all who leave their teens alive - like I have survived some secret rite of passage. It is a fruitless exercise - Pia has already survived all passages. And she has the look of someone who experienced something deep and other many years ago. Long before she was born.

We are at the crossroads. I am utilising my superior and more mature highway awareness skills to guide her across. Pia likes this. She is extraordinarily terrified of traffic. She has become a tiny rabbit - beautiful, slender and exotic. She looks wet: sharp bones, fat lips, fearful and wet. I marvel at what a baby she is at main roads. Especially as I have seen her club pigeons to death with a brick.

Once we leave the crossing she straightens up. Her frailty grows sleek and sinuous, her frightened steps become fast and urgent. She is hard on my arm, like a panther. Now she is leading me, as she says, to sink a brew. To sink a brew ! Pia does eight hour shifts dissecting the meaning of a single word. Her mind is clear as a bell, with a bright mental vision that runs in a straight white line and selects every word with rigour. She is not a girl to sink a brew. When she first said it, my horror and incomprehension made her laugh so long and so dry I knew the joke was on me. Maybe it's a double bluff, perhaps it is strangely ironic. Either way that's where we're going, and I must say I'm rather thirsty.

Although I've only known Pia six weeks, I am aware of her propensity to be at the centre of dramas of at least Greek proportions. We arrive at her flat and I know she has a new one. She paces up and down, marking out its gravity. I had hoped that she might breath warmth into my neck and kiss my chest with her tongue. As things stand - it looks like I'll be lucky to get that brew.

Pia says she loved a girl who loved her back. Next the girl is raped. Trouble is the girl is only 15, so as well as police there are social workers, welfare persons and all manner of poking about. The rapist is caught. He too is under-age and what with all the prying and uncovering they soon discover Pia: 18 and fully adult. In their wisdom, those in a position to judge, judge that all things considered (perversion, inversion, the corruption of minors; society, wisdom, intelligence quotient), everything all told - Pia and the rapist are roughly to blame. Everyone gets rehab, confab, aversion and the cure. One day Social Services visit the girl and discover her father abusing her with a hairbrush. This is not part of the programme. They send her to a home. Two weeks later she is raped by a care assistant. A few days later she kills herself.

I am punctuating the drama. "What ?" I say. "O no !" "My God!!" and I know I am no where. I am a pudgy student with chaffed thighs, offering flabby words with nothing behind them. Rape and suicide are not in my frame. The nearest I can get is A level English: she is King Lear and I am the Fool. Minus the wit. This is the worst thing about being a student - real life only really makes sense when it's been covered on the syllabus.

But Pia forges on without me. She swells with vehemence as she blasts. Now it's social workers: short men, weasel eyes, coarse suits and shrunken shirts - they open their mouths to recite dimly comprehended clichés, and all they do is disturb the balance of her finely bred nostrils with the foul stench of their unkempt teeth. They come with bovine, flat-headed women in worn heels and inadequate bras. Unfamiliar with the concept of rationality, the women spew out an unconnected collection of slogans. *Daring* to come here, *presuming* to tell her. Coming here, ordering her about - her - *Pia* - with their inferior knock-kneed rubbish.

I am lost for breath, stunned by this wall of passion which shoots through her story and steers it·in a new direction. Really I think, seeing her now, you can't blame them. Pia has never moved a paper, cleaned a pot or even acknowledged the inches of sticky dust that cover every surface she owns. She is rooted in dirt. Her feet are buried in sludge and debris. The dirtiest girl in the known world is also the most beautiful. Right now she is like a tropical flower - rare and promising, rising up and thrusting out of a steaming bed of rich manure. Maybe the social workers wanted her to tidy up. Maybe they thought it would help her case, it is their job after all. But something tells me it would be wiser not to say.

Now she has changed gear. Like an engine she switches herself up and over: the boy rapist. There is a gurgling inside her, like a motor. I can't hear all her words... ...Revenge she says ... it must be... done... A deed ... she... has to do to spill the ...blood. It must be done and she... will... make the cut.

I am lurching, stifled and dizzy, with a movement in my stomach like a live fish beating to get out. This is a step too far. I will leave, but it will not be permitted. Pia will make me stay. My head is wet with sweat and looking over to where she is - I see that I have gone already. Pia has shut me out, she has talked herself into another place. There is a heat around her, a light curtain covers her eyes, a strange liquid feeling hangs in the air. Something so close and private is happening that I feel I am intruding. Free to go I move slowly, half regretful, out onto the street, where I am surprised to find daylight burning and mothers shopping like before. The thing I understand is - those roaring passions, that gaping hunger, the urgent need for blood: no wonder she didn't stick at being a vegetarian.

I have never seen her since. Not till now. I look up and there she is, across the table in a small café. Three years later she amazes me all over again with the force of her sculptured bones, the polish on her skin, and eyes with such a large and lazy slant. She sits down with an easy smile, but with a look that burrows inside my head. I get the old feeling that she knows my secret: there is nothing more in me, nothing more than what you see. And immediately I am gauche. I had forgotten just how gauche she makes me. That's something at least that teaching does - provides a whole class of people more gauche than you.

There is something different about her. As she moves I am mesmerised by her fluidity - like someone undid a key in the back of her neck. Her bones seem to be in perfect balance across her spine, with open, easy, well oiled joints. It gives her whole person a surging sparkling confidence. Like magic. A broad man approaches her from behind. She reaches backwards for his hand, knowing exactly where he is. He leans down and whispers. "Pia" he says. "Yes Pia". I feel so odd I have to say it. "He called you Pia"; I sound petulant. "That's not your name." She looks at me and laughs but only the sound, nothing else. She is laughing hard while the rest of her body is perfectly poised and still. Laughter is streaming down through her nostrils, like a horse, but her head is unmoved. Strangely, her stillness seems to burst with life. Her eyes are up inside me. I lock glances with the woman behind the counter, she nods at me, and Pia is at my neck. She is breathing warm air down my jumper. "Come on," she whispers. "Back to mine." And off we go, to sink a brew.

Brian Howell

The Imagist

Though his initial wanderings in the city and the subjects of his study were arbitrary, he eventually restricted himself to the area of the Gallery. He never went in; he didn't need to. The girls who came out provided enough visual material for him. For a good while he was unable to distinguish sufficiently between them. But eventually one had dominated, and he would need to be closer.

He caught the bus home, thinking only of Irina. He had to give her a name. In an effort to remember her features he did not look out of the window or at anyone on the bus. He closed his eyes, but it was too early for darkness. He took out a book, and read it backwards, so that although his fovea had to work and his mind was active, ultimately they took in nothing. He did not even risk looking out of the window for his stop. He preferred to estimate his arrival by his watch. This was always the most taxing part.

He proceeded to the bedsit in a hallucinatory fug of recollection. His skin at this point started to prickle, his bowels pumped momentarily. It would be ruined if he met anyone in the hall.

He was in his room. The Venetian blinds were still closed. He opened them a tiny degree, enough for him to reach the kitchen without stumbling and make a tea. The flat was compact, with the toilet and kitchen jutting off either side of the bedroom. There was one window.

The walls were blank save for a few reproductions of abstract paintings. Anything figurative, too large, or clustered, would hinder his concentration, his nightly striving for that envied state of nocturnal emmetropia.

He sat opposite the barest wall in a chair which determined the correct focal length, won through much experiment. Stretching out his hand he closed off the light completely with ease, and the room assumed a comforting hood of darkness.

It started with a blur, a filmy wash of mixed colours running into each other. He remembered her height, the size of every limb, her clothes. It became sharp, except for her face. That he would have to work harder on. He closed his eyes for a moment, and opened them again. Now she was naked, as if posing for a nude painting. He realized that she was in fact very skinny, the cunea of pubic hair was scraggly, like a pencil drawing. Her gaze was distracted, her eyes were given a pointedness by her circumflex eyebrows. This was the

196

one, he knew. He was roused momentarily, and his hand made a tentative journey down to his lap, but stopped short of stimulation. The image was not ready. This was the closest in a long while, but he would have to get closer.

*

He had time, he was under no pressure. It was a relief to allow his eyes to wander now. He ate up people's free time, he devoured their lunch breaks. He was certain she would come here again.

When he closed his eyes he saw her head suspended in a gilt frame, superimposed over a skid mark of paint. It was the first time he had seen this far. She was inside the Gallery. He opened his eyes again, to make sure he hadn't lost his hold on the outside world. The square and its traffic of vehicles and people were a fish rippling in the darker, less defined currents of a stream. He closed his eyes again. She was still there looking at the painting. Then she moved. It became a blur. She was no longer concentrating. She was moving to the entrance. No, she had stopped in front of another picture, this time without a glass covering. It was dark, it allowed her to dream, she clung to the ridges of ribbed impasto. He would go in. If only she stayed with the picture long enough.

He paid, reluctantly, feeling superior and disdainful. It was the first time he had been in such a place. He went through three or four rooms until he saw her, coming directly towards him. For a moment he could have mistaken her expression for a look of recognition. But she continued on. That was enough for now.

Back in the flat he went through the routine. The blinds, the adaptation to the dark, the retinal adjustment. Her body was still pale and gaunt but the whole was taking on greater substance, no longer the eidolon of his thoughts. The lips, which were thin like the silhouette of a distant bird in flight, moved, but the only sound, which could not be synced to them, was a continuous mumble that seemed as if it were being played backwards on a tape. He concentrated on her as she moved about a restricted angle of view, the background giving no clue to her whereabouts. She continued to talk. This was more than a mumble; she was talking to someone in her room.

Then he saw someone's hand and forearm edge into view, as jarring as a boom microphone disturbing the illusion of reality in one of their archaic 'films'. He played this part back in a small window inset in the corner while the main image continued in real time. Yes, it was a man's, he established. And it was holding her tight, trying to stop her leaving. Just as abruptly, the hand disappeared. She stopped speaking, and seemed less distracted. He must have left the room.

The image started to fade, its detailed lines diminishing co-terminously with his memory. His exposure to her had been too little. He had been cheating himself to think that it could have lasted longer. He still did not even know what she did. He would try the Gallery the next day, but this time the contact would have to be longer.

He watched a few of their pathetic 'videos' to help him take his mind off her and help him fall asleep. During the second, the neighbour above him, whom he had never seen since he had moved in three months earlier, banged on the ceiling for him to turn the volume down. He did not normally rile easily but the thought of someone he never saw living in his box room, complaining about noise coming from another box, grated. He almost went upstairs to confront the hidden complainer, but he did not want anything to interfere with his plans. Even a simple verbal exchange might throw his visual balance off kilter, fill his mind with the image of a new face it might take days to be rid of.

He turned the volume down, eventually slipping off into a no-man's-land that had for its impressionable surface a dark umber goo to which, he feared, anything might attach itself, but which, if undisturbed, would spread over him pleasantly like syrup.

In the night he woke to sounds whose provenance he knew instinctively was not located in the dimensions of the room surrounding him. At first he supposed that it was an overlap from a dream carried on into his barely woken state. Then, as the sounds persisted, he listened, sitting up in bed. It was a rustling sound with a hint of a struggle. Although he could see nothing in the projection, it was clear to him now that the rising moans and sighs were coming from a cone of darkness on the wall. The thought that she was reaching him now in the middle of the night without knowing it, while she made love to another man, made him feel almost dizzy with restlessness. He pulled the blanket over him and shut out the sounds as much as possible. Mercifully, the projection soon faded.

In the morning he took the underground in to the Gallery in an attempt to cut out even more stimuli than usual. It was easy on the system to fix on a meaningless furrow of space and occupy oneself with this mentally without fear of disturbance, or simply to close one's eyes. The only infringement was that of body temperatures, whose individual identities registered with him like so many pleading patients in a doctor's surgery during an epidemic. He had to remain oblivious, calm.

He arrived at the Gallery before it opened. He would have a chance to spot her before she went in and follow her movements. But she did not arrive with the first swell of tourists, and his vision was soon overcrowded with extraneous information. He walked over to the fountain to relax and concentrate, closing his eyes. For an hour or so he inhabited a tunnel of darkness which yielded nothing but a weak pulse like a bleep on an old-fashioned radar screen. The outside light threatened all the time to flood his delicate construction and wipe it clean, like a hand peeling back the skin of a fruit, but eventually she got nearer, and this strengthened his determination.

He did not look up when she entered the Gallery. He was content to wait for her to finish. Today she stayed longer in front of the painting, a whole hour. Then, when she moved, it was quickly, intently, without any distraction, as if she too were wary of an infecting influence.

He moved up to the entrance as if his path were through a corridor which would allow no possible deviation. The people around him seemed to sense his determination and gave shape to his pursuit. As he reached the Gallery's revolving door, she was coming out. Without demur, he went straight in and followed the door round the whole 360 degrees, letting the blur of flickering images wash over him, to find her briskly descending the steps. He trailed her all the way to her home.

*

Her place was a terraced house on the outskirts of the capital which, it seemed, she shared with a group of people her age. He did not want to go in, he merely wanted to establish what kind of people she lived with, whether, in particular, there was a boyfriend.

He could not wait outside her house. He would be noticed immediately. However, he had noticed that a bus passed by her house and he had found out from the driver that it went in a circle that lasted roughly one-and-a-half hours. In this way, with little effort he could gain a cross-section of the daily movements of the inhabitants of the house. In any case, he did not feel like going home till dark.

When he had familiarized himself with the route enough to trust

199

his watch and look out the window a minimum of times, he concentrated more on recalling her features, her quizzical dark eyebrows, her lank blonde hair, her thin lips. The first two times he passed he saw nothing. The third he saw a young girl crouching by her bicycle pumping up a tyre. The next activity was some hours later when he saw a motorbike outside the house and the thin form of a young man edging into the front door. Here he got off.

It was nearly dark. They had not pulled the curtains. He recognized her and the other girl with the bicycle as well as the still leather-jacketed man who had just gone in. The latter was pacing around the living room with a can of lager in his hand.

Now was the time to focus in on the scene before he was shut out for the evening. He enlarged the pacing man's features first, then those of the two girls who were sitting on the sofa. The man was gaunt, his face feral and rat-like. He seemed to be arguing, possibly raising his voice. The bicycle girl was leaning forward on the edge of the sofa, as if concentrating hard on his words. The girl, his girl, was slumped back, her face tense; she replied occasionally to what was becoming ever more evidently a rant. After fifteen minutes the man calmed down. The other girl went out of the room. The man put his arms around the remaining girl, who resisted weakly. The bicycle girl came back, passed around a clutch of lager cans, and switched off the light. A silvery blue glow bathed the room and the three sat curled up on the sofa, their faces shining, convex vessels of reflecting light.

As the street and shop lights came on, threatening to neutralize his stored images, he made his way home, holding her face in his mind's eye as if he were handling precious Delftware. He analyzed its concavities and convexities, turning it through 180 degrees till it disappeared into a mnemonic ellipse, then came back through the full circle, its every detail checked and itemized. He was close now, as close as he would ever be. He took no stimulant of any kind that night, not even tea. He was confident.

*

He fell asleep in the armchair, the blank rectangle of white wall already delineated by expectancy. He knew it would not come immediately. He estimated it would take between two to three hours.

It came in spite of him. He had not needed to project. Her image woke him. The man lay on her, pumping like a piston. She stared

200

past at him. Could she see him? She started to shout at the heaving body, then hit her fist on his back. He continued mechanically, unswayed.

He proceeded to follow the outline of the man, up his sides and over the diving head which was foreshortened to near invisibility. When the process was complete, his dark silhouette brightened suddenly and in a flash was gone. She was left grasping air, her clenched hands falling onto her breasts.

He spoke to her through thoughts and dreams, caressing her form with these and a soft pillow of energy which was all that separated them. She fell asleep and dreamt of a planet where people were insubstantial beings who survived from a resource of memories and images copied from another time. In the night she remembered having made love some hours before, but now Rat was gone.

*

That night she dreamt of the man in the Gallery. She recalled his pallid complexion and his hare-like awareness of everything that was going on around him. She was attracted to his boniness; he was like Rat but a benevolent version. She liked his thin beard that reminded her of a gentleman in a seventeenth century Dutch painting. Though she had not seen him except inside the Gallery, he seemed more familiar than chance eye contact would have led her to think.

*

She did not go to the Gallery for five days. Rat was gone; Sheila seemed more affected than her. They hadn't told the police. They couldn't. For days afterwards Sheila watched the video constantly. In the video Rat repeatedly penetrated the two of them from behind, came over them, came in their faces, struck them. They still hadn't got any money. And now it was not likely they would.

Later that day two large-set men in tweed jackets and jeans turned up asking for the video. Stephanie didn't want to give it, but Sheila rushed back into the living room to get the master tape. When Stephanie asked about the money, one of the men hit her in the face, and as they went back to the car, said, 'Tell Rat he still owes, hear?' Sheila moved out the next day, leaving no forwarding address.

For the next two days his trips to the gallery and the house were fruitless. Her image had weakened. He was restive. His armchair investigations were no more satisfactory. He felt himself a captive of the room, he was the view, subtended by two opposing walls; he could not see the pictures.

Finally, he went out at night and wandered around the immediate vicinity of the Gallery, then along the embankment, under bridges, looking for the unlikely. Nothing happened, but when he returned to the flat her image was there on the wall, radiating its own life, or death. Was she moving, indeed? She was staring out at him, her arms wrapped around her breasts, like a pin-up, except that here was no pose. It was a defence against something, someone.

He went back to the house. It was dark. No one answered the bell. The front window was unlocked. He climbed in with ease. Staleness and stagnation were in the air. In the hallway was the other girl's bicycle, in the kitchen some rotting Camembert and a glass of milk circled by a squadron of flies.

Upstairs, in the first room, pastel walls contained rudimentary furniture, some posters of contemporary idols, a cassette player and tapes. A toy animal's projecting button eyes were the only hint of menace.

In the adjacent room he recognized the peripheries of the one he had glimpsed in the vision. The man's skin lay like an old shrivelled condom across the bed. She lay next to this as he had last seen her.

Downstairs he went back into the living room. He saw the video on the floor, and slipped it into the machine. He saw the man and the girls, his girl, in their physical contortions. His imaginings had been tame in comparison to this.

Special Fiction Supplement

LANCASTER UNIVERSITY CREATIVE WRITING DEPARTMENT FICTION COMPETITION 1995

Judges: Janice Galloway, Linda Anderson, David Craig, Alan Burns

NOTES ON THE PRIZEWINNERS

Chris D'Lacey lives in Leicester and this is his first published story. His children's book *A Hole At The Pole* came out with Heinemann last year. He has been shortlisted for *Stand* and *Sunk Island* competitions.

Siri Hansen has an MA in Creative Writing and is currently doing a PhD in the same subject. She has a novel in progress, but this is her first published story. She lives in Edinburgh.

Karen Stevens had her first story printed in *The Big Issue* (London) in July. She lives in Hampshire and holds an MA in Creative Writing.

Jude Weeks is married with two sons and lives in Gateshead. She had a story in *Iron* last year and has won numerous local literary prizes. She was recently shortlisted for both the Ian St James and Sid Chaplin Awards. She is working on a novel at the moment.

Foreword	*Linda Anderson*	206
All Gone	*Siri Hansen*	208
A Good Clean Edge	*Chris D'Lacey*	216
Aunt Selma And The Witch Doctor	*Jude Weeks*	222
Fighting For It	*Karen Stevens*	230

Lancaster University Department of Creative Writing Short Story Competition 1995

WINNERS

First Prize: **Karen Stevens** of Hayling Island with *Fighting For It.* £500 plus publication.

Second Prize: **Jude Weeks** of Gateshead with *Aunt Selma And The Witch Doctor.* £200 plus publication.

Joint Third Prize: **Chris D'Lacey** of Leicester with *A Good Clean Edge.* £100 plus publication.

Joint Third Prize: **Siri Hansen** of Edinburgh with *All Gone.* £100 plus publication.

RUNNERS-UP

Chris Kenworthy, Preston: *Blue Glass*

Heather Leach, Manchester: *Smashing Patriarchy*

COMPETITION REPORT

We had no idea what to expect when we set up this competition. There was a great deal of local interest and publicity. Leaflets displayed in Lancaster cafés favoured by the literati vanished overnight! We wondered if the entries might come predominantly from our own patch but we need not have worried. 872 entries arrived from all over Britain and Ireland, with a fair number from as far away as New Zealand and South Africa.

As the three internal judges (Linda Anderson, Alan Burns, David Craig) have worked with so many writers, not only in Lancaster, but in London, Wales, and East Midlands, we used the safeguards of anonymous entry and an external judge for the shortlist, to prevent any possibility of discrimination, positive or negative. After shortlisting, we looked up identities and found that four of the twenty-two writers listed were former or current students of ours. It confirms our sense that adding 'training' to talent gives some writers the edge, though it has to be said that the vast majority of our students and alumni who entered were not placed.

The internal judges had a huge task, each reading hundreds of manuscripts, many of a good standard and few less than competent. Janice Galloway, who judged the shortlisted stories, again without writers' names revealed, had in some ways the most difficult and agonising task. We would like to thank her for the careful, conscientious way she carried it out. She found the stories of an excellent standard and said that 'trying to compare chalk with cheese

206

with curtain hooks was just awful', especially when many of the writers had virtually equal levels of technical skill. She asked us to award two third prizes and has named two runners-up. The four winning stories are all original, exciting, and very well written. *Fighting For It* is an account of an ugly compelling relationship, like something written by a streetwise Strindberg. *Aunt Selma And The Witch Doctor* is a funny, ultimately poignant story about a sister's permanent loss of her runaway brother. *A Good Clean Edge* is about bullying and bonding in a harsh world of boys and men. *All Gone* charts the self-diminishment of a young woman in a humiliating affair.

Of the excellent runners-up, Chris Kenworthy's *Blue Grass* is about a man's achingly futile love for a lesbian woman. It contains memorable images of her contact lenses which are a different colour from her eyes. Her blue-on-brown eyes come to symbolise her elusive, volatile personality, and her shifting sexuality. Heather Leach's *Smashing Patriarchy* subverts the simplicity of its title. She shows the contradictions by exploring the unconscious longing for the father (or The Father) and a loving portrayal of the narrator's actual father. We publish the full shortlist here, to give recognition to the writers who made it so far against fierce competition.

As part of the Lancaster LitFest, we will be holding a celebration on Sunday, 29 October, 2-4 p.m., at Lancaster Town Hall. Janice Galloway will be there and the winners will read their stories.

Our thanks go to John Murray for joining in this venture, for practical advice throughout, and for his generous agreement to publish four stories instead of the three originally planned. We also thank everyone who entered our competition.

Linda Anderson

THE SHORTLIST

Hilary Shields, Doncaster
Terry Tinthoff, London
Chris Culshaw, Lancaster
Alan Shorrock, London
David Rose, Ashford, Middlesex
Jude Weeks, Gateshead
Tim Love, Cambridge
Siri Hansen, Edinburgh
Paul Lenehan, Dublin
Chris Kenworthy, Preston
Chris D'Lacey, Leicester

John F. Deane, Dublin
Robert Graham, Manchester
Karen Stevens, Hayling Island
Judy Sharman, Ripon, N. Yorks
Richard Barlow, Leicester
Susan Davis, Shropshire
Maria Murphy, Olney, Bucks.
Peter S. Gillott, Mere
Stephen Ormsby, Lewes
Heather Leach, Manchester
Tom Scalway, Lancaster

JOINT 3rd PRIZE

All Gone

Siri Hansen

I can't see anything in this swelling white. The lights are shining right in my eyes. I turn and look at Dad: he's staring straight ahead, his face bleached in the headlights of the cars coming towards us. If I can't see where the car's pointing, how can he? Still we hurtle on at a steady seventy and we don't crash. At every moment I'm both afraid we will and afraid we won't.

Dad kisses a cigarette from the packet and lights up. He doesn't offer me one. I'm twenty-four years old and still can't smoke in front of my parents. It's simple. Children do not smoke. I am a child. Therefore I do not smoke. I ran away, of course, but that is to be expected of some children. I'm coming back, too, as you would also expect.

I think I'm dead.

"Coffee break," says Dad and takes the exit to the services.

*

The table has a lace cloth printed onto the top. I push crumbs around the pattern and watch Dad eating. The chips he insisted on buying me have begun to stick together as they cool; a greasy film makes them look covered in plastic. I told him I didn't want anything to eat but he decided I did. I can see him shooting the plate a glance now and then but perhaps he'll let it go. I sip my coffee and set the saucer down on the crowd of crumbs I have gathered in front of me. All gone.

"You've never had much luck with your friends, have you?" he says.

He shakes his head and reaches for the cigarettes. I mumble something about the toilet and leave the table, trying not to run. In the too-bright, too-tiled room I feel the smoke smack into my lungs and for a moment, just for a moment, everything seems alright. But when I've finished the fag I'll be getting back into that car and heading straight for the place I started off from eight months ago. I'll be polite. I'll tell them what they want to hear, that is what I'm here for.

Dave would love this.

*

"Come with me, hen," he said when he told me he was going back to Scotland. I thought then he was asking me, but it could have been a command. I loved his accent, though, the shape of his words.

"I'm going to Scotland," I told my mum and dad. I had then to tell them about Dave. He was my evenings; my visits to the library, the meetings with girlfriends I didn't have and, once, a Bible class I had seen advertised on a poster although my true religion was this secret from my parents.

"You've deceived us. How *could* you? And how can you go away with someone we don't know?" asked Mum. "This is your home." She cried. I cried, too. It seemed contagious, like a yawn.

Dave was a musician. At least, he played the guitar and sang and I thought he was wonderful. He played a few local pubs in England and I couldn't believe the way people talked over him as though he was a jukebox. They were ignorant and I told him so. "Thanks, hen," he said. "Maybe the English just aren't ready for me, eh?" He smiled. "Except one, of course. You're ahead of your time, that's what it is."

Anyway.

I went to Edinburgh. It was April and the sky kept a tight grey lid over the city, reluctant even to squander rain on it. Occasionally the cover would lift and sudden sun would make us all blink but it snapped back down again soon enough. We lived in a grubby tenement on Leith Walk, stuffed with the sound and smell of traffic. We put up rainbowed sheets over the windows and sealed out the daylight. The naked bulb in the living room burned constantly and from time to time we would talk about buying a shade for it

People called in at all hours; I smiled a lot, sitting on the floor at Dave's feet, and he would play with my hair from time to time and ask me to fetch another can. I thought this crowd was exciting and bohemian. I smoked hash and giggled wisely at appropriate intervals.

One night in July when the last straggler had gone, Dave gave me a long look across the living room wreckage.

"You've let yourself go," he said. "You want to take a good look in a mirror." He belched softly through the lager fizz as he drained his can.

My heart felt squashed into my throat.

Dave narrowed his eyes. "You know, I think you're getting fat."

I don't think I'd put on weight; we didn't seem to eat much outside of the nightly take-away. I hadn't exactly been a sylph to begin with: Dave had fondly described making love to me as bathing in a sea of woman, and now he was afraid of drowning.

"I'm sorry, I don't want to disappoint you. I'll do something about it, Dave. Honest I will."

"Come here," he said. "You're just a wean." He wound his hands gently into my hair. "You get on my fucking nerves, d'you know that?" He pulled me upright and I could feel the crackle of hairs snapping at the root. His empty can rang on the floorboards.

"I'm sorry, Dave. I'm sorry."

"No, no, *no!*" he bellowed and the wall came up and hit me in the back of the head. And again. And again. I heard this thin, sad sound and realized it was me; a wail somehow too polite to turn itself into a scream. And Dave banging my head hard enough for it to hurt but not hard enough to knock me out which is what I wanted after I stopped being surprised. And the naked light scrubbing at my eyes, and then the thumping from the other side of the wall and Dave dropping me on the floor so we wouldn't disturb the neighbours any more. And my head fuzzy with pain and me telling Dave, "It's alright - it was the drink, it's alright, it's not your fault, it's not your fault".

*

"You should eat," says Dad, when I get back to the table.

"I'm not hungry," I say. "Really."

"I bought you some fresh chips."

"I just -"

"Come on, do it for your Dad." He pushes a plastic sachet across the table. "I even got you some ketchup."

I can see my hand picking up the fork and the tines pushing into the chip and feel the floury food in my mouth.

I'll need another visit to the toilet before we go.

*

It didn't happen again. Things went on much as usual. To me, Dave was still the greatest guy in the world, even more so because he didn't keep hitting me. He played his guitar but wasn't trying to get gigs; I wasn't looking for a job either so I can hardly criticize. It meant we were together virtually all the time. And when you love someone you want to be with them. This was the real thing.

Pete, a drummer who spent most of the time admiring his own tattoos, came by frequently with his girlfriend, Shona. Occasionally he would look hungrily at the pale, blank arms snaking out from her black clothes. I gradually noticed that when Shona and I talked, she smiled only when I did, a kind of disconnected shadow. The rest of the time she just looked; an Edinburgh-grey gaze pressing down on me so that sometimes I had to go into the kitchen just to breathe. When she began to come alone, I tried hard to think of ways to dazzle Dave with my good points.

One day we were going down Leith Walk when we met Shona on her way to visit. I found myself trailing behind them, a child shut out of the adults' conversation. The screeching and rumbling of the buses pushed through my head and the red sari of an Asian woman outside a shop was a wound bleeding into my eyes. The wind, the constant push of the wind, was slicing my skin, carving me away until I felt I would slip between the paving stones. My chest was beginning to split open. I looked down, appalled, compelled to watch my heart burst out and slop down into the dog shit and fag ends and gobbets of spit.

The world snapped back as suddenly as tinnitus. Up ahead Shona and Dave were looking in the window of a second-hand shop that sprouted a tangle of mountain bikes outside. They had just passed a toilet which someone had put out for the rubbish collectors. There it was, complete with seat and lid, standing under a telephone pole. A good laugh, that's what Dave and I had shared from the start - so I pulled a newspaper from the bin on the pole, lifted up the toilet lid and took a seat. I opened up the newspaper. A lorry going past tooted me. Dave and Shona turned. His expression dried onto his face like a mask.

"You're an embarrassment," he said. "A fucking embarrassment." He looked at me as though I'd smeared his disgust on him myself. Shona grinned. I hadn't noticed before what sharp little teeth she had.

She easily kept up with Dave as he strode away. I trotted after them.

*

Dad grunts as I down the last chip with its coating of scarlet slime.

"Good girl," he says. "There'd be hell to pay if your mum thought I wasn't looking after you properly." He jangles his keys. "Right then, we'd best be off."

"I think I'd better go again, just to be sure."

He gives me a look.

"Touch of tummy trouble," I say. "You know, woman's - "

He does a little cough to drown me out. "I'll wait by the newsagent," he says.

Set into the white tiles of the toilet is a plastic case containing plastic flowers, with a notice telling you that you can buy this Ideal Gift in the services shop. The case is blurry with fingerprints. Why do we want to touch them when we know they're not real? I try too.

In the cubicle I purge myself of the starch and grease. It's the only way to deal with it. The first time I did this in Edinburgh I was surprised when I was sick, even though I had put my fingers down my throat with this precise result in mind. It struck me, though, that this had a purity other bodily functions lacked: this was something I could control. It was only me, but I could control it.

I flush the toilet and sit on it for a minute to compose myself. Someone comes into the cubicle next door. She's crying. She closes the door and keeps on crying, huge sobs to decorate the desolation of the motorway services.

I have to leave. I don't have room for this. I don't have room.

*

I was taking control of my life.

My clothes began to hang off me.

"You look ill," he said after another joyless fuck brought on by drink and boredom.

"Do I?" My cheekbones had made an appearance.

"And... oh, forget it."

"What?"

"Nothing. Just drop it."

"Come on, Dave, you can't just pretend you weren't going to say something. Tell me."

He began to get out of bed. I could feel crumbs niggling my backside. He found his jeans and stepped into them.

"It's your breath," he said. "It smells." His zip going up made a curt ripping sound. "You asked me."

I began to buy mints.

*

I decided to try to get a job. I could get some money together and we could take a holiday. A change of scenery was what we needed. Great gouts of Festival-hungry tourists had erupted over Edinburgh and the streets were ragged with flyers that rustled like insects.

I got the first job I applied for, selling tartan tat on Princes Street.

212

I went home to tell Dave. Things are moving now, I thought.

It was just after noon. Dave had to sign on at two so I made him a coffee and took it into the bedroom.

The room pulsed with a warm, animal smell. Beside the sleeping Dave lay Shona, one hand stroking into the light fur of her pubic hair. She looked at me, blinked like a long white cat, and took a toke on her joint. We both watched the smoke stream unhurriedly from her nostrils.

"Shall I wake him?"

"No, I... I... "

She raised an amused eyebrow. "What's the matter?" she said, mimicking my accent impeccably. "Cat got your tongue?"

*

We drive on southwards.

"Your mum and I have been worried about you," Dad says. "Not hearing from you, not knowing where you were. It's been preying on your mother's mind. You know she's not a well woman."

Mum has never been well; it's hard to think anything about it. I should have stayed, I suppose, looked after her. Her need was always bigger than me; finally I'd left her alone with it.

Mum's life.

My life.

I don't feel anything.

I keep watching the cats' eyes, squinting against the occasional blare of headlights from the other side of the motorway.

"We did everything we could think of for you," says Dad. "You've wanted for nothing."

But still want had blossomed in me.

"I know, and I'm grateful. Really I am."

"You've a funny way of showing it."

"I've made a mess of things, Dad, but I *am* grateful. You must believe me."

"I thought we'd brought you up better."

"You did, you did. It's not your fault. It's me." Me, looking for.

Looking for.

*

Shona didn't actually move in but she might as well have. I slept on the sofa and she and Dave had the bed. She took the sheets to the laundrette. I listened to them fuck.

"Let me give you a little piece of advice," said Alex, a friend

213

twice-removed who came round to pick up his guitar. He spoke at length about self-determination and pride and not getting shat upon. I agreed.

"Then leave, you daft bitch."

I felt my face smile. "We're out of biscuits," I said. "I'll just run to the shop."

When I got back he was gone. He was right, I knew that; but at least I knew these people, understood the routine that wound around us. I put the custard creams in the kitchen where Dave could find them easily. I didn't eat biscuits. I didn't eat anything much.

I took long walks through the city. The worse the weather got the more I went out. Christmas mania thrust shoppers from the dark afternoons into radiant displays, warmed air stinging them into sweat inside their coats. Princes Street was thronged with dazed people lurching from one present to another. In the Gardens lines of empty benches looked down into dark pools of grass and the wind battered the odd bit of rubbish along the paths. It was cold, cold, *cold* sitting there, a perfect painful balance between feeling and not feeling. My ears pulled an ache out through my teeth and clamped it to my head; my hands and feet were fat, dulled copies of themselves.

I was looking up at the castle floodlights smearing out into the sky when a woman walking past dropped some coins onto the carrier bag on the seat beside me. I felt like a fraud. I called out to her, to tell her to take her money back, but she quickened her pace and left me behind.

To prove my point I went home.

It wasn't there. Outside the door was a black bin liner; stuck to it was a piece of paper with my name on it. On the back - nothing. Just my name on the front. Inside the bag were my clothes and a little pink furry pig I bought Dave when we came to Edinburgh. And a bath brush that had been in the flat when we moved in.

The new lock on the door shone in the gloom of the stairway.

"I thought you were away for a couple of weeks," said the old guy from upstairs as he passed me. "That's what the young man said. Forget something, did you? Don't worry about the rubbish, I'll put it out for you on the day."

I sat on the stairs. I should have been thinking about what to do next but everything seemed a monumental effort and anyway I was waiting for some kind of emotion to arrive. After a bit it occurred to me that I was tired and I rested my head on my knees and shut my eyes. The wash of not-knowing was just creeping through me when the old guy passed me on his way back.

"You alright, hen?" he said. He put his hand on my shoulder; a kindly gesture that seemed to be happening to someone else. "Come up for a cup of tea," he said. "A nice cup of tea'll do you good." He was so kind; too kind. I had to get away.

As I stumbled down the stairs I heard his tutting and the rustle of the bin liner as he took it to his flat. He'd look after it for me until I came for it. How I hated him and the stare of his unsolicited concern.

Outside the cold slapped at me again. I prepared myself for what I knew I was about to do. I used one of the coins the woman had given me in the Gardens to phone my parents. There wasn't anyone else.

"I'm coming to get you," said Dad. "Wait there. Don't move."

For a second I saw myself with absolute, horrible clarity: Christ, Daddy, I thought, where would I go?

*

We're off the heartbeat of the motorway, no longer punctuated with the rhythm of bridges flattened into cardboard cut-outs by the headlights.

We pass along roads that bulge with sudden shops and then smooth out into houses and back into knots of shops. I'm beginning to recognize where we are. Dad is humming under his breath and drumming his fingers on the steering wheel. Nearly home. Past the café where I first saw Dave. Somehow Dad seems to be driving faster than we ever went on the motorway. I can picture my mother waiting in her chair, refusing to go to bed until we arrive, her patience an extra blanket in the already too-hot room. That tune Dad's humming, it's familiar. Can't quite place it; it's a nursery rhyme, I think. Nearly home. Round the roundabout. Turn left, turn right, into the drive. Tum tum te tum what is it what is it out of the car small woman framed by the light tum tum te tum she's reaching for me there's almost nothing of you she's saying and I think you're right there and it's worse than you can know all gone and that tune that tune is a lullaby looking for me but I'm all gone all gone.

She has hold of my hands, her thin grip as sure as the elastic bands I wound around my fingers as a child. Still using me to support her she pulls me into the hall, and I follow her onto the deep-pile, tongue-coloured carpet which sinks under my feet with a give like flesh.

JOINT 3rd PRIZE

A Good Clean Edge

Chris D'Lacey

There's this blond-haired boy I see in the mornings. He goes to the school down at my end of town. The big white building. The senior school. I go to the juniors at the other end of town.

So this is how it is: every morning we pass. He goes to one school, I go to the other. So maybe you're thinking I look for him coming? But I keep my head down. I stay close to the shopfronts. I don't look up. I don't pull faces. I concentrate instead on the cracks in the pavement.

But this boy sees me.

Somewhere near the butcher's. Or Wheeler's garage. Or the boarded-over place all stuck with posters. I can always tell he's coming by the clip of his shoes.

"You," he says.

He bangs his hand through my shoulder. Spins me off balance. Into the shopfronts.

"What?" I say. But I know the answer.

"What?" he says. "What? You *what?*"

"Nothing," I say.

"Whadd'you mean, *nothing?*"

I take a sideways step. He takes a bigger step. I step the other way. We dance on the pavement. The two boys with him, they snort at the sky. One of them lights up a fag for the other.

"Please," I say.

"*Please*," he says back.

"I'll be late for school."

"What do I care?" He says this up to my face. He smells of tobacco, cold stale beer. Sometimes I get to taste this on spit.

*

You see how it is? The corner I'm in? You understand now why I don't talk at breakfast? Why I hate that my father doesn't have money? Buses pass. I want to tell my father that. Buses pass. They don't stand and talk. My mother has money, a civil service job. My mother has my sisters. She doesn't have me.

*

216

My grandmother got to know something was up. She knew when the blond boy got too rough. She wanted the story on the hole in my shirt.

"How did you get this, here?" she said.

"What?" I said, looking. "It's nothing. A tear." I was reading a comic. I didn't want to talk.

"You'll have to use the other shirt tomorrow," she said. She sat in the rocking chair, threading a needle.

She needed an explanation, I knew. She was using small-talk to squeeze it out. I read. She talked small. Some stuff about the hole. The size of it. The edge. Clean, was what she said, the edge was clean. So I made up a story. I made up a lie. "We were running in the yard and I fell, that's all. I ripped it on the gravel. I was meaning to tell you."

"No," she said, "you didn't do that."

Then I let it out, about the blond-haired boy. I folded like a flower. I rolled on my side. My grandmother moved the shirt off her knee. She opened her arms. She acted like my mother.

I was still cleaning up when my uncle walked in.

"What's with him?" He said it to his mother.

She said, "Some boy, some boy at school."

"Not *school*," I said. I think I shouted.

"Boy?" said my uncle.

"A senior," she said.

My uncle came over, held me by the chin. He twisted my face up into the light. "Where," he said, "where's he been hit?"

My grandmother said, "This boy doesn't hit." She showed him the line of stitches in my shirt.

My uncle nodded. He let go of my face.

"We have to deal with this, put this right." He opened up the clock on the centre of the mantelpiece, drilled the key tightly, restored the tick.

His mother said, "His father is the one who should deal with it."

"His father drives lorries," my father's brother said.

*

It was the weekend. No school. It was all to our advantage. We had time to work it out, my Uncle Billy said. Give that bastard what bastards deserve. Turn him whiter than the stiffs, okay?

He was talking about the bodies in the fridge next door.

"It's like this," he said. He held up a fist and he faced it with a palm. "You just have to crack him. One big punch."

There we were, on the forecourt of my grandfather's business, between the long coffin store and the chapel of rest: me and Uncle Billy, cracking palms.

He stole a piece of gravel from the top of an urn. "Here, squeeze this. Close your hand right around it. When he starts up next time, you stand back, you swing. You get him on the chin. And you do it *hard*."

"But he'll beat me," I said. "He'll beat me flat!"

My Uncle Billy smiled. He spat on the ground. He threw gravel at the crows on the roof of the chapel. I was his brother's son, he said. He told me everything was going to be all right. He had that look in his eye, the look I've seen before when they gave him medals. Uncle Billy has medals for outdoor survival. He rescues people from mountains sometimes.

*

So I walked to school on the Monday morning. I didn't wear a satchel. My arms were swinging free. I had to get a really good swing at this boy. Uncle Billy took care of the little things, the satchel. All I carried was the gravel in my palm.

My uncle had said it would all be all right. We'd turn him whiter than a stiff, okay? But I couldn't think straight. I couldn't walk straight. I was thinking of penknives, holes in shirts; cold, dead bodies; stiffs in the store; my uncle, driving up behind me in the hearse. It would only seem odd if I looked back, he said. I should act like normal. Do what I do. Look at the cracks in the pavement, perhaps.

At Wheeler's garage I saw the blond boy coming. He nudged his friend, nodded me out. He's a smart-looking boy: wide, square shoulders; shortish, stocky; crisp black jacket; the blue and yellow tie that the seniors wear. His blond hair rolls in waves across his forehead. It hides his eyes and the dangers there.

"You," he says, approaching. "You looking at me?"

This is the first time proper, yes. I didn't know before, he has a dimple in his chin. I stand back. I swing. One big punch. I hit him clean. In the dimple. In the chin. Gravel bites my palm. My knuckles feel hurt. The blond boy staggers. His bottom lip drops. His bottom lip judders and he can't close his mouth. His face changes colour. Whiter than a stiff.

"Jesus, Frankie..." his one friend says. The lighted cigarette drops out of his fingers. He looks around for guidance. What the hell should he do?

A hearse pulls up beside Wheeler's garage. Uncle Billy leaps out of the seat.

"You," he says, pointing hard at Frankie. "I'm talking to you. I want your *name*."

Now this boy looks whiter than his shirt. He stares at the hearse. He says his name. I wonder if he wonders if the box is for him. There are tears in his eyes as my uncle warns him, You'd better not touch this boy again.

But that's not all. There is punishment worse than a punch to come.

My uncle says, "Here's what you're going to do..."

*

We get into the hearse, Uncle Billy and me. He drives me to school in a funeral car. A slow, smooth ride all the way down the road. People nod. They take off their hats.

"We gave him a taste," my Uncle Billy says. He blows smoke into the car, leans his elbow out the window. "That chicken-shit won't go near you again. You should practise, though, on a bag or something."

"Practise?" I say.

"You could have hit him harder."

I don't know. I don't know about that. I've got this feeling, this afterburn of nerves. I'm getting to understand what it is I've done. I don't get a ride to school every morning.

"Ronnie'll give him some pain, you'll see."

The car pulls up at the gates of the school. "Mr Pulson?" I say. "You mean, Mr Pulson?" When Frankie gets to school, he has to report.

Uncle Billy says, "He ought to thank Christ he's not in the mountains. We might stuff him down a rabbit hole, leave him there."

I lean on the door and get out of the hearse. I do the longer walk, round the back of the car. My uncle hands me my satchel through the window.

He says, "It's done. We sorted this out. When your Dad gets home, we'll show him that punch."

He winks at me, proud, and the hearse pulls away.

The bell rings for school. I walk through a playground emptying of boys. On the way I'm thinking this to myself: how will I look in a

219

crisp black jacket, badge on the pocket, blue and yellow tie?
In five months time, I won't have to think.

*

So maybe you're wondering, is this how it ends? I go to the seniors? I get beaten flat? I go to the seniors, that part's right. But it doesn't end there. It just gets different.

I meet Ronnie Pulson, my uncle's friend. Physical Education on a Wednesday afternoon. Ronnie makes us run in a never-ending circle. For nearly an hour we jog around his gym. We're wearing our shorts. The rest is bare. We're miserable specimens, lily-skinned boys. At the end of the lesson we don't know which is worse, our bursting lungs or the medicine ball Ronnie Pulson throws - the contact that tells us we're now allowed to shower.

In the playground, I stay out of Frankie's way. I see him sometimes. He sees me. He'll throw me a glance but he never comes over. He looks no different to the day I hit him. I never tell anyone about that day.

And then, the weirdest thing.

My turn comes up with Joey Johnson.

"Oi you!" Joey says. "You lanky streak of piss. You got any money? I fancy a coke."

We're on the ground floor, in the well of the stairs. Joey slaps a hand in the centre of my chest. He pushes me back. My head hits the wall. Two of his mates take hold of my arms. Some other kids get wise, move away from the machine.

Joey says, "R'you deaf? I said I fancy a coke."

"I heard you," I say.

"You cocky shit," he says.

He feels my pockets. Then my balls. I'm readying to scream when a gold-ringed finger taps Joey on the shoulder.

Frankie hits him hard, just as he turns. One good punch like a cracking palm. Joey drops down with blood in his mouth.

Frankie says to Joey, "You leave this boy alone."

That's all he says. It's over in a punch. He pulls the sleeves straight on his crisp black jacket, runs a hand back through his curled blond hair. He nods, as if some favour is returned. I stay silent. Frankie turns and walks away. What's the point of words?

Now we have a bond.

*

220

I was thinking of that bond last night before I wrote this. I was thinking of the way this story never ends.

It was late, and Janet had already gone up. I was locking up the house when I heard this commotion. Some boys in the street. Bawling it out.

I stepped outside. There were four of them at it. Spraying lager on the cars. They'd had too much.

I said, "Hey, you boys. Move away from the cars."

"We weren't near the cars," these boys said to me. They laughed and hung loose in the centre of the road. Then one of them, the biggest, sat down on a bonnet.

I looked at each of these boys in turn. They were fifteen, no more. Just kids from a school. I picked up a piece of gravel from the road.

I said, "It's simple."

These boys said, "What?"

"Either you move or I have to move you."

Then they didn't shake their lager anymore. They could see I was serious. I had a look in my eye, gravel in my palm. Maybe they thought: this guy climbs mountains. Three of them moved as I stepped across the road. The guy on the bonnet, he slid off fast.

"I've got a knife," he said, but he was twitching, nervous.

"Leave it, Yabba," another boy said.

"Knife?" I said.

He said, "I'll use it."

And I got mad then, madder than I've ever been before.

I said, "You're gonna end up in a ditch, you jerk. Just like Frankie, face down in the dirt. If I punch you out, you're gonna learn nothing. Why don't you fucking people ever learn? You'll end up in dirt, at the side of a road. A hole in your shirt. A good clean edge."

But I was talking to myself, to the light of the lamps.

Away down the road some boys were running. They were splashing lager. Over the cars.

SECOND PRIZE

Aunt Selma And The Witch Doctor

Jude Weeks

I look into my heart, and she is always there. Wherever I am, whatever I am doing, my heart can still see and hear her, hear the footfall I used to listen for, and her voice so near to me it could be in the same room... "What's the matter with you, child?" Thoughts of me and for me, which were always with her... She is wearing the orange stripey dress that flaunted her generous belly and midriff, what she called her womanly curves. Around her head is wound the turban made of sparkly stuff with golden tassels, which dangled and tangled constantly with her golden earrings. On the wide span of her wrists gilt bangles hung; when she was in a temper, they jangled and clicked as she shook her fist. But not at us; never at us.

We lived in a house with a green front door, but never used it. We all went in and out through the back, less chance for Her Next Door to neb into our business, she would say, touching the side of her nose with a fat brown finger, nodding knowingly. Her earrings would swing and ring like little golden bells. To me, our lives began anew each day like the first act of a play, with no history, and what was before us was unguessed. I was much younger then. However, I went along with her espionage act. I knew what she meant.

"Mrs Next Door has her own way of doing things, but it's not my way," Aunt Selma would mutter darkly, "and who shall touch pitch and not be defiled?" What riches there were in living with her!

Me and our Eddy lived with Aunt Selma, in the house where we were born, and where Mam had died, worn out with the pain of being torn apart every five minutes, and the effort involved in trying to pull herself together, over and over again. Our Dad had died in this house too, by mistake. He had jumped out of the upstairs window when he thought the house was afire, and he fell on his head. It was a mistake, because the house wasn't on fire, Aunt Selma just told him it was, and he was drunk again and believed her, more fool him.

Mrs Next Door saw it all. She just stood there with her pinny wrapped round her hands, watching. "Well," she said to the polis, "What can you expect?"

*

Our Eddy loved writing letters. We used the backs of packets, old bills, anything, and he would sit and write to people he'd read about. Most of them were dead, and the others were mainly cartoon characters, so it didn't much matter how many people he asked to stay, the notes all went on the fire when he'd gone to bed. Once, when Batman and Robin wrote back, he told us what they said. In beautiful English.

I see him now, one Christmas long ago, wearing his old green jumper with the holes in, writing his letter to Santa. Every year, he asked for the same thing, a cat to cuddle or a dog to take for walks. "A dog, just what I need to send me right round the bend, can't afford it, can't trust Eddy anyway, forget it," Aunt Selma cried irately, as if anyone was going to argue with her! Eddy jumped up on to the stool, and stood wobbling - I remember his long pants were too short again - and spoke up loudly. "I'm going to read what I've written. It's a list but not of the things I want off Santa, it's what I've got already, all the people I love best in the world, and you and our Bernadette are number one and two."

*

Aunt Selma and I chose the dog without him knowing, partly as a surprise, and partly "to stop him wanting an Alsatian, or some other horse what would eat us out of house and home, just his way, he'd choose the biggest because it was a pretty colour. We want a smallish one we can control."

So we came home with an Old English Sheepdog. Aunt Selma had had one when she was little, and this was a dead ringer. When we brought it home, Her Next Door was watching again, her pale face pressed against the window, flat as a bloater.

When Eddy saw it snuffling through the front door, he burst into tears, "Mop, it's our Mop, my Mop," he cried, although to the best of my knowledge he'd never clapped eyes on a dog like it before, let alone owned one. He was a queer lad, Aunt Selma said, gazing at him with a strange expression.

"The dog we had was called Mops," she said, not looking at me. Aunt Selma not looking meant quite a lot. I watched Eddy hanging around the dog's neck, and Mop responding to his kisses with hot tonguey smiles. A cold shiver slid down my spine.

Her Next Door was on to us straight away. "You've not got a dog in there have you? What a racket I nearly knocked on the wall sounded like elephants charging all over me ceiling the bulb swung like the pit and the pendulum you know you're not supposed to have pets in here and if my lot gets fleas I'll know where to come and if it bites one o' me bairns I'll get the polis on you." She never stopped to draw breath.

*

All that winter, Mop took our Eddy for walks every day. When I close my eyes, I can see them still, like an old jerky black and white film, hurtling down the road, Eddy hanging off the back like streamers, clinging to the leash. He got a bit better, more sensible, less confused, as if some essence of him was becoming distilled and concentrated, restoring some facsimile of the man he might have been.

As the months went by, I watched him grow happier and stronger. Off he would go down the street, the dog panting by his side, with the old red bag, and a shopping list. With Her Next Door watching every move, just looking for trouble, Aunt Selma said, and I'm just the woman to give it to her. Eddy soon recognised tins of dog food, and how much it cost; very soon, he knew which brand Mop preferred. He could go to the butcher and beg for bones, and saved his coppers to buy broken biscuits. And I wondered if I dared hope, dared relax; if the worry about anything happening to me would ever become unnecessary.

Aunt Selma said "Don't get your hopes up, it's only a dog, not a miracle cure, there's nothing really there, pet, the Doctor says so, it's just a new interest, a distraction, like, and the dog's tiring him out, he hasn't got the energy for twistin' on like he used to." I knew there was more to it than that. His voice grew deeper, and a faint fuzz crept over his upper lip. His knees lost their childish knobble, and an Adam's apple settled under his chin. My brother was drawing away from me, drawn into tardy manhood by another love, stronger than his love for me. I wanted to say good for him, I really did.

Now that Mop crammed upstairs with him, there was no fight at bedtime, and no incessant begging for the old stories I had read so often I knew them by heart. I never thought I would miss those characters, King Arthur, Aladdin, Superman, Alice in Wonderland, all finished with. Me and Alice, both redundant. My tears were shed in secret - I was ashamed of them.

*

One morning we got a note, scrawled on an old envelope. 'Plese keep

224

yor dog of our garden, or I will be forced to take it farther.' For a moment I thought it was Eddy playing the fool. Aunt Selma laughed at first, but when she thought again, she got mad. "I can tell her just where she can take it, and the further the better," she said, and sent the note back with all the spellings corrected. In red biro.

We tried to make Eddy understand about being quiet, and he tried, he really did. He would shake his head at Mop, his finger over his lips, and his eyes like organ stops... as if the dog understood! So we tried putting him out in the yard, but that was even worse, everyone who passed by got the full treatment, and the plaster started coming off our walls because of Them Next Door banging through with the broom. That set him off worse than anything, but try and explain to them. "It'll be a fine, and don't say I didn't warn you I've stood as much as flesh and blood can bear but that dog's got to go." Aunt Selma banged the door in her face.

The policeman was nice, young, with blue eyes, fair curly hair and big shoulders, quite handsome really, but I was too worried to notice him much. The dog loved him at first sight, and flew to embrace him. When we rescued him out of the fireplace, he was okay, just a few cinders on his pants, and only a small burn on his sleeve. He tried to be nice to us, he tried so hard his neck nearly vanished into his collar. When I reached the door with him, he held out his hand and I saw how white it was.

Of course, she was there. "Got any more spanners you want to throw?" I asked, but of course it went right over her head.

"It's no good blamin' me it can't go on it's been snappin' at the bairns and barkin' till they're terrified to come home."

"That's because they torment him and throw stones, you should of brought them up proper, not like little hooligans what they are, and you so stuck up with your lace curtains, only there for you to snoop behind and filthy dirty into the bargain." Aunt Selma was shouting. Mrs was bright red and spitting. The dog shot upstairs. The handsome young polis jumped into his car and vanished. I wondered how far he'd get before he'd notice his aerial and back number-plate were missing.

We showed Eddy the letter. He could read a little bit and I explained the rest. He soon understood. Mop had to go away, and he could not go with him. He sat down on the old chair and looked at his feet. "You should of thought of it before you give 'im to me." How often had I prayed for such lucid thought from him. But now I

wept and touched his face. He looked up at me. His eyes were empty
again. When I went up later, he was tucked up in bed, his head at the
top, and Mop's head sticking out at the bottom. They both smiled at
me. I went away comforted.

*

In the morning they were both gone. The bed was cold. He had left a
note. I still have it in my jewellery box. 'Me and Mop has gon away
to a farm in the country were I can keep him. I can work I am strong.
Goodby our Bernie and Auntie Selma, I will see you soon. Love
Eddy'

So we had the polis at the door again. Same young lad,
"following it up," he said. I thought that was kind, considering.
Seemingly, a little lad had seen our Eddy with his 'horse' up by the
allotments. Eddy always thought that was the country. The polis
wanted us to wait in, they said it was best in case he came back. I
made tea, so much tea I never drank it again. The hours went by and
we sat on the green chairs by the hearth and stared at each other and
at the fire until it went out. Noises outside faded and the sounds of
the traffic receded. As night fell, the orange lights in the streets flared
out like marigolds against the dark blue sky. After a while, I left the
curtain open so's I could see out of our prison to the world outside.
Just to see that other life existed made me feel that anything was
possible.

It seemed like a moment, and I opened my eyes and the sky was
grey. The bright flowers of light went out, and slowly the birds began
to sing. It was not their fault, they knew nothing about fear and loss
and grief. I had written the words upon the darkness over and over in
the quiet night, and now was glad to see the rising sun wipe them
out. It might still not be true.

A movement from the window. I looked up and Her Next Door
was peering in. I sprang to the door before Aunt Selma could hear.
We stood shivering together on the front step. I noticed her rough
red hands as she handed me a covered plate. "I've made you a bit
breakfast, I know you must be fretted sick. I want to do what I can.
Mebbes I was in the wrong." Her tears were real. I took the plate
from her. "We'll be glad of it, Mrs Sewell, thank you." Then she
went into her house and I went into ours. Through the front door.

*

The factory hooter sounded. It was one o'clock. "I can't stand it no
longer I'm not born to sit still I gotta go and look," Aunt Selma

226

cried, and rushed out without her coat or scarf. I chased after her and caught her just before the number one bus would have sent her quickly to heaven. Mrs Sewell came panting up after us, chins wobbling. "I've got your key, you left the place wide open and I'm comin' with ye to search." She looked away. "Now no argyin!"

But no matter where we looked, how many alleyways we searched, how many people we asked, there was no trace. Churches yawned emptily, and once or twice, Aunt Selma chose to kneel at the altar. She lit a candle, too. It was so long since I'd seen her do that. Garages surrendered their dead cars, and garden sheds their lawnmowers and rusty old bikes. Attics were denuded, and tons of dust, crumbs and paper showered over the town like confetti. Estate agents jumped to attention, and rattled keys at empty factories and shops; derelict warehouses were scoured. A crypt in the churchyard was found to have a broken latch, and we stood in the rain while the polis shone his torch into the house of the dead. Eddy was not there. He was not anywhere.

As the days went by, we waited. The young polis came round regularly, but had nothing new to suggest. Father Doyle came to visit and held Aunt Selma's hand. He knelt in front of the fire, placed his hands together and closed his eyes. I got a sudden vision of his prayers vanishing up the chimney like wishes to Santa, and I nearly burst out laughing. I had to run upstairs, but once there, I found out that it wasn't laughter after all.

At first, the neighbours were in and out all the time, but that fizzled out as we all lost hope... all except Aunt Selma. She had given up on the Sally Army, the Polis and the church, it didn't matter how kind they were, there was nothing they could do, she said. It was a miracle we needed. But she had one more ace up her sleeve. "I never thought I'd live to see the day I'd revert, but it's been taken out of me hands, I gave the polis, the good Lord and St. Anthony every chance and they've all let me down, so it's bruja now. I should of done it sooner." I didn't know what the hell she was on about.

The night he came, I sat up with her. We turned out the light about eleven, and lit two candles in the window. Aunt Selma sat gazing out of the window. I gazed at her. At the edge of her turban, white hairs poked free and lay against her cheek like a question mark. There was a permanent pink line around her eyes now, and lines around her mouth. My Aunt, she was getting old. I drew nearer to her in the darkness. She turned and smiled, dark eyes glowing, reflecting the candlelight. "It's everybody's turn one day, don't worry about me. It's Eddy. It isn't his time yet. But the man'll know, he'll tell us what to do."

"What man, what are you going on about?"

She shook her head and pointed. And there he stood in the street, straight out of Rider Haggard. He was half naked, and barefoot on the cold pavements, he, who surely graced the wilds of Africa. I swear to God he was ten foot tall, and as black as ebony. He gleamed all over, slippery as a snake, writhing and jerking, dancing around the lamp posts. He wore leopard skin, and gold bangles; gold rings hung from his nose and from his ears. Around his neck swung huge teeth from some mighty animal. He held a spear which shone brazen in the darkness.

We all went outside, Mrs Sewell too, and stood watching. Steam rose from his back, sweat poured down his face, as on he went, up and down the path, shaking his spear and chanting. When he opened his mouth, his teeth gleamed white, and his eyes shone like golfballs.

"A witch-doctor," I breathed.

"Rubbish, it's him from the launderette, he's no witch-doctor, he's a Presbyterian, I know it for a fact".

He stopped gyrating for a moment, and looked pained. "Madam, if you don't mind." Mrs Sewell subsided.

On and on he went, until even he flagged. His feet grew less nimble, and his steps faltered; once or twice he staggered. He slowed down to a rhythmic shuffle and then fell to his knees. Rocking back and forward, he cried out, holding his arms up to the sky. A cloud raced forward and threw itself over the moon. He was lost to sight. When he reappeared, he was peering into an old cloth bag. Aunt Selma started forward. He looked at her once, and shook his head silently. He began to sing, a strange, haunting yodel which stirred the air with melancholy. He took off his head-dress and placed a square of cloth over his head. And I knew what it meant, I just knew, before Aunt Selma told me. It was the song of the dead.

*

No one ever found him. A man and a dog had vanished into thin air without a trace. Each day, I walked down to the allotments and searched, hoping against hope. Looking forward, looking back, looking for clues, wondering what I did wrong, what else I could have done, what if, what if?

*

Now I live in another place, another time, and Aunt Selma is long since dead. But my mind still takes me back to the house with the green front door, to Eddy and Mop and the allotments, and to the great mystery of it all. He would be forty now, and I wonder what he would look like - perhaps I would pass him in the street. But he would never pass me by as a stranger, I know it: My little brother, my little brother forever. What more can I do but watch and wait and hope?

FIRST PRIZE

Fighting For It

Karen Stevens

Marshall wished he could tell her to fuck off. He wanted to get out;
go down the pub and leave this oppressive atmosphere behind. He
hated it when she came around and lay on her fucking back, refusing
to move, not talking, just lying there dominating his room with her
sullen presence. At first he had tried talking to her nicely, explaining
how he needed his own time, his own space. But she would lie there,
on her back, red hair sprawled across his cushions. She visited his
basement flat at least four or five times a week, and seemed to think
she had the right to interrupt his life whenever she wished. She never
telephoned to ask if it was convenient to drop by. She never knocked
on the door and asked if it was alright to come in. She never
apologised and left if he was busy, or if he told her that he already
had friends inside. When she visited she expected to come in, and if
he ignored her familiar knock she would bang his window harder and
harder. He had to let her in before she smashed through the glass. So
there she lay. He sipped his tea silently, willing her to leave, while she
stared into the gloomy room beyond him.

"Do you believe in telepathy?" Marshall asked at length.

"Why?" she replied as she stared above. Marshall freed his long
blonde hair from the piece of elastic in which it was tied, and secured
the band onto his wrist.

"Because I wondered if you ever felt another person's thoughts
without being literally told." The tone was acid.

"Sometimes I think I must be clairvoyant," she replied slowly.

"Why's that, then?" Marshall asked coldly.

"Because I can see certain things."

"Like what?"

"Like how you play games with me."

"I don't play games with you." He was somewhat amused by her
answer. "You play games with yourself."

Marshall looked at the girl and felt angry. He didn't know why he
thought of her as a girl. She was at least twenty. Perhaps it was her
tireless nature, or her thick skin that usually belonged to those

230

pubescent girls who never seemed to get the hint. Three months ago she'd started talking to him in a pub. They went out a few times and he'd fucked her once or twice. That was it - no big romance, no words of love, flowers or cards - just a few drinks and the occasional fuck. She'd rung his home constantly for two days after the first time. The messages had filled up the tape of his answering machine, but he hadn't bothered to ring her back. So she'd sent silly letters to his work address instead. He watched her closely as she stubbed out her cigarette in an ashtray by her side.

*

The first time they met he had been sitting alone in the pub, minding his own business, drinking Guinness, looking at the video screen above, wondering what to teach his 'A' level students the next day, or whether to just stick on a video. Which video? Perhaps he could show them a video on racism and the undercover work of two men - one white and one black - both seeking employment and accommodation ...

"You look deep in thought," she said, out of the blue, as she sat down next to him. He had to bring his senses back to the pub.

"I am," he replied with a quick shake of his head, and because she obviously expected him to expand on this, he told her about the video he was planning to use the following day.

"The video is supposed to make us aware of how racism exists on every level - from housing to employment," he told her. "A hidden camera shows a typical white landlady telling a coloured guy that the spare room in her house is taken - and yet, ten minutes later, she shows the white guy around the vacant room."

"But don't you think that the growing racism in this country is Thatcher's fault?"

Marshall smiled at her question and continued. "Next, the hidden camera highlights how the coloured guy is discriminated against in the work force. When he personally answers a job advertisement to work in a bar, the landlord tells him the job is already taken. However, ten minutes later, he offers the white guy an interview."

"But don't you think that Thatcher has a lot to answer for where racism is concerned?"

Marshall smiled again, and humoured her as she told him her somewhat unsophisticated theories.

"So you don't think the video, itself, could be considered racist?" Marshall asked in a superior manner, which he often adopted when

231

speaking to people he considered less knowledgeable than himself.

"Why?" she asked.

"Well, for instance, do you think that the response would have been any different if the white man had knocked on a black person's door?" Marshall saw her brows knit together as she thought about his question. He noticed that when she moved under the light the roots of her hair were not naturally red, but lighter - almost blonde. She had an unusual face. It was quite attractive, but it was strangely flat, and when she smiled, her small, straight teeth seemed an extension of that flatness. She laughed at almost everything he said - quick, high and nervous - yet when she spoke she seemed to become quite intense as she laboured her point of view, forehead deeply furrowed, fist banging periodically upon the table to punctuate her argument.

*

Later that night, when he'd rolled away from her, turned onto his side and stared into the darkness of his room, he'd felt her long slender arms circling his neck, like snakes slipping across his bare skin, until her hands met and her fingers clasped tightly shut.

*

"I think you'd better go." Marshall shook his head and turned his attention back to the darkened room. "I've got a long day tomorrow." He got up from the floor and switched on a small lamp that stood on a round table in the furthest corner of the room. The lamp merely lit that corner - the television, the giant rubber plant - and cast the rest of the room in shadow. The tall bookcase that lined the two walls opposite appeared almost black in the dimness, and the girl's expression was difficult to distinguish in the shadow that was cast onto the floor from the old corduroy settee. Marshall collected the cups and put them onto the tray with the matching teapot.

"Are you always so precise?" she asked out of the gloom.

"What do you mean?"

"I mean, do you always have to tidy things away nice and neatly, like they had never been?" He could not see the expression on her face but her voice attacked.

"It avoids having to clear up any mess at a later date," he replied.

"And we don't want anything 'messy' hanging around, do we?"

"Of course, tidying up one mess means that there's always room for more."

There was a prolonged silence in which she made no attempt to

232

leave.

"You'd better go." Marshall was tired of her. "I've got to get up early in the morning." She was so exhausting.

"Make me," she dared as she stretched leisurely.

"Don't be stupid!"

"I'm not."

"I don't have time for your games."

"If you want me to get out, you're going to have to make me." She feigned another stretch. She was like a sly ginger cat that had managed to claim the warmest place in his house. Something snapped inside Marshall. He lunged across the room and grabbed her arm and began to pull her. The ashtray spilled its contents as she was dragged across the floor. Marshall made a mental note to clean it up later. She screamed and kicked, but his grip was surprisingly solid for someone so slight, and he continued to pull her across the room. She twisted and turned and, finally, his fingers slipped. She slithered away on her stomach, but he was after her, over her, and when he managed to turn her onto her back her flat face smiled up at him - laughed at him, the bitch - and so he fucked her there and then. Savage and quick.

*

After, Marshall rolled onto his side, tired, depleted, and when she spoke to him in a low dreamy voice, he merely answered in bland sentences while he stared vacantly ahead. He felt her hands slide up his back, across the thickly folded skin of his shoulders, curling around the front of his neck until her hands met and her fingers joined together firmly.

"You like it when you have to fight for it, don't you?" she whispered close to his ear. He felt her warm breasts squash against his back, and he shifted to avoid their touch.

"I knew it the first time ..." she said. "Knew you couldn't've stood it without the struggle ..."

*

"I'm cooking spaghetti bolognese tonight," she told him soon after they had first met. She had begun to wait for him outside his flat every night. It was cold, and she was shuffling her feet. He dreaded turning that corner and seeing her there, in her long black coat.

"I'm going out," he said bluntly.

"But I'm cooking us dinner," she persisted, eager, waiting for the door to be opened. Marshall remembered looking up into the clear, black winter sky. The twin lights of an aeroplane blinked from high above as it cut across the blackness.

There seems to be some sort of confusion," he began.

"Well, let's talk about it inside." She moved towards the door and he caught her arm.

"What I'm trying to say, is that I don't want to have dinner with you. I don't want you to come inside my flat, and I don't want you to assume that I do."

"Well, I'm here now."

For the first time he caught that hard edge to her voice. It surprised him momentarily, just long enough for her to pull her arm from his grip.

She picked up the box of groceries she had brought and looked straight at him. "Open the door, then."

"You don't listen, do you?" A vein pulsed in his temple. "Just fuck off!" Marshall pushed past her and slammed the door. Through the frosted glass panels he could see the indistinct shape of her white oval face and red hair as she waited patiently outside.

In the morning, as he left for work, he saw something red on his carpet. A trail of spaghetti sauce dripped from the letter box, down the front door and onto the floor. Marshall scrubbed hard, but the deep red would not shift from his beige carpet.

*

He didn't see her for about a week after he'd told her to fuck off. Sometimes, as he put the key in the door, he thought he heard a sound from behind, felt there was someone waiting, but dismissed this feeling as paranoia when he twisted around and found nobody there. After three or four days he began to relax, visited a few friends, went down the pub, even joked about this crazy red-haired bitch who'd posted spaghetti sauce onto his carpet.

"One day ..." His friend, Tom, lifted his pint towards his lips. "One day the tables will turn." His upper lip curled over the rim of his glass as he sipped the froth from the top of his pint.

"What do you mean?" Marshall couldn't see Tom's expression clearly in the shadowy corner of the dingy pub.

"I mean that your humanitarian ethics seem to end in the classroom."

"Bullshit!"

The pub was quiet, and the couple sitting at a table nearby stopped talking and looked at Marshall.

Tom moved forward in his seat, out of the shadows, and lowered

234

his voice. "Alright then, what about the girl you met in here last year
…"

"Which one?" Marshall lowered his voice, too.

"The one you met here that Friday night, took home, fucked, and then refused to acknowledge when she told you she was pregnant."

"How do I know it was anything to do with me?" Marshall asked. "She'd probably fucked half of this pub before she got to me." Marshall saw Tom's brown eyes widen as his mouth dipped disapprovingly at the corners.

"Did you bother to find out that it wasn't anything to do with you?"

Marshall sighed and picked up his pint.

"All I'm saying is that you should treat women with a little more humanity."

"Are you saying I don't treat women like human beings?" Marshall raised his voice again, and the woman at the table nearby turned her back on them.

"Of course I'm not." Tom leaned across the table and said quickly, "I just think that a little more respect might prevent any more 'spaghetti sauce' episodes."

Marshall's lips were pinched with anger. Tom looked at Marshall and smiled slowly, slowly, until he was grinning. "Thank God you weren't having fish!" he said, and laughed, rocking his whole body from side to side. Marshall laughed too, as he watched his friend's huge Adam's apple rise and fall. He felt good that night. It felt as if he'd got out of a relationship that had been dominating his life for years, and that he'd left behind something unnatural, something quite repellent.

*

Then the bitch turned up at college. At first he didn't notice because he was talking to a blonde student about Functionalism. The student listened intently, big blue eyes focused upon his face. When his other students went quiet, Marshall turned around to look at the unknown figure who waited, arms folded, in the doorway of his classroom. He excused himself and walked into the corridor with her. He asked her to leave, but she wouldn't go.

"I'll see you down the pub tonight," he said hurriedly.

"I want to see you now," she said.

"Not now." He shook his head. "I've got a class."

"Then I'll wait."

Marshall returned to his class who were, by now, talking loudly among themselves. He sensed their unspoken questions. She stood in the middle of the corridor while Marshall's lesson deteriorated. He finished early. When his students had left, he grabbed her arm, guided her down the stairs that led to the exit of the building, and into his car. He drove away fast, away from those inquiring eyes, and did not consider stopping until they were speeding along the small, empty country roads which led away from the town.

"Don't ever do that again!" Marshall pulled into a lay-by and stopped the car. He breathed in and out loudly, exaggerating the rise and fall of his chest, as he attempted to control himself. He tried to speak slowly to steady the anger in his voice. He wanted to know what the hell she was playing at, what the hell she thought she was doing. He wanted to sort this thing out once and for all. When he turned to face her, he saw that she was smiling, almost laughing, laughing, the bitch, the bitch. He got out of the car, ran around to her side and wrenched open the door. He wanted her out of his car, out of his life, and so he began to grab at her arm, her hair, anything, anything to get the bitch out. She was screaming, screaming, arms flying out at him, fending him off, feet wedged up high against the dashboard to make it all the more difficult. And then he was in the car, actually inside the car, trying to grab hold of the front of her shirt, trying to yank her out. Instead, he pulled the shirt apart, ripped the tiny buttons from their holes, and she pulled him towards her.

*

"Why don't you answer me?" she asked. Marshall stared at the upturned ashtray and the grey ash that scattered across his carpet. The ash had probably ground into the fibres. He'd have to be careful when scrubbing that out. He thought about the car incident, of how, like that sly ginger cat, she had smiled appreciatively while he ground himself into her. She was like the Cheshire Cat - one big mocking flat smile that spread from ear to ear. His hands bunched into fists as he felt her hold tighten around his neck.

"Why won't you answer me?" her voice persisted from the blackness behind. "I know you're not asleep." She accompanied her words with the sharp butt of her knee which went straight into the back of his upper leg. Marshall winced and instantly pulled his leg up and away from her. He tried to yank her hands away from his neck.

"Get off me!" Marshall yelled while he rubbed the back of his leg, and her hands and arms seemed to tighten all the more.

"Answer my question," she commanded, and the hardness in her voice told him she would not drop the subject until he had answered.

"What fucking question?"

"You like it when you have to fight for it, don't you?"

"That's a statement - not a question." He continued to pull at her hands.

"You still haven't answered me." She pulled her arms back so that her hands pressed against his Adam's apple, restricting his breath, making him gasp. The vivid image of Tom's Adam's apple, rising and falling as if in slow motion, came to him briefly.

"You assume so much where I'm concerned ..." Marshall managed to splutter, "that I thought you would be telling me what I like, rather than asking ..."

Before Marshall could say anything more she pulled her arms back suddenly, cutting off his air supply. As he wriggled backwards, forwards, sideways, in his attempt to breathe, her legs moved up to his waist and curled around him tight. Marshall yanked her arms forward and gulped for air. He thought that he must have pulled her arms out of their sockets, but when he grabbed at her wrists, forcing them apart with all his might, her fingers remained clamped together as before. He panicked, and his legs and arms moved frantically on the carpet as he attempted to escape. She followed him, dragging heavily behind, laughing at his attempt to get away.

"You fucking crazy bitch!" Marshall struggled to turn his head, but as he turned, from the corner of his eye, he saw her red head fly towards him and felt a blow to the side of his temple which made him reel, made the room spin.

"Bitch! Bitch!" Marshall clawed at her hands, tugging at the white knuckles. he attempted to slip his head through her arms but her arms were not loose enough, and her legs, wrapped so tightly around his waist, restricted his movements. How can she be so fucking strong? Marshall grunted and groaned as he tried to roll onto his front in order to drag himself onto his hands and knees. He fell back on his side. She was a dead weight wrapped around his neck and waist like a huge pink wrapper in which he was encased. He couldn't seem to dislodge her, whichever way he moved.

"Get off me!" He tried, again, to roll onto his front. As he struggled, he felt her weight shift just enough to enable him to quickly scrabble onto his knees and elbows. She moved dangerously above from side to side as he hoisted himself up and, briefly, he thought he was going to topple back down as the weight of her body dragged heavily down his left side. His blonde hair fell forward, covering his face. Sections of his hair were wet with sweat, probably where it had been trapped between their bodies. And then he noticed her long red strands of hair which intermingled with his own. Her head must be close to his. He remained still and heard her breathing near his left ear. He was suddenly afraid to move. Any movement could start her off ... the slightest twitch. He breathed as silently as he could, while his back and knees and elbows ached with her weight. He thought that he heard a low, low growl in the back of her throat. He imagined her upper lip curling back ... Oh God ... dear God ... her lip curling up her straight little teeth like a Dobermann's before the pounce. He smelled her breath and found that it had changed; it had become foul and rancid, and she rasped heavily into his ear. They remained still, silent. The muffled sound of a television crept into the silence from the flat above.

*

In the distance, Marshall heard a child calling out.

"Poppy! Poppy!" the child called, and Marshall thought it must be the small child who lived in the house opposite. He imagined him, sandy-haired, standing on the gate, feet wedged between the black wrought-iron, calling, calling - Poppy! Poppy! - blue eyes searching the gloomy road as the gate swung backwards and forwards with his movements. Marshall thought about calling out, but what would a small boy - Adrian, that was his name - what would Adrian think of such a thing? What would he think of the nakedness, the indignity of their position, the mad thing strapped to his back, cunt opened wide as her legs wrapped tightly around him? ... Our Father who art in heaven ... hallowed by Thy ... Would the people have heard upstairs? No one had knocked, or banged, the police had not arrived. He thought of the old couple above, sitting there, watching television, volume turned up loud.

*

"Why don't we stop all this," Marshall said slowly, carefully. "Why don't we talk about this."

A pain shot up the left side of his head as she sank her teeth into his earlobe. She bit so hard, she must have bitten straight through the soft flap of skin. Marshall screamed, raised his hand and punched the side of her head. Her mouth sprang open and she howled. Marshall lost his balance and crashed to the floor and heard the quick crack of

238

her hip. She squealed a high animal yelp, and then she began to snarl and snap at the back of his head and shoulders. He attempted to loosen her legs but they remained tightly shut. She snapped at him; nipping at his skin, biting at his neck, snarling and growling in her frenzy. Marshall struggled to fend her off with his free fist, and punched aimlessly behind his head. But she was so quick, so agile as she moved her head backwards and forwards, backwards and forwards as she bit into his skin, and yanked at his hair with her teeth. She stopped. Marshall could not move. His arms hung useless from his shoulders as they rested against the cool carpet, and his legs felt as heavy as lead. Where was the blood? Was the carpet covered in big red stains? A strand of red hair lay across his face, but he did not have the energy to brush or blow it away ... Our Father who art ... He could hear her quick rasping breath from behind; feel the heat of her breath on his back; smell the stench of her breath in the room.

*

"Come on, then!" Marshall heard Adrian call, and he could see the dog, part labrador, part something else, running out of the semi-darkness, up the road, running towards the boy, tail a-wagging, pink tongue lolling out of its big black head.

"Good boy," Adrian called, and he heard the sound of the boy jumping from the gate he so often swung upon; jumping to the floor, patting the dog's thick coat before going inside.

*

Marshall felt cold. Alone. He began to sob, and his shoulders heaved as he cried loudly into the room. If only Tom would burst through the front door; smash his fist through the frosted glass, or kick the door down with his long, powerful legs. He'd done it before ... at school ... kicked the toilet door in ... A car drove up the quiet road, slowing at the end to turn left or right. Marshall sobbed convulsively, painfully, as his Adam's apple pushed itself up and down against the restrictions of her hands. He felt her move. She was still behind, still there, still retaining him in her grip.

*

Marshall went quiet. He felt something warm, something coarse and long that brushed his skin upwards harshly. Fleetingly, he thought of an inquisitive cow he'd once enticed towards a barbed wire fence; how the animal lifted her heavy head, sniffed the air with her wide black nostrils and then, suddenly, darted her rough tongue against the back of his hand. A film of sweat covered Marshall's forehead, and

239

his thighs, pressed tightly together, became hot and wet. He heard her sniff the air, felt her head move forward slightly, and the small, regular puff of air as she smelt his skin. A car turned the corner of the road again. Should he shout out? The old couple above would never hear over the noise of the telly. He thought of the numerous parties he had thrown in his flat. They had never complained. Perhaps they were deaf. Parties, people, all seemed to belong to someone else. If he spoke to her, would she bite him again? Snot streamed from his nostrils. He didn't bother to wipe it away. Again, Marshall felt something warm, something damp, perhaps wet, something that brushed like sandpaper against his skin. He tentatively moved a hand across to feel her leg, testing to see whether her hold had loosened. Her leg, which lay under his side, must have lost all feeling by now with his weight on it for so long. Perhaps he could loosen its grip. Marshall moved his hand cautiously up the other leg, trailing slowly across her skin. Her leg felt rigid. His hand continued up to the top and across the big muscle that bulged from her thigh. Marshall began to whimper like a young rabbit caught in a snare. His slight frame felt helpless in her grip. His bones were twigs between her loins. If she gripped him any tighter he would snap like a wishbone. He heard a low, guttural sound in her throat, and sensed that she was waiting, waiting patiently behind.

*

Marshall put his hand to his head and cried, and he felt something warm, something wet, something that lingered roughly against his battered skin as it brushed again and again in a long, rhythmic motion. He quietened slowly and the heaving of his body became still. He stared into the room vaguely, and heard the sound of someone shouting outside, somewhere in the distance. He felt strangely calm and no longer noticed the coldness of the room as the rhythmic motion continued across his back, over his shoulder, down his arm, and his cuts and bruises were licked gently, slowly, methodically clean.